W9-DEY-889

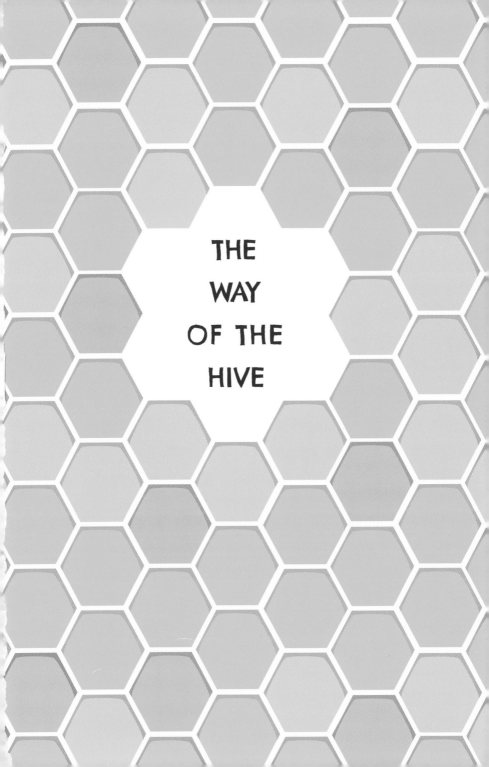

THE
WAY
OF THE
HIVE

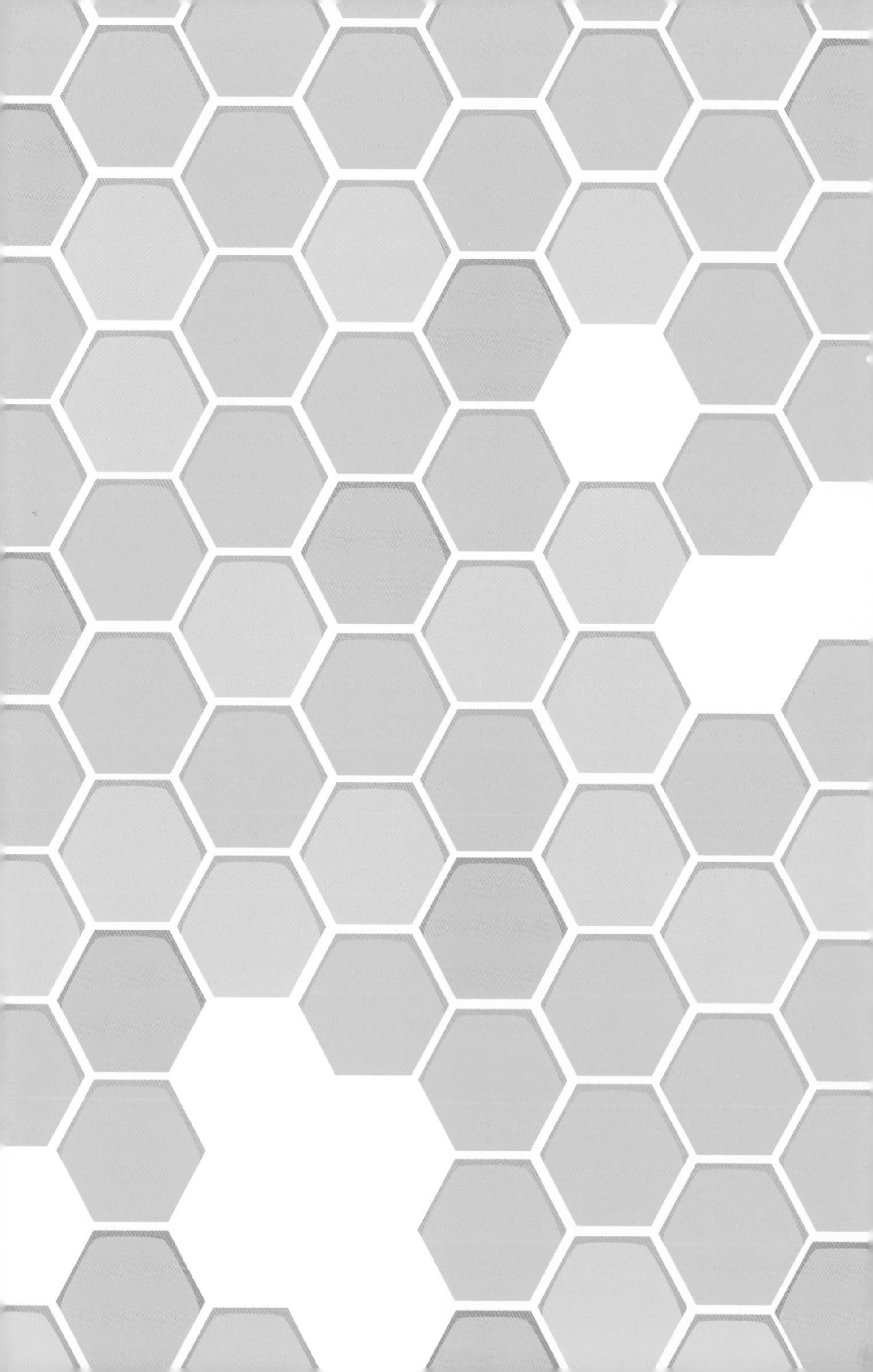

THE
WAY OF THE
HIVE

A HONEY BEE'S STORY

JAY HOSLER

An Imprint of HarperCollinsPublishers

1

TRANSITIONS

Once upon a time
there was a whole
lot of nothing.

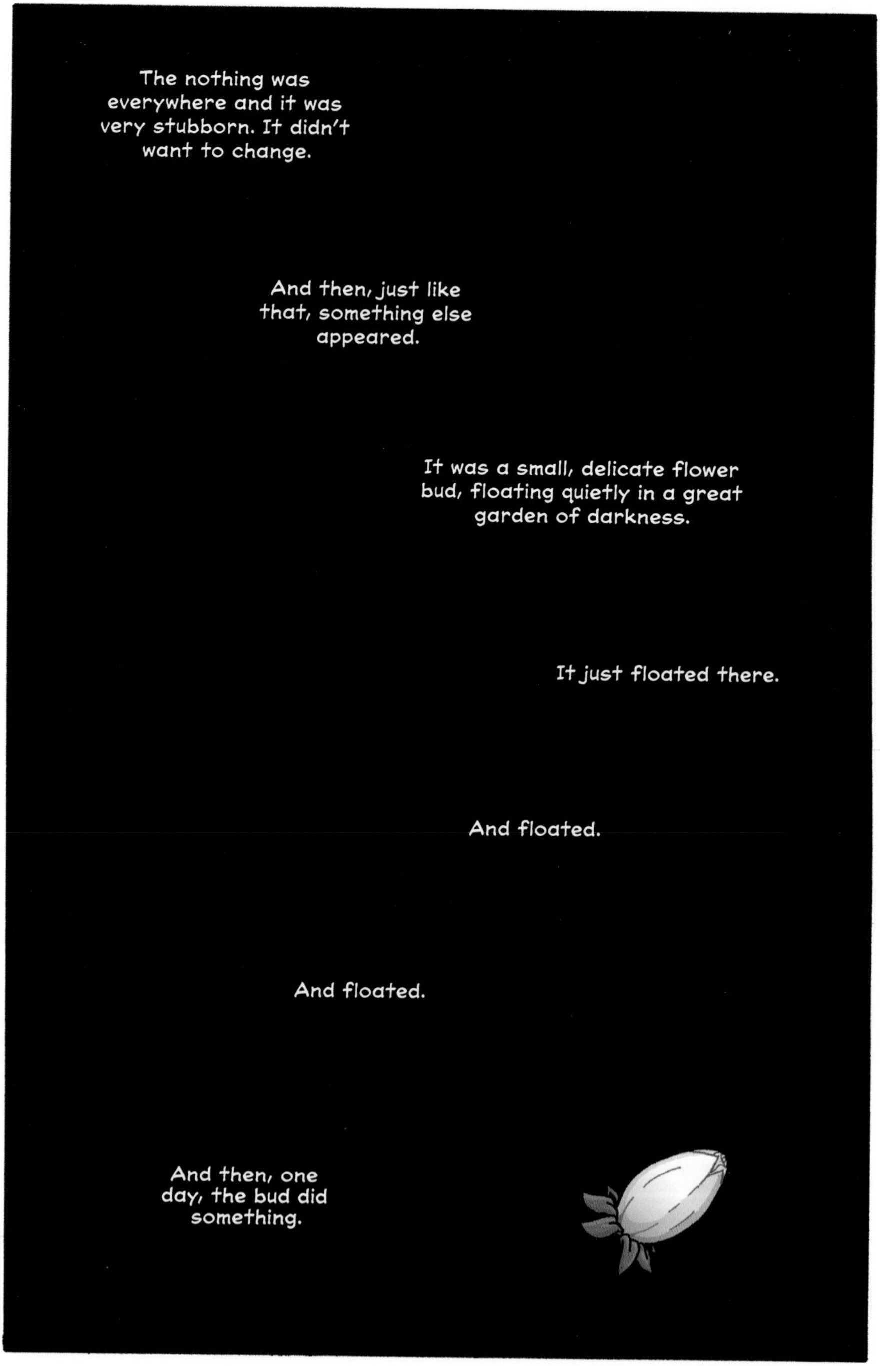
The nothing was everywhere and it was very stubborn. It didn't want to change.
And then, just like that, something else appeared.
It was a small, delicate flower bud, floating quietly in a great garden of darkness.
It just floated there.
And floated.
And floated.
And then, one day, the bud did something.

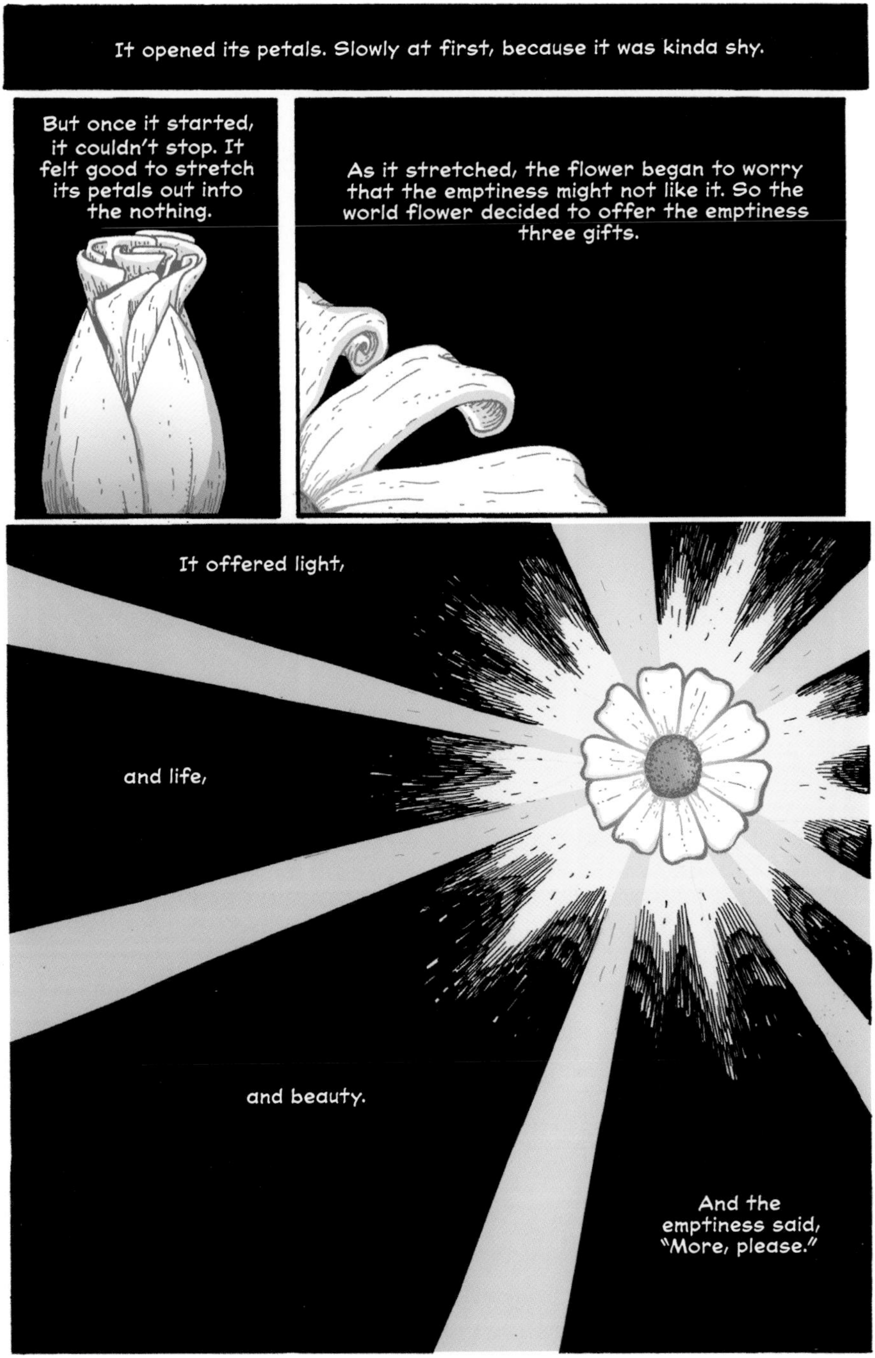
It opened its petals. Slowly at first, because it was kinda shy.
But once it started, it couldn't stop. It felt good to stretch its petals out into the nothing.
As it stretched, the flower began to worry that the emptiness might not like it. So the world flower decided to offer the emptiness three gifts.
It offered light,
and life,
and beauty.
And the emptiness said, "More, please."

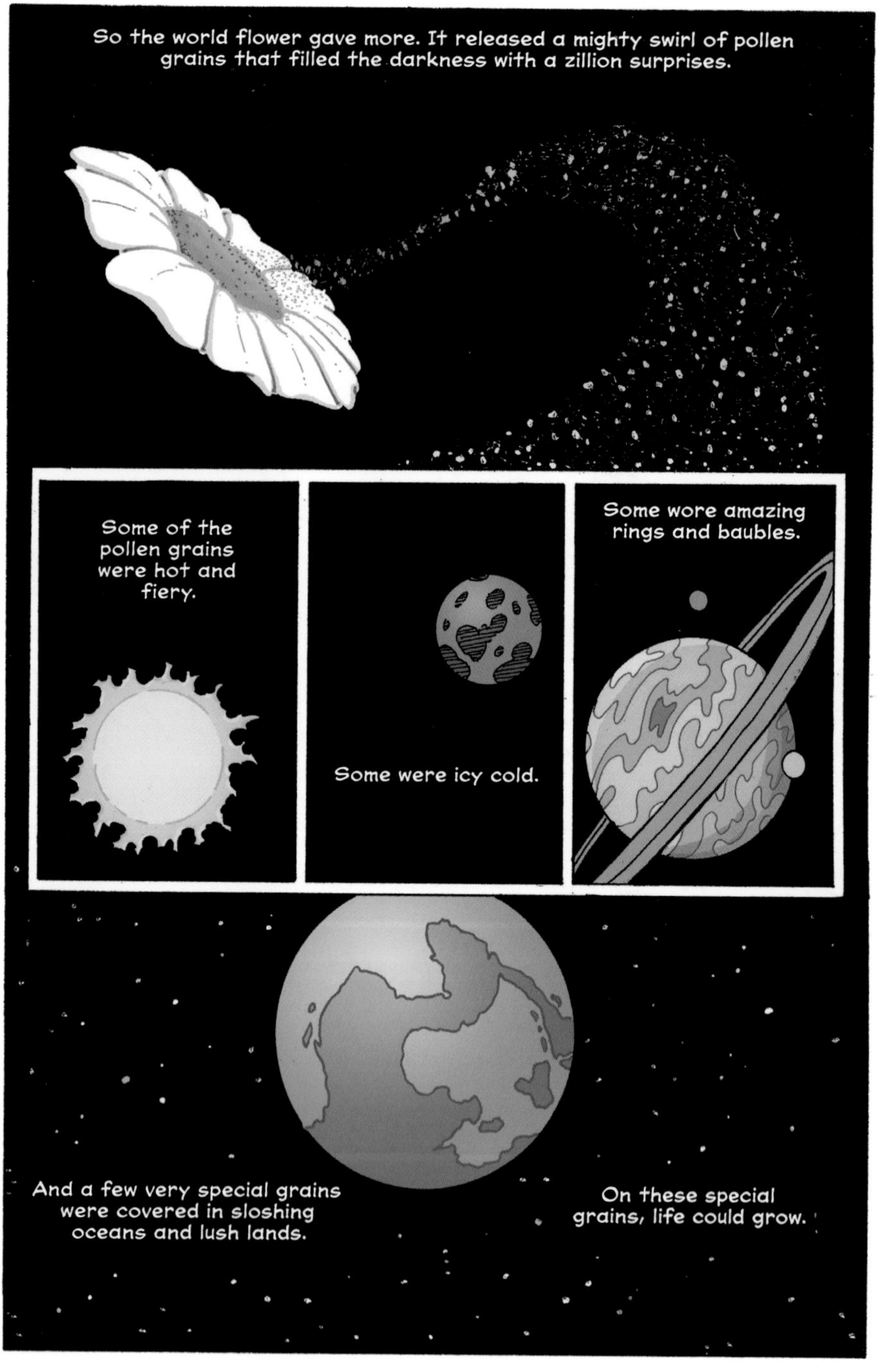
So the world flower gave more. It released a mighty swirl of pollen grains that filled the darkness with a zillion surprises.
Some of the pollen grains were hot and fiery.
Some were icy cold.
Some wore amazing rings and baubles.
And a few very special grains were covered in sloshing oceans and lush lands.
On these special grains, life could grow.

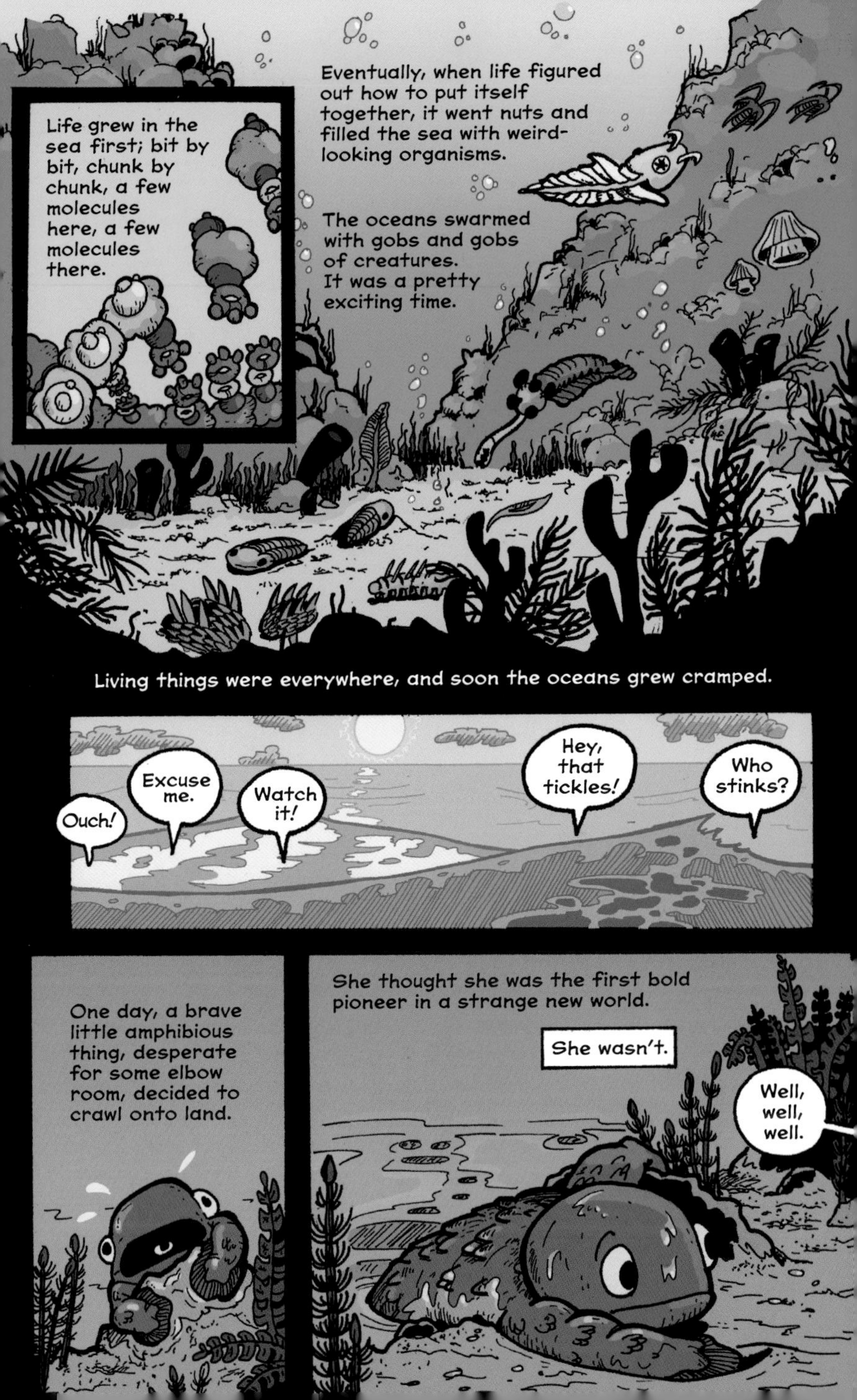
Life grew in the sea first; bit by bit, chunk by chunk, a few molecules here, a few molecules there.
Eventually, when life figured out how to put itself together, it went nuts and filled the sea with weird-looking organisms.
The oceans swarmed with gobs and gobs of creatures. It was a pretty exciting time.
Living things were everywhere, and soon the oceans grew cramped.
Ouch!
Excuse me.
Watch it!
Hey, that tickles!
Who stinks?
One day, a brave little amphibious thing, desperate for some elbow room, decided to crawl onto land.
She thought she was the first bold pioneer in a strange new world.
She wasn't.
Well, well, well.

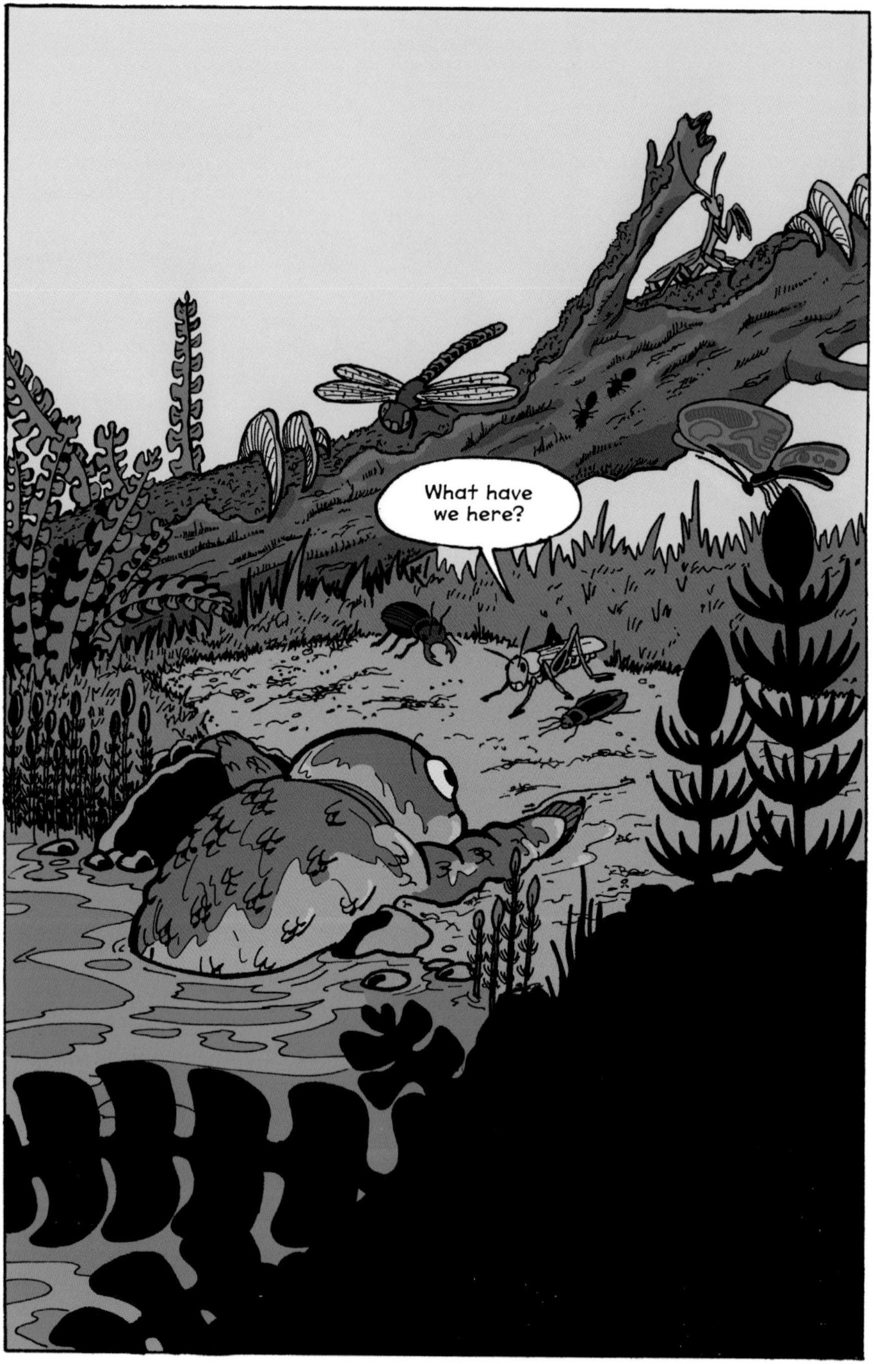
What have we here?

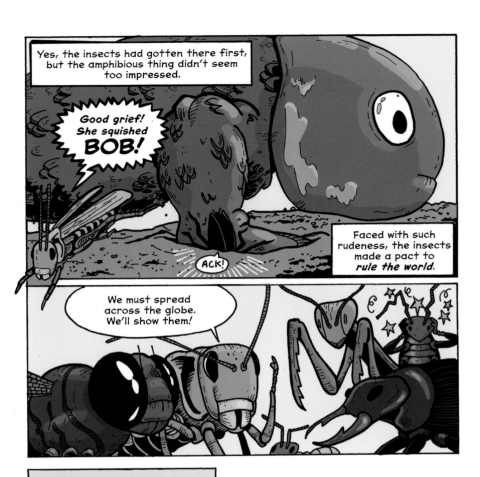

Yes, the insects had gotten there first, but the amphibious thing didn't seem too impressed.

Good grief! She squished BOB!

ACK!

Faced with such rudeness, the insects made a pact to *rule the world*.

We must spread across the globe. We'll show them!

The plan worked. Eventually, 10 quintillion insects covered the planet.

Most lived alone, but a few found that they had better success surviving if they worked together.

One group, known as the honey bees, cared for the children of the world flower in exchange for nectar and pollen.

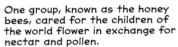

9

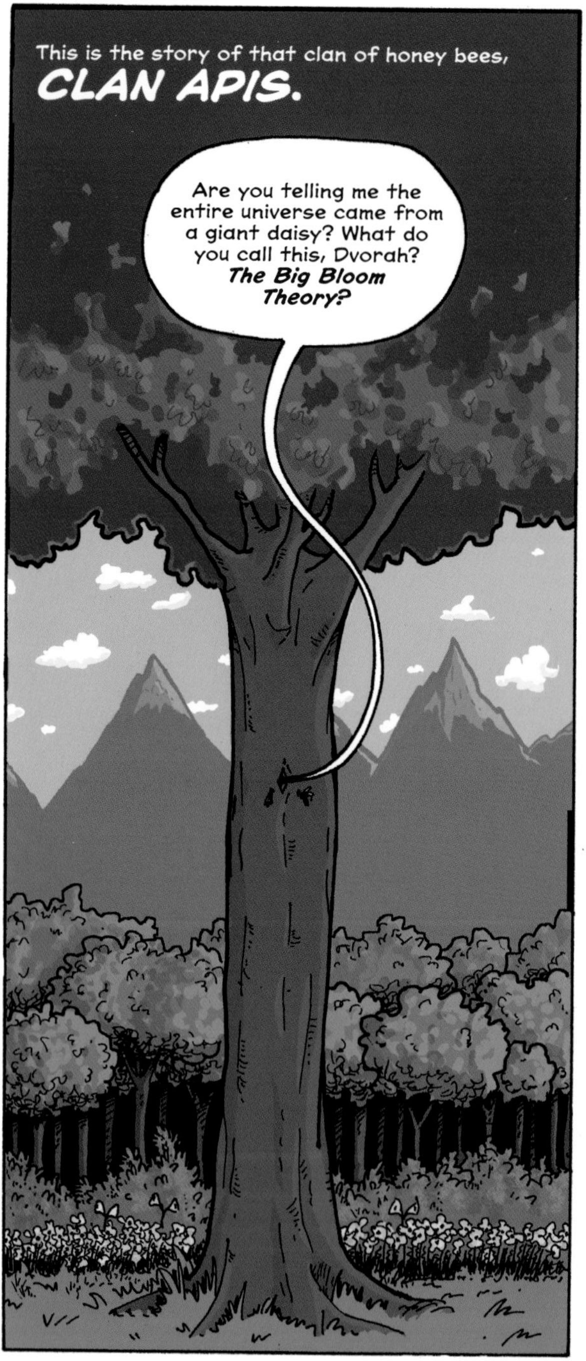
This is the story of that clan of honey bees,
CLAN APIS.
Are you telling me the entire universe came from a giant daisy? What do you call this, Dvorah? ***The Big Bloom Theory?***

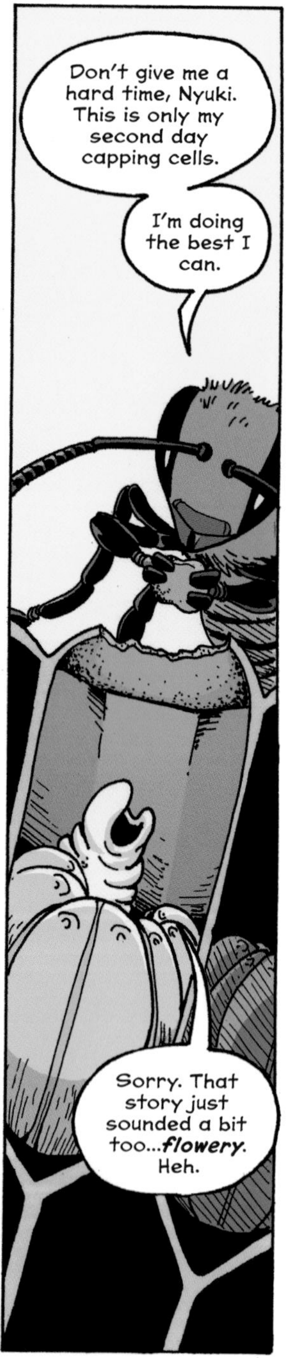
Don't give me a hard time, Nyuki. This is only my second day capping cells.
I'm doing the best I can.
Sorry. That story just sounded a bit too...***flowery***. Heh.

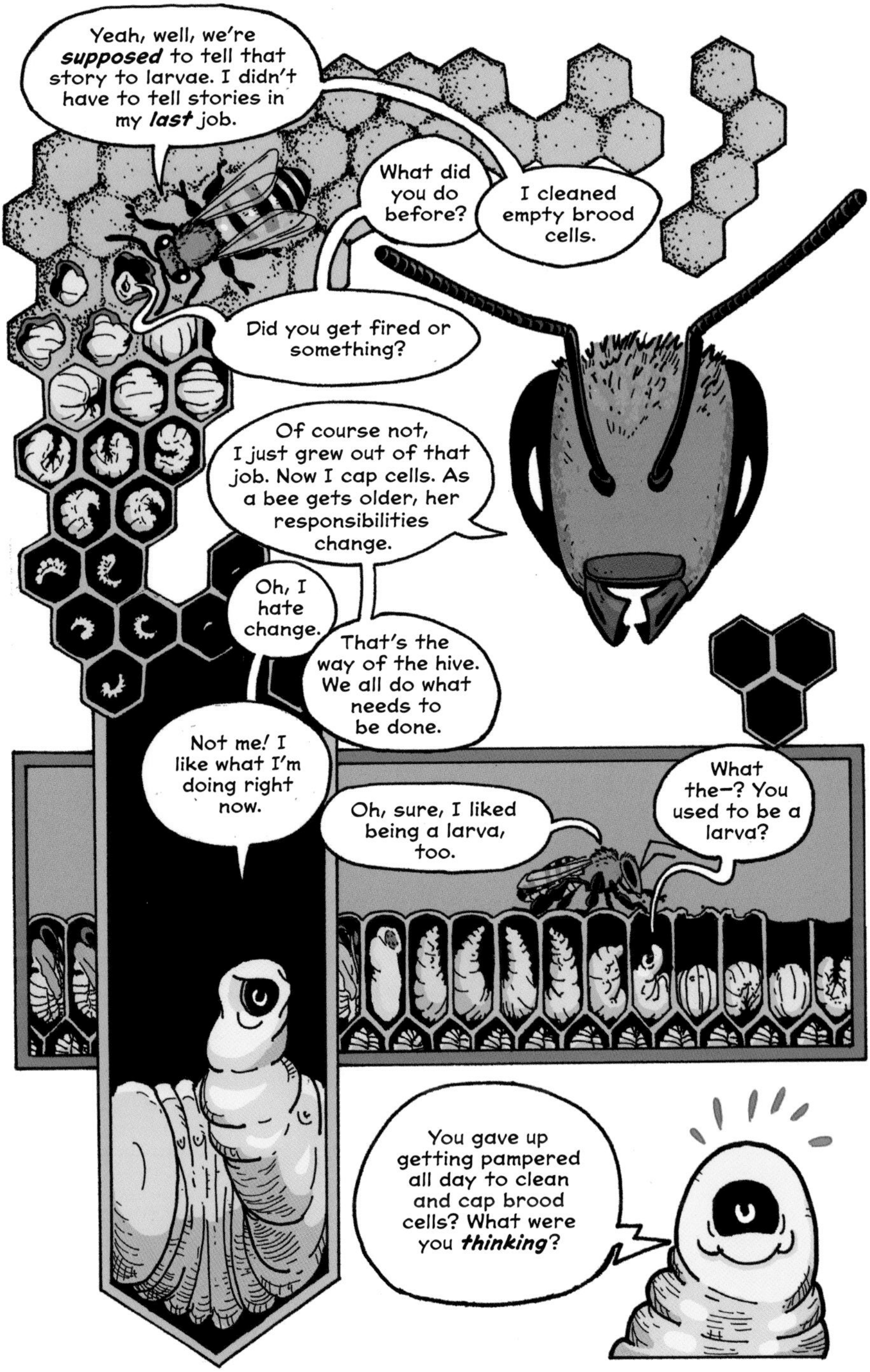
Yeah, well, we're ***supposed*** to tell that story to larvae. I didn't have to tell stories in my ***last*** job.
What did you do before?
I cleaned empty brood cells.
Did you get fired or something?
Of course not, I just grew out of that job. Now I cap cells. As a bee gets older, her responsibilities change.
Oh, I hate change.
That's the way of the hive. We all do what needs to be done.
Not me! I like what I'm doing right now.
Oh, sure, I liked being a larva, too.
What the—? You used to be a larva?
You gave up getting pampered all day to clean and cap brood cells? What were you ***thinking***?

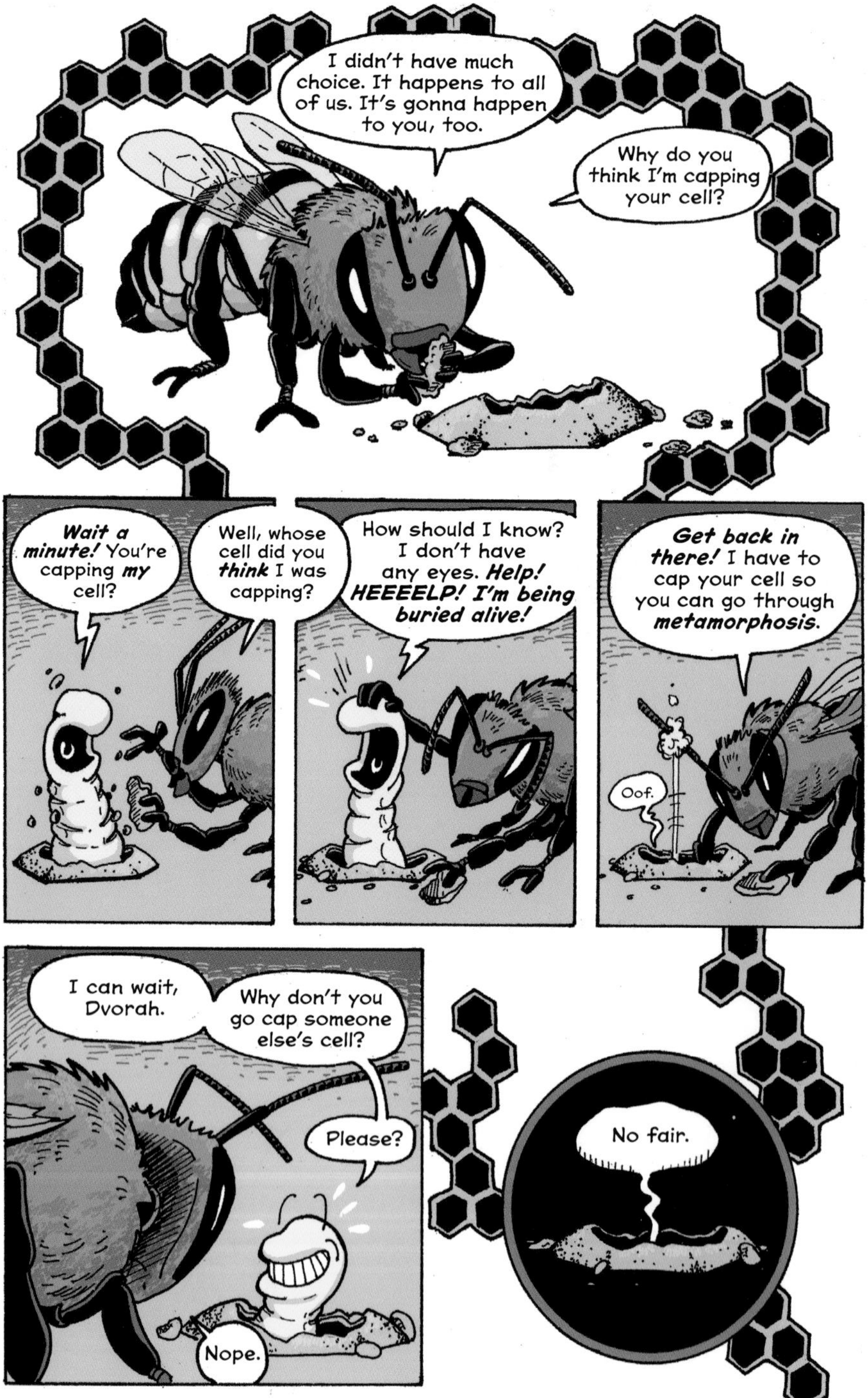
I didn't have much choice. It happens to all of us. It's gonna happen to you, too.
Why do you think I'm capping your cell?
Wait a minute! You're capping **my** cell?
Well, whose cell did you **think** I was capping?
How should I know? I don't have any eyes. **Help! HEEEELP! I'm being buried alive!**
Get back in there! I have to cap your cell so you can go through **metamorphosis**.
Oof.
I can wait, Dvorah.
Why don't you go cap someone else's cell?
Please?
Nope.
No fair.

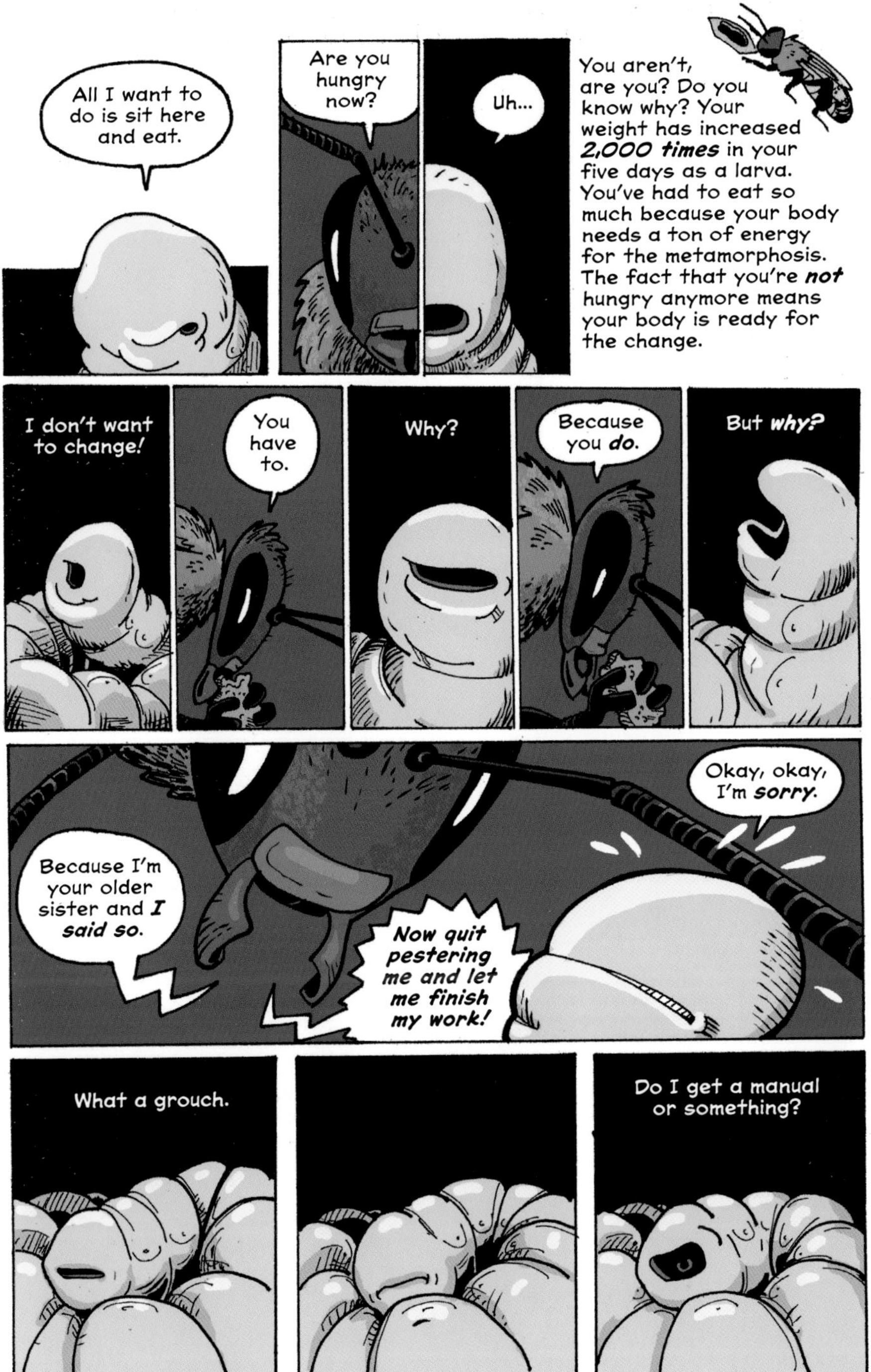

All I want to do is sit here and eat.
Are you hungry now?
Uh...
You aren't, are you? Do you know why? Your weight has increased **2,000 times** in your five days as a larva. You've had to eat so much because your body needs a ton of energy for the metamorphosis. The fact that you're **not** hungry anymore means your body is ready for the change.
I don't want to change!
You have to.
Why?
Because you **do**.
But **why?**
Because I'm your older sister and **I said so**.
Now quit pestering me and let me finish my work!
Okay, okay, I'm **sorry**.
What a grouch.
Do I get a manual or something?

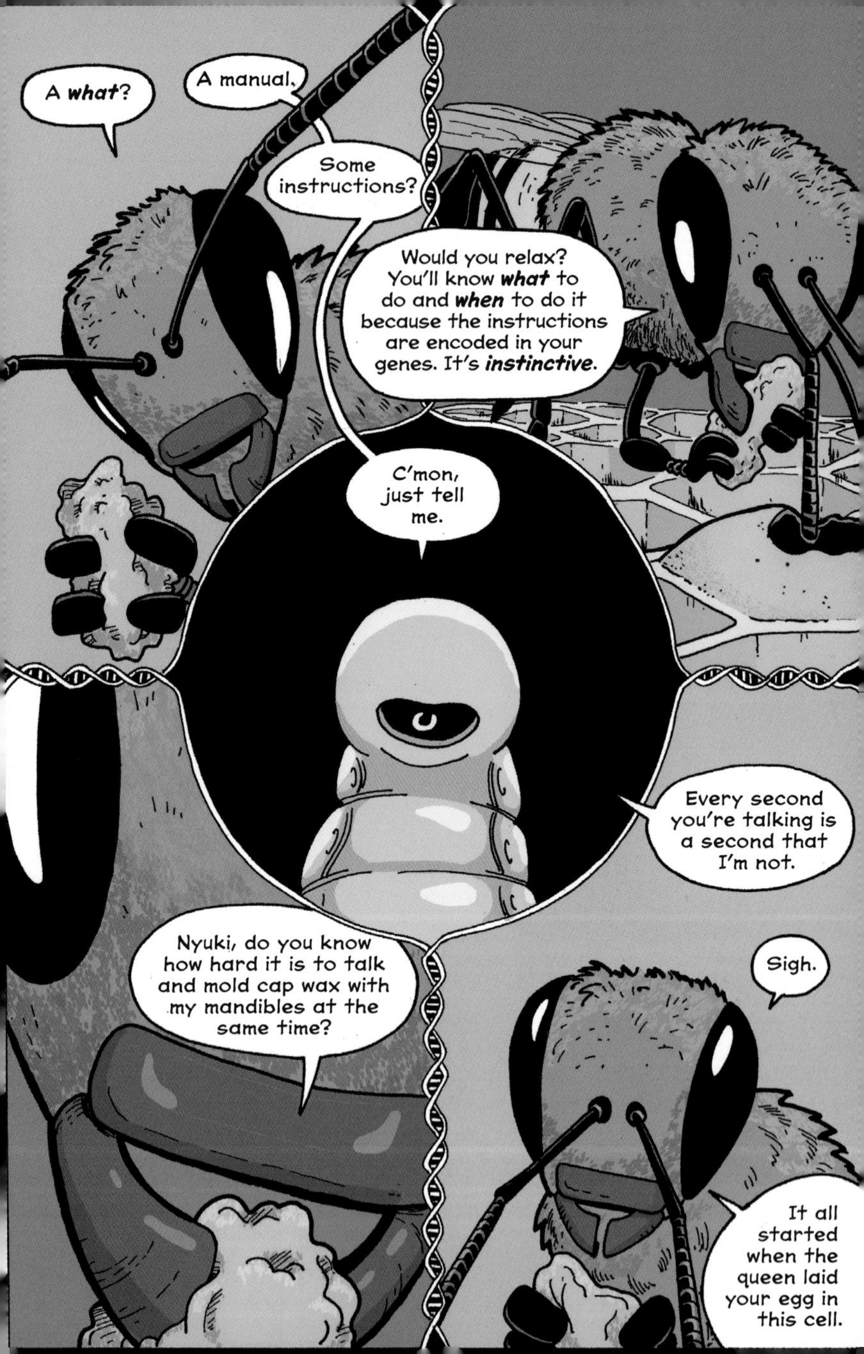
A *what*?
A manual.
Some instructions?
Would you relax? You'll know *what* to do and *when* to do it because the instructions are encoded in your genes. It's *instinctive*.
C'mon, just tell me.
Every second you're talking is a second that I'm not.
Nyuki, do you know how hard it is to talk and mold cap wax with my mandibles at the same time?
Sigh.
It all started when the queen laid your egg in this cell.

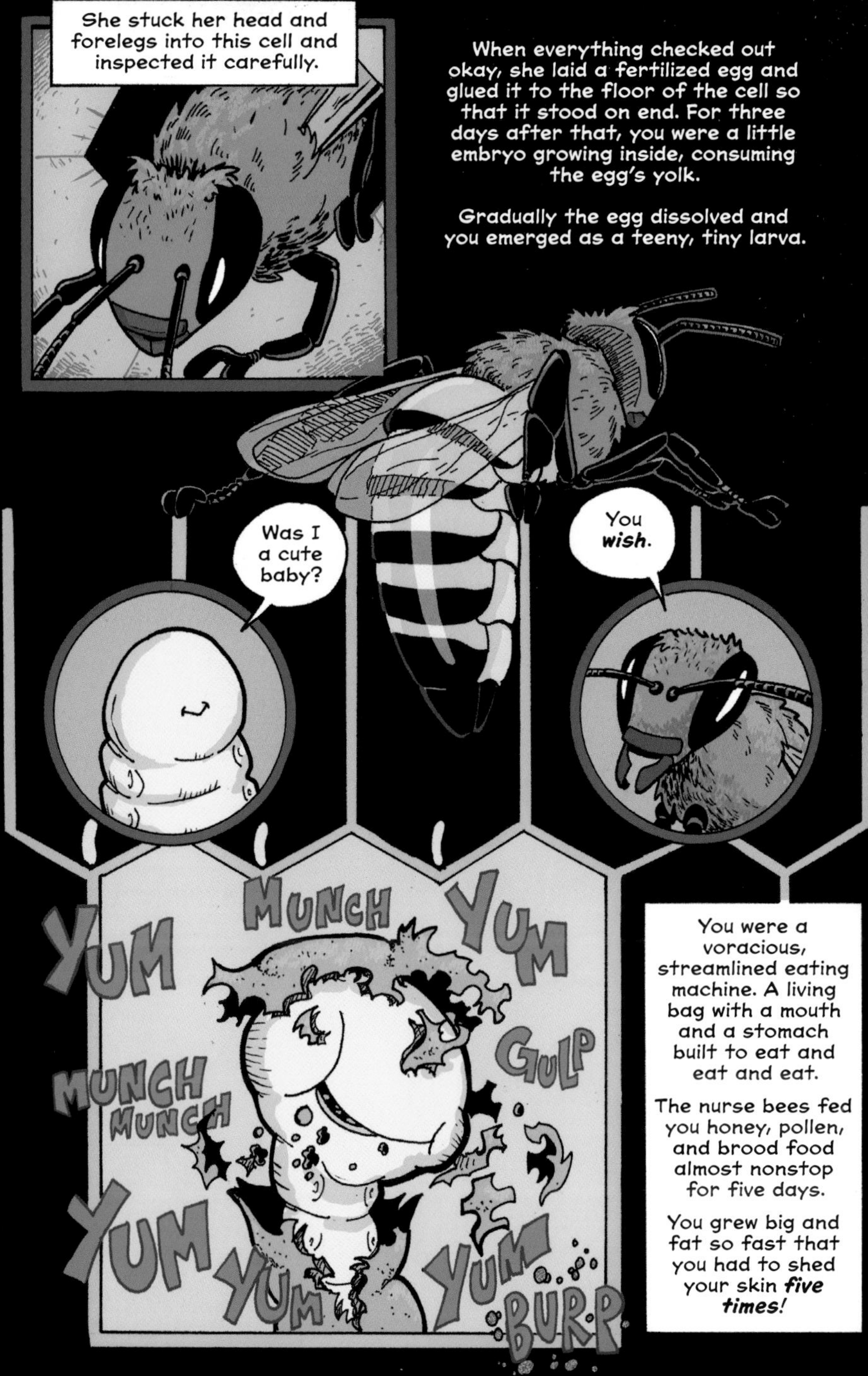

She stuck her head and forelegs into this cell and inspected it carefully.
When everything checked out okay, she laid a fertilized egg and glued it to the floor of the cell so that it stood on end. For three days after that, you were a little embryo growing inside, consuming the egg's yolk.
Gradually the egg dissolved and you emerged as a teeny, tiny larva.
Was I a cute baby?
You *wish*.
YUM
MUNCH
YUM
GULP
MUNCH MUNCH
YUM
YUM
YUM
BURP
You were a voracious, streamlined eating machine. A living bag with a mouth and a stomach built to eat and eat and eat.
The nurse bees fed you honey, pollen, and brood food almost nonstop for five days.
You grew big and fat so fast that you had to shed your skin *five times!*

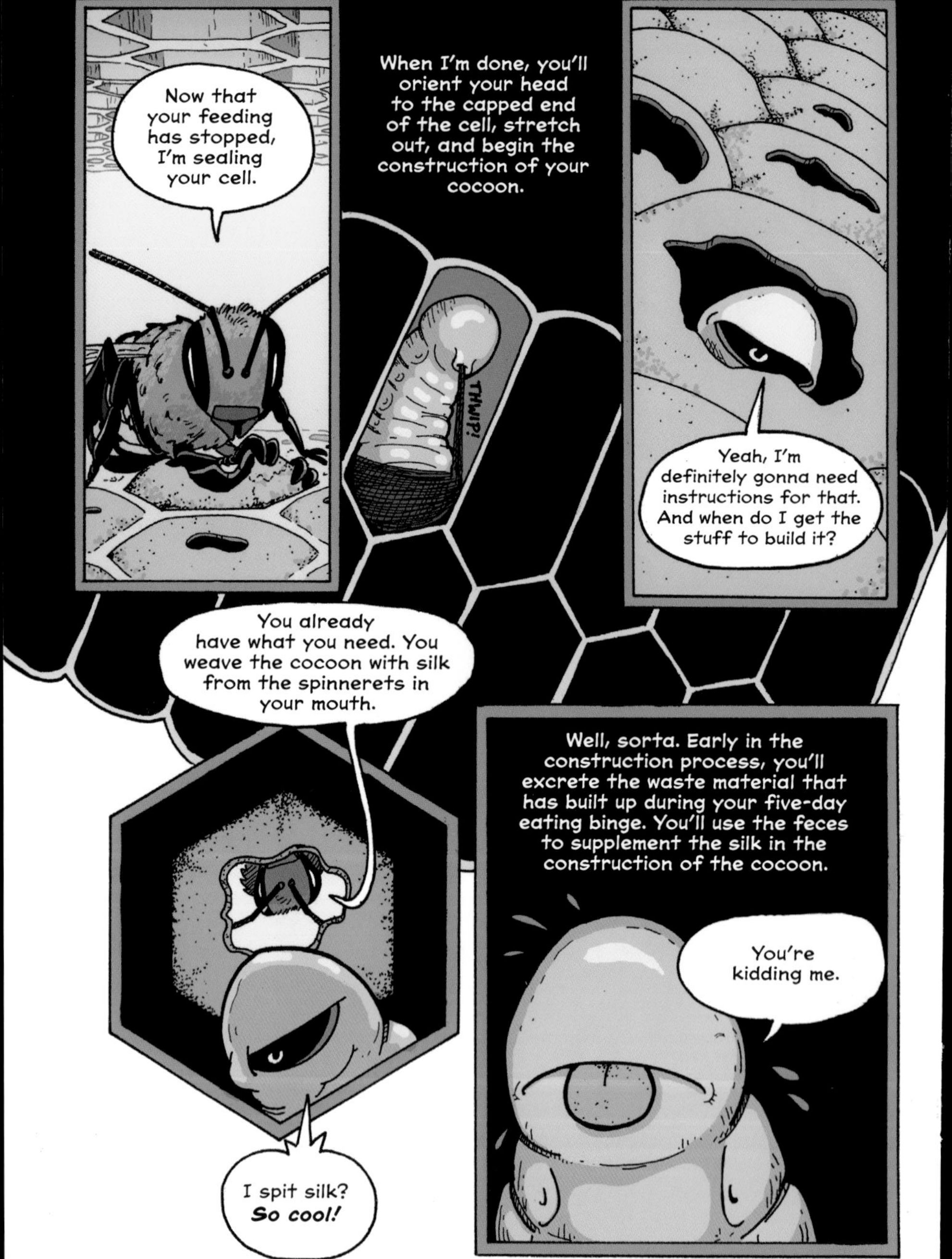
Now that your feeding has stopped, I'm sealing your cell.
When I'm done, you'll orient your head to the capped end of the cell, stretch out, and begin the construction of your cocoon.
THWIP!
Yeah, I'm definitely gonna need instructions for that. And when do I get the stuff to build it?
You already have what you need. You weave the cocoon with silk from the spinnerets in your mouth.
I spit silk? ***So cool!***
Well, sorta. Early in the construction process, you'll excrete the waste material that has built up during your five-day eating binge. You'll use the feces to supplement the silk in the construction of the cocoon.
You're kidding me.

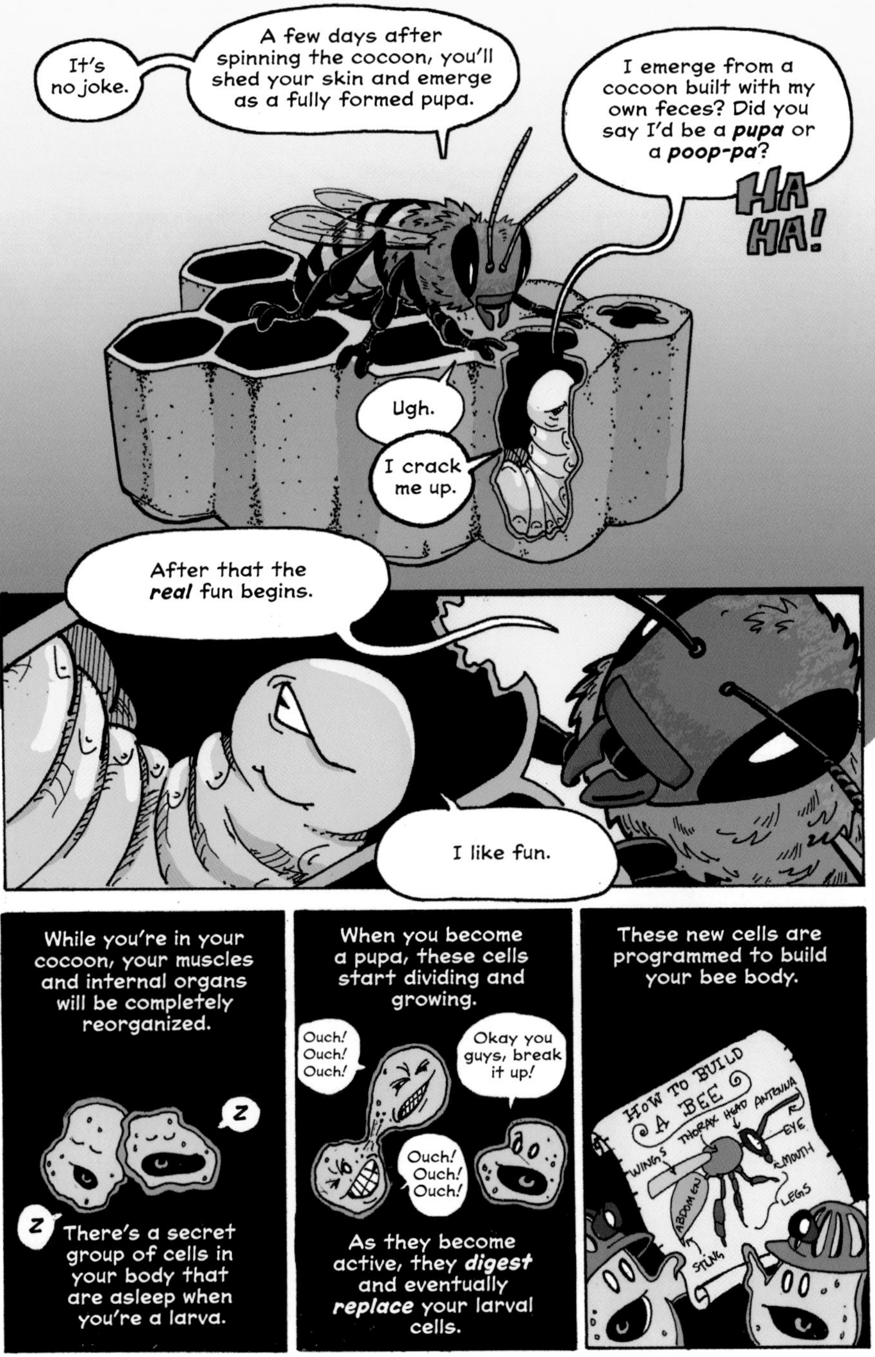
It's no joke.
A few days after spinning the cocoon, you'll shed your skin and emerge as a fully formed pupa.
I emerge from a cocoon built with my own feces? Did you say I'd be a *pupa* or a *poop-pa*?
HA HA!
Ugh.
I crack me up.
After that the *real* fun begins.
I like fun.
While you're in your cocoon, your muscles and internal organs will be completely reorganized.
Z
Z
There's a secret group of cells in your body that are asleep when you're a larva.
When you become a pupa, these cells start dividing and growing.
Ouch! Ouch! Ouch!
Okay you guys, break it up!
Ouch! Ouch! Ouch!
As they become active, they *digest* and eventually *replace* your larval cells.
These new cells are programmed to build your bee body.
HOW TO BUILD A BEE
THORAX
HEAD
ANTENNA
EYE
MOUTH
WINGS
LEGS
ABDOMEN
STING

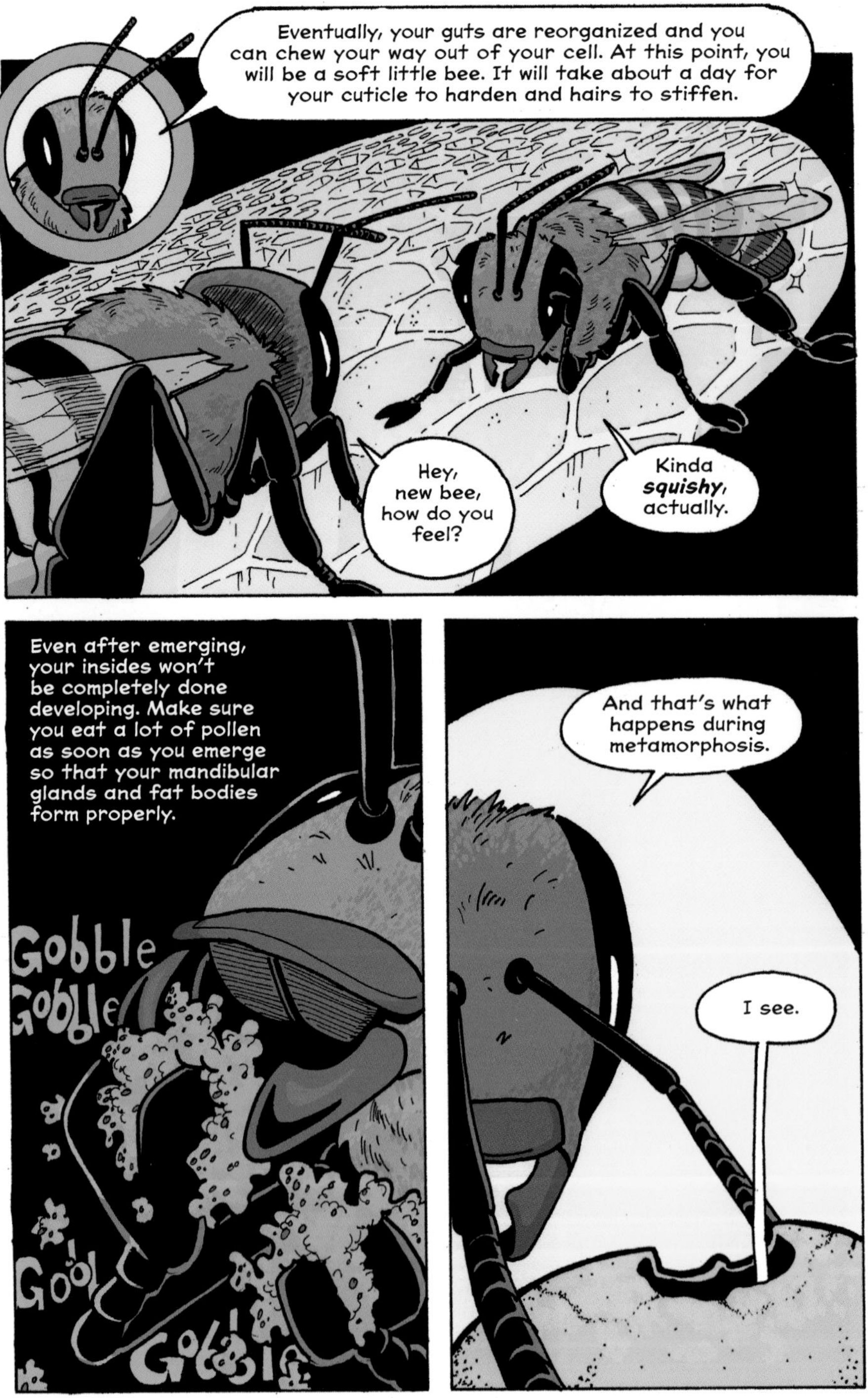
Eventually, your guts are reorganized and you can chew your way out of your cell. At this point, you will be a soft little bee. It will take about a day for your cuticle to harden and hairs to stiffen.
Hey, new bee, how do you feel?
Kinda *squishy*, actually.
Even after emerging, your insides won't be completely done developing. Make sure you eat a lot of pollen as soon as you emerge so that your mandibular glands and fat bodies form properly.
Gobble Gobble
And that's what happens during metamorphosis.
I see.

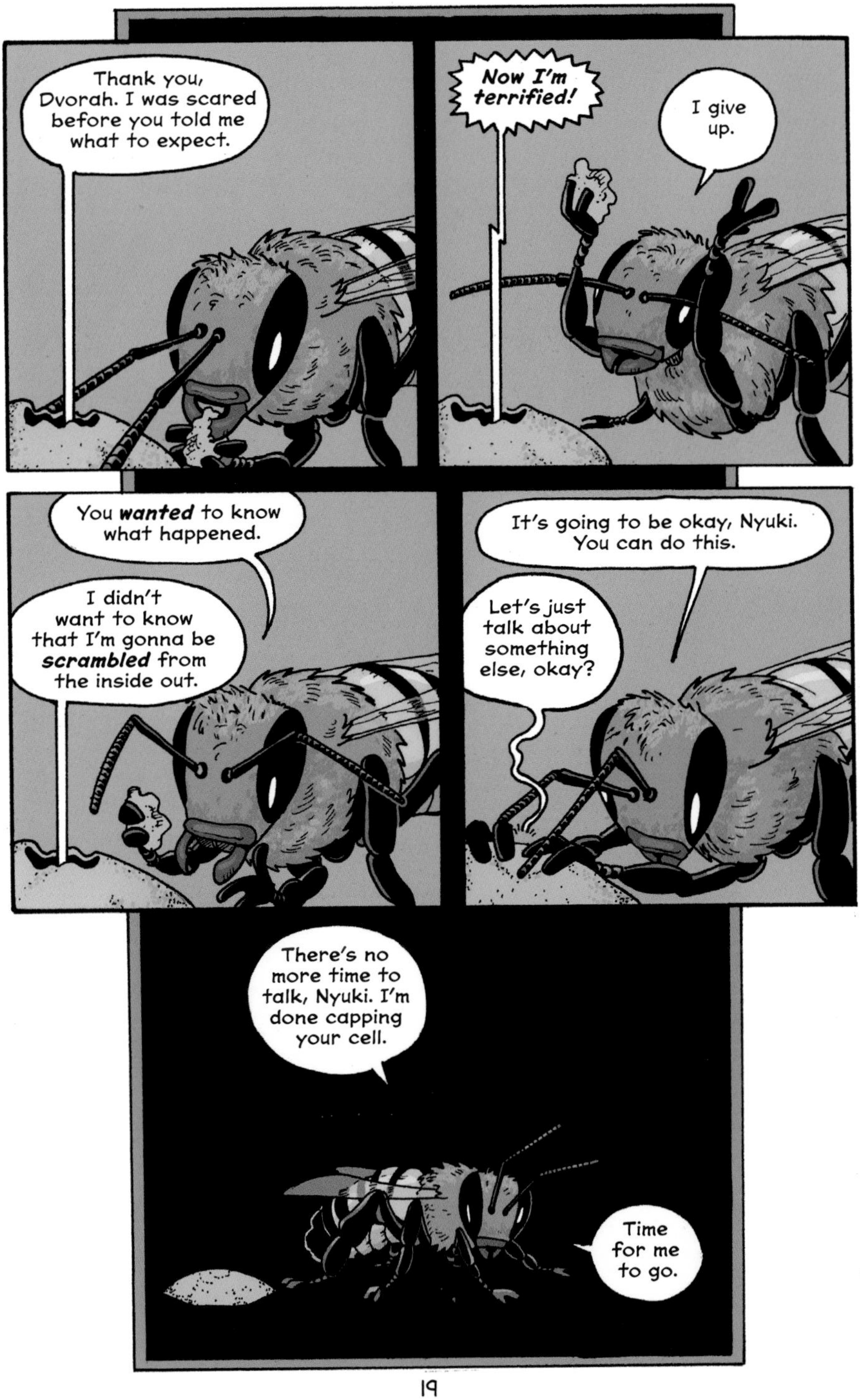
Thank you, Dvorah. I was scared before you told me what to expect.
Now I'm terrified!
I give up.
You *wanted* to know what happened.
I didn't want to know that I'm gonna be *scrambled* from the inside out.
It's going to be okay, Nyuki. You can do this.
Let's just talk about something else, okay?
There's no more time to talk, Nyuki. I'm done capping your cell.
Time for me to go.

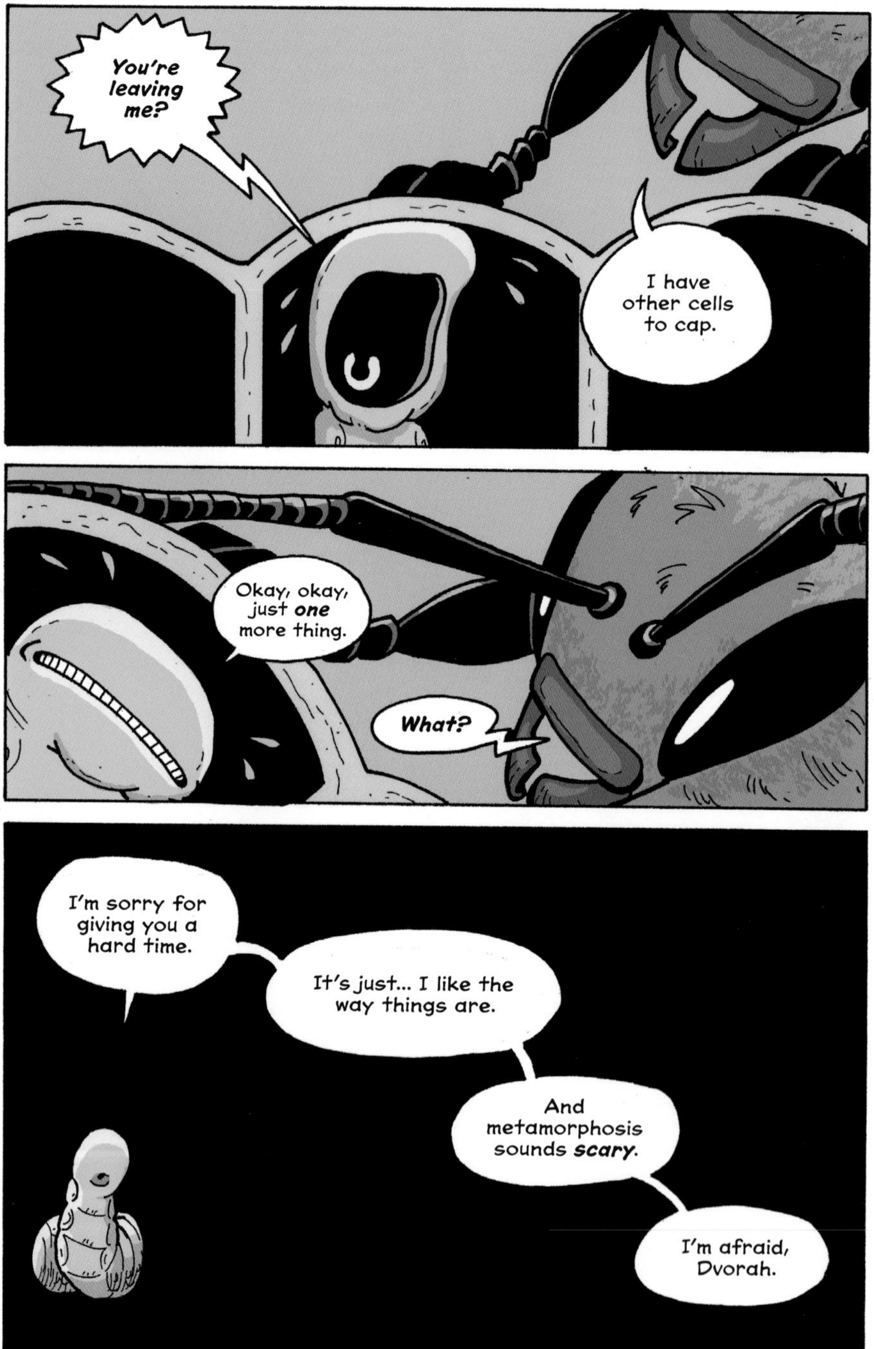
You're leaving me?
I have other cells to cap.
Okay, okay, just **one** more thing.
What?
I'm sorry for giving you a hard time.
It's just... I like the way things are.
And metamorphosis sounds **scary**.
I'm afraid, Dvorah.

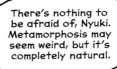

There's nothing to be afraid of, Nyuki. Metamorphosis may seem weird, but it's completely natural.

And when it's all done, I'll be here waiting for you.

I promise.

But it's so dark in here.

I feel so *alone*.

I know.

I felt the same way at your age.

Unfortunately, you have to do this on your own.

But trust me, Nyuki. When this is all over and you crawl out of this little cell...

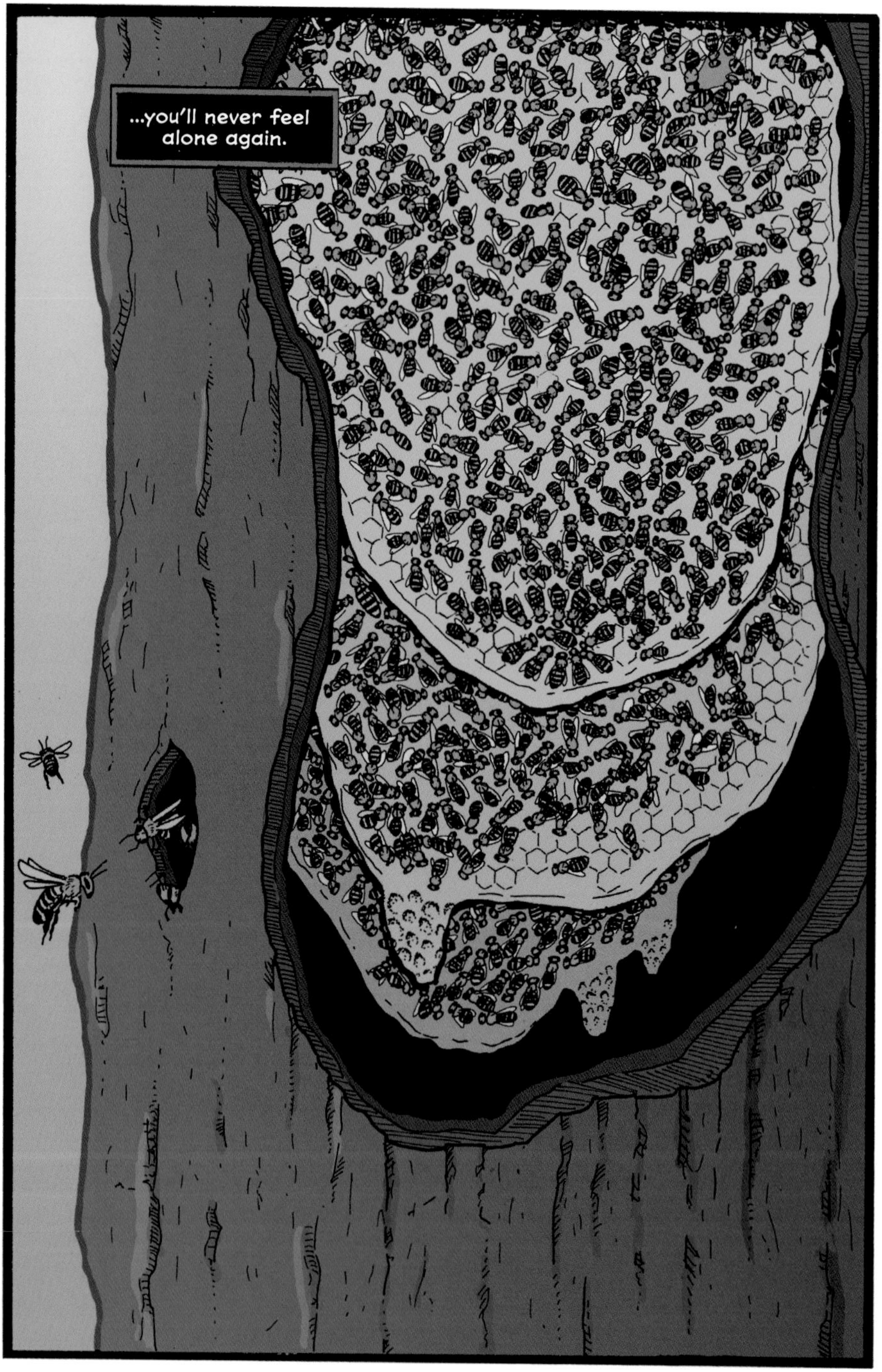
...you'll never feel alone again.

2

SWARM

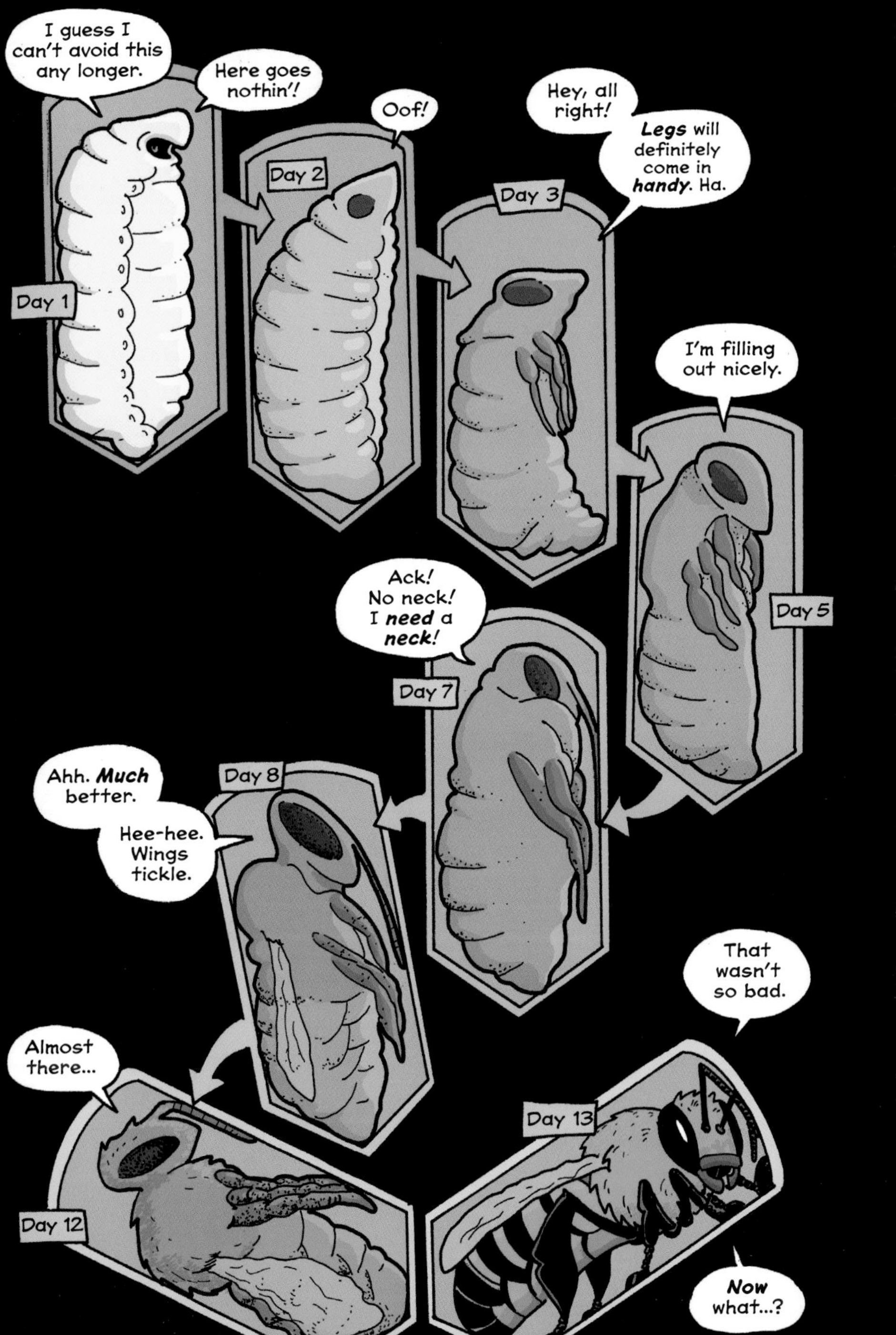
I guess I can't avoid this any longer.
Here goes nothin'!
Day 1
Oof!
Day 2
Hey, all right!
Legs will definitely come in ***handy***. Ha.
Day 3
I'm filling out nicely.
Day 5
Ack! No neck! I ***need*** a ***neck***!
Day 7
Ahh. ***Much*** better.
Hee-hee. Wings tickle.
Day 8
Almost there...
Day 12
That wasn't so bad.
Day 13
Now what...?

Day 13 of metamorphosis (twenty-one days after Nyuki's egg was laid).
GNAW! GNAW! GNAW!
GNAW! SCRITCH! CRACK!
Gah!
GNAW! SCRITCH! GNAW!
Ta-daaaa!

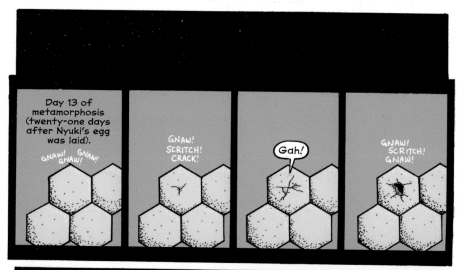

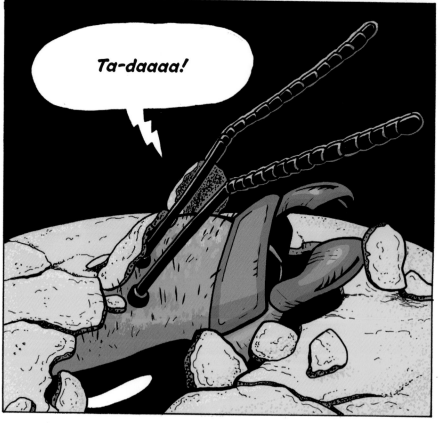

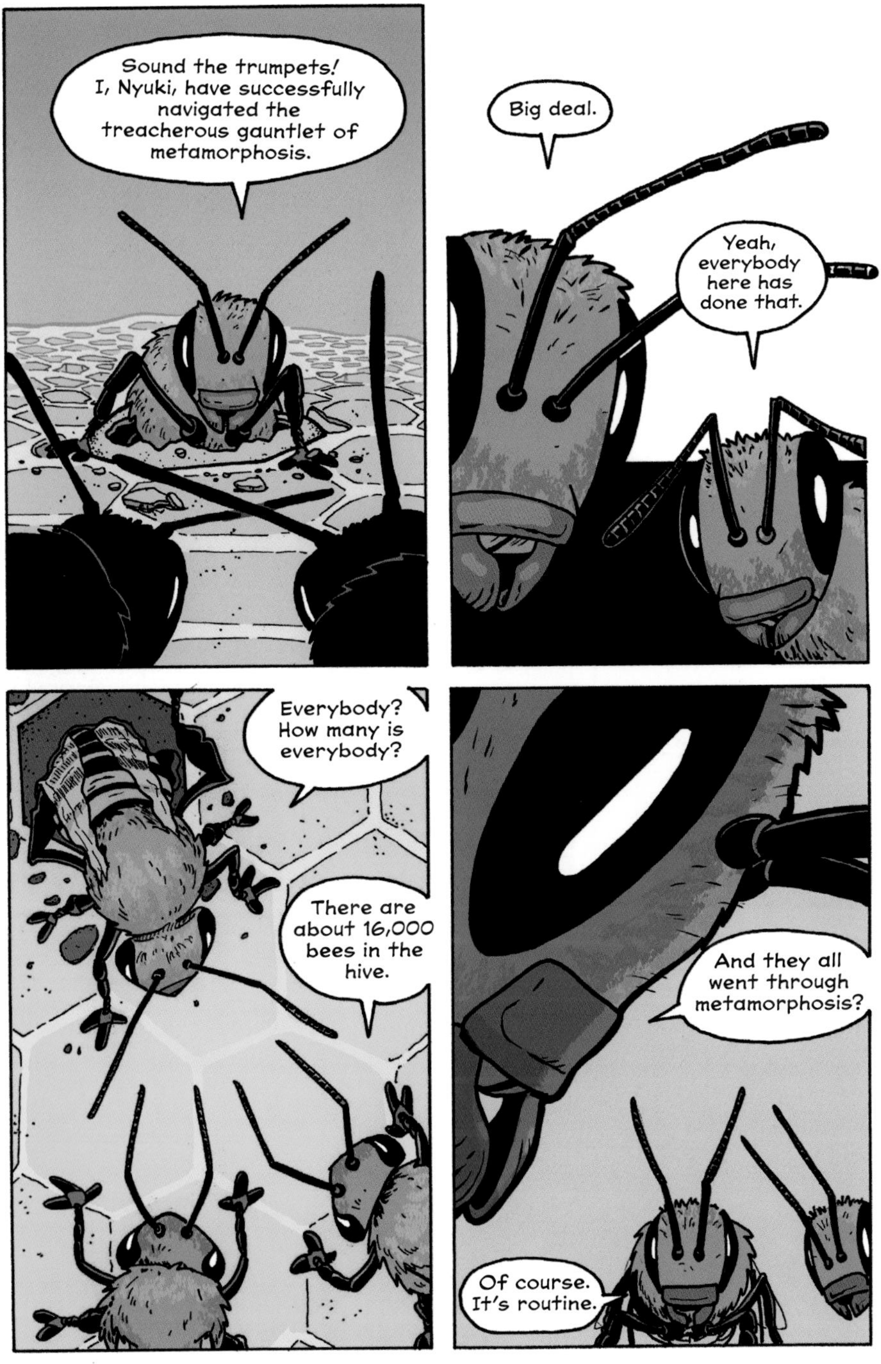
Sound the trumpets! I, Nyuki, have successfully navigated the treacherous gauntlet of metamorphosis.
Big deal.
Yeah, everybody here has done that.
Everybody? How many is everybody?
There are about 16,000 bees in the hive.
And they all went through metamorphosis?
Of course. It's routine.

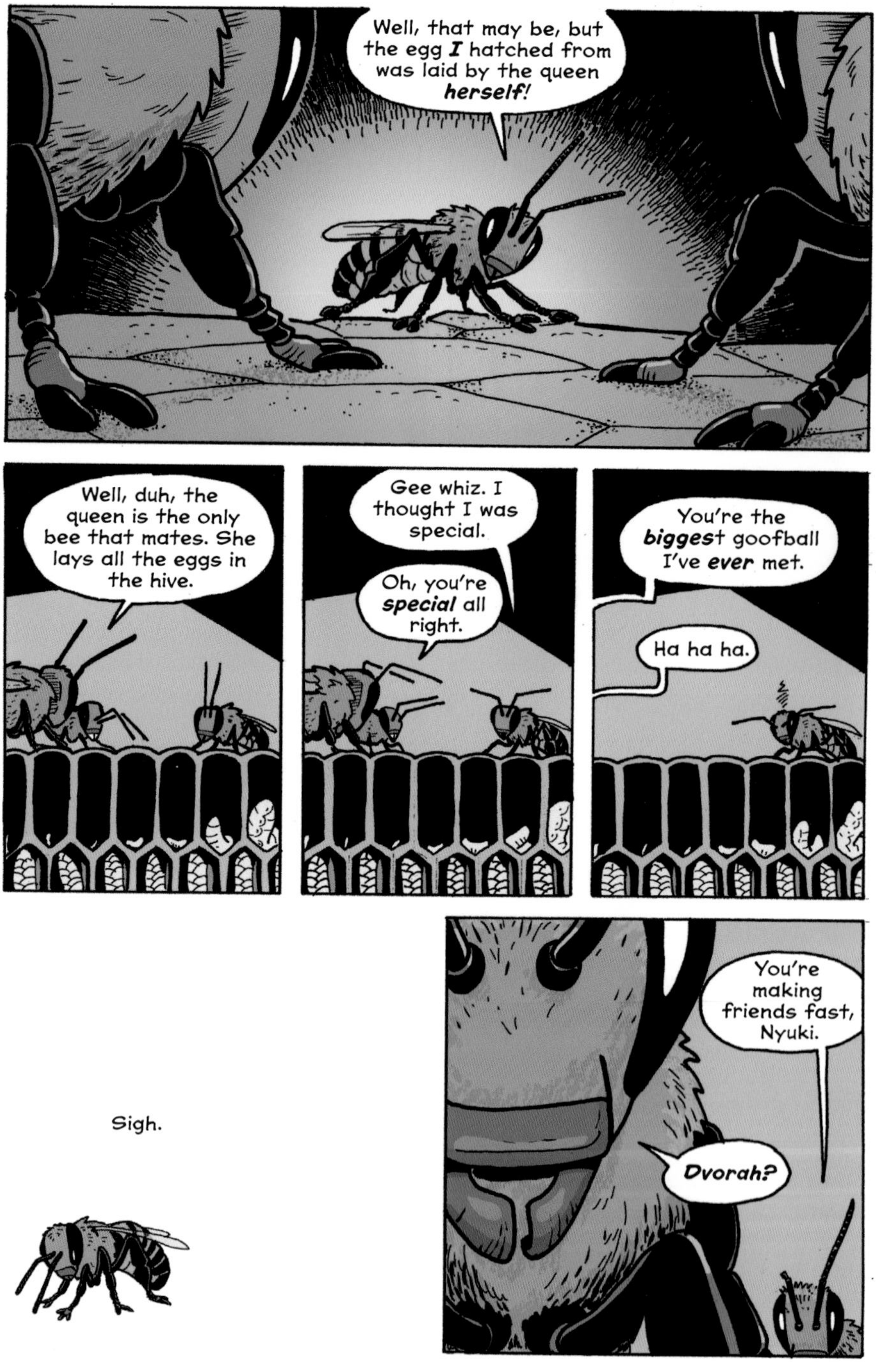
Well, that may be, but the egg *I* hatched from was laid by the queen *herself!*
Well, duh, the queen is the only bee that mates. She lays all the eggs in the hive.
Gee whiz. I thought I was special.
Oh, you're *special* all right.
You're the *biggest* goofball I've *ever* met.
Ha ha ha.
Sigh.
You're making friends fast, Nyuki.
Dvorah?

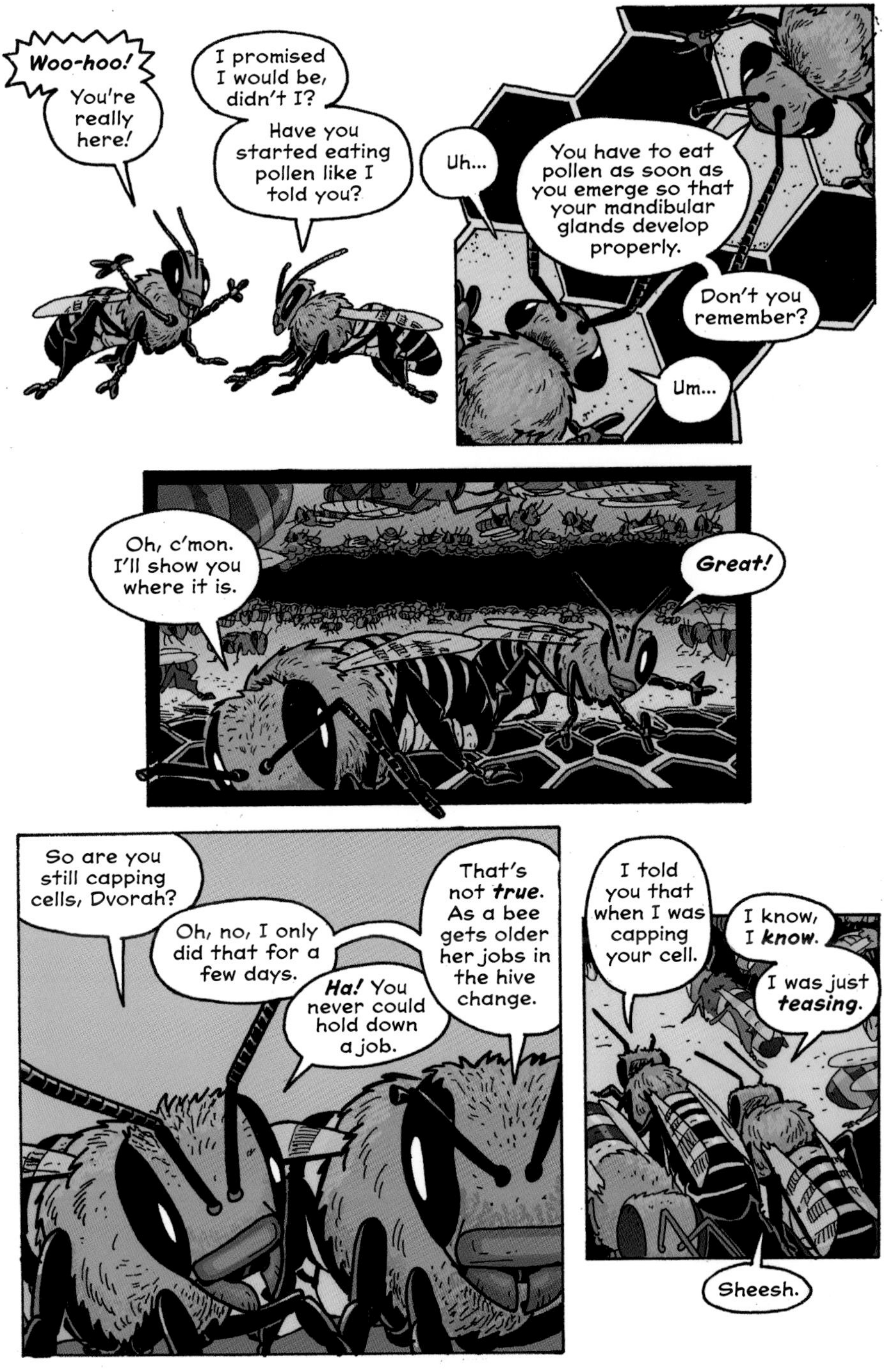
Woo-hoo! You're really here!
I promised I would be, didn't I?
Have you started eating pollen like I told you?
Uh...
You have to eat pollen as soon as you emerge so that your mandibular glands develop properly.
Don't you remember?
Um...
Oh, c'mon. I'll show you where it is.
Great!
So are you still capping cells, Dvorah?
Oh, no, I only did that for a few days.
Ha! You never could hold down a job.
That's not true. As a bee gets older her jobs in the hive change.
I told you that when I was capping your cell.
I know, I know.
I was just teasing.
Sheesh.

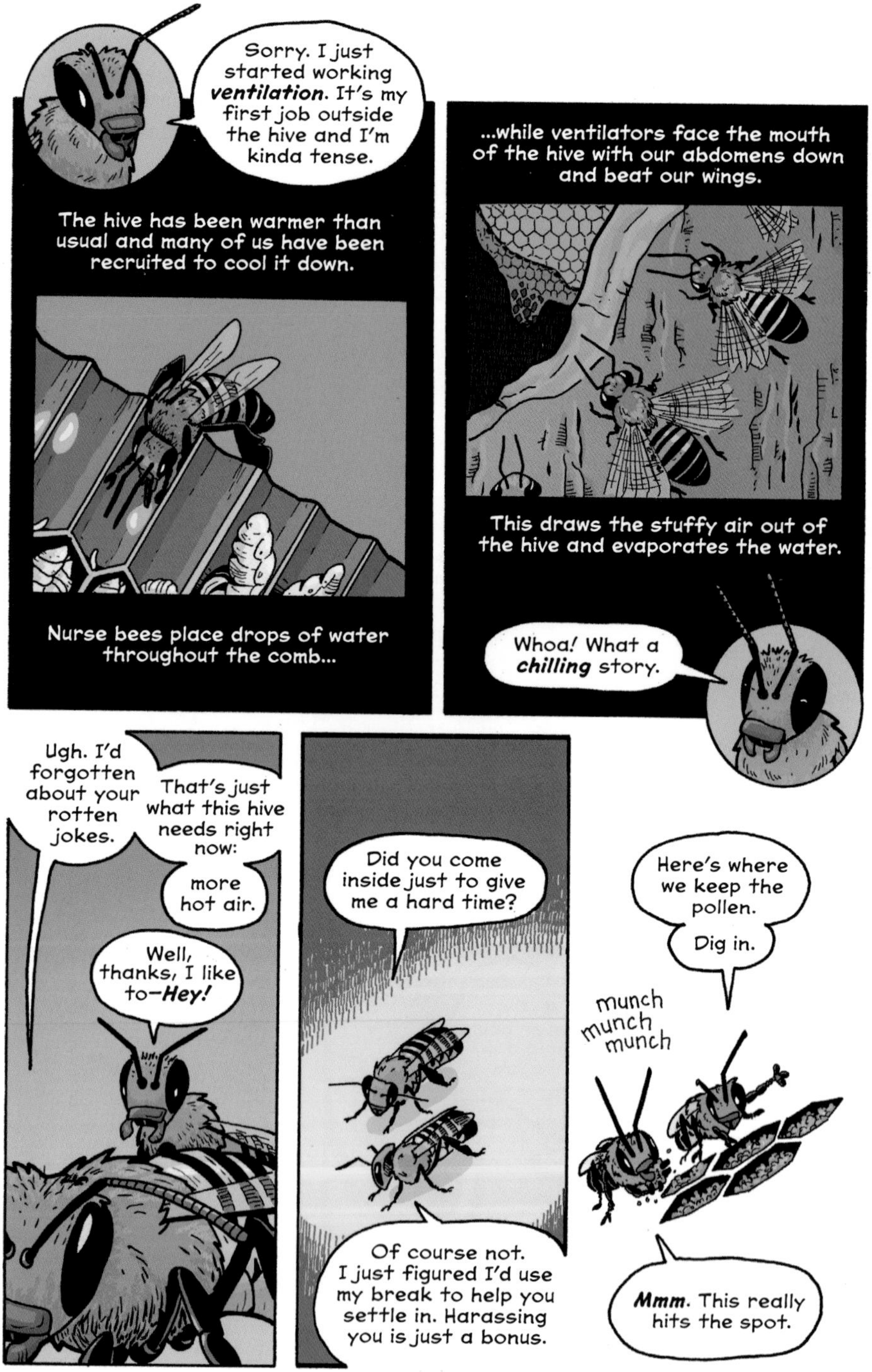
Sorry. I just started working *ventilation*. It's my first job outside the hive and I'm kinda tense.
The hive has been warmer than usual and many of us have been recruited to cool it down.
Nurse bees place drops of water throughout the comb...
...while ventilators face the mouth of the hive with our abdomens down and beat our wings.
This draws the stuffy air out of the hive and evaporates the water.
Whoa! What a *chilling* story.
Ugh. I'd forgotten about your rotten jokes.
That's just what this hive needs right now:
more hot air.
Well, thanks, I like to—*Hey!*
Did you come inside just to give me a hard time?
Of course not. I just figured I'd use my break to help you settle in. Harassing you is just a bonus.
Here's where we keep the pollen.
Dig in.
munch munch munch
Mmm. This really hits the spot.

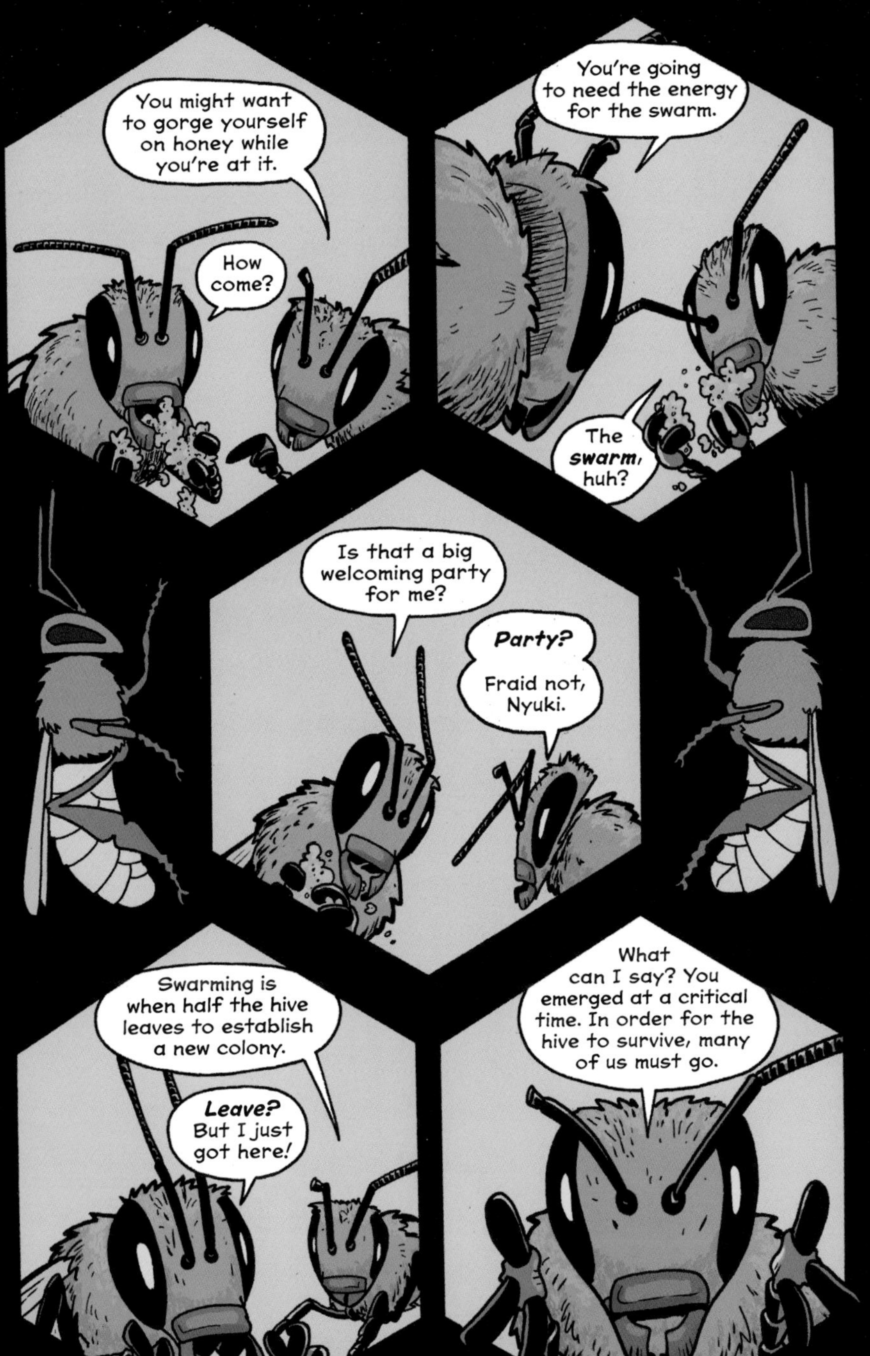
You might want to gorge yourself on honey while you're at it.
How come?
You're going to need the energy for the swarm.
The *swarm*, huh?
Is that a big welcoming party for me?
Party?
Fraid not, Nyuki.
Swarming is when half the hive leaves to establish a new colony.
Leave? But I just got here!
What can I say? You emerged at a critical time. In order for the hive to survive, many of us must go.

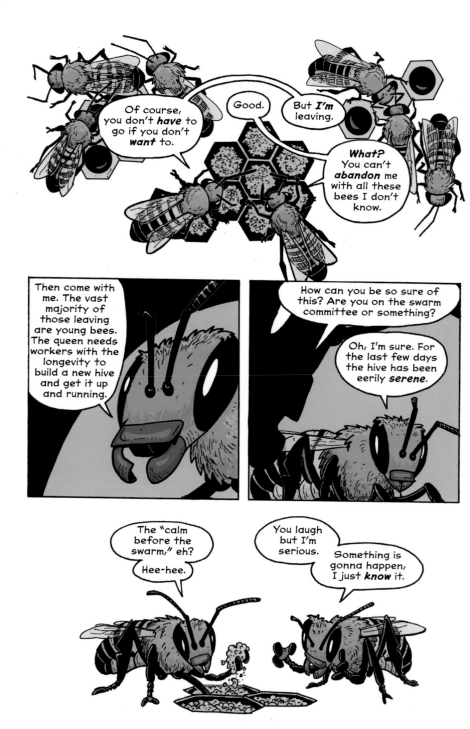

Of course, you don't **have** to go if you don't **want** to.

Good.

But **I'm** leaving.

What? You can't **abandon** me with all these bees I don't know.

Then come with me. The vast majority of those leaving are young bees. The queen needs workers with the longevity to build a new hive and get it up and running.

How can you be so sure of this? Are you on the swarm committee or something?

Oh, I'm sure. For the last few days the hive has been eerily **serene**.

The "calm before the swarm," eh?

Hee-hee.

You laugh but I'm serious.

Something is gonna happen, I just **know** it.

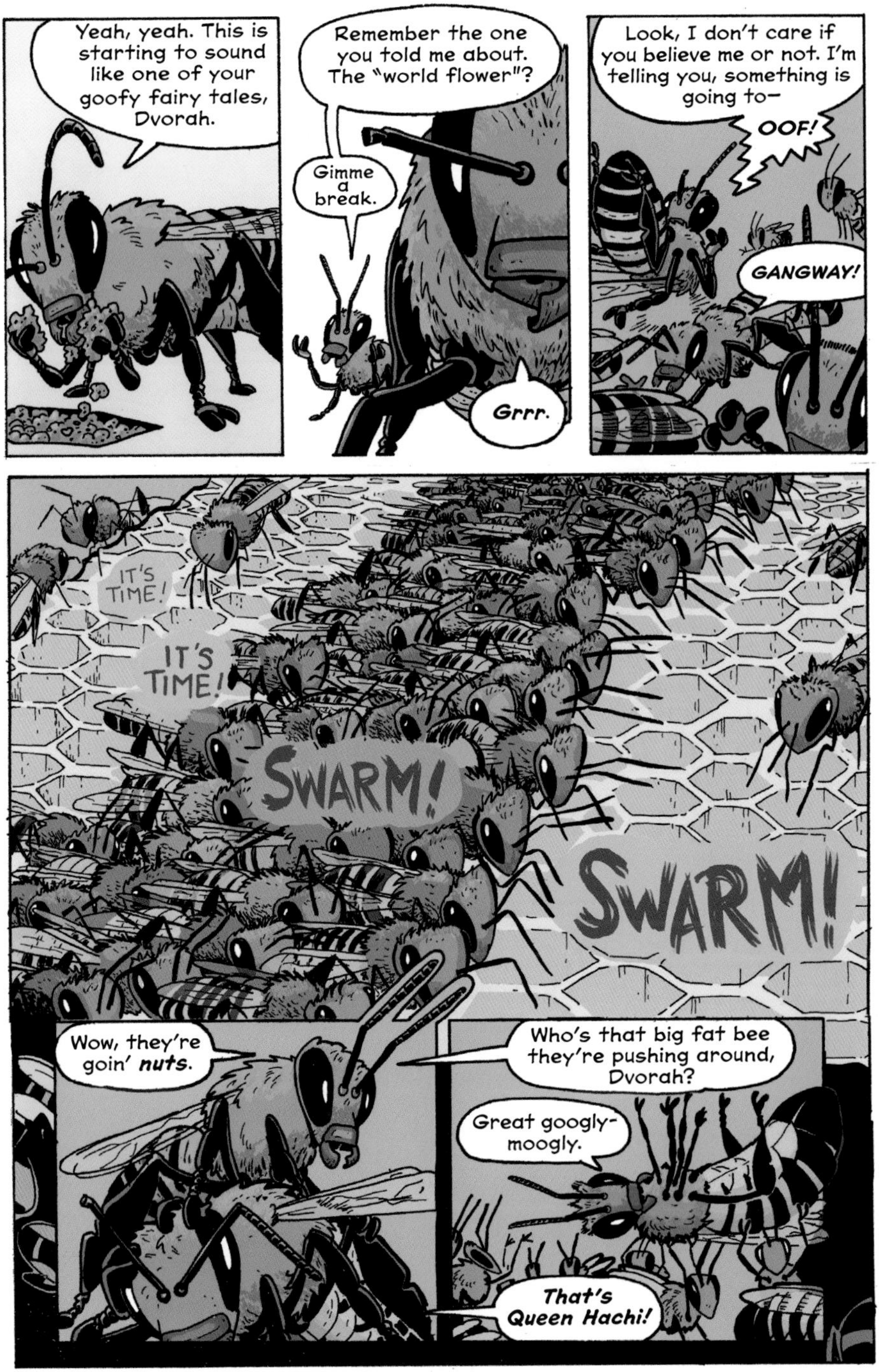
Yeah, yeah. This is starting to sound like one of your goofy fairy tales, Dvorah.
Remember the one you told me about. The "world flower"?
Gimme a break.
Grrr.
Look, I don't care if you believe me or not. I'm telling you, something is going to–
OOF!
GANGWAY!
IT'S TIME!
IT'S TIME!
SWARM!
SWARM!
Wow, they're goin' *nuts*.
Who's that big fat bee they're pushing around, Dvorah?
Great googly-moogly.
That's Queen Hachi!

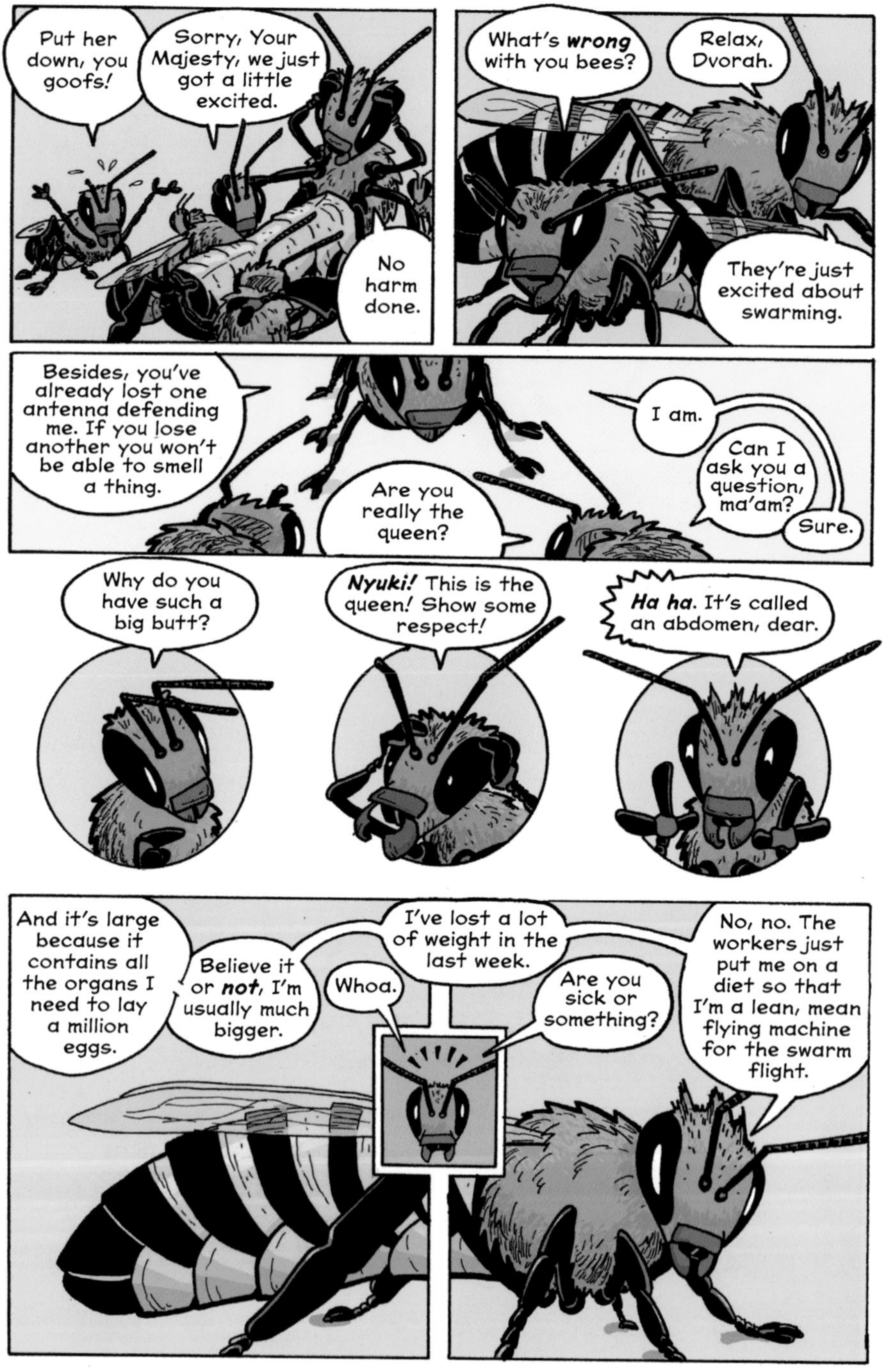

Put her down, you goofs!
Sorry, Your Majesty, we just got a little excited.
No harm done.
What's **wrong** with you bees?
Relax, Dvorah.
They're just excited about swarming.
Besides, you've already lost one antenna defending me. If you lose another you won't be able to smell a thing.
I am.
Can I ask you a question, ma'am?
Sure.
Are you really the queen?
Why do you have such a big butt?
Nyuki! This is the queen! Show some respect!
Ha ha. It's called an abdomen, dear.
And it's large because it contains all the organs I need to lay a million eggs.
Believe it or ***not***, I'm usually much bigger.
I've lost a lot of weight in the last week.
Whoa.
Are you sick or something?
No, no. The workers just put me on a diet so that I'm a lean, mean flying machine for the swarm flight.

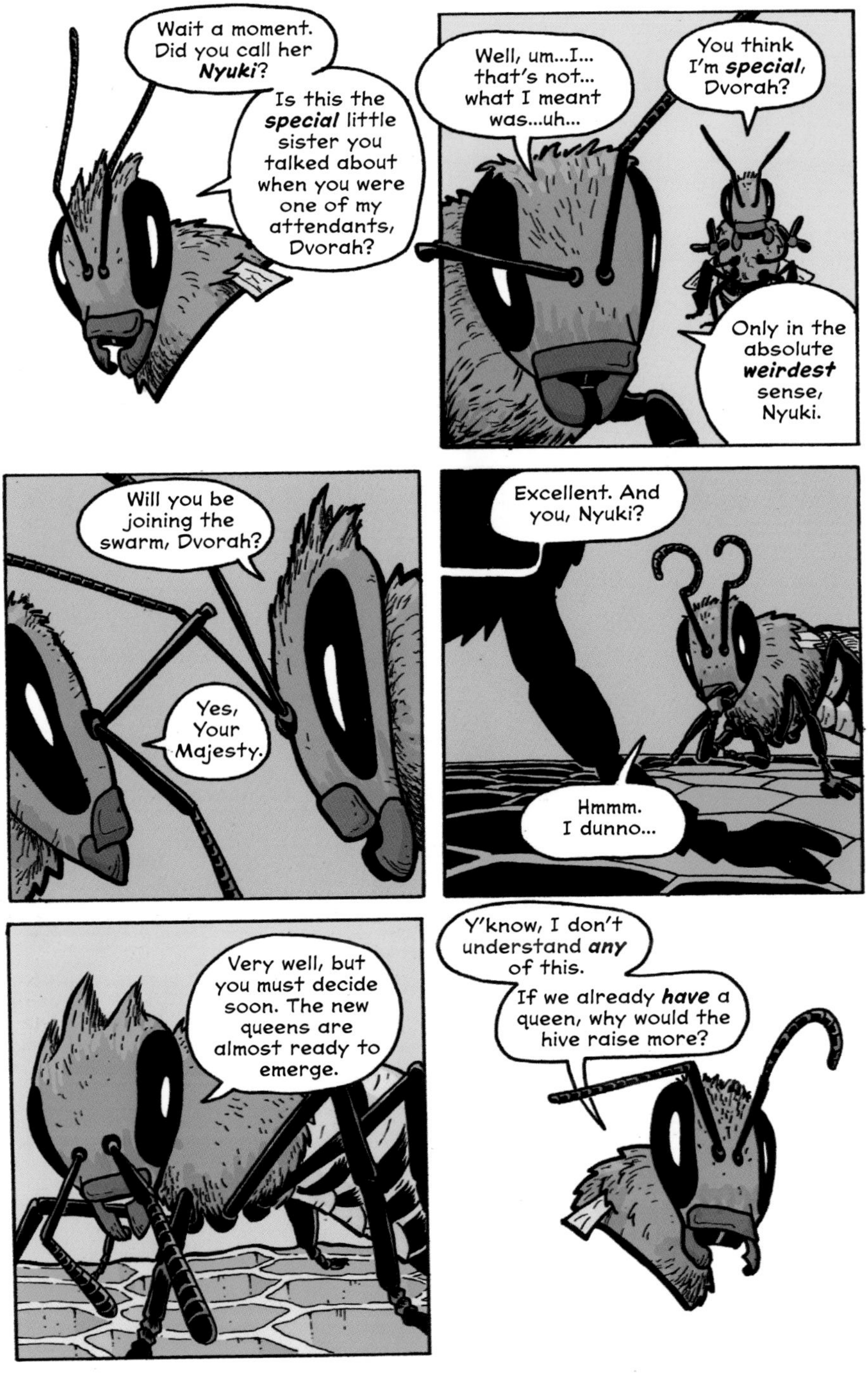
Wait a moment. Did you call her *Nyuki*?
Is this the *special* little sister you talked about when you were one of my attendants, Dvorah?
Well, um...I... that's not... what I meant was...uh...
You think I'm *special*, Dvorah?
Only in the absolute *weirdest* sense, Nyuki.
Will you be joining the swarm, Dvorah?
Yes, Your Majesty.
Excellent. And you, Nyuki?
Hmmm. I dunno...
Very well, but you must decide soon. The new queens are almost ready to emerge.
Y'know, I don't understand *any* of this.
If we already *have* a queen, why would the hive raise more?

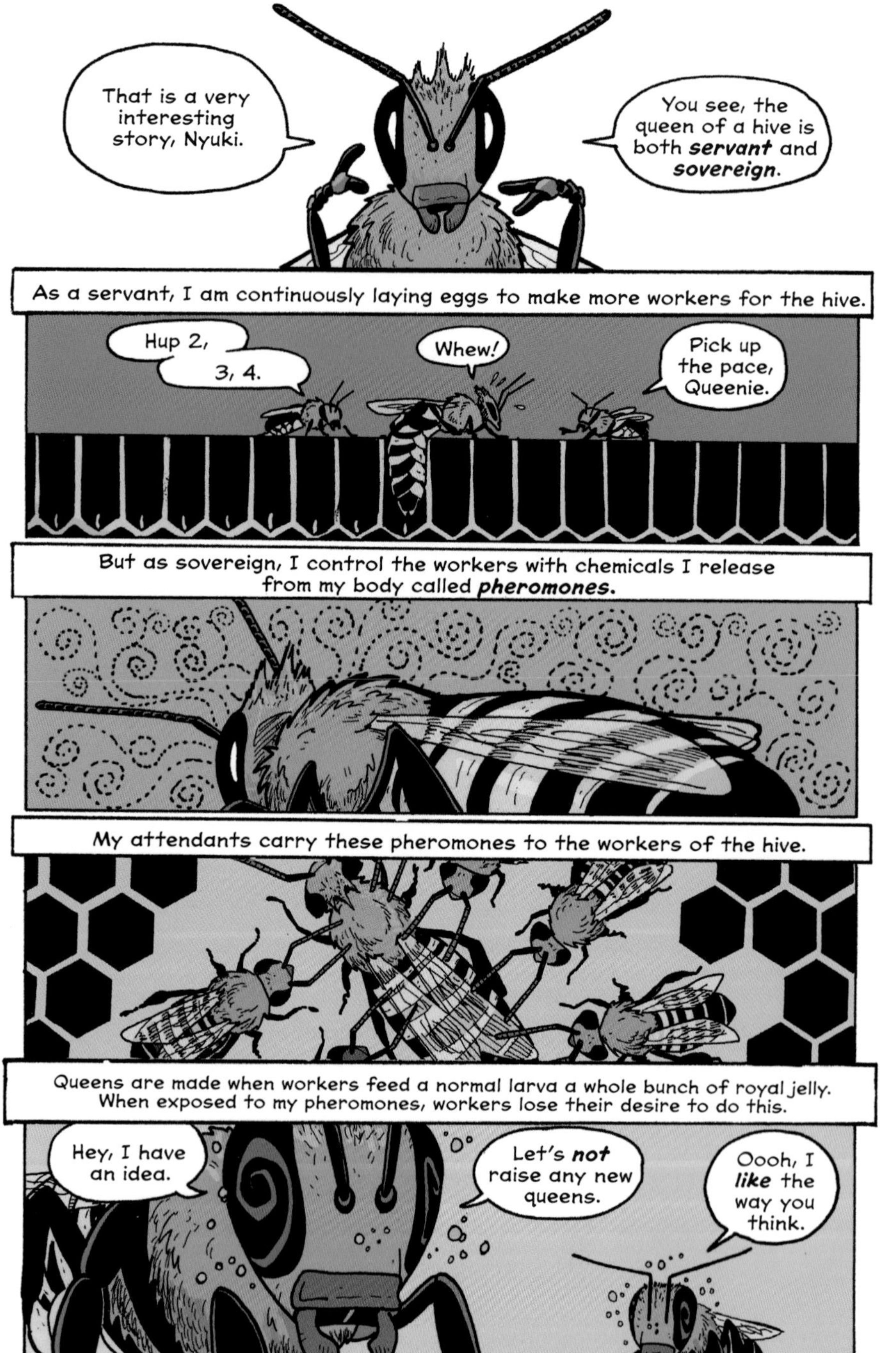
That is a very interesting story, Nyuki.
You see, the queen of a hive is both ***servant*** and ***sovereign***.
As a servant, I am continuously laying eggs to make more workers for the hive.
Hup 2,
3, 4.
Whew!
Pick up the pace, Queenie.
But as sovereign, I control the workers with chemicals I release from my body called ***pheromones***.
My attendants carry these pheromones to the workers of the hive.
Queens are made when workers feed a normal larva a whole bunch of royal jelly. When exposed to my pheromones, workers lose their desire to do this.
Hey, I have an idea.
Let's ***not*** raise any new queens.
Oooh, I ***like*** the way you think.

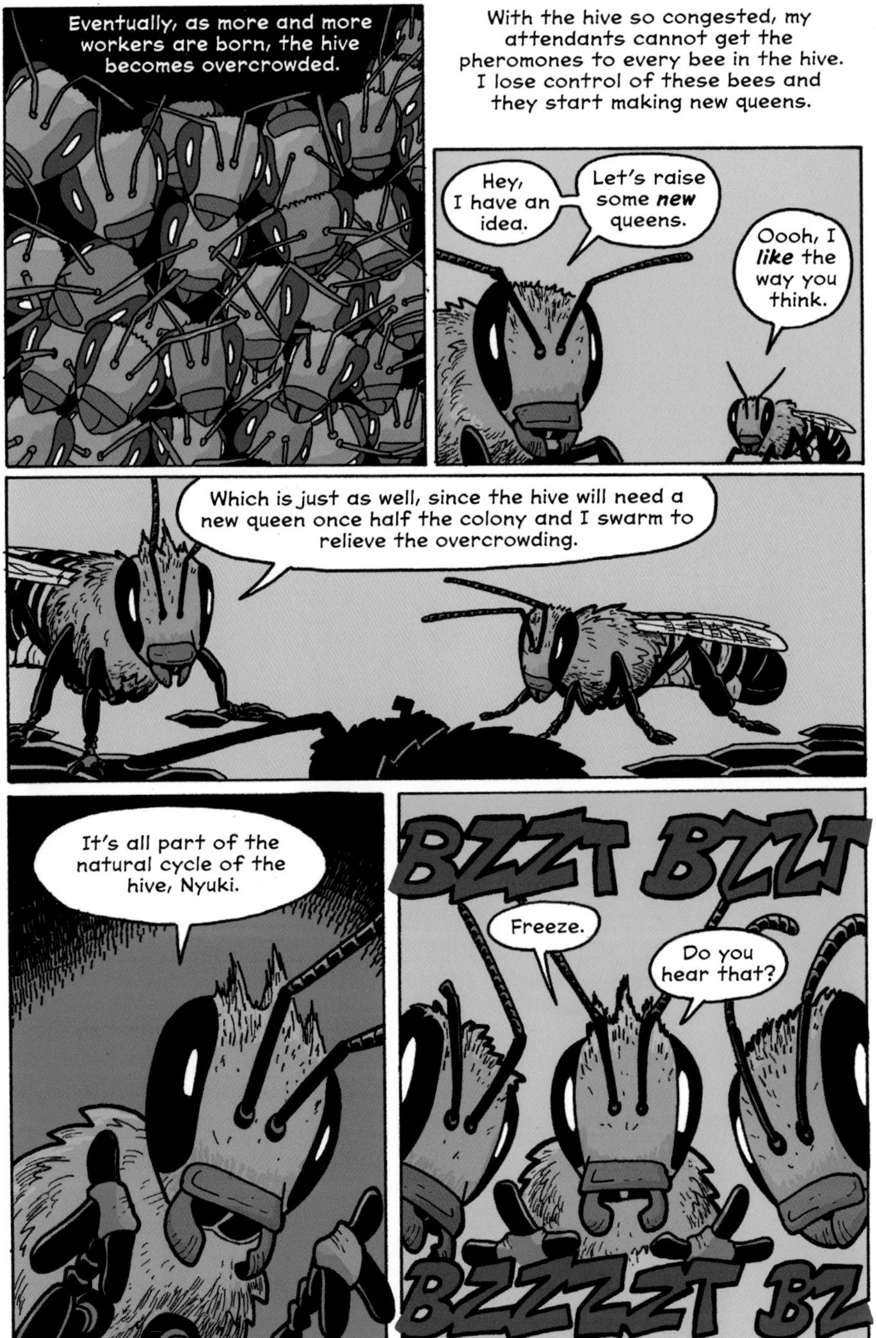
Eventually, as more and more workers are born, the hive becomes overcrowded.
With the hive so congested, my attendants cannot get the pheromones to every bee in the hive. I lose control of these bees and they start making new queens.
Hey, I have an idea.
Let's raise some *new* queens.
Oooh, I *like* the way you think.
Which is just as well, since the hive will need a new queen once half the colony and I swarm to relieve the overcrowding.
It's all part of the natural cycle of the hive, Nyuki.
BZZT BZZT
Freeze.
Do you hear that?
BZZZZT BZ

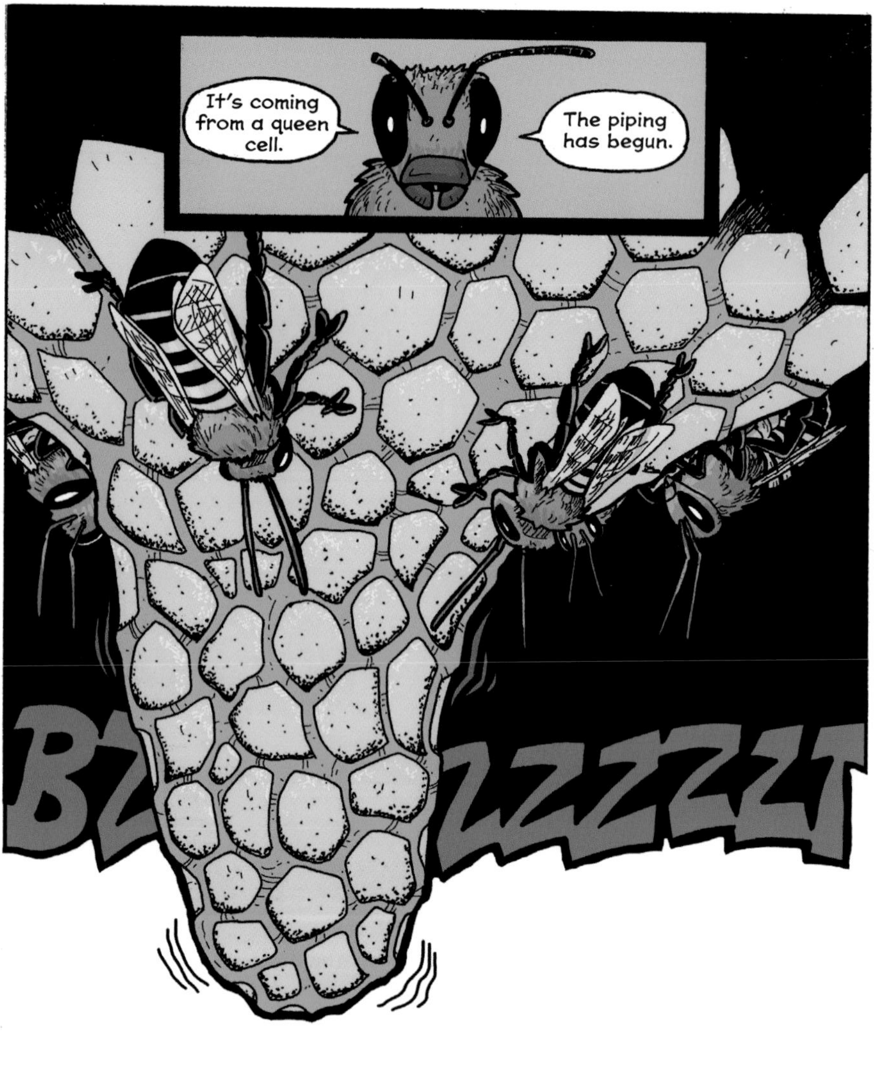
It's coming from a queen cell.
The piping has begun.
BZZZZZZT

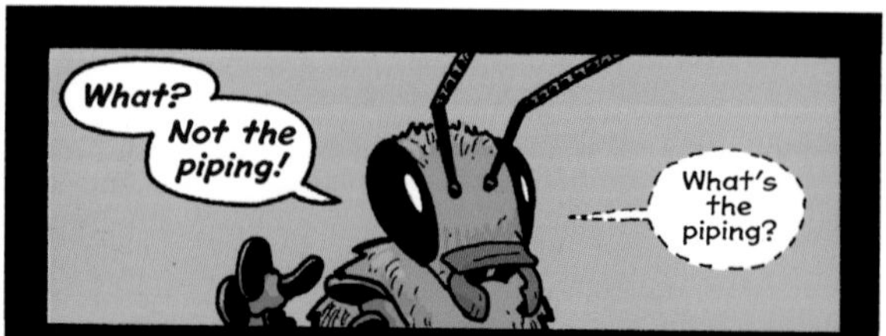
What? Not the piping!
What's the piping?

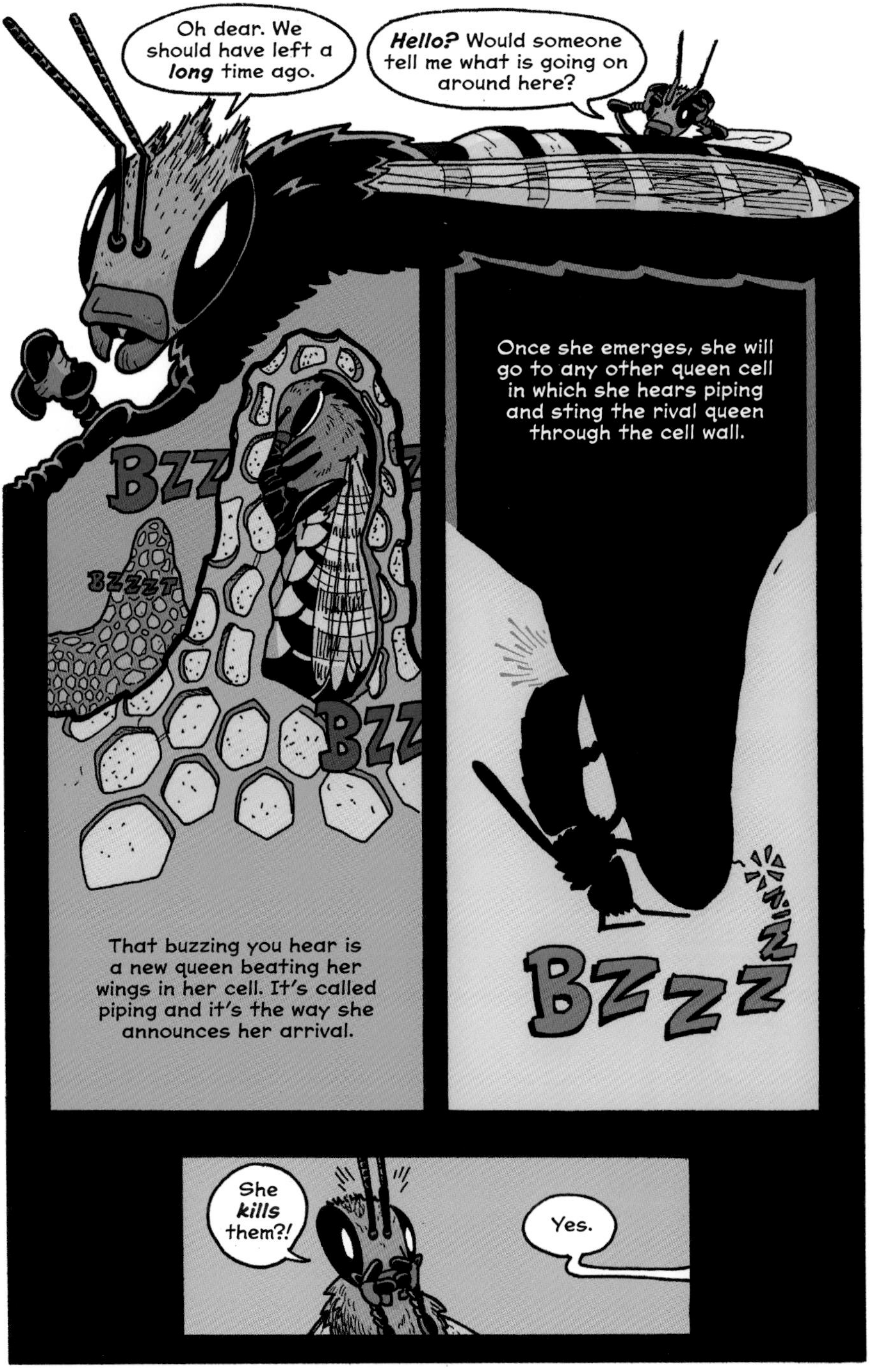

Oh dear. We should have left a **long** time ago.
Hello? Would someone tell me what is going on around here?
BZZ
BZZZT
BZZ
That buzzing you hear is a new queen beating her wings in her cell. It's called piping and it's the way she announces her arrival.
Once she emerges, she will go to any other queen cell in which she hears piping and sting the rival queen through the cell wall.
BZZZZ
She **kills** them?!
Yes.

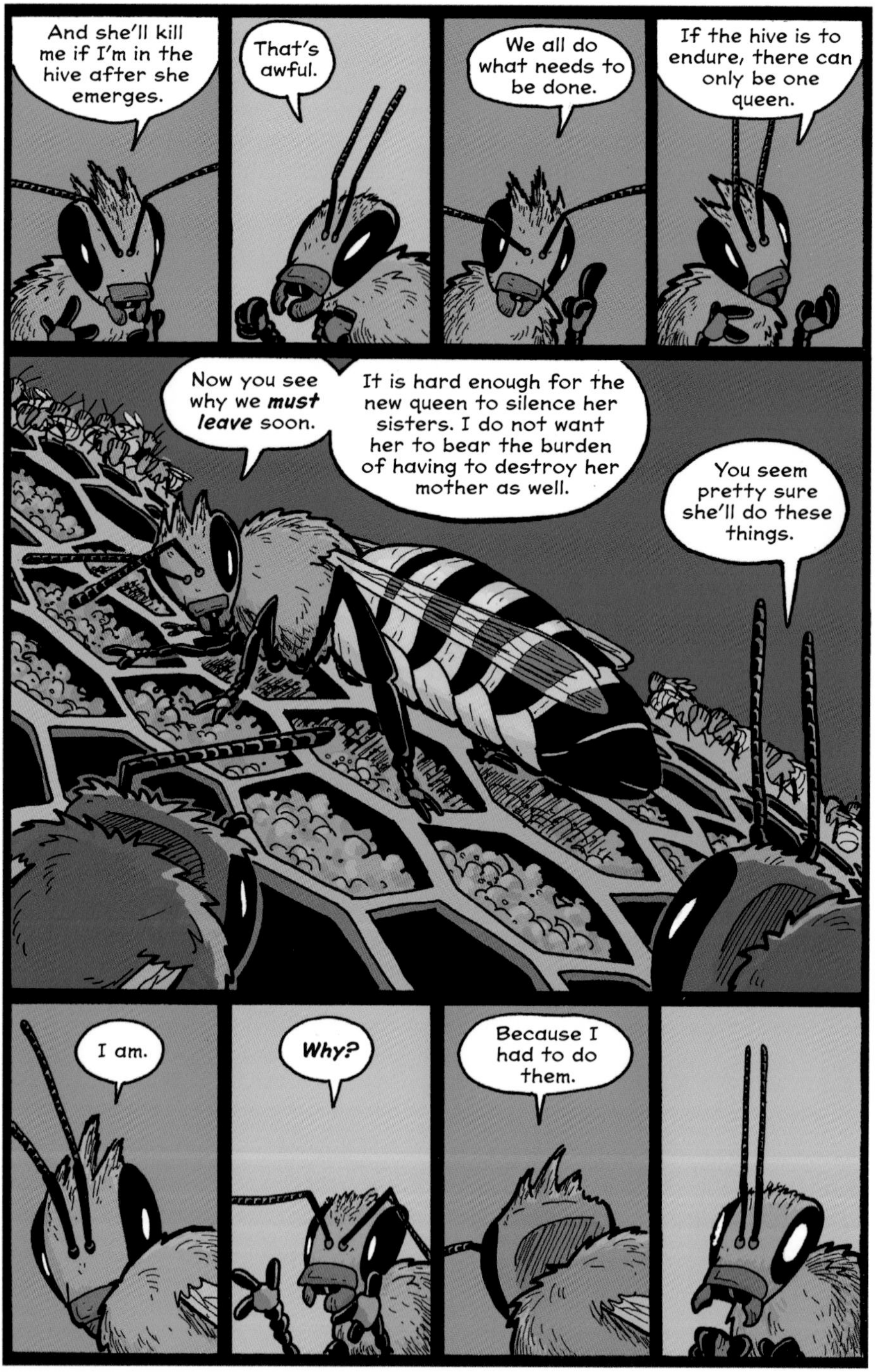
And she'll kill me if I'm in the hive after she emerges.
That's awful.
We all do what needs to be done.
If the hive is to endure, there can only be one queen.
Now you see why we ***must leave*** soon.
It is hard enough for the new queen to silence her sisters. I do not want her to bear the burden of having to destroy her mother as well.
You seem pretty sure she'll do these things.
I am.
Why?
Because I had to do them.

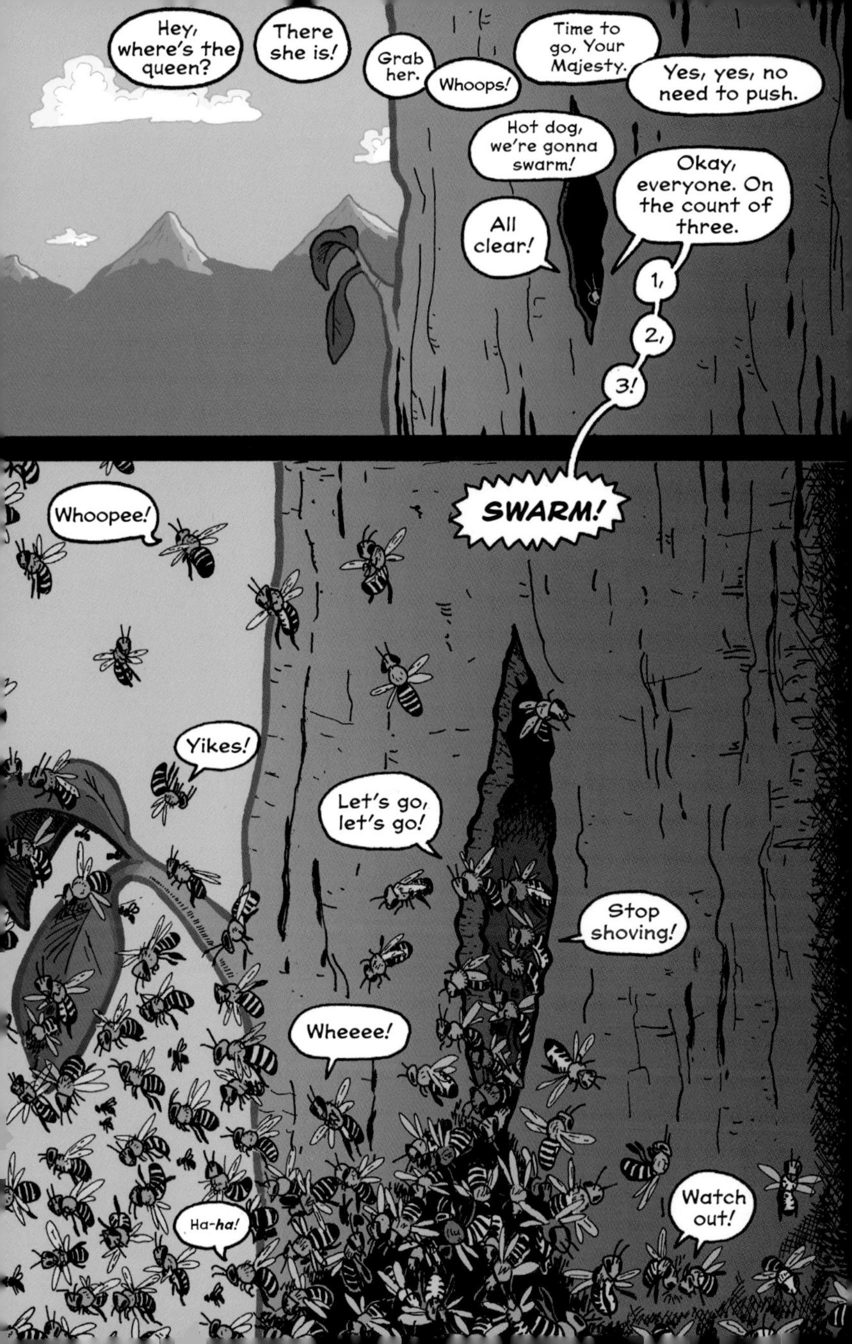
Hey, where's the queen?
There she is!
Grab her.
Whoops!
Time to go, Your Majesty.
Yes, yes, no need to push.
Hot dog, we're gonna swarm!
All clear!
Okay, everyone. On the count of three.
1,
2,
3!
SWARM!
Whoopee!
Yikes!
Let's go, let's go!
Stop shoving!
Wheeee!
Ha-*ha*!
Watch out!

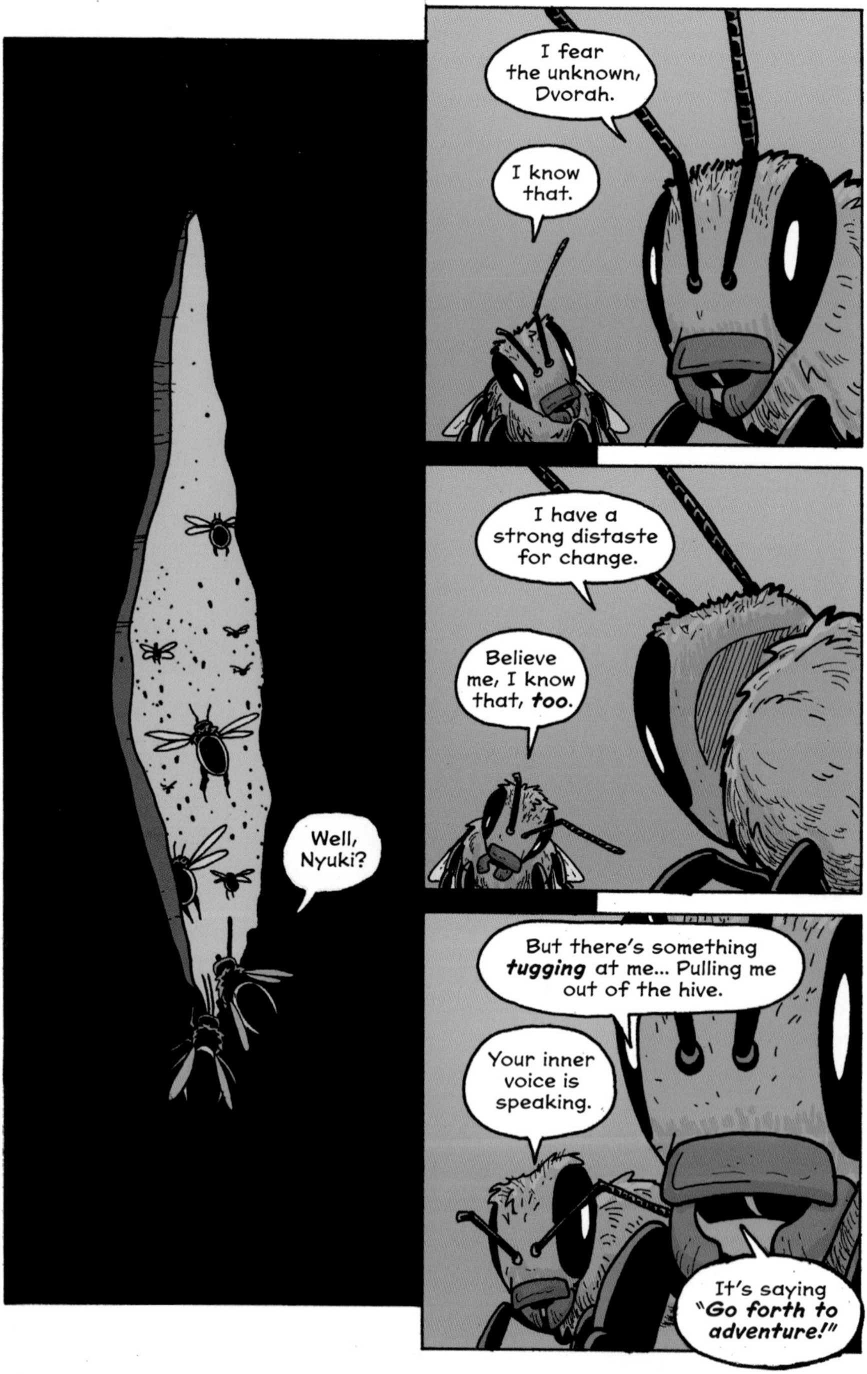
Well, Nyuki?
I fear the unknown, Dvorah.
I know that.
I have a strong distaste for change.
Believe me, I know that, *too*.
But there's something *tugging* at me... Pulling me out of the hive.
Your inner voice is speaking.
It's saying "*Go forth to adventure!*"

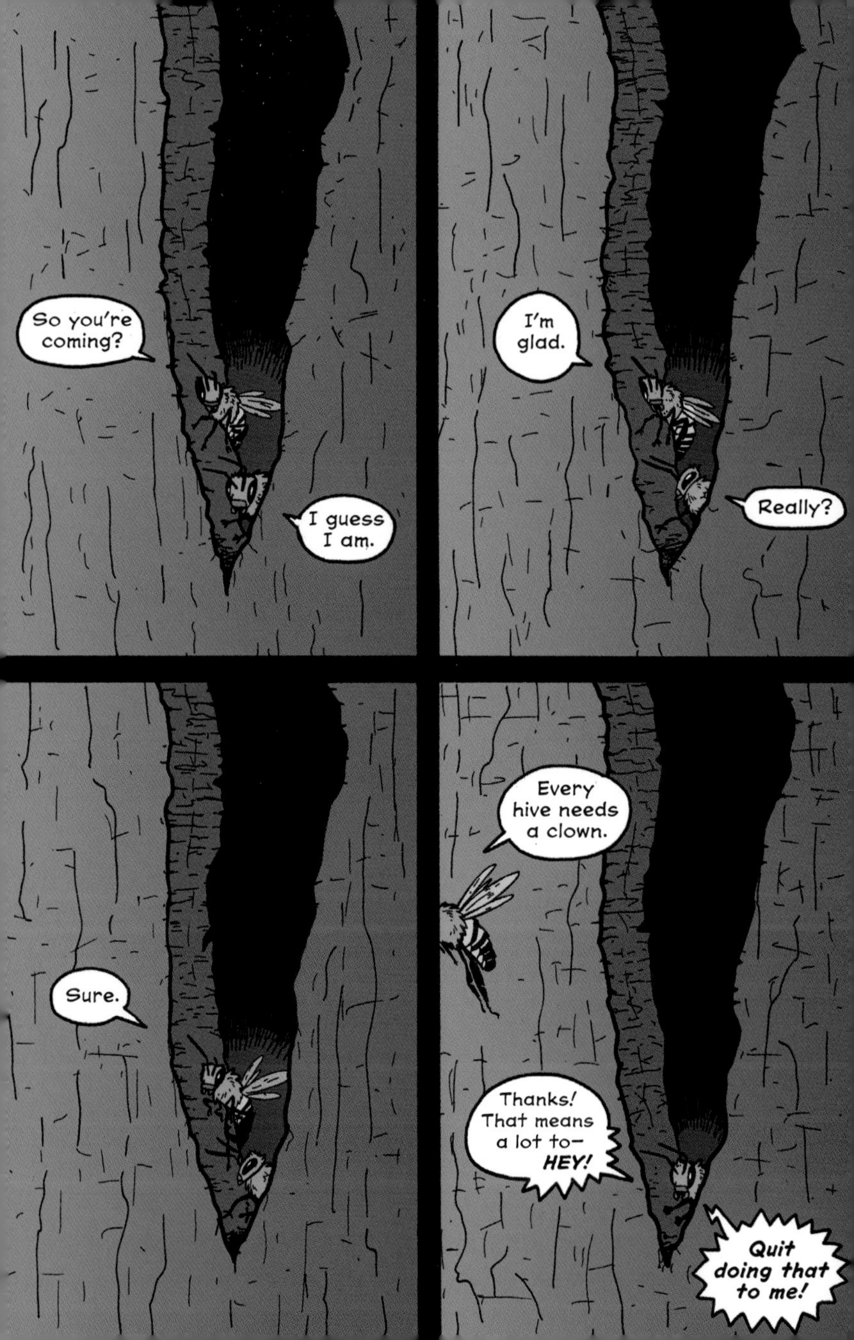
So you're coming?
I guess I am.
I'm glad.
Really?
Sure.
Every hive needs a clown.
Thanks! That means a lot to— HEY!
Quit doing that to me!

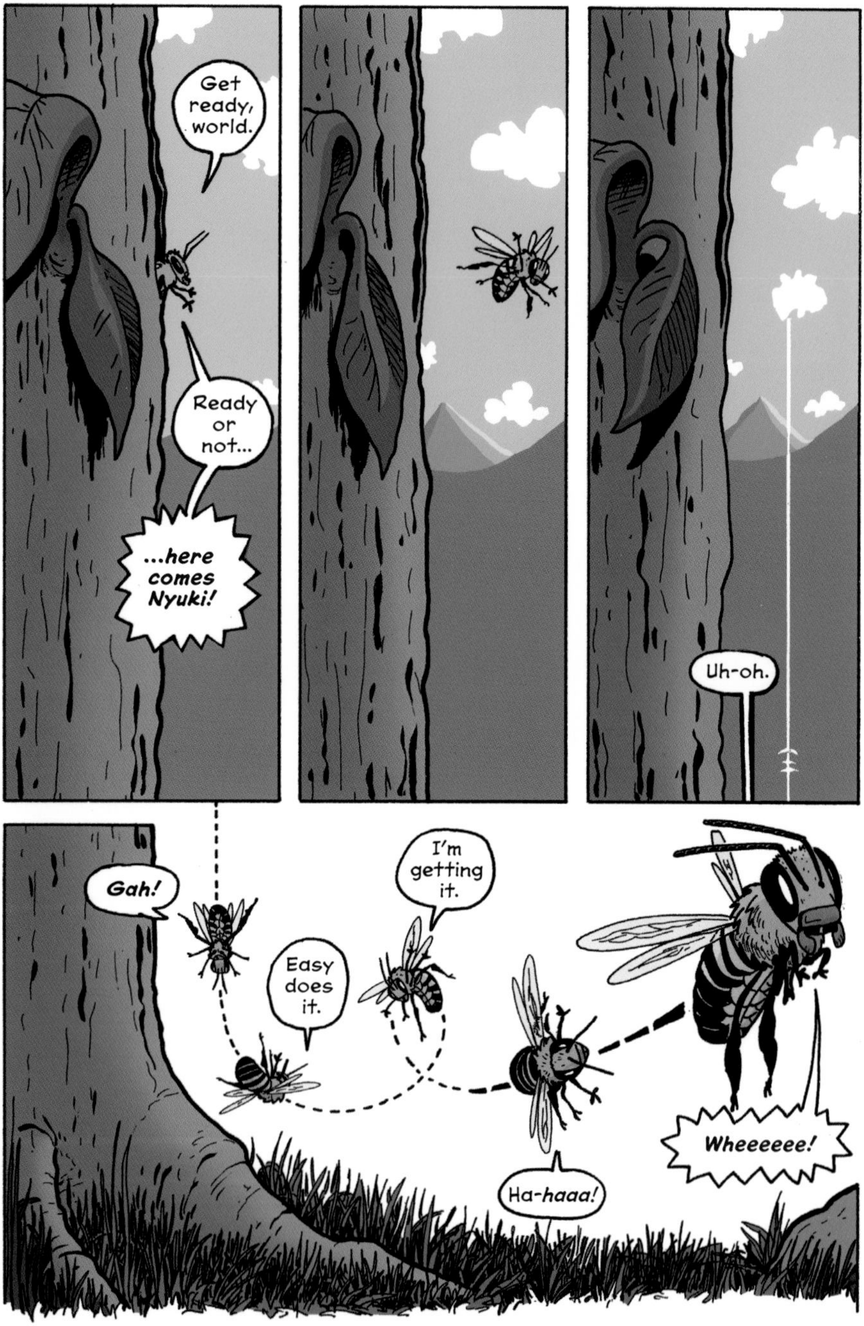
Get ready, world.
Ready or not...
...here comes Nyuki!
Uh-oh.
Gah!
Easy does it.
I'm getting it.
Ha-haaa!
Wheeeeee!

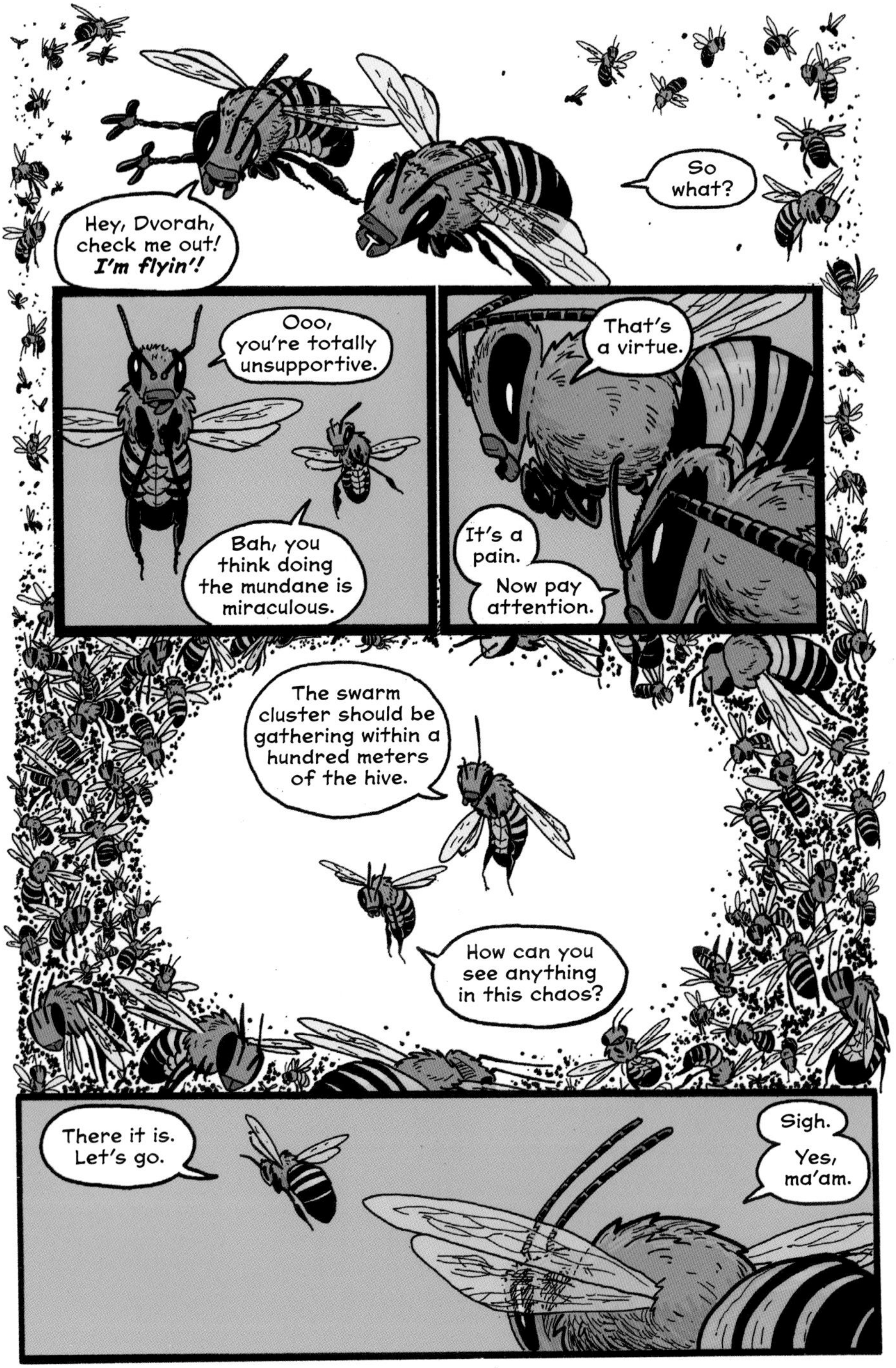
Hey, Dvorah, check me out! *I'm flyin'!*
So what?
Ooo, you're totally unsupportive.
Bah, you think doing the mundane is miraculous.
That's a virtue.
It's a pain.
Now pay attention.
The swarm cluster should be gathering within a hundred meters of the hive.
How can you see anything in this chaos?
There it is. Let's go.
Sigh.
Yes, ma'am.

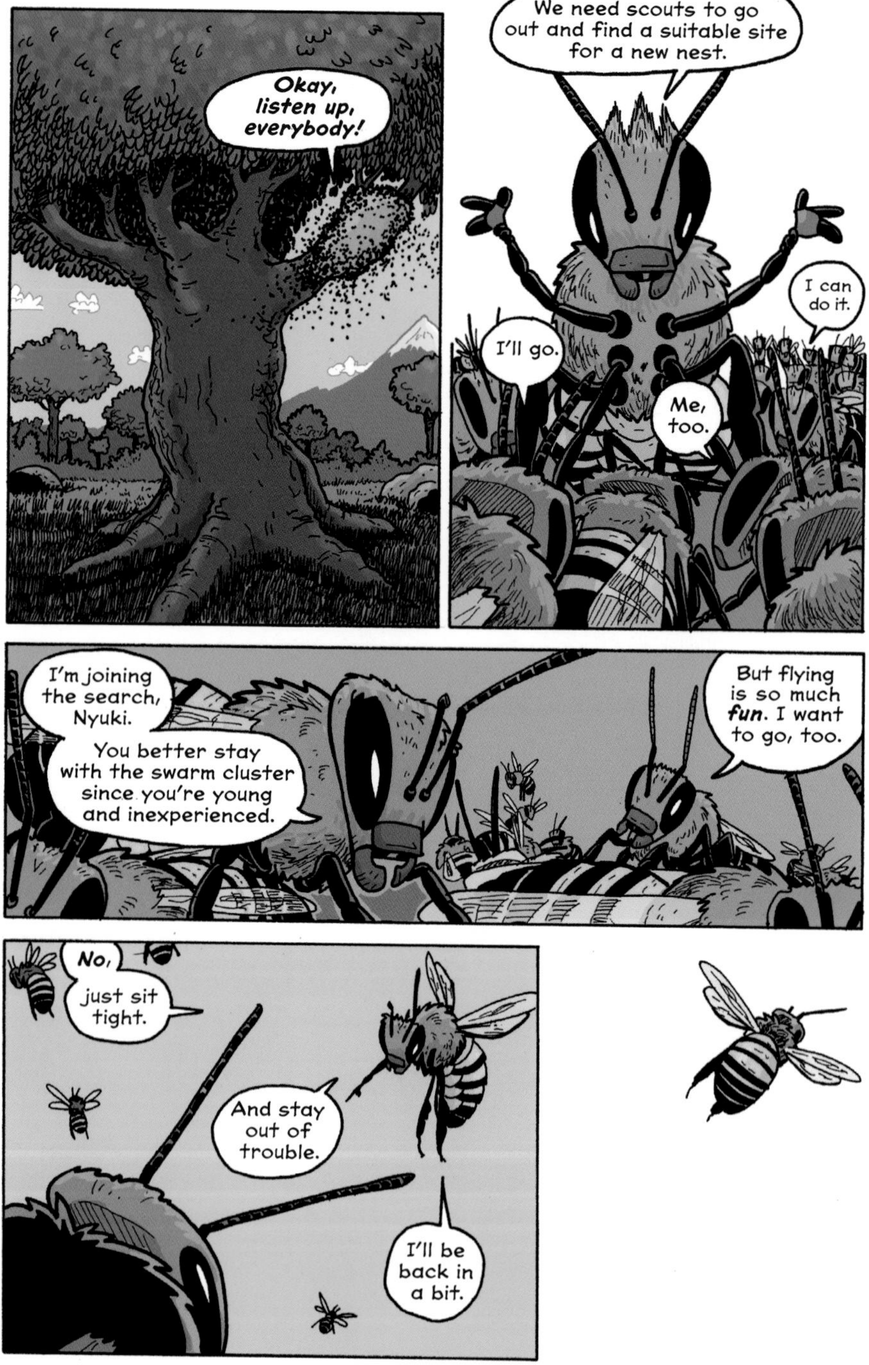
Okay, listen up, everybody!
We need scouts to go out and find a suitable site for a new nest.
I'll go.
I can do it.
Me, too.
I'm joining the search, Nyuki.
You better stay with the swarm cluster since you're young and inexperienced.
But flying is so much **fun**. I want to go, too.
No, just sit tight.
And stay out of trouble.
I'll be back in a bit.

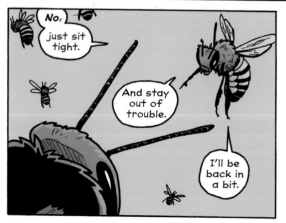

Hello, sister!

Yipe!

I am your brother Zambur.

You scared me.

But it is only I, your brother **Zambur.**

Sorry, Zambur. My name's Nyuki.

So we just sit here and wait, huh?

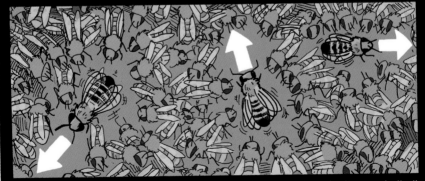

Ah, yes. Soon the scout bees will return with many possible nest sites. They each will do a dance that points in the direction of the nest site they have found.

The better the nest site, the more exciting the dance. Eventually, we shall all attend to the scout with the best dance and follow her to the new nest.

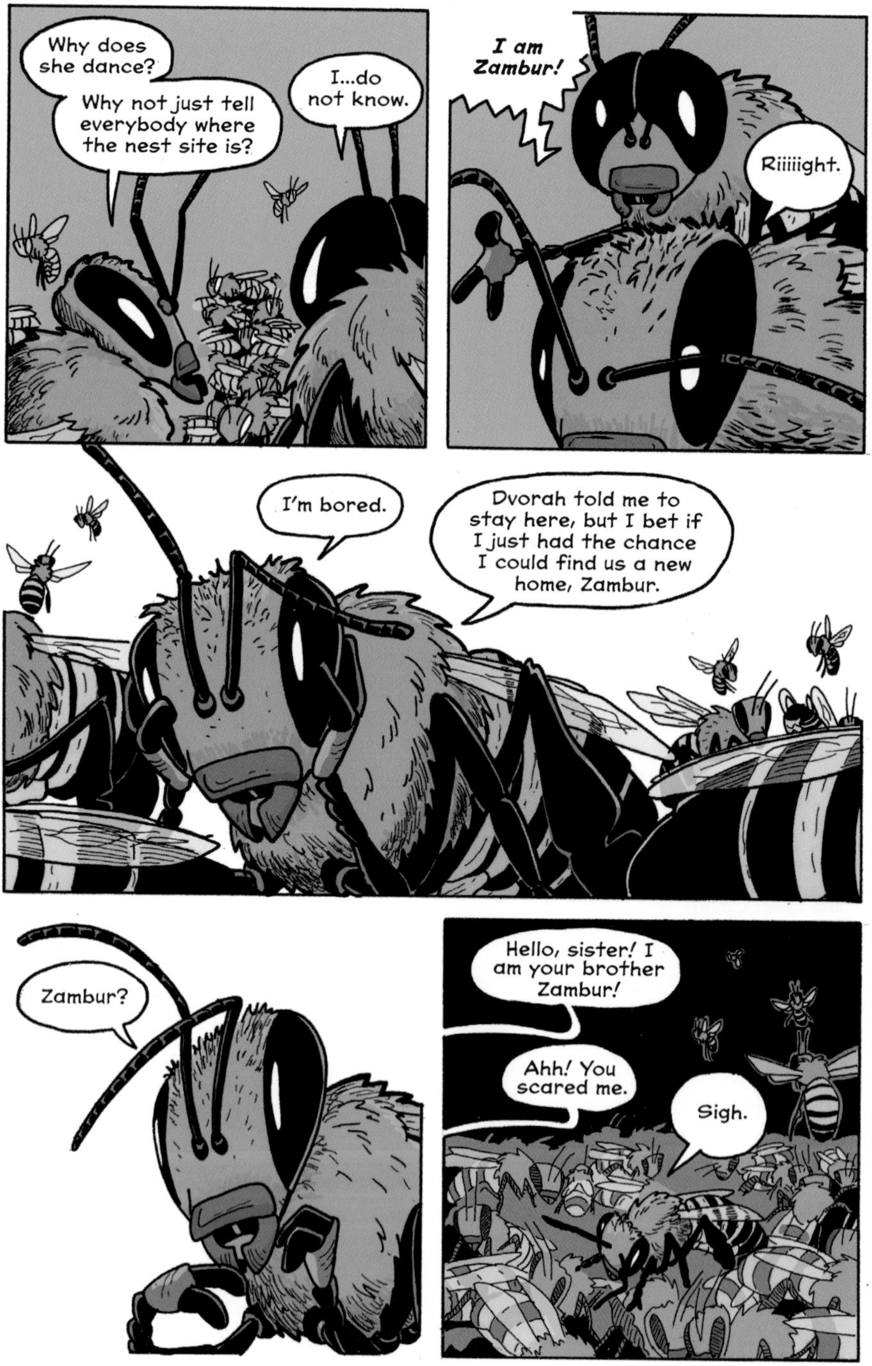
Why does she dance?
Why not just tell everybody where the nest site is?
I...do not know.
I am Zambur!
Riiiiight.
I'm bored.
Dvorah told me to stay here, but I bet if I just had the chance I could find us a new home, Zambur.
Zambur?
Hello, sister! I am your brother Zambur!
Ahh! You scared me.
Sigh.

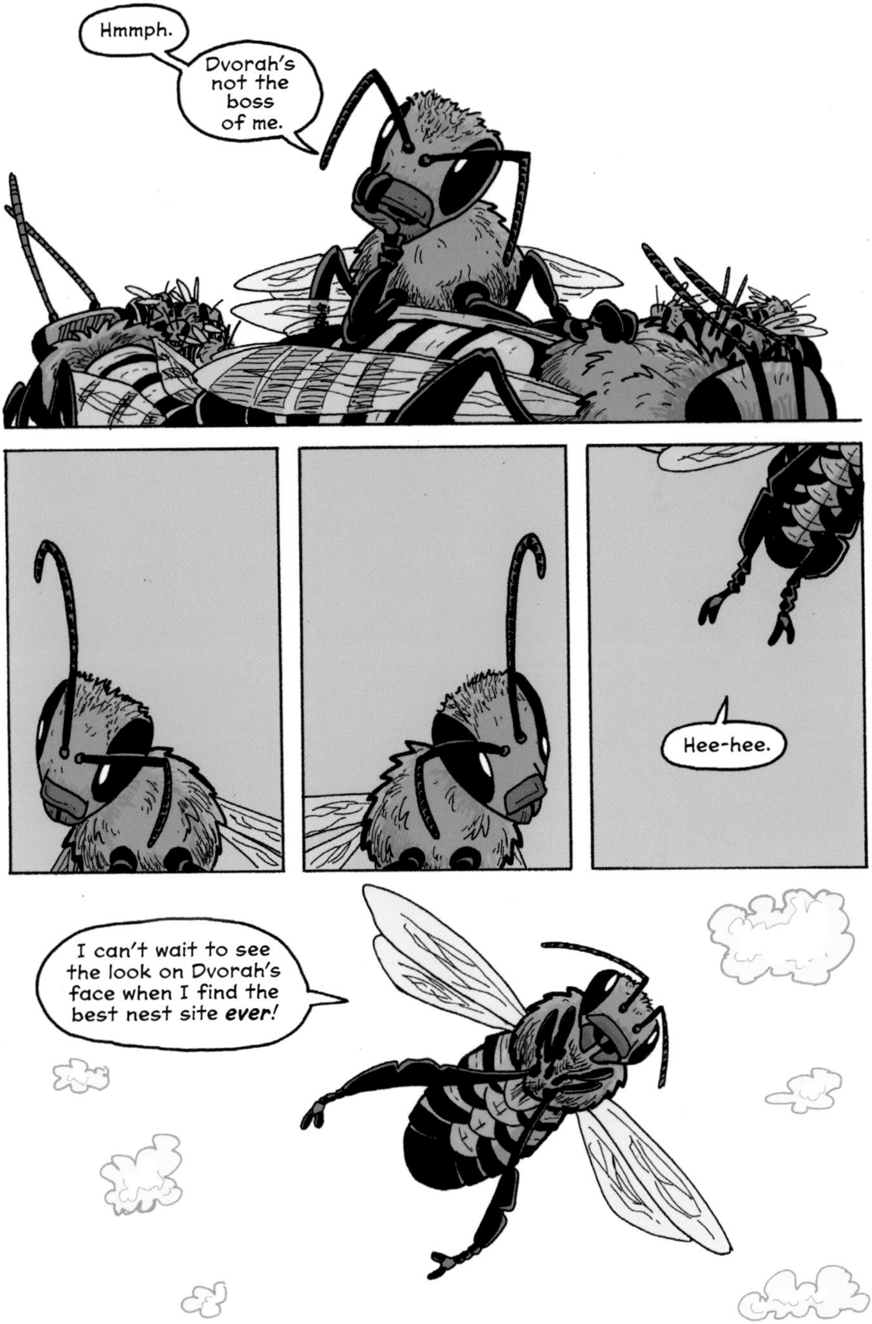
Hmmph.
Dvorah's not the boss of me.
Hee-hee.
I can't wait to see the look on Dvorah's face when I find the best nest site *ever*!

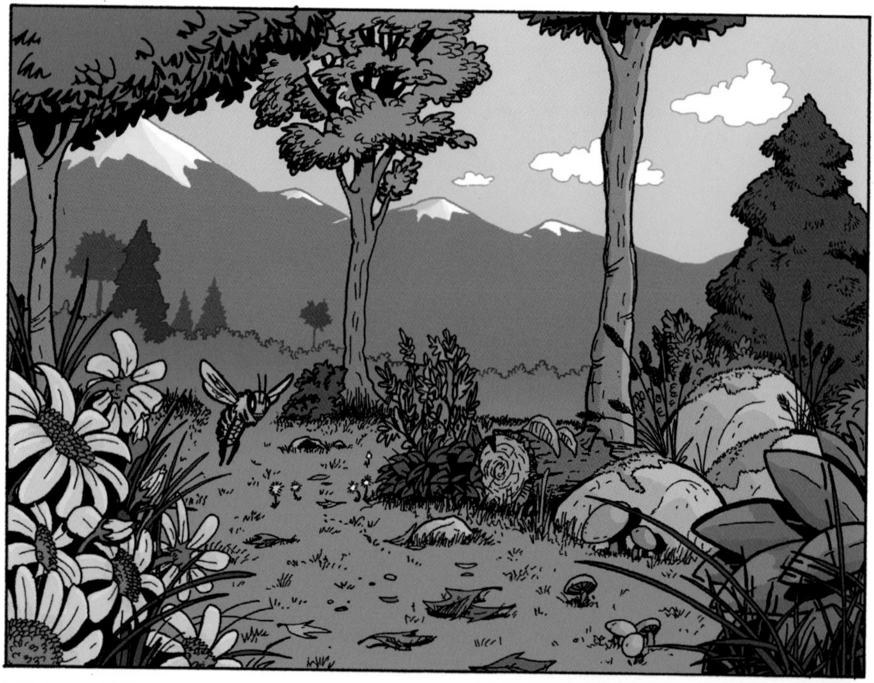

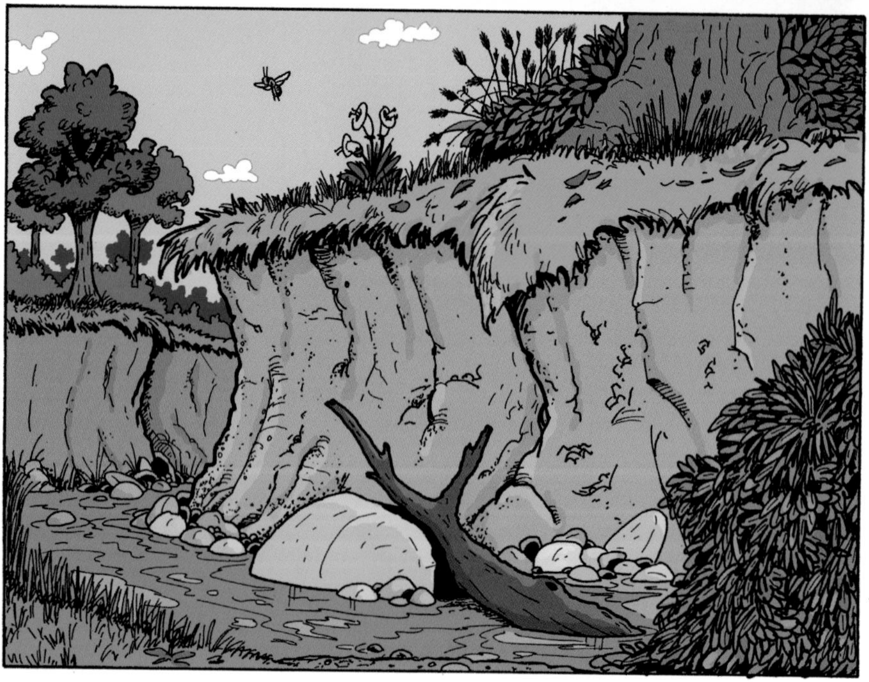

Wow. Look at *that* one!

Big solid tree.

Roomy interior.

And lots of flowers around.

Hot diggety! I can't wait to tell the others!

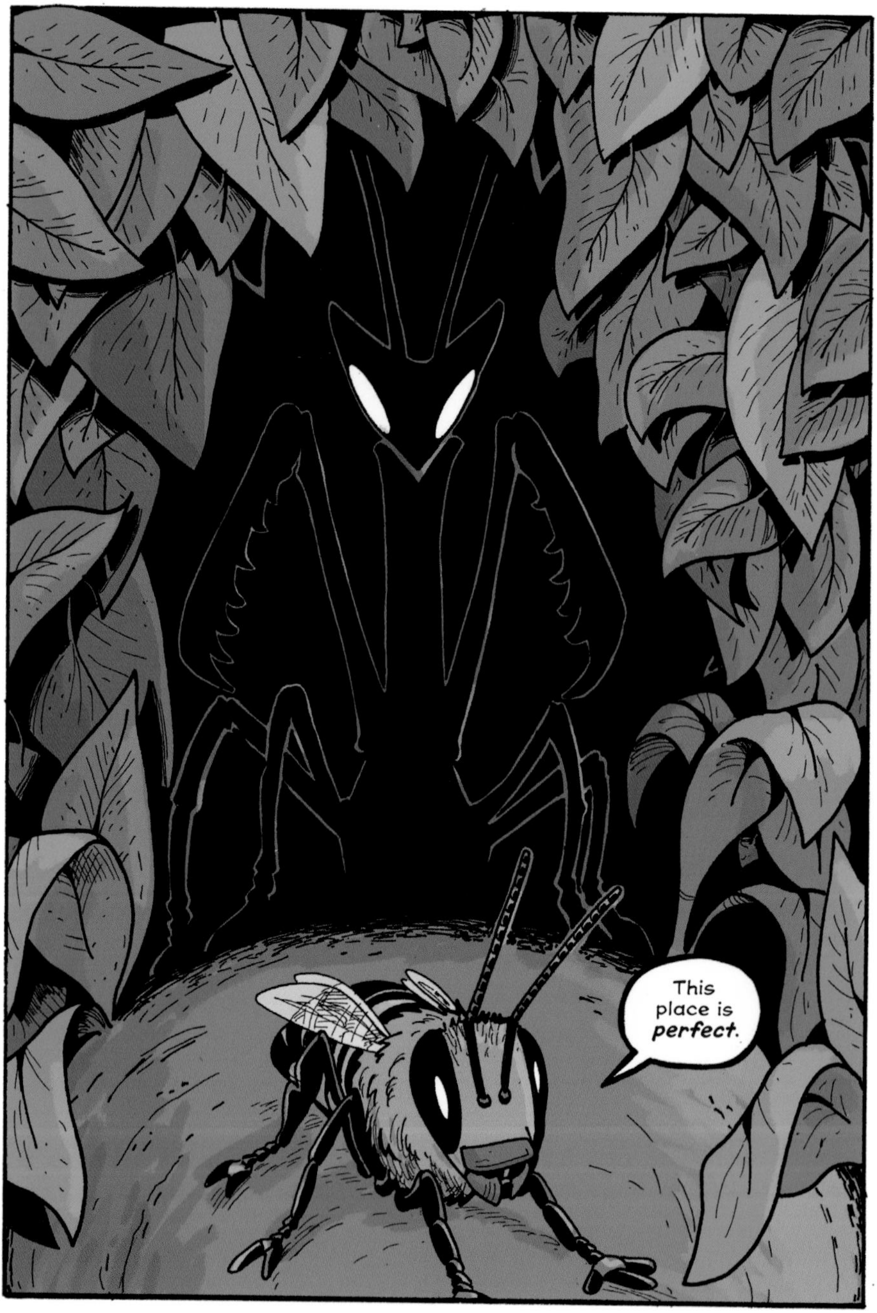
This place is *perfect*.

HIDE & SEEK

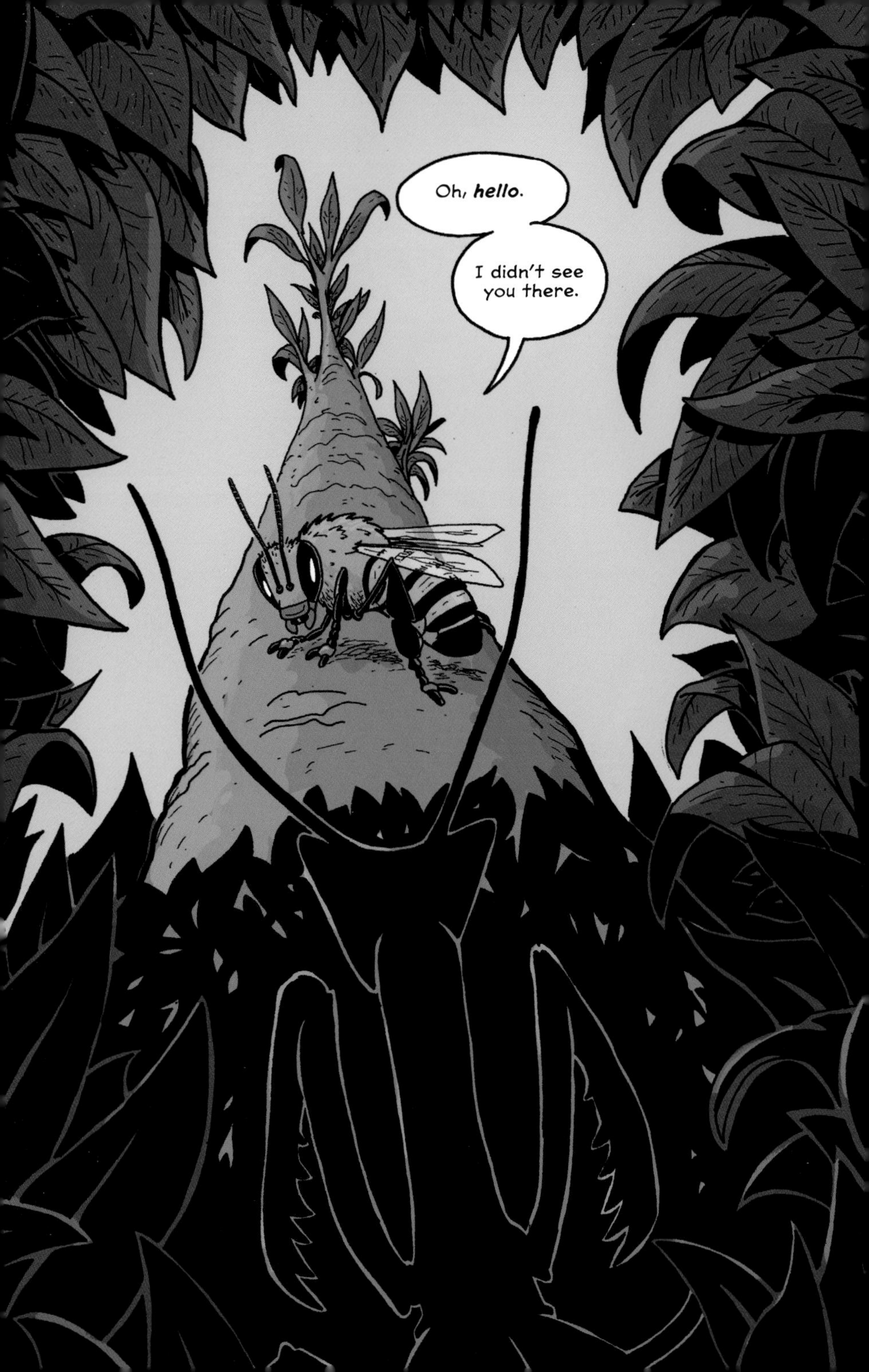
Oh, ***hello***.
I didn't see you there.

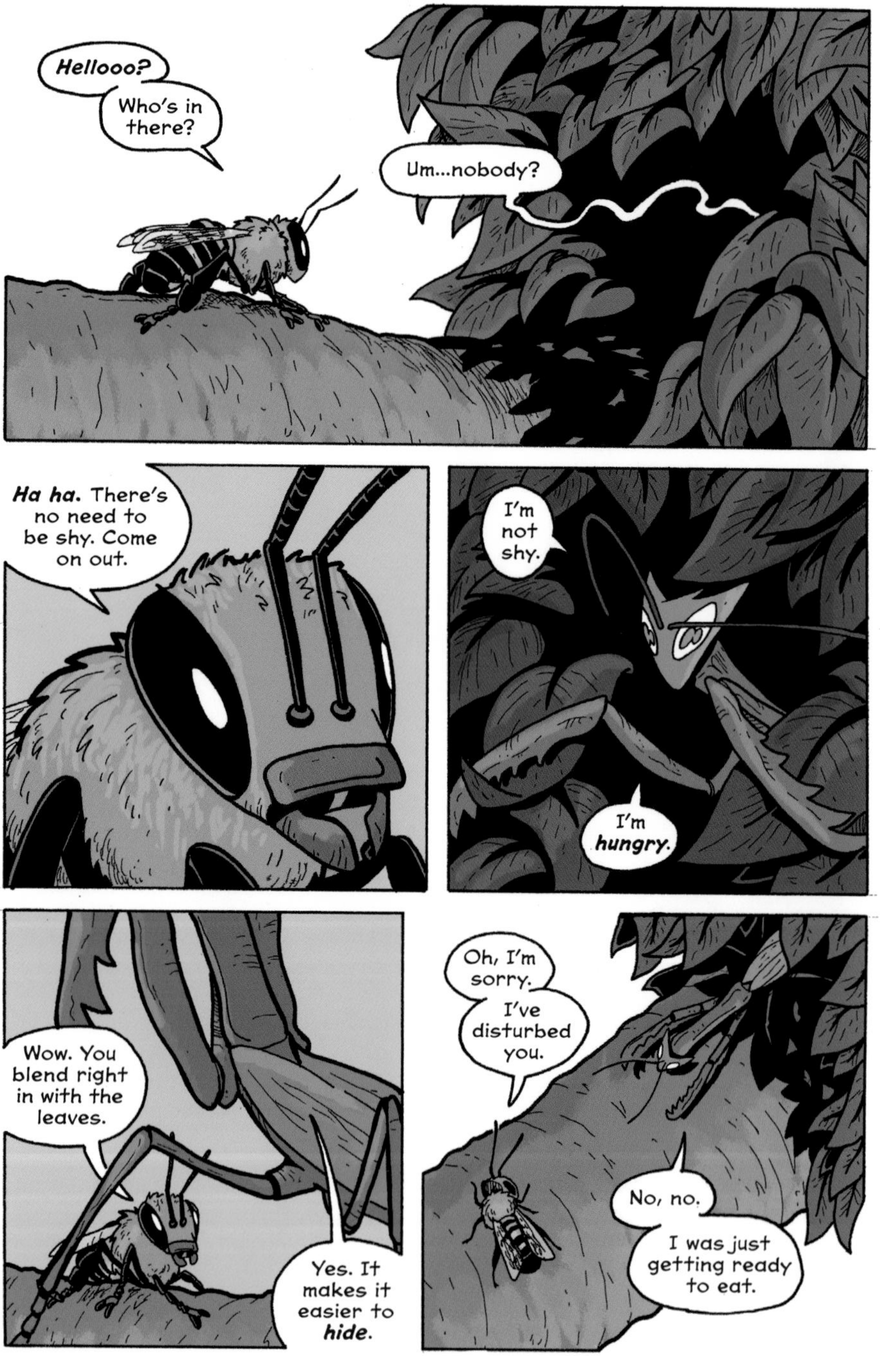

Hellooo?
Who's in there?
Um...nobody?
Ha ha. There's no need to be shy. Come on out.
I'm not shy.
I'm ***hungry***.
Wow. You blend right in with the leaves.
Yes. It makes it easier to ***hide***.
Oh, I'm sorry.
I've disturbed you.
No, no.
I was just getting ready to eat.

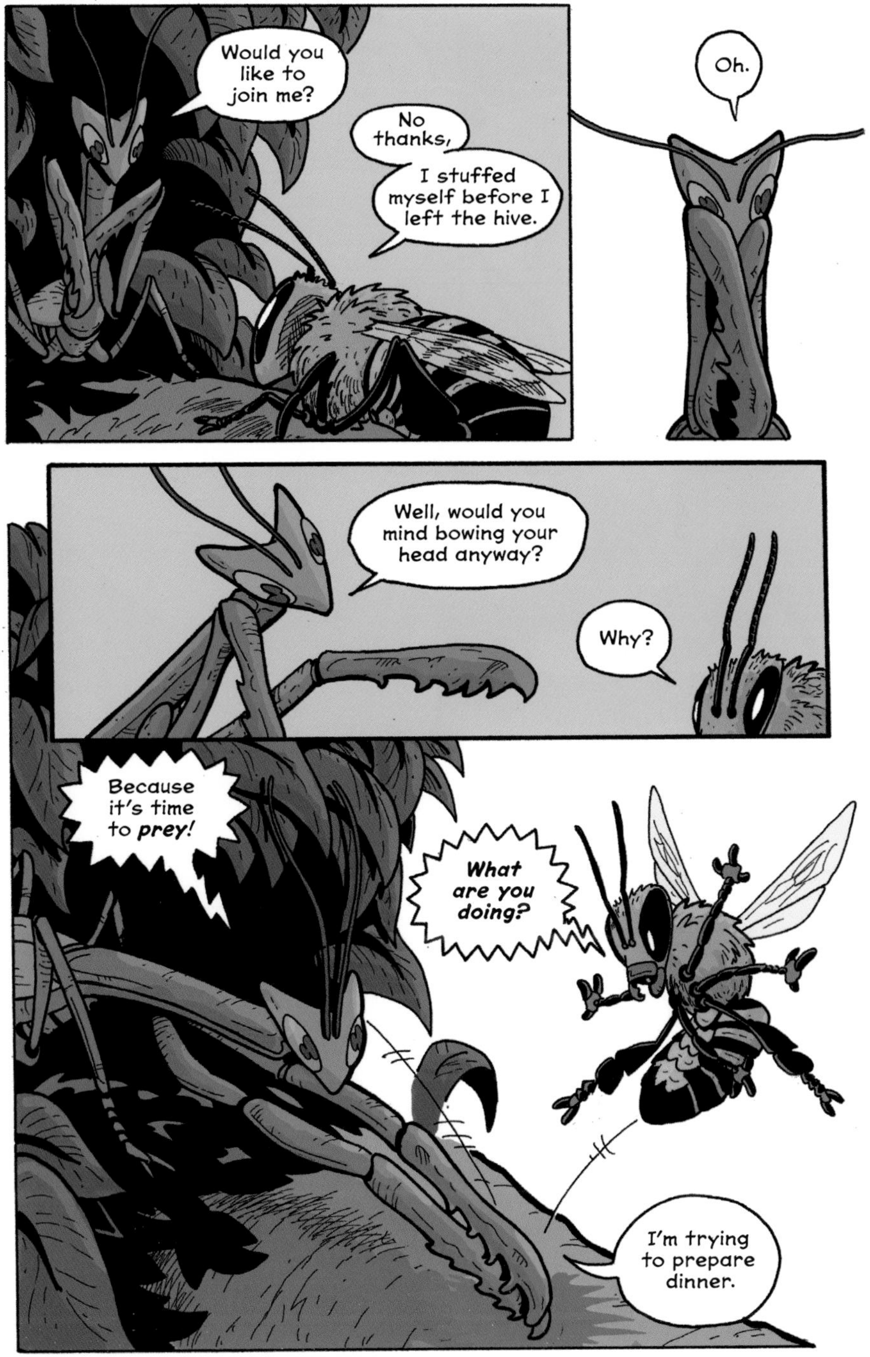
Would you like to join me?
No thanks,
I stuffed myself before I left the hive.
Oh.
Well, would you mind bowing your head anyway?
Why?
Because it's time to ***prey!***
What are you doing?
I'm trying to prepare dinner.

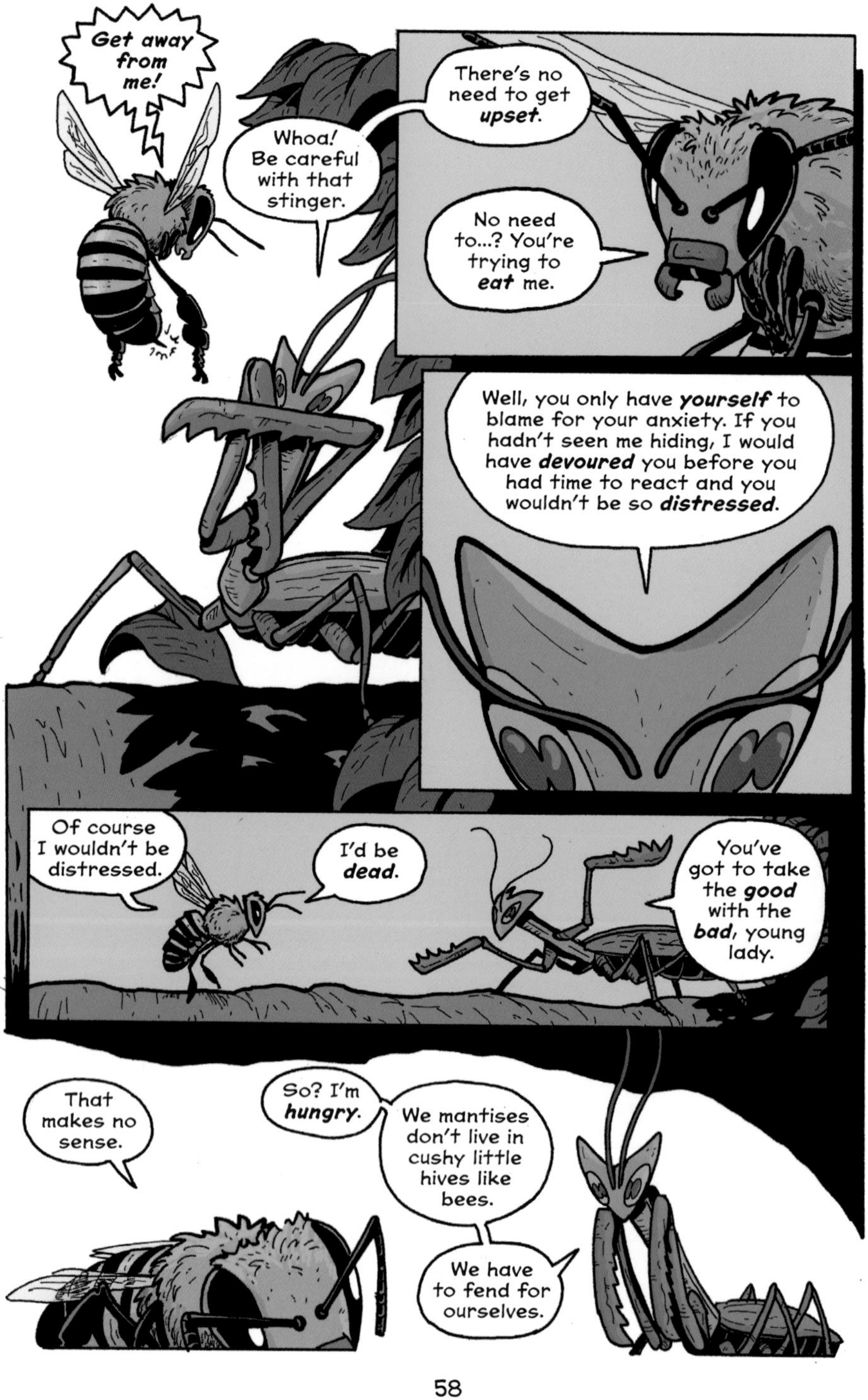
Get away from me!
Whoa! Be careful with that stinger.
There's no need to get upset.
No need to...? You're trying to eat me.
jut jmf
Well, you only have yourself to blame for your anxiety. If you hadn't seen me hiding, I would have devoured you before you had time to react and you wouldn't be so distressed.
Of course I wouldn't be distressed.
I'd be dead.
You've got to take the good with the bad, young lady.
That makes no sense.
So? I'm hungry.
We mantises don't live in cushy little hives like bees.
We have to fend for ourselves.

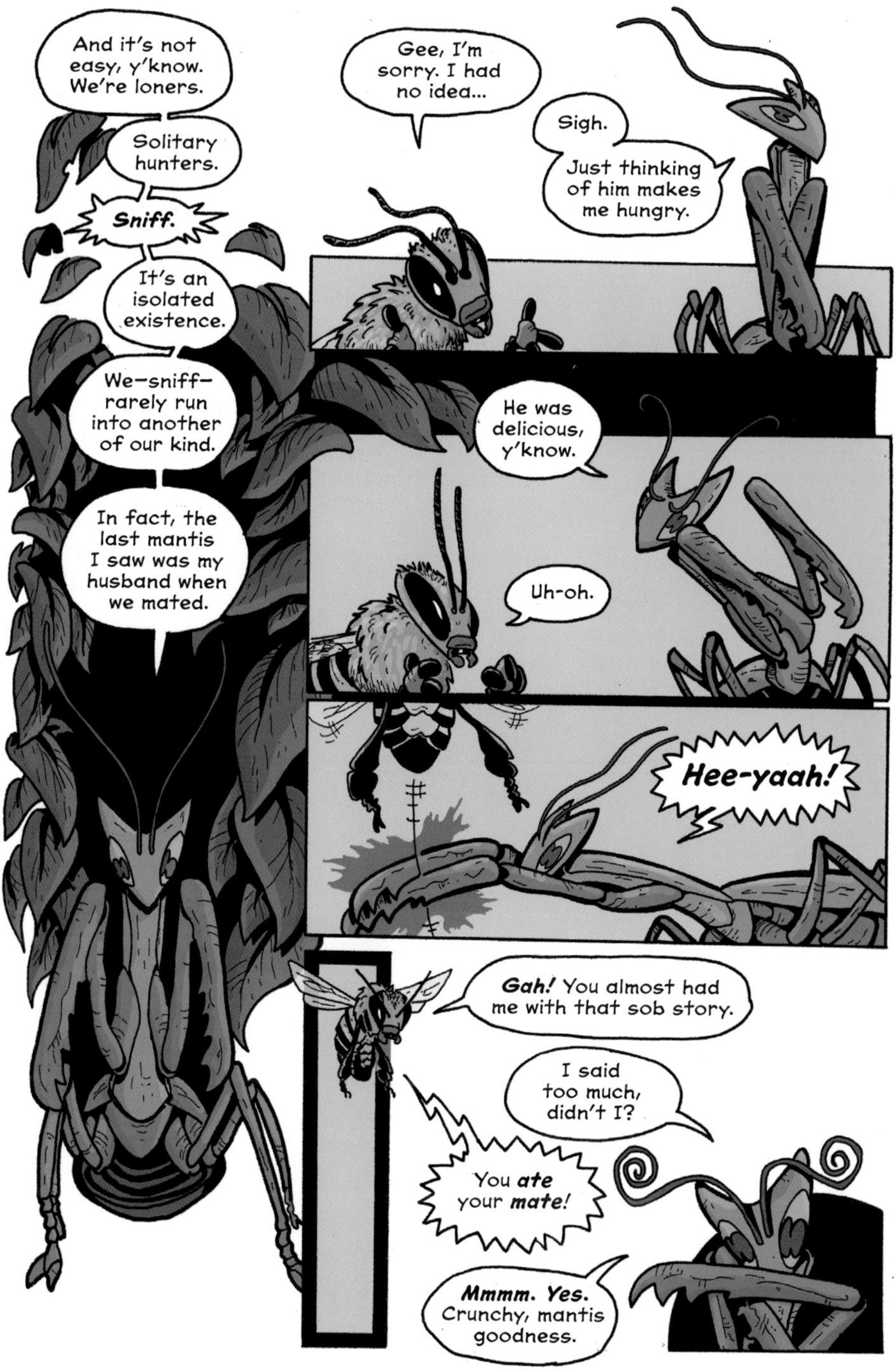
And it's not easy, y'know. We're loners.
Solitary hunters.
Sniff.
It's an isolated existence.
We—sniff—rarely run into another of our kind.
In fact, the last mantis I saw was my husband when we mated.
Gee, I'm sorry. I had no idea...
Sigh.
Just thinking of him makes me hungry.
He was delicious, y'know.
Uh-oh.
Hee-yaah!
Gah! You almost had me with that sob story.
I said too much, didn't I?
You ate your mate!
Mmmm. Yes. Crunchy, mantis goodness.

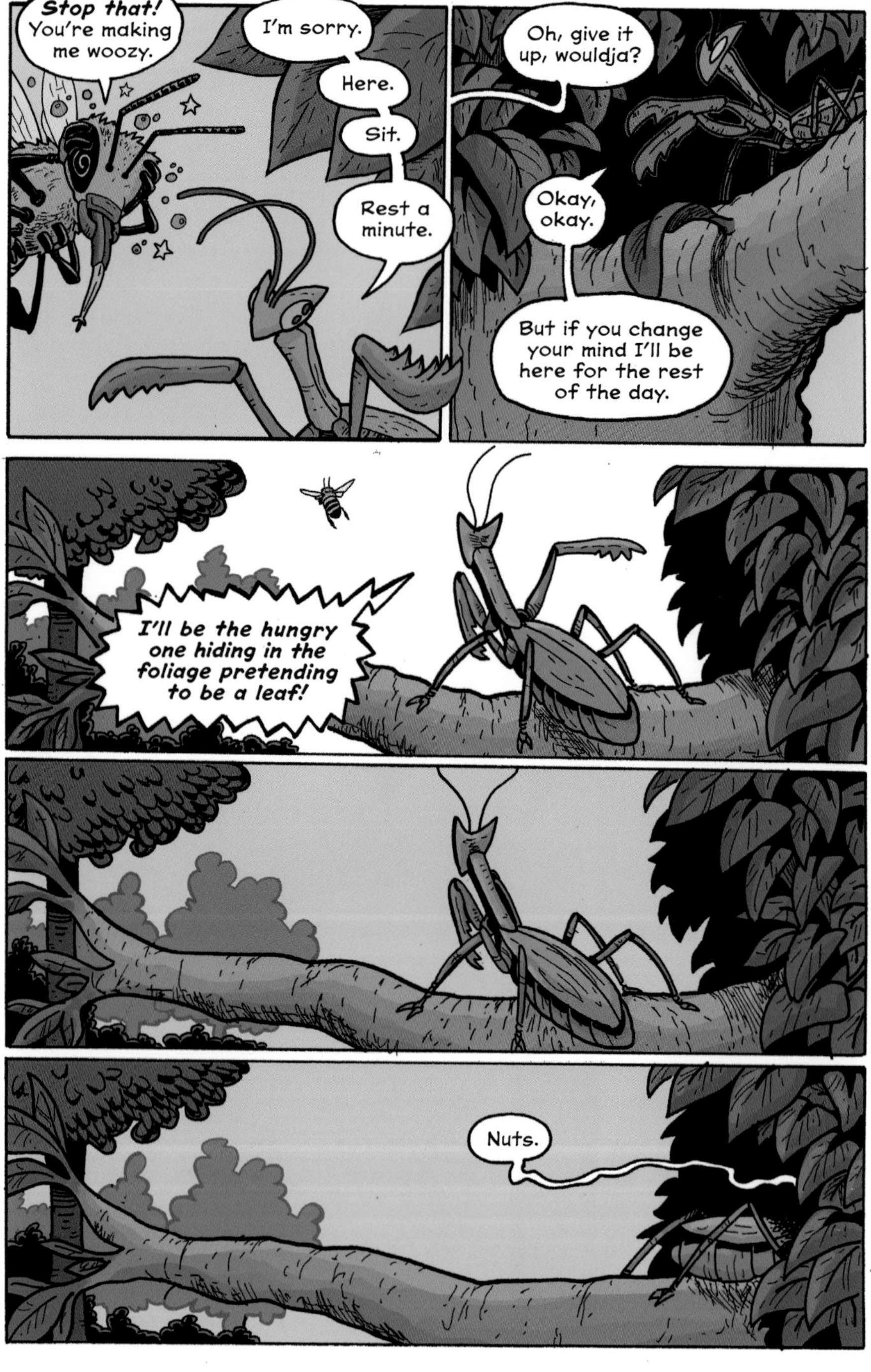
Stop that! You're making me woozy.
I'm sorry.
Here.
Sit.
Rest a minute.
Oh, give it up, wouldja?
Okay, okay.
But if you change your mind I'll be here for the rest of the day.
I'll be the hungry one hiding in the foliage pretending to be a leaf!
Nuts.

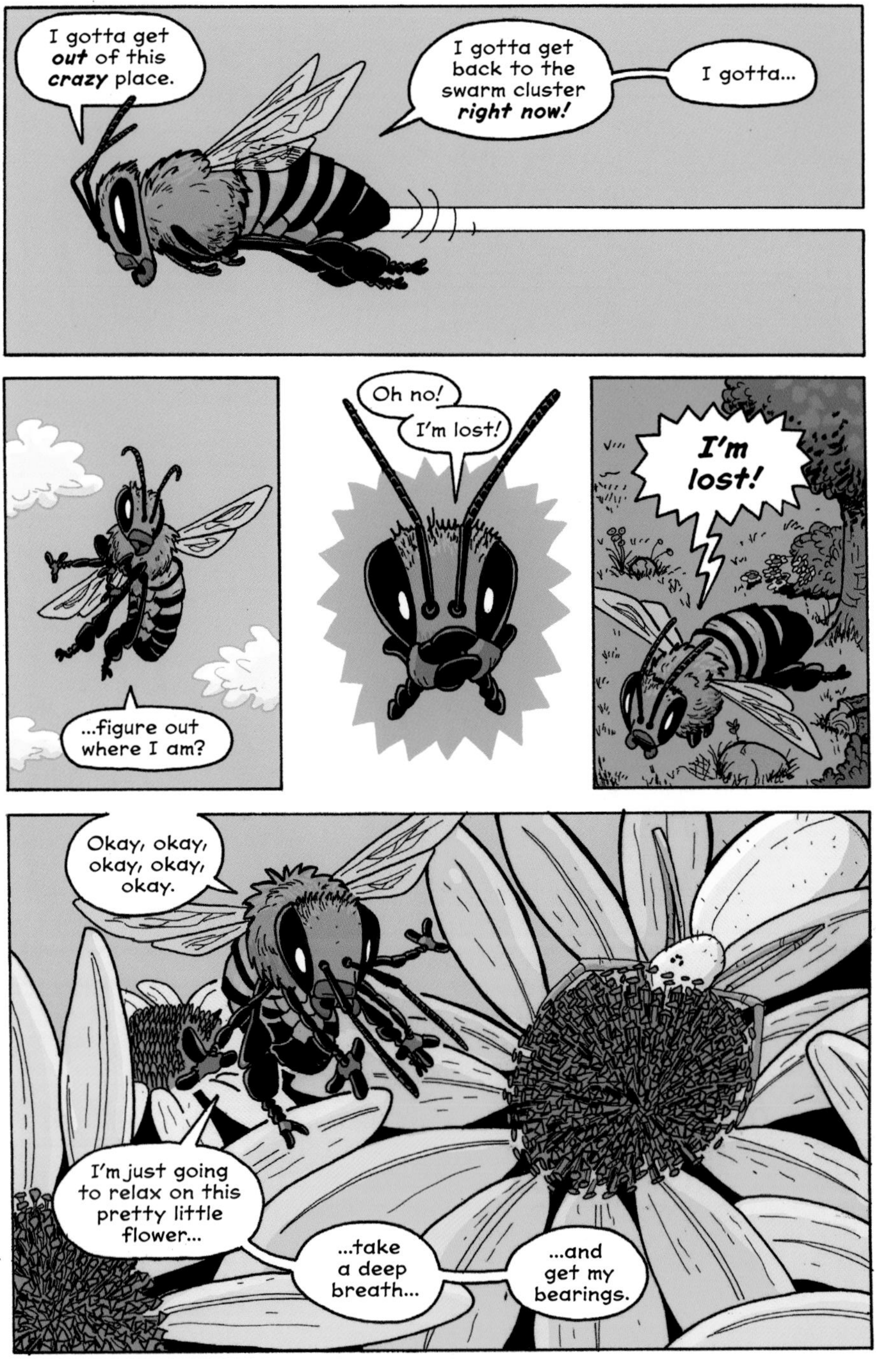
I gotta get **out** of this **crazy** place.
I gotta get back to the swarm cluster **right now!**
I gotta...
...figure out where I am?
Oh no!
I'm lost!
I'm lost!
Okay, okay, okay, okay, okay.
I'm just going to relax on this pretty little flower...
...take a deep breath...
...and get my bearings.

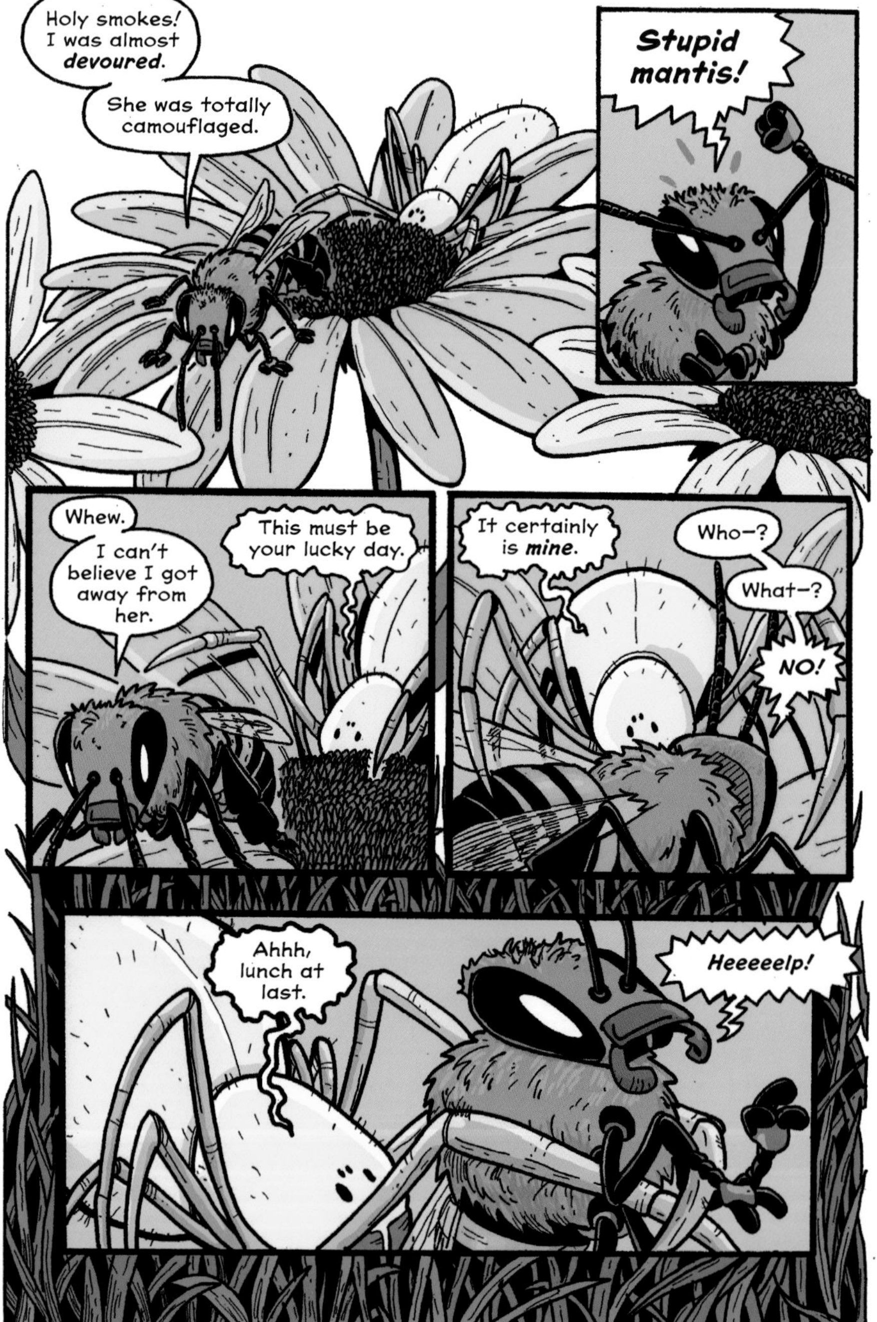
Holy smokes! I was almost *devoured*.
She was totally camouflaged.
Stupid mantis!
Whew.
I can't believe I got away from her.
This must be your lucky day.
It certainly is *mine*.
Who–?
What–?
NO!
Ahhh, lunch at last.
Heeeeelp!

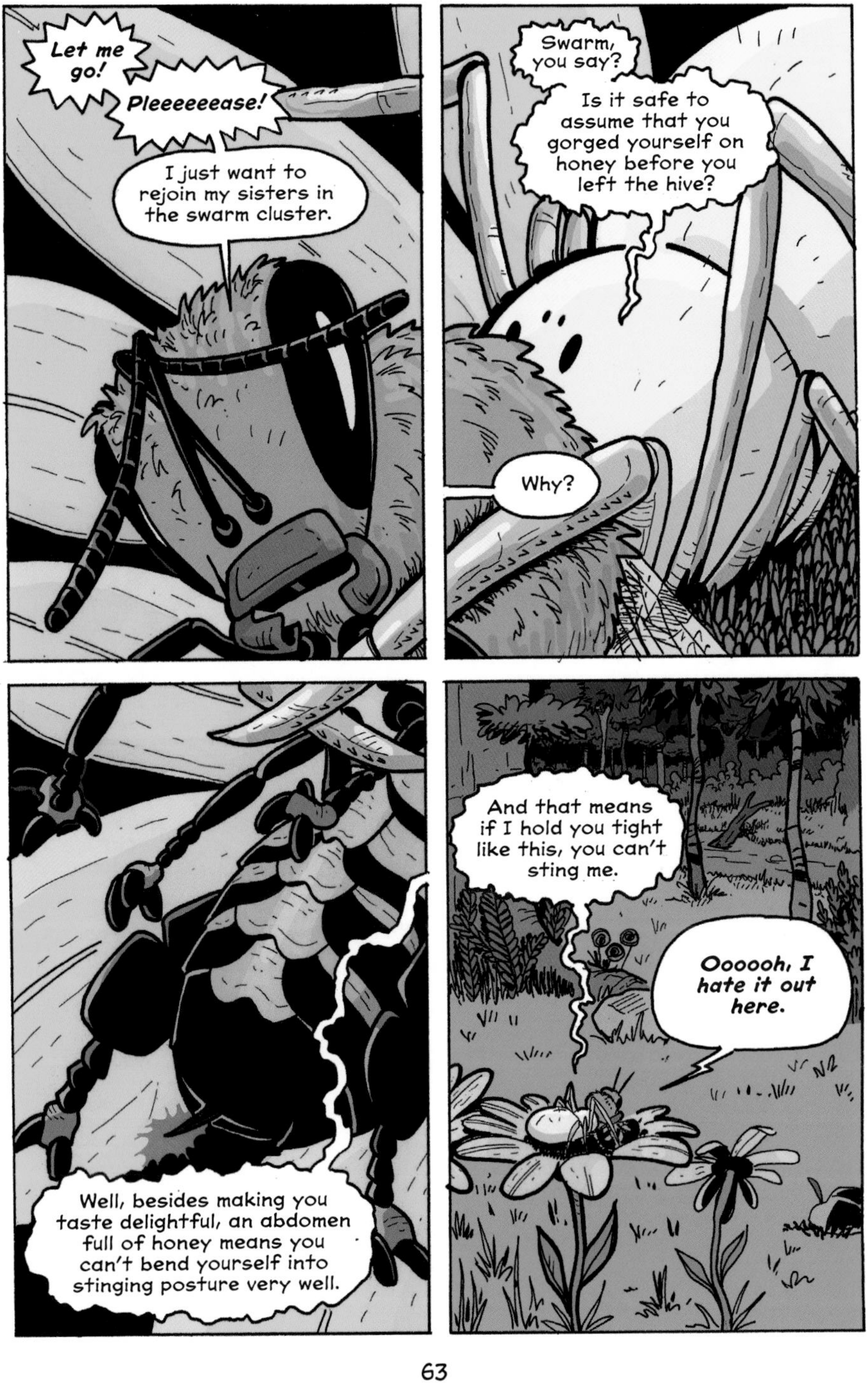
Let me go!
Pleeeeeease!
I just want to rejoin my sisters in the swarm cluster.
Swarm, you say?
Is it safe to assume that you gorged yourself on honey before you left the hive?
Why?
Well, besides making you taste delightful, an abdomen full of honey means you can't bend yourself into stinging posture very well.
And that means if I hold you tight like this, you can't sting me.
Oooooh, I hate it out here.

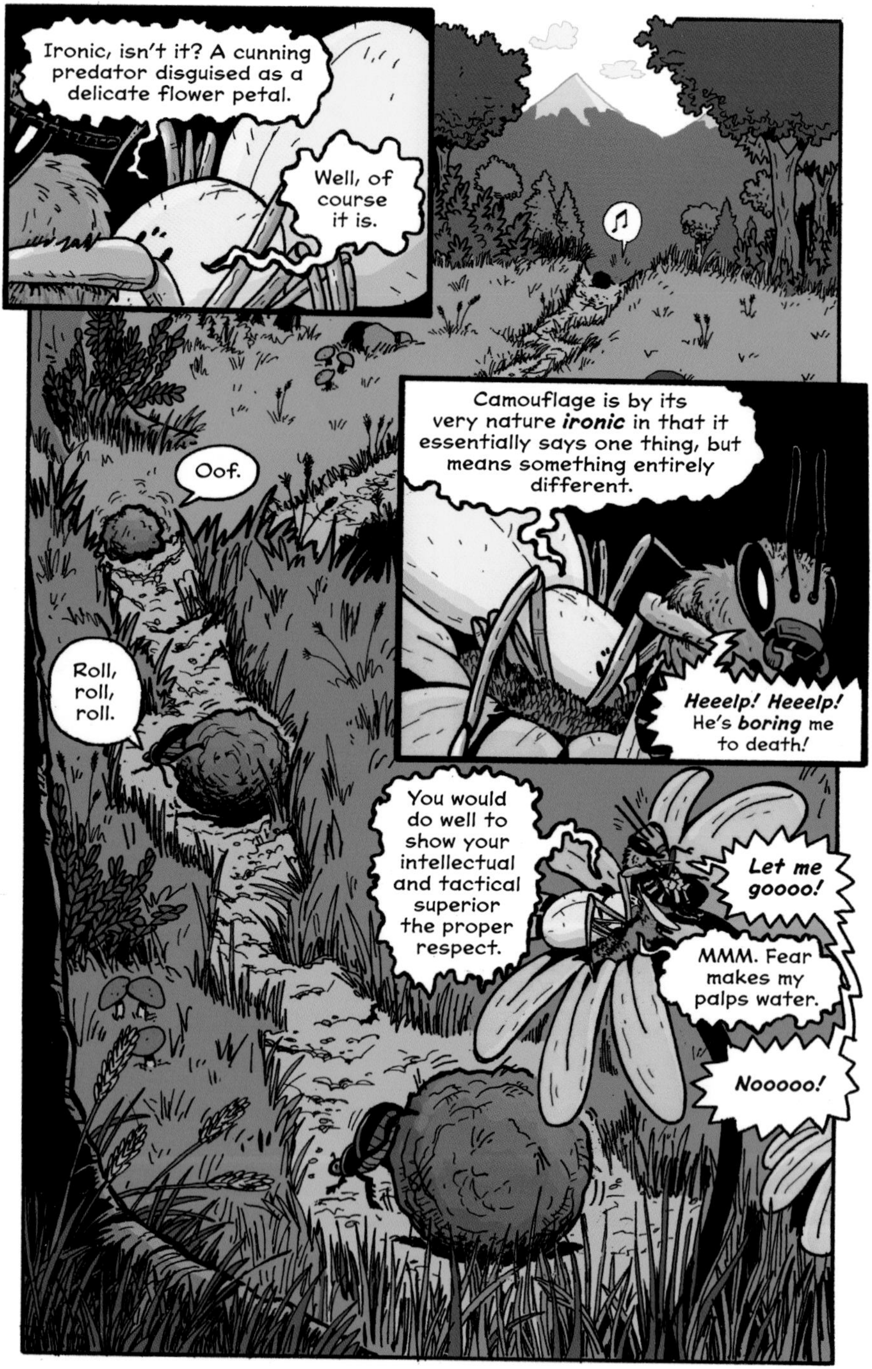
Ironic, isn't it? A cunning predator disguised as a delicate flower petal.
Well, of course it is.
♫
Oof.
Roll, roll, roll.
Camouflage is by its very nature *ironic* in that it essentially says one thing, but means something entirely different.
Heeelp! Heeelp! He's *boring* me to death!
You would do well to show your intellectual and tactical superior the proper respect.
Let me goooo!
MMM. Fear makes my palps water.
Nooooo!

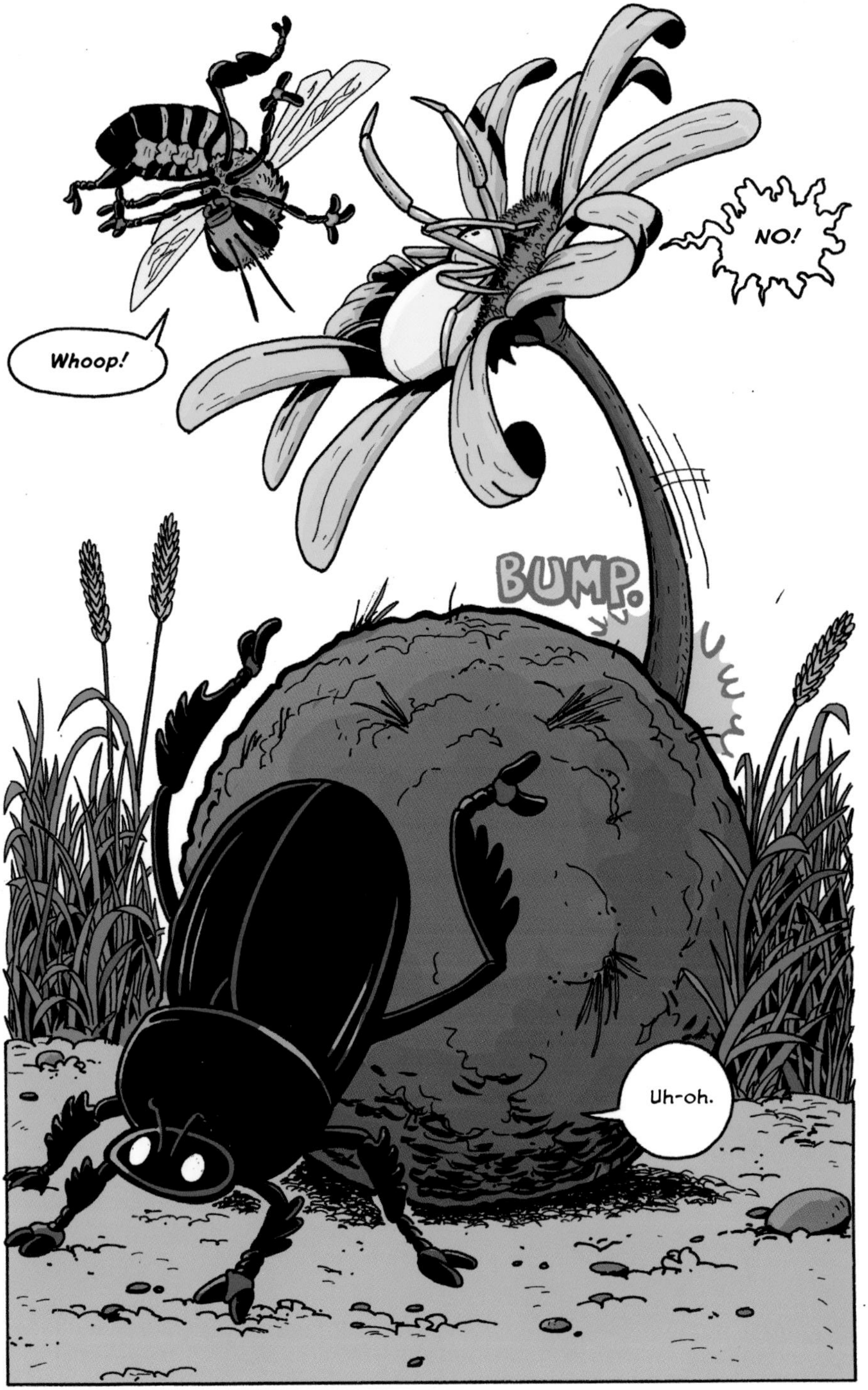
Whoop!
NO!
BUMP.
Uh-oh.

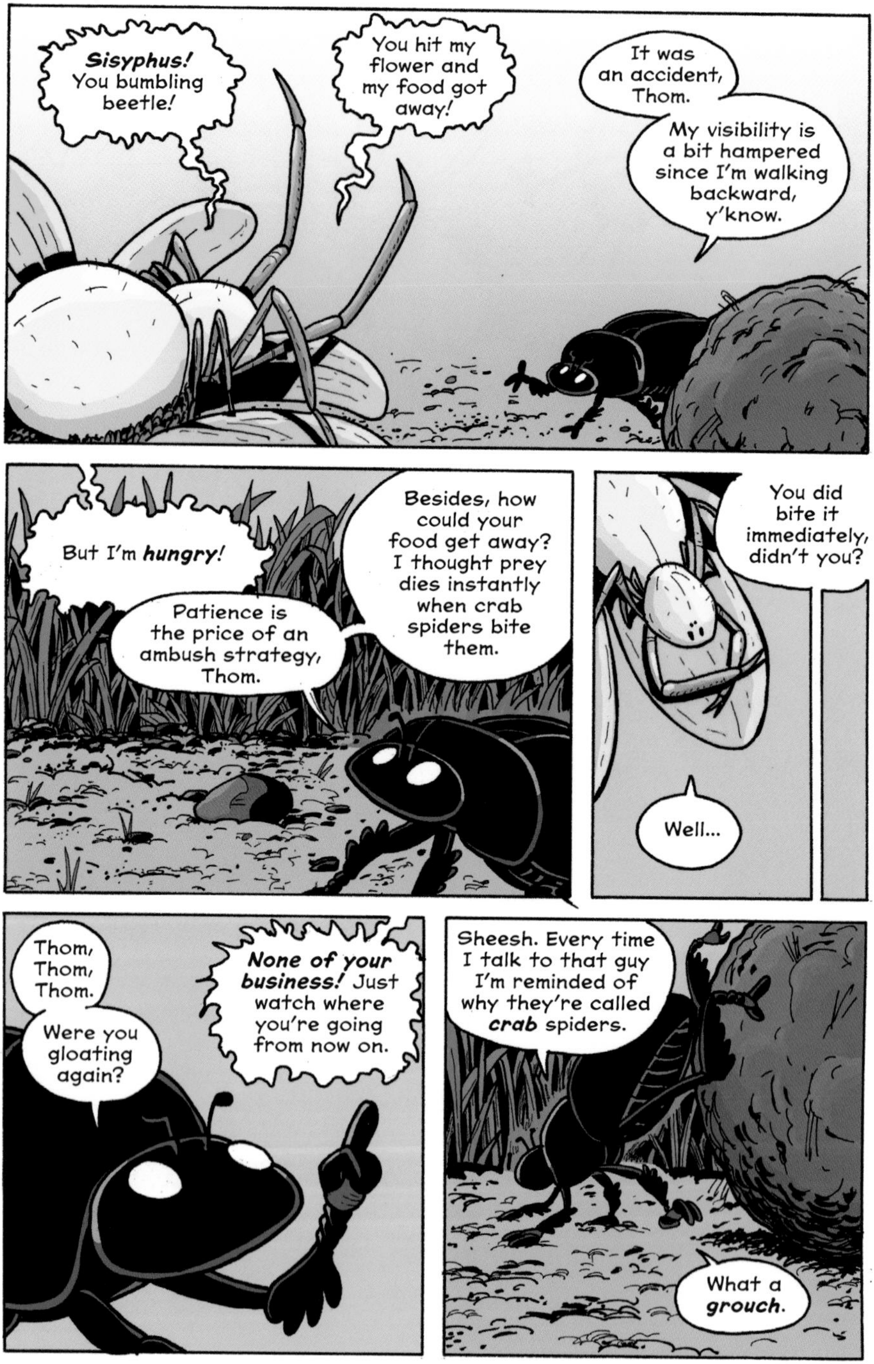
Sisyphus! You bumbling beetle!
You hit my flower and my food got away!
It was an accident, Thom.
My visibility is a bit hampered since I'm walking backward, y'know.
But I'm hungry!
Patience is the price of an ambush strategy, Thom.
Besides, how could your food get away? I thought prey dies instantly when crab spiders bite them.
You did bite it immediately, didn't you?
Well...
Thom, Thom, Thom.
Were you gloating again?
None of your business! Just watch where you're going from now on.
Sheesh. Every time I talk to that guy I'm reminded of why they're called crab spiders.
What a grouch.

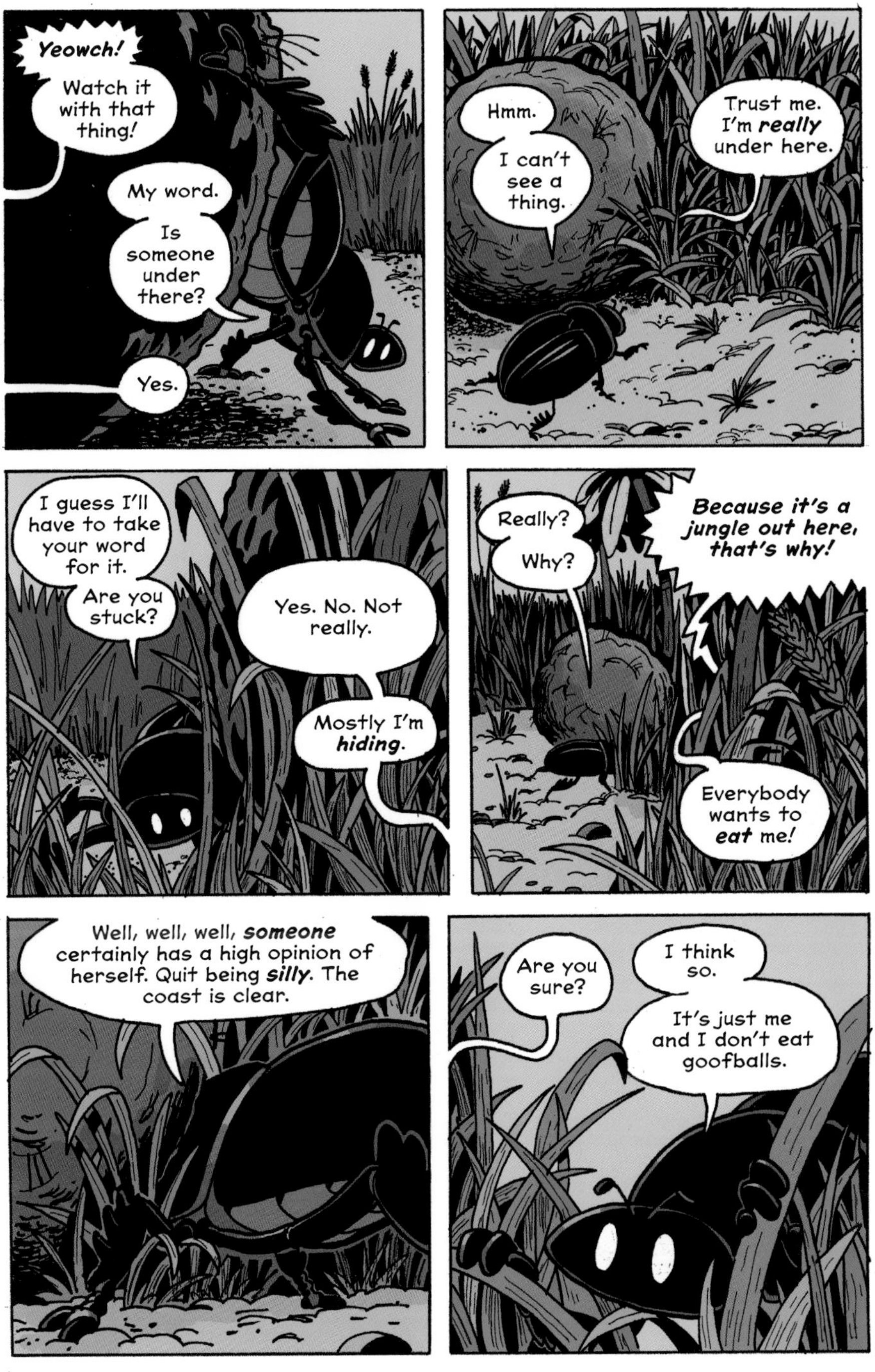
Yeowch!
Watch it with that thing!
My word.
Is someone under there?
Yes.
Hmm.
I can't see a thing.
Trust me. I'm *really* under here.
I guess I'll have to take your word for it.
Are you stuck?
Yes. No. Not really.
Mostly I'm *hiding*.
Really?
Why?
Because it's a jungle out here, that's why!
Everybody wants to *eat* me!
Well, well, well, *someone* certainly has a high opinion of herself. Quit being *silly*. The coast is clear.
Are you sure?
I think so.
It's just me and I don't eat goofballs.

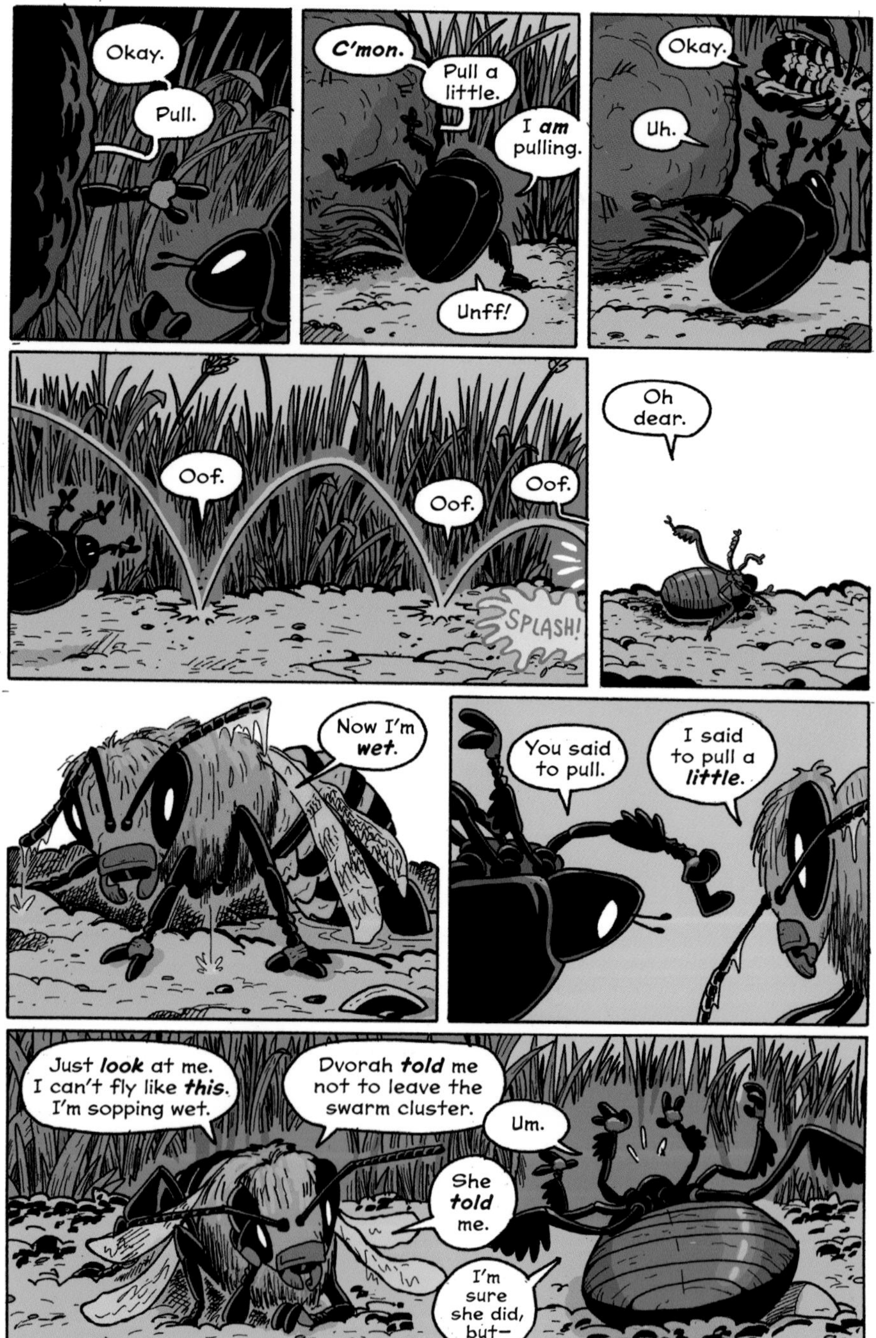
Okay.
Pull.
C'mon.
Pull a little.
I am pulling.
Unff!
Okay.
Uh.
Oof.
Oof.
Oof.
SPLASH!
Oh dear.
Now I'm wet.
You said to pull.
I said to pull a little.
Just look at me. I can't fly like this. I'm sopping wet.
Dvorah told me not to leave the swarm cluster.
Um.
She told me.
I'm sure she did, but—

Now I'm lost, disoriented, **and** drenched.

Could you just—?

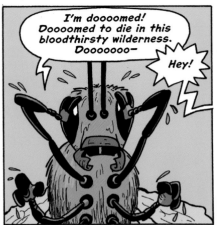

I'm doooomed! Doooomed to die in this bloodthirsty wilderness. Doooooooo—

Hey!

What?

Could I get a little help here?

Oh.

Sorry.

Y'know, you're on the verge of making a very *lousy* first impression.

I said I was sorry.

Fair enough.

Let's start over.

My name is Sisyphus.

I'm Nyuki. Nyuki of Clan Apis.

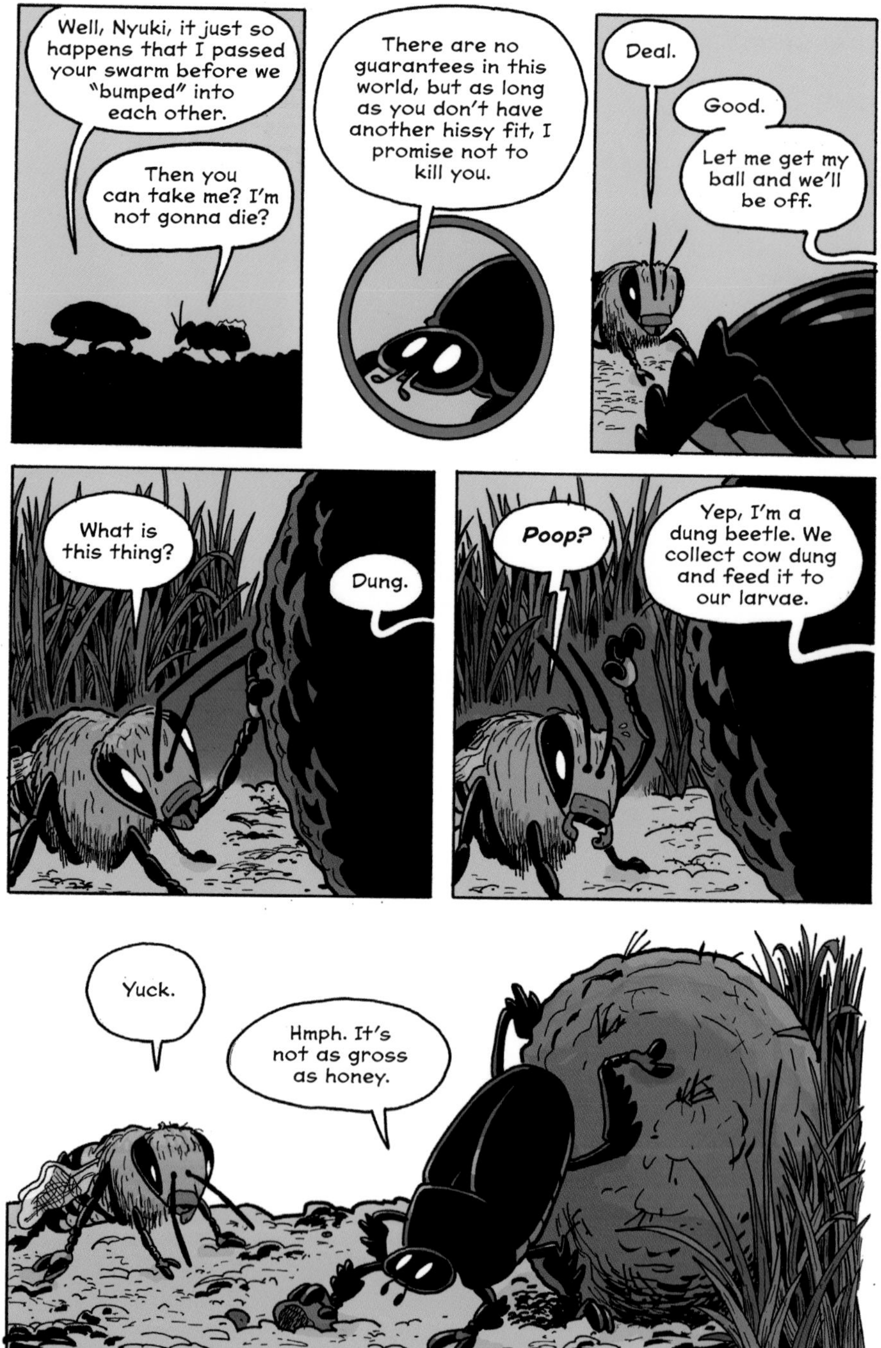
Well, Nyuki, it just so happens that I passed your swarm before we "bumped" into each other.
Then you can take me? I'm not gonna die?
There are no guarantees in this world, but as long as you don't have another hissy fit, I promise not to kill you.
Deal.
Good.
Let me get my ball and we'll be off.
What is this thing?
Dung.
Poop?
Yep, I'm a dung beetle. We collect cow dung and feed it to our larvae.
Yuck.
Hmph. It's not as gross as honey.

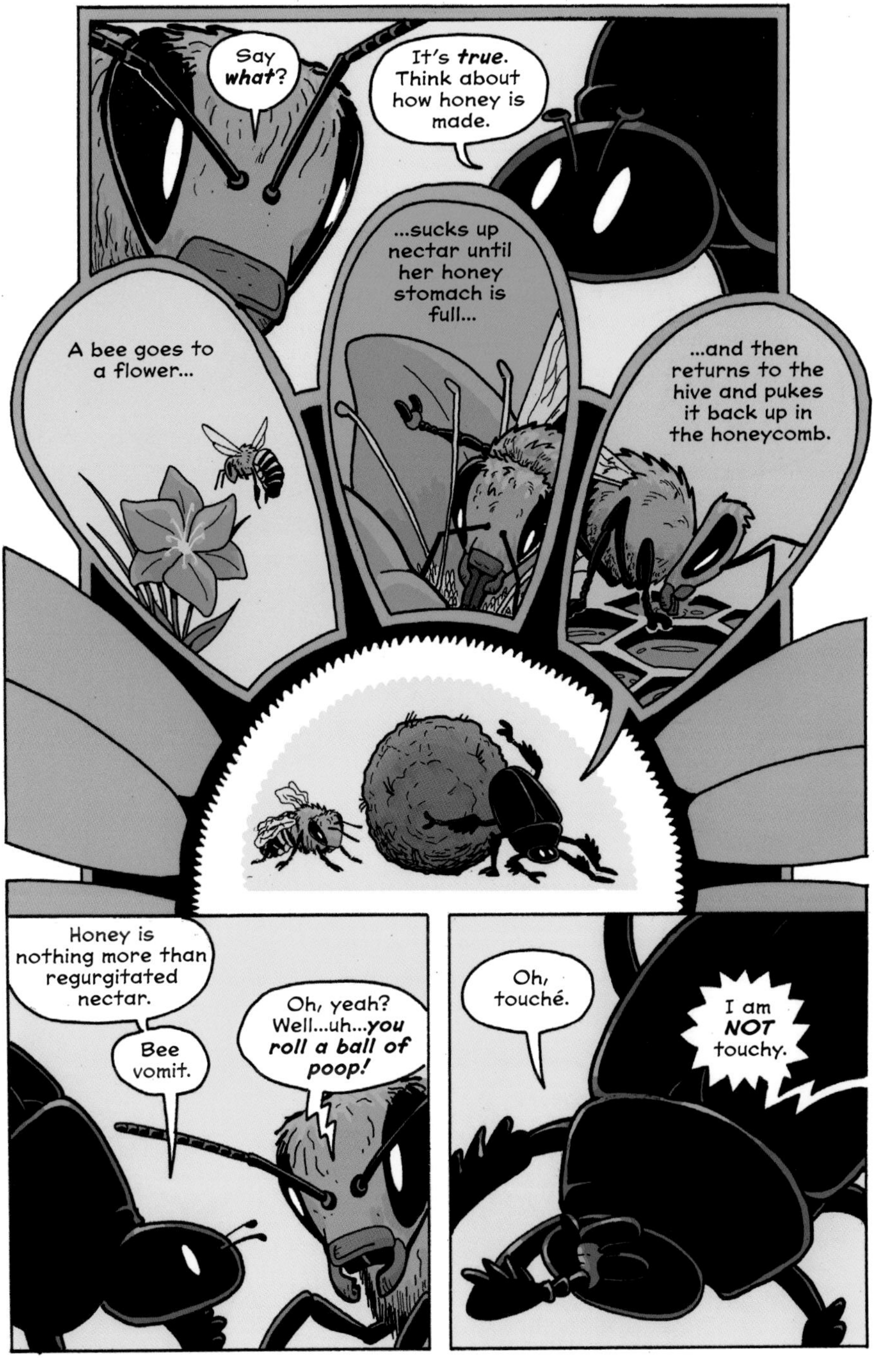

Say what?
It's true. Think about how honey is made.
A bee goes to a flower...
...sucks up nectar until her honey stomach is full...
...and then returns to the hive and pukes it back up in the honeycomb.
Honey is nothing more than regurgitated nectar.
Bee vomit.
Oh, yeah? Well...uh...you roll a ball of poop!
Oh, touché.
I am NOT touchy.

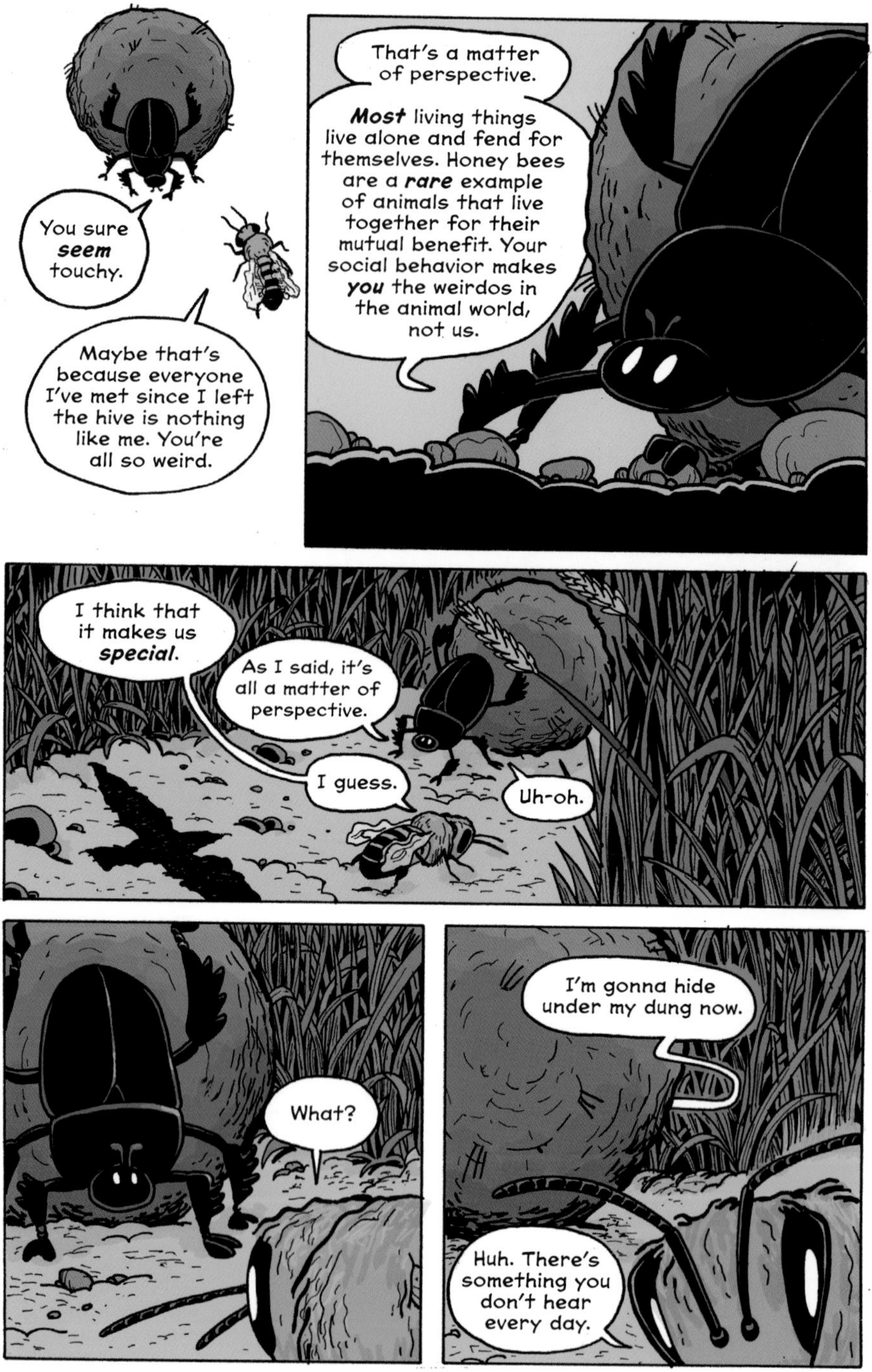
You sure *seem* touchy.
Maybe that's because everyone I've met since I left the hive is nothing like me. You're all so weird.
That's a matter of perspective.
Most living things live alone and fend for themselves. Honey bees are a *rare* example of animals that live together for their mutual benefit. Your social behavior makes *you* the weirdos in the animal world, not us.
I think that it makes us *special*.
As I said, it's all a matter of perspective.
I guess.
Uh-oh.
What?
I'm gonna hide under my dung now.
Huh. There's something you don't hear every day.

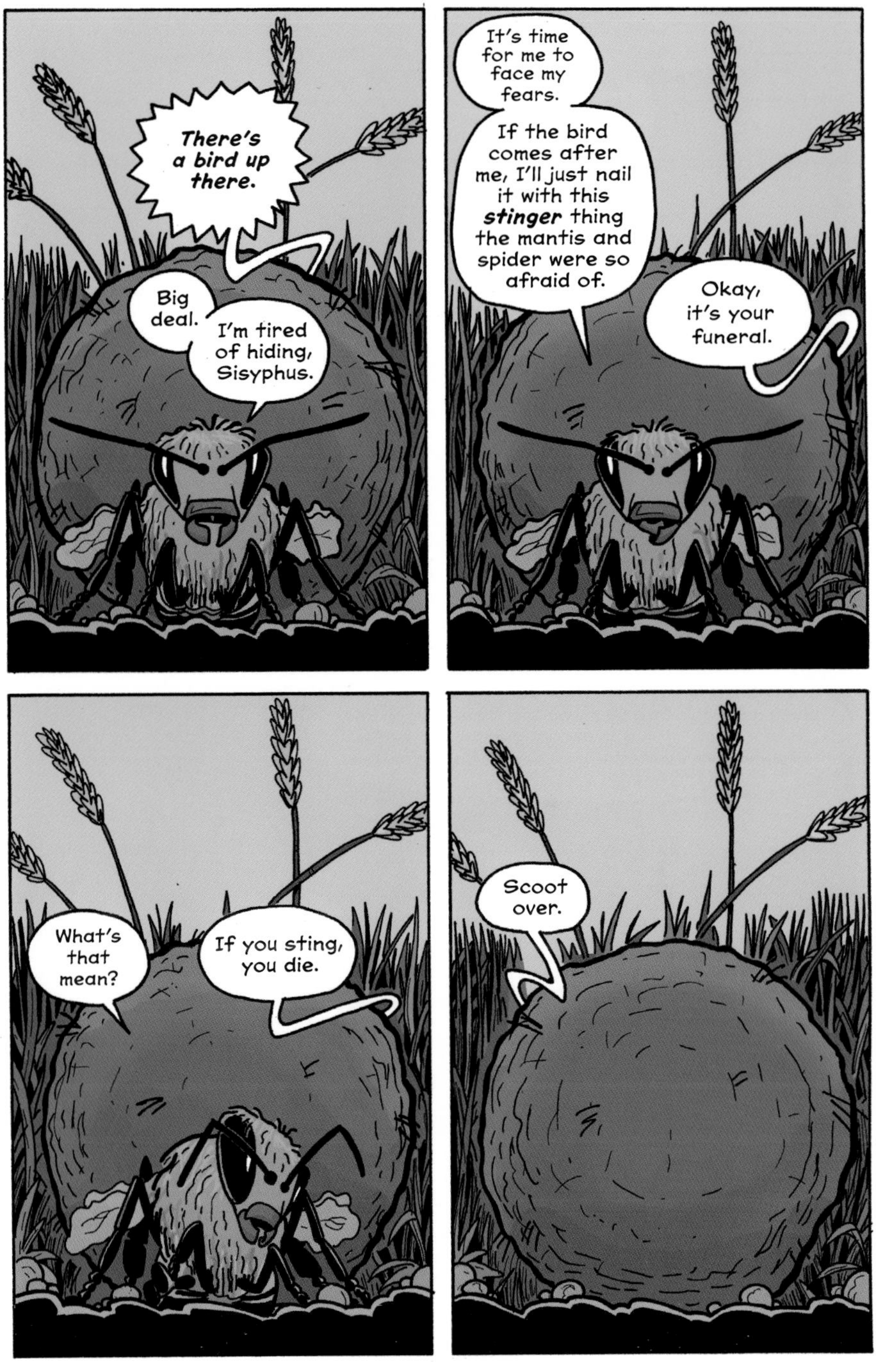
There's a bird up there.
Big deal.
I'm tired of hiding, Sisyphus.
It's time for me to face my fears.
If the bird comes after me, I'll just nail it with this *stinger* thing the mantis and spider were so afraid of.
Okay, it's your funeral.
What's that mean?
If you sting, you die.
Scoot over.

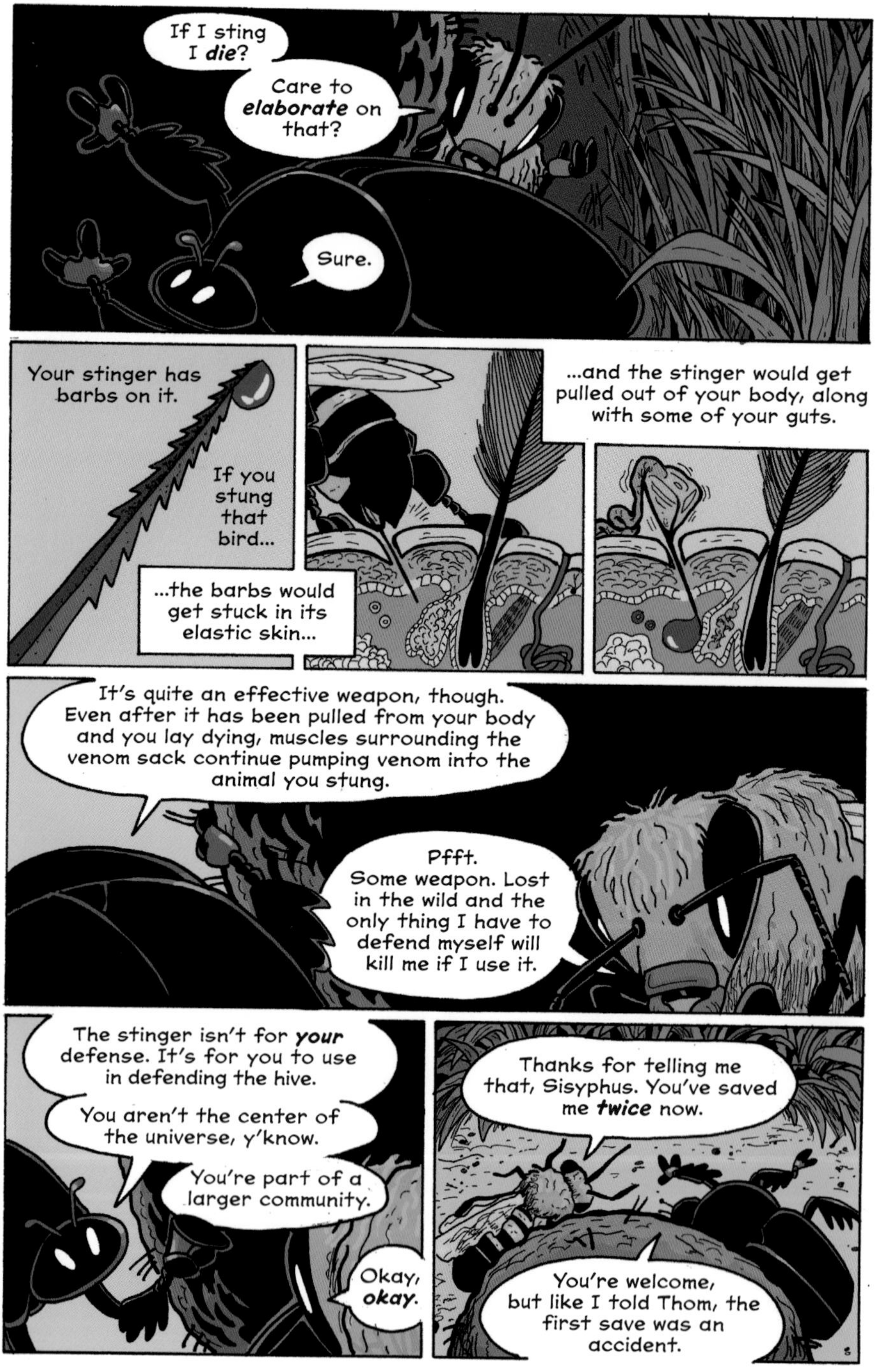

If I sting I *die*?
Care to *elaborate* on that?
Sure.
Your stinger has barbs on it.
If you stung that bird...
...the barbs would get stuck in its elastic skin...
...and the stinger would get pulled out of your body, along with some of your guts.
It's quite an effective weapon, though. Even after it has been pulled from your body and you lay dying, muscles surrounding the venom sack continue pumping venom into the animal you stung.
Pfft. Some weapon. Lost in the wild and the only thing I have to defend myself will kill me if I use it.
The stinger isn't for *your* defense. It's for you to use in defending the hive.
You aren't the center of the universe, y'know.
You're part of a larger community.
Okay, *okay*.
Thanks for telling me that, Sisyphus. You've saved me *twice* now.
You're welcome, but like I told Thom, the first save was an accident.

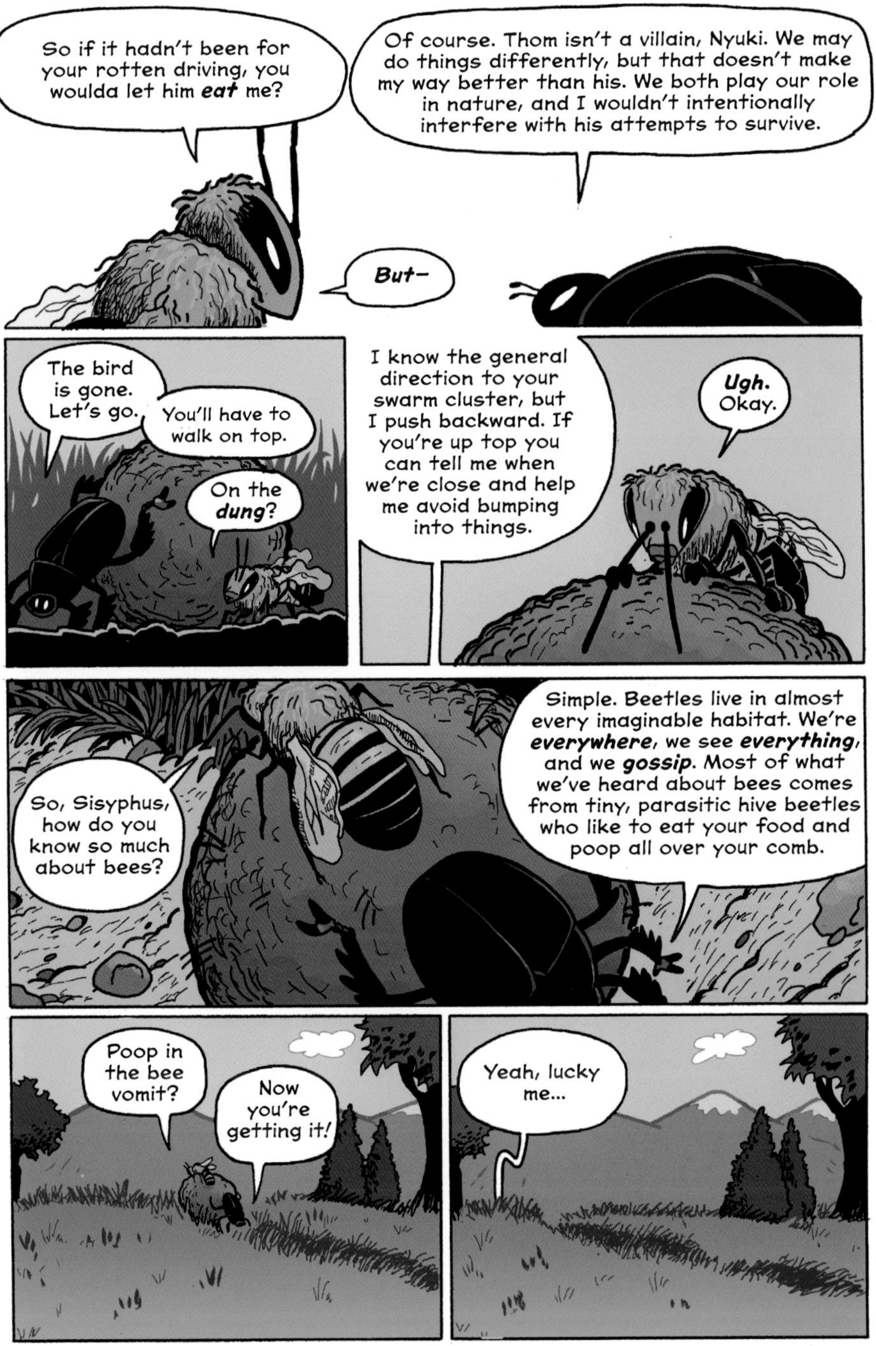

So if it hadn't been for your rotten driving, you woulda let him *eat* me?
Of course. Thom isn't a villain, Nyuki. We may do things differently, but that doesn't make my way better than his. We both play our role in nature, and I wouldn't intentionally interfere with his attempts to survive.
But–
The bird is gone. Let's go.
You'll have to walk on top.
On the *dung*?
I know the general direction to your swarm cluster, but I push backward. If you're up top you can tell me when we're close and help me avoid bumping into things.
Ugh. Okay.
So, Sisyphus, how do you know so much about bees?
Simple. Beetles live in almost every imaginable habitat. We're *everywhere*, we see *everything*, and we *gossip*. Most of what we've heard about bees comes from tiny, parasitic hive beetles who like to eat your food and poop all over your comb.
Poop in the bee vomit?
Now you're getting it!
Yeah, lucky me...

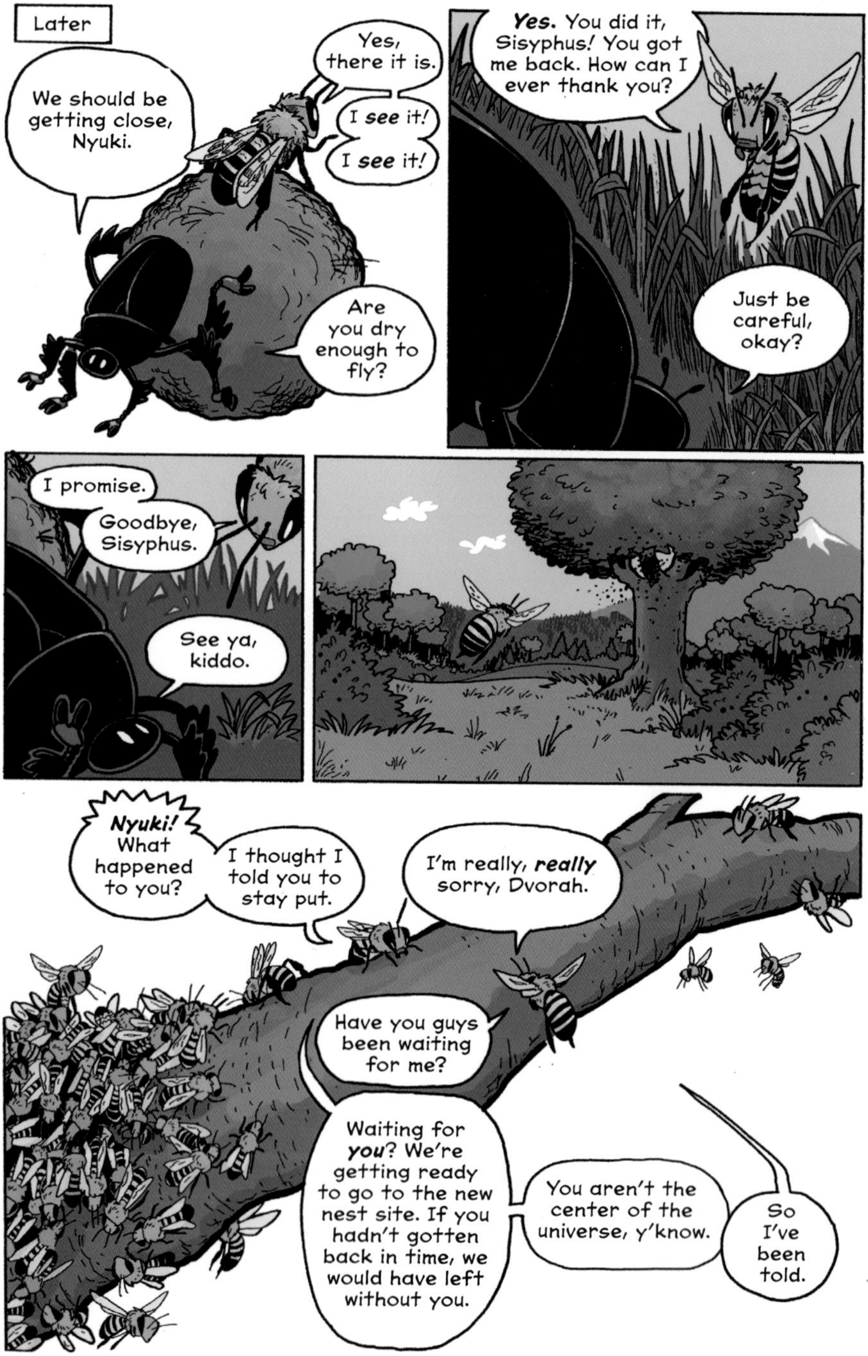
Later
We should be getting close, Nyuki.
Yes, there it is.
I see it!
I see it!
Are you dry enough to fly?
Yes. You did it, Sisyphus! You got me back. How can I ever thank you?
Just be careful, okay?
I promise.
Goodbye, Sisyphus.
See ya, kiddo.
Nyuki! What happened to you?
I thought I told you to stay put.
I'm really, really sorry, Dvorah.
Have you guys been waiting for me?
Waiting for you? We're getting ready to go to the new nest site. If you hadn't gotten back in time, we would have left without you.
You aren't the center of the universe, y'know.
So I've been told.

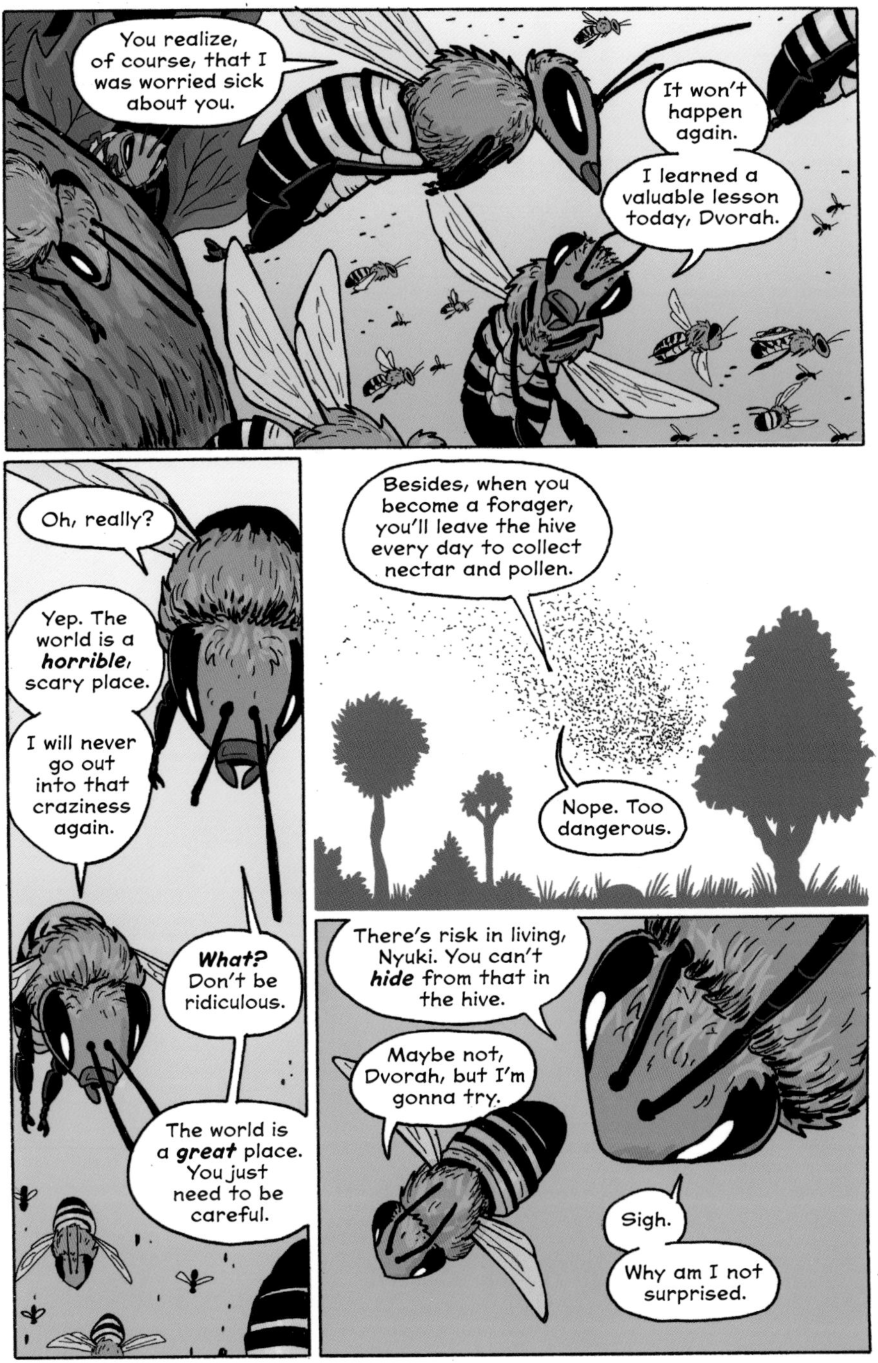
You realize, of course, that I was worried sick about you.
It won't happen again.
I learned a valuable lesson today, Dvorah.
Oh, really?
Yep. The world is a *horrible*, scary place.
I will never go out into that craziness again.
What? Don't be ridiculous.
The world is a *great* place. You just need to be careful.
Besides, when you become a forager, you'll leave the hive every day to collect nectar and pollen.
Nope. Too dangerous.
There's risk in living, Nyuki. You can't *hide* from that in the hive.
Maybe not, Dvorah, but I'm gonna try.
Sigh.
Why am I not surprised.

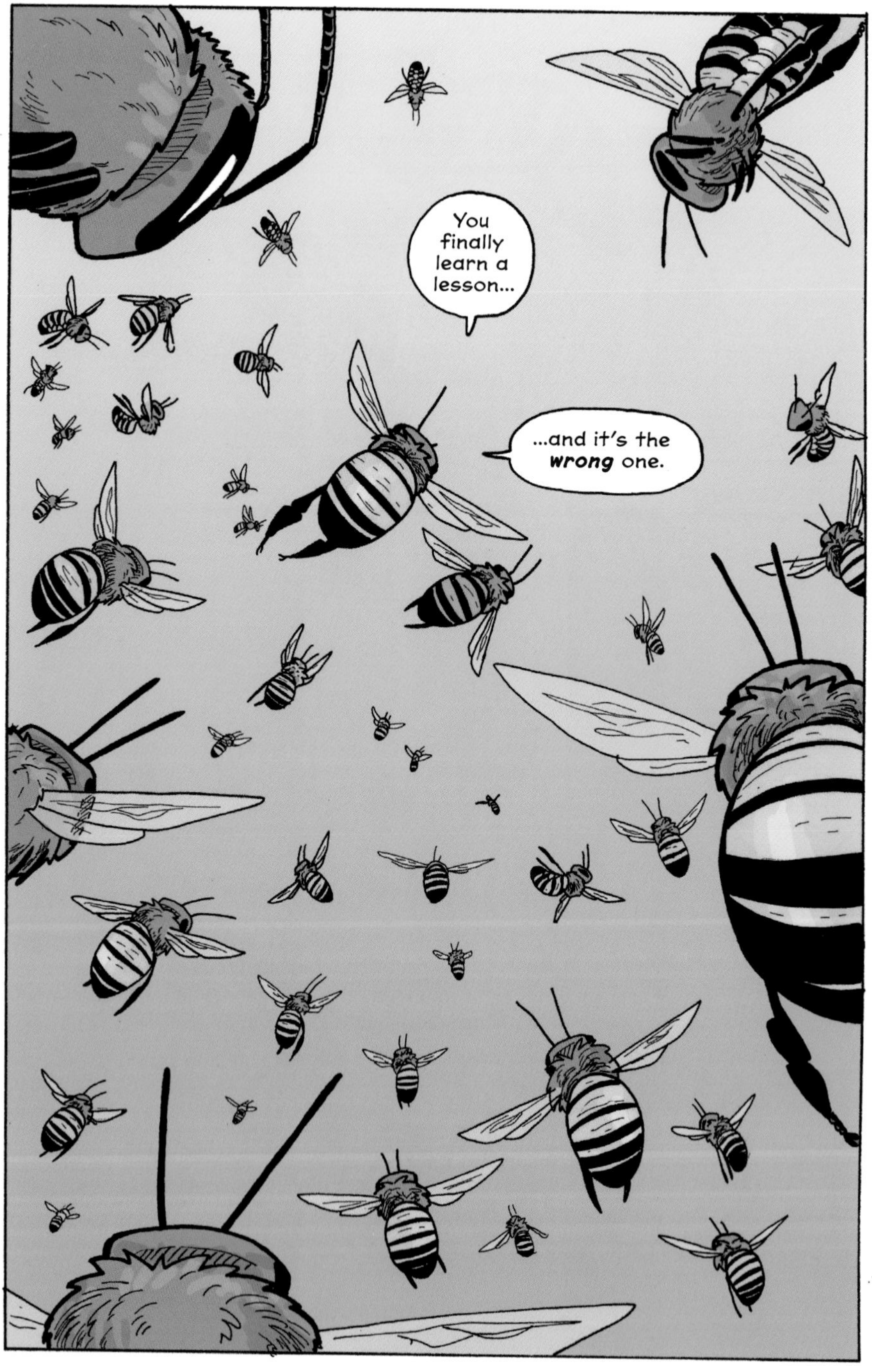
You finally learn a lesson...
...and it's the **wrong** one.

HOMEFRONT

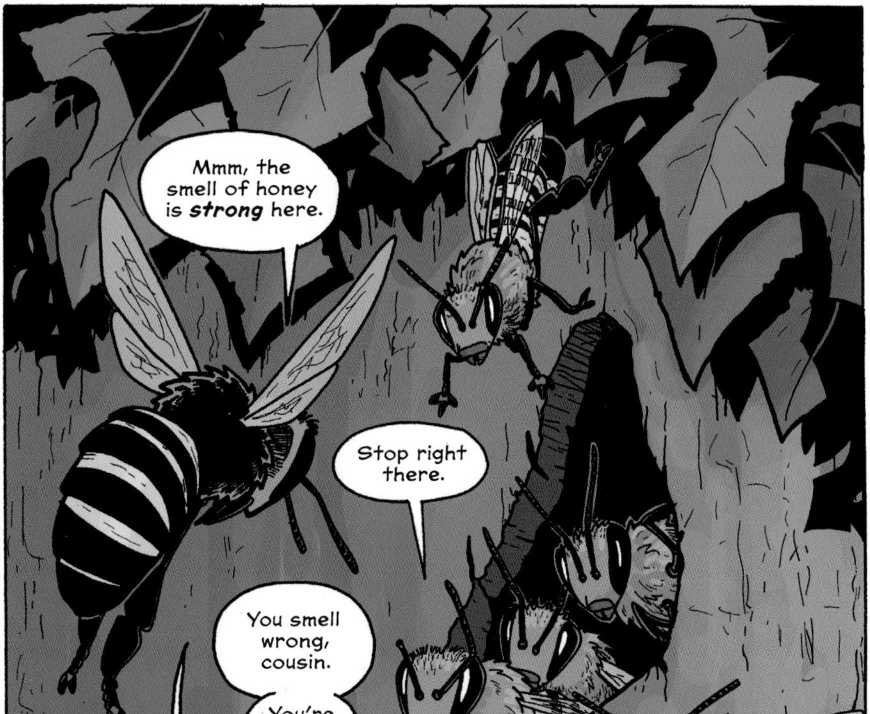
Mmm, the smell of honey is **strong** here.
Stop right there.
You smell wrong, cousin.
You're not from our hive.
My hive is far from here.
I'm just passing by.

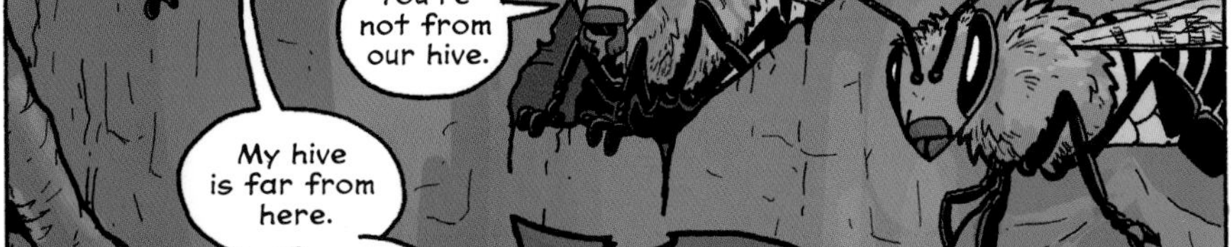
You're casing the joint and we know it.
Now leave.

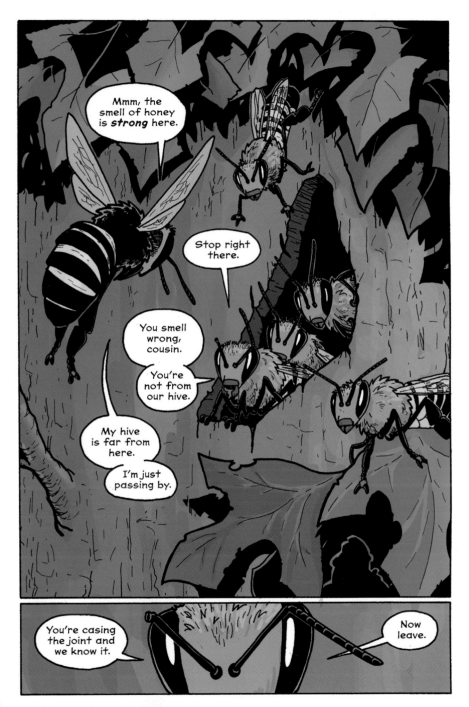

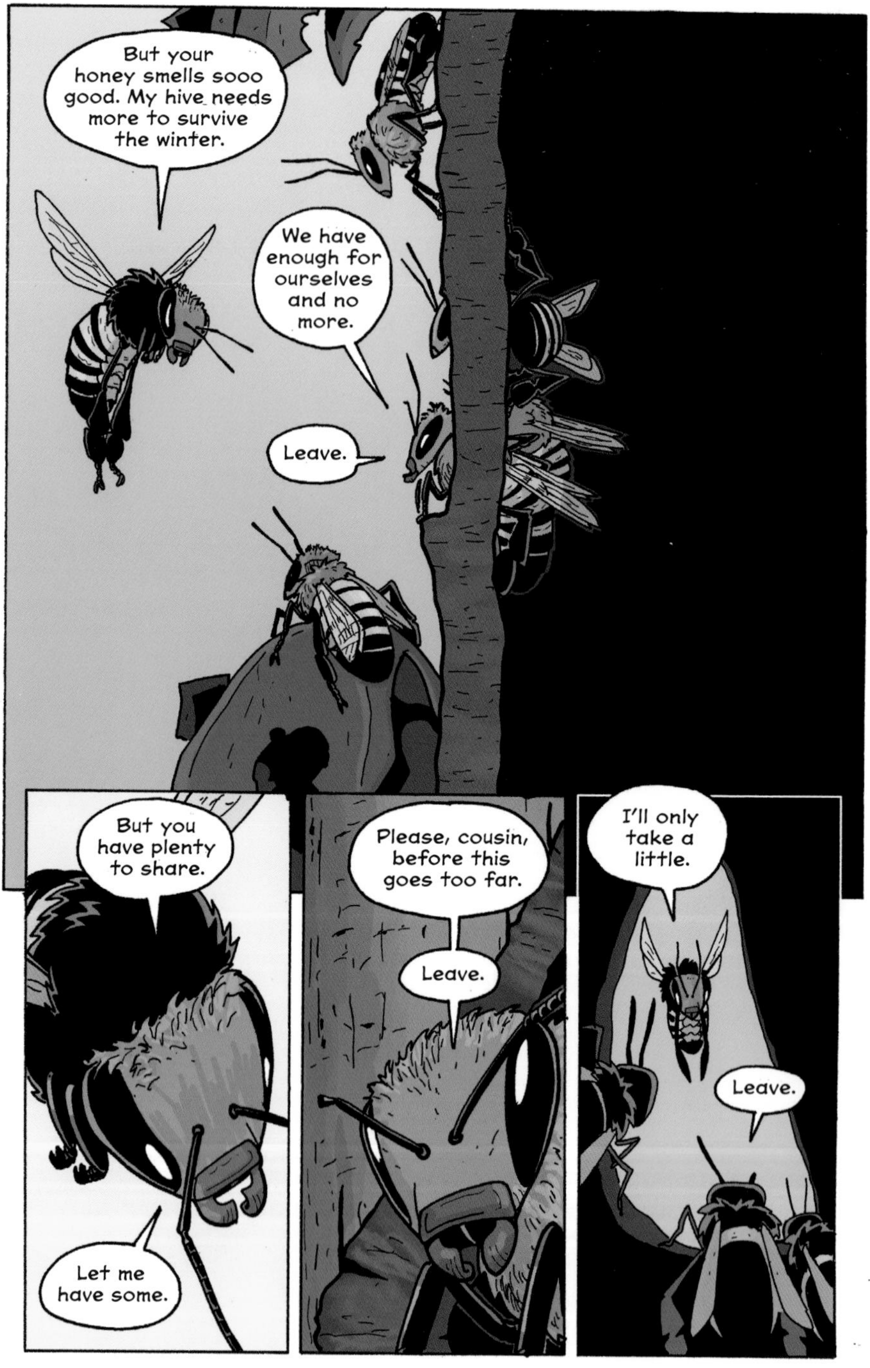
But your honey smells sooo good. My hive needs more to survive the winter.
We have enough for ourselves and no more.
Leave.
But you have plenty to share.
Let me have some.
Please, cousin, before this goes too far.
Leave.
I'll only take a little.
Leave.

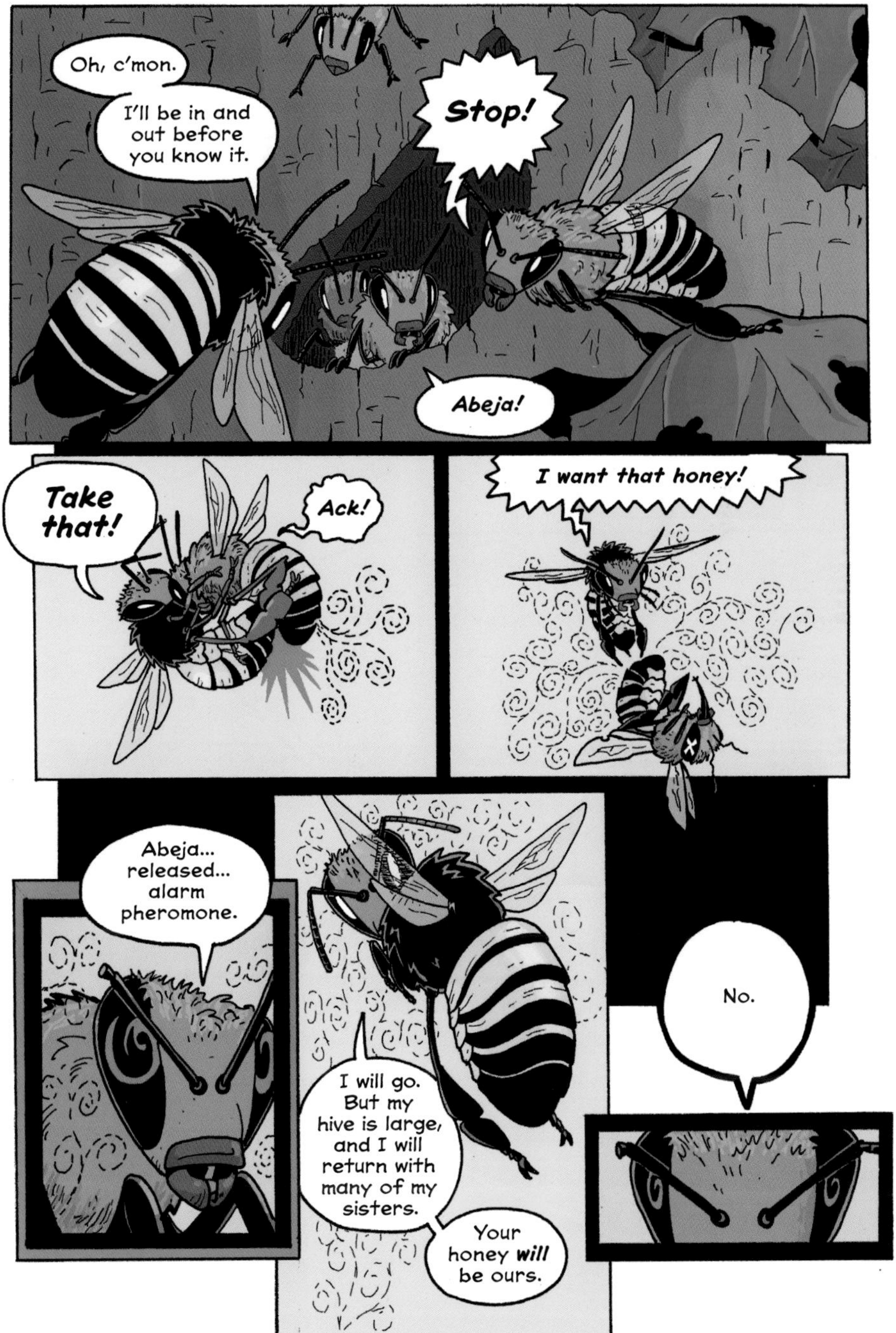
Oh, c'mon.
I'll be in and out before you know it.
Stop!
Abeja!
Take that!
Ack!
I want that honey!
Abeja... released... alarm pheromone.
I will go. But my hive is large, and I will return with many of my sisters.
Your honey will be ours.
No.

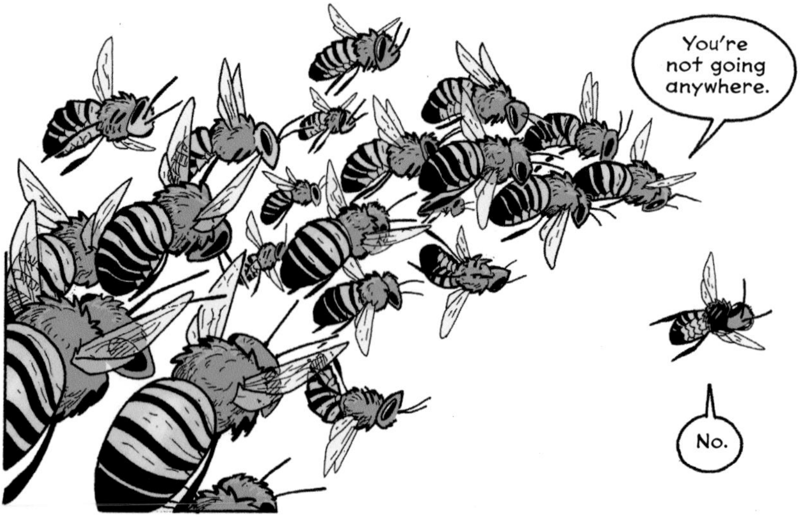
You're not going anywhere.
No.

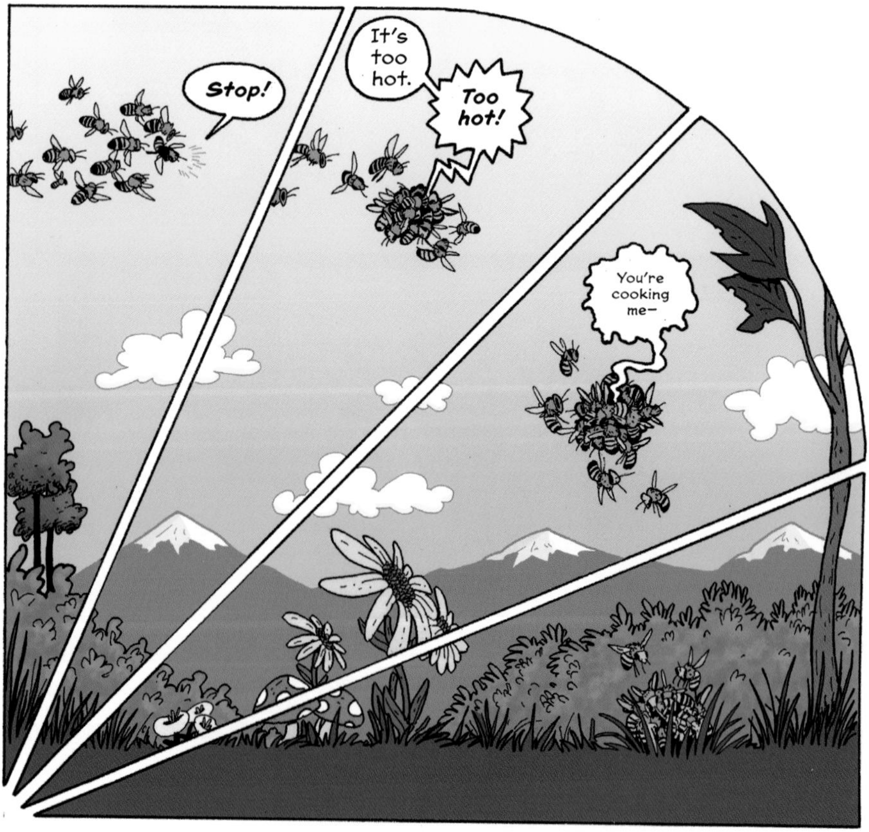
Stop!
It's too hot.
Too hot!
You're cooking me–

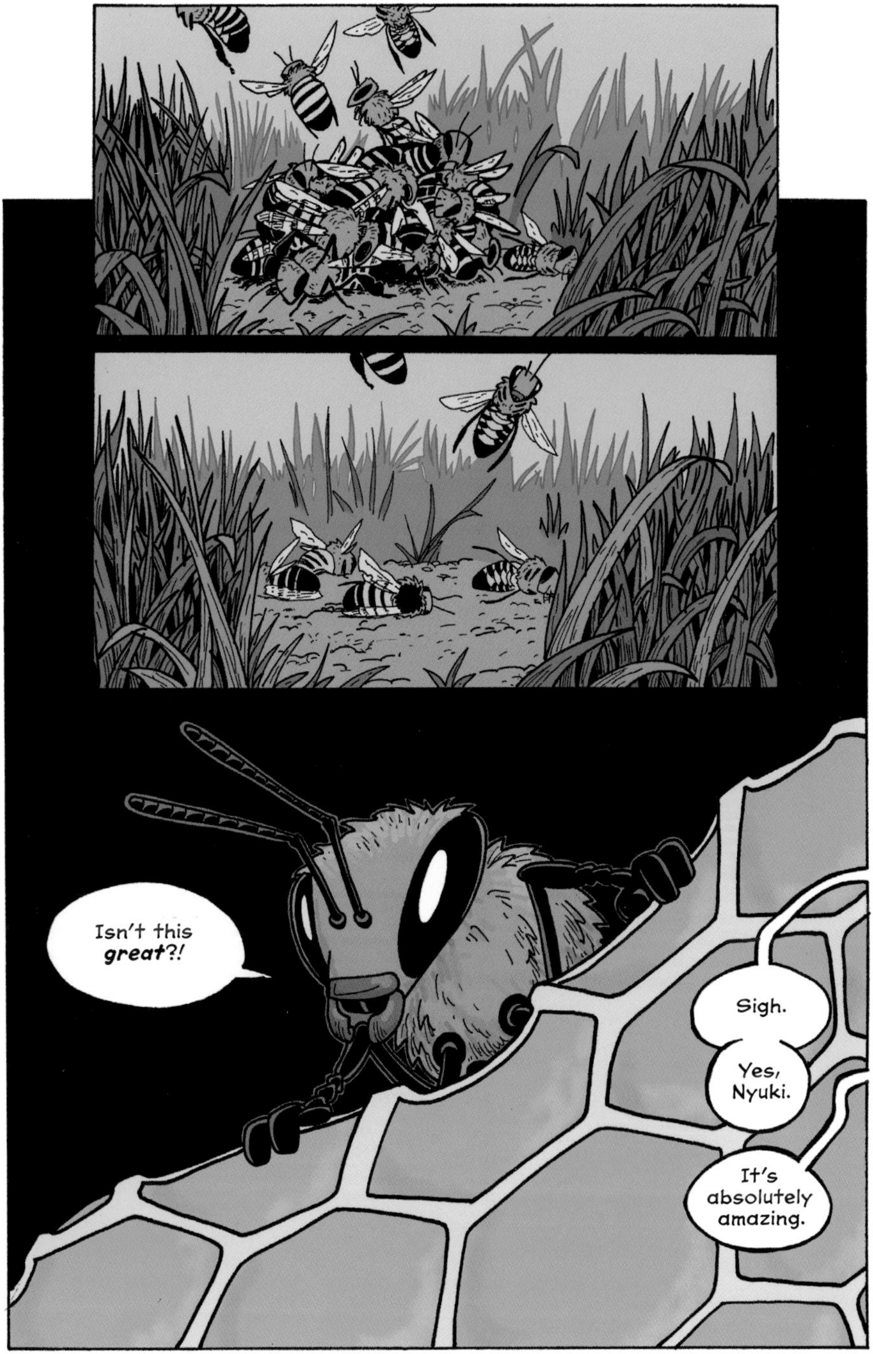
Isn't this *great*?!
Sigh.
Yes, Nyuki.
It's absolutely amazing.

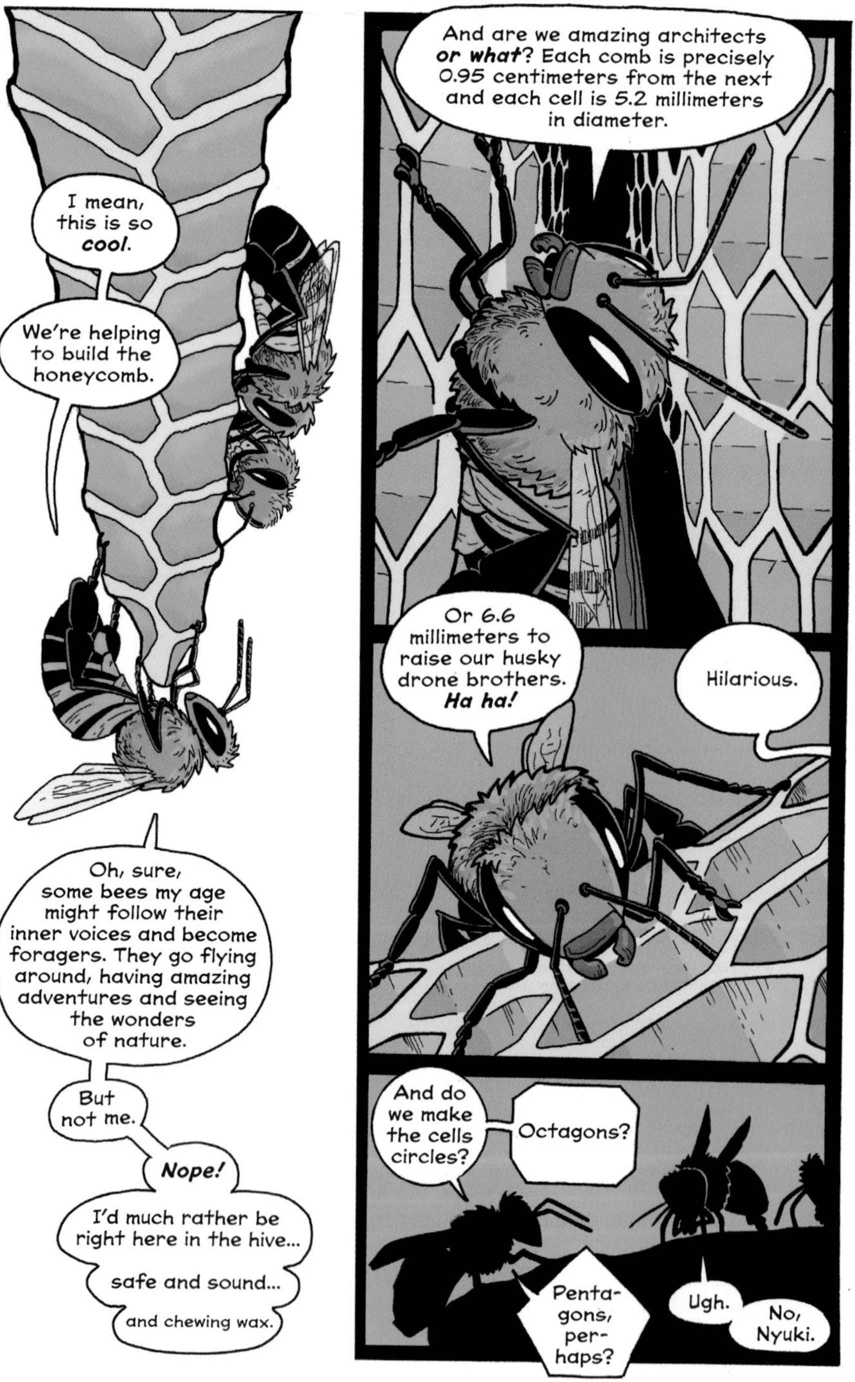
I mean, this is so *cool*.
We're helping to build the honeycomb.
Oh, sure, some bees my age might follow their inner voices and become foragers. They go flying around, having amazing adventures and seeing the wonders of nature.
But not me.
Nope!
I'd much rather be right here in the hive...
safe and sound...
and chewing wax.
And are we amazing architects ***or what***? Each comb is precisely 0.95 centimeters from the next and each cell is 5.2 millimeters in diameter.
Or 6.6 millimeters to raise our husky drone brothers. ***Ha ha!***
Hilarious.
And do we make the cells circles?
Octagons?
Pentagons, perhaps?
Ugh.
No, Nyuki.

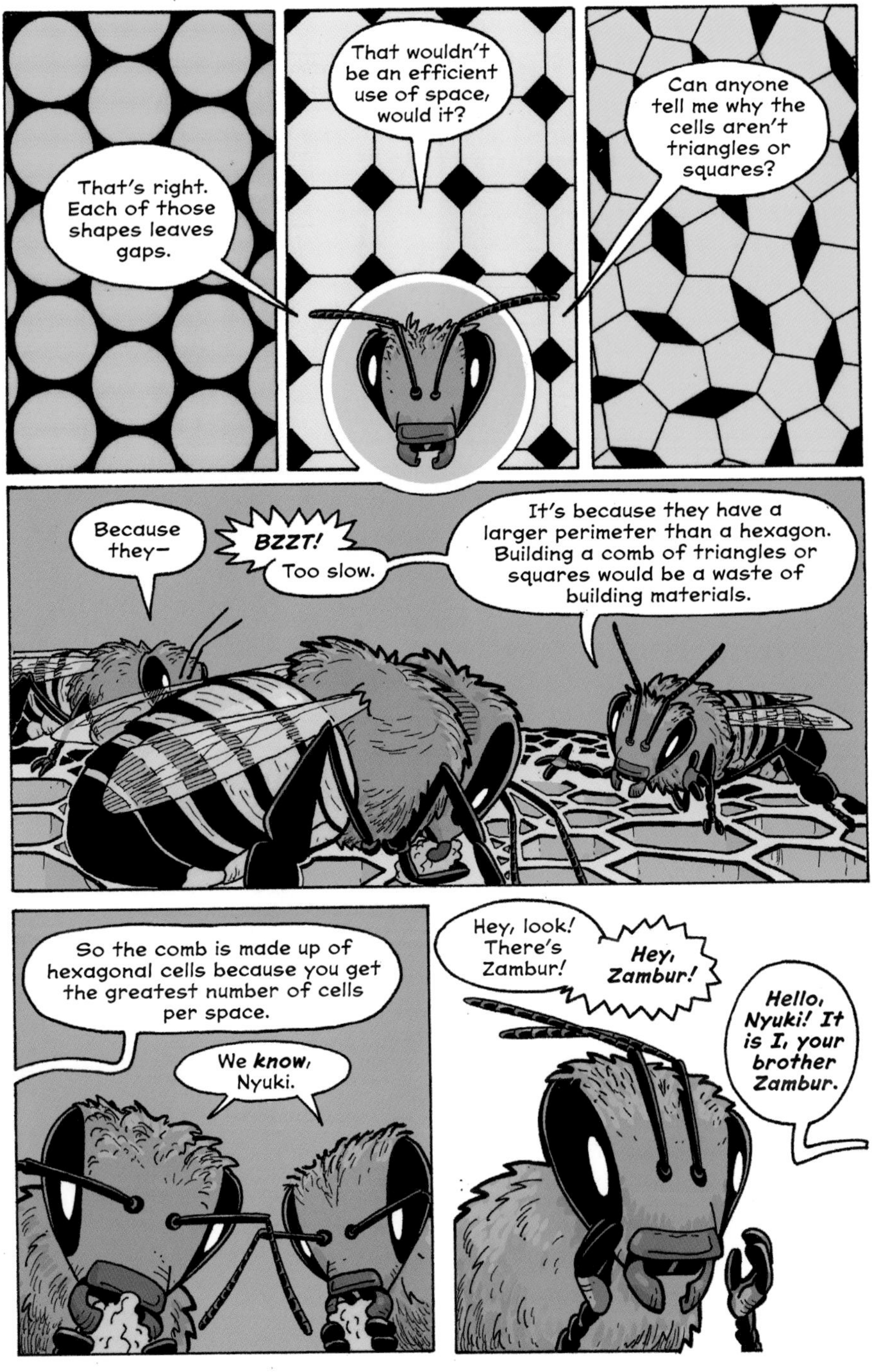
That's right. Each of those shapes leaves gaps.
That wouldn't be an efficient use of space, would it?
Can anyone tell me why the cells aren't triangles or squares?
Because they—
BZZT!
Too slow.
It's because they have a larger perimeter than a hexagon. Building a comb of triangles or squares would be a waste of building materials.
So the comb is made up of hexagonal cells because you get the greatest number of cells per space.
We *know*, Nyuki.
Hey, look! There's Zambur!
Hey, Zambur!
Hello, Nyuki! It is I, your brother Zambur.

Hey, Big Z, did you know we live on a structure built from our own glandular secretions?

Ha ha! You are full of such **whimsy**, little one.

I'm **serious**. Our honeycomb is made from wax that we secrete from wax glands in our abdomens.

Ha! Silly sister. Zambur does not have a wax gland.

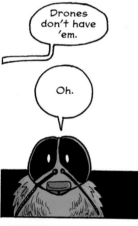

Drones don't have 'em.

Oh.

See?

I just secreted a little flake of wax.

Glorious!

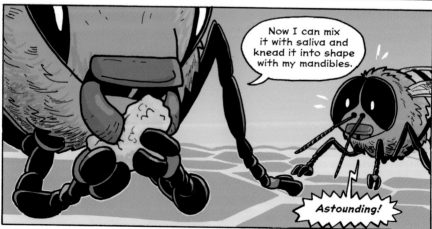

Now I can mix it with saliva and knead it into shape with my mandibles.

Astounding!

Or I can give it to younger bees who can't make as much as I do.

Here you go, girls.

Heads up!

Gah!

BONK!

She's *really* driving me crazy, Ari.

Well, y'know, Bij, I've heard that our stinger doesn't get stuck in insects like it does in other animals.

Really?

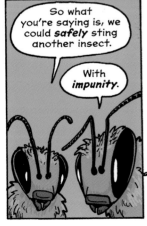

So what you're saying is, we could *safely* sting another insect.

With *impunity*.

We better not.

Yeah, well, I'm just sayin'.

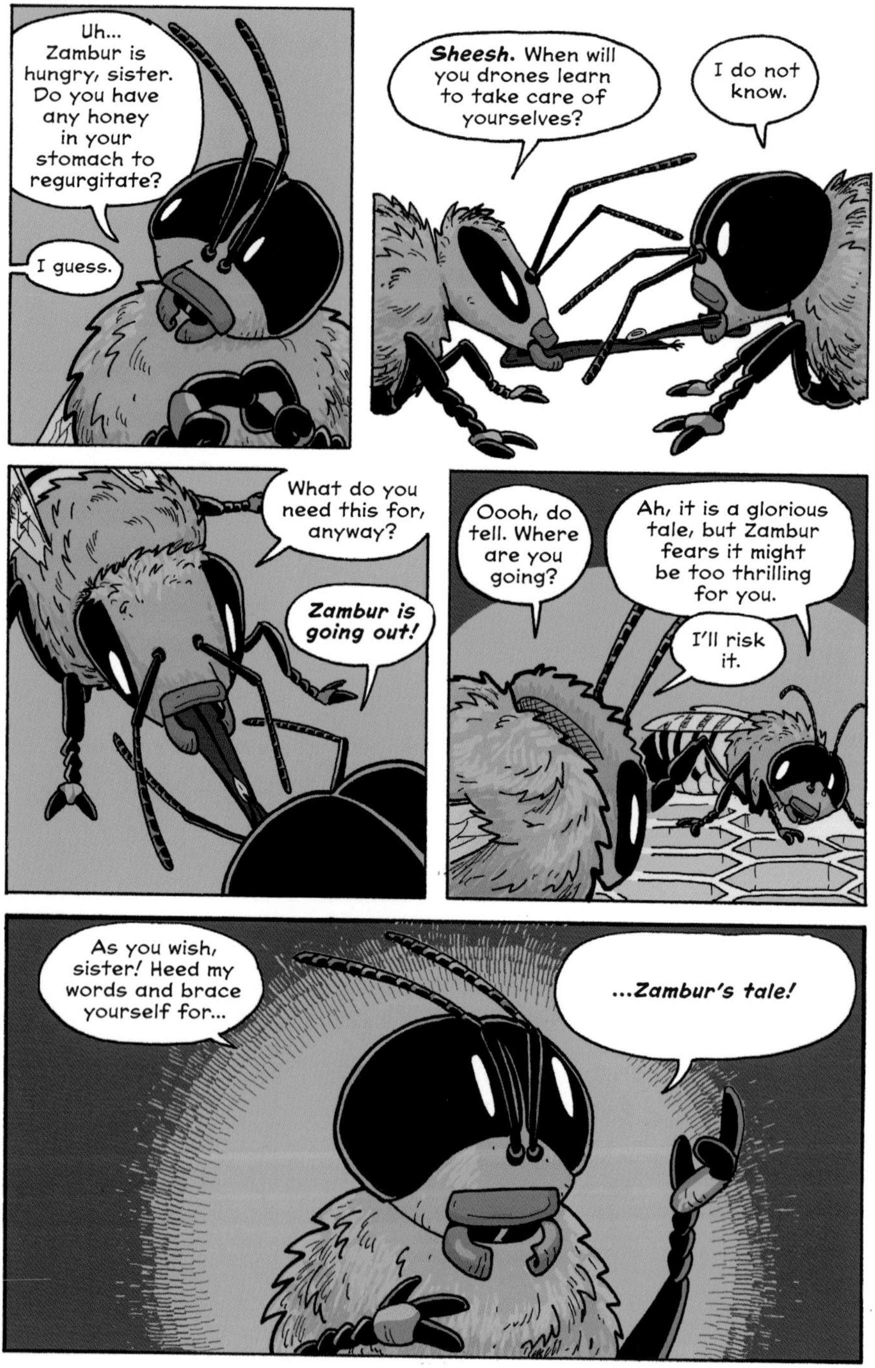
Uh... Zambur is hungry, sister. Do you have any honey in your stomach to regurgitate?
I guess.
Sheesh. When will you drones learn to take care of yourselves?
I do not know.
What do you need this for, anyway?
Zambur is going out!
Oooh, do tell. Where are you going?
Ah, it is a glorious tale, but Zambur fears it might be too thrilling for you.
I'll risk it.
As you wish, sister! Heed my words and brace yourself for...
...Zambur's tale!

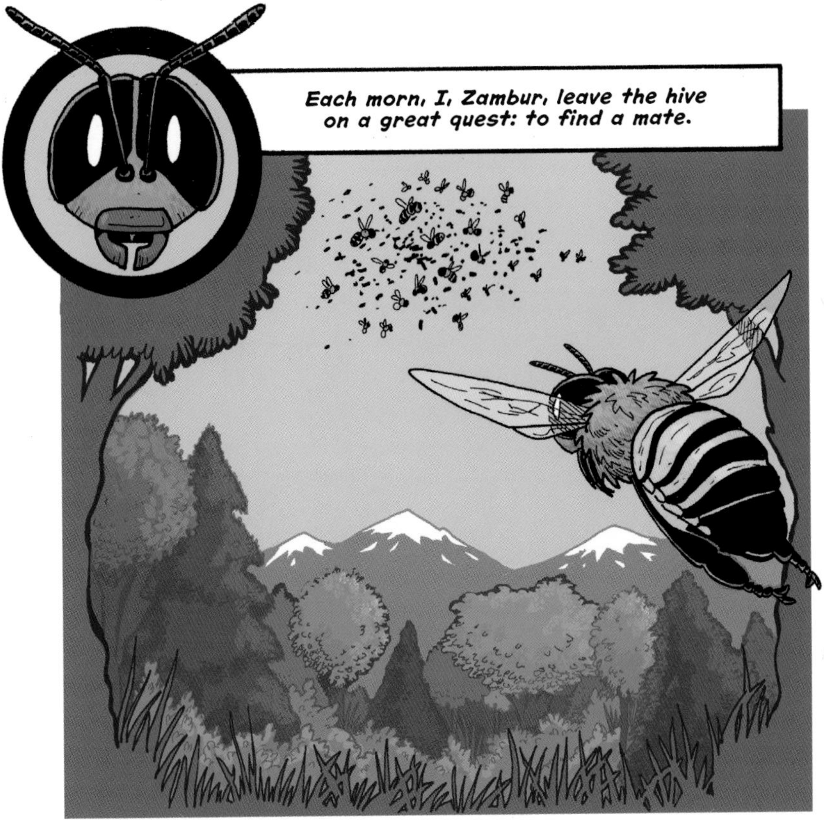
Each morn, I, Zambur, leave the hive on a great quest: to find a mate.

I join my fellow drones high in the air above a clearing in the forest for the great gathering. There we circle and swirl and swirl and circle as we wait for the arrival of a new queen.

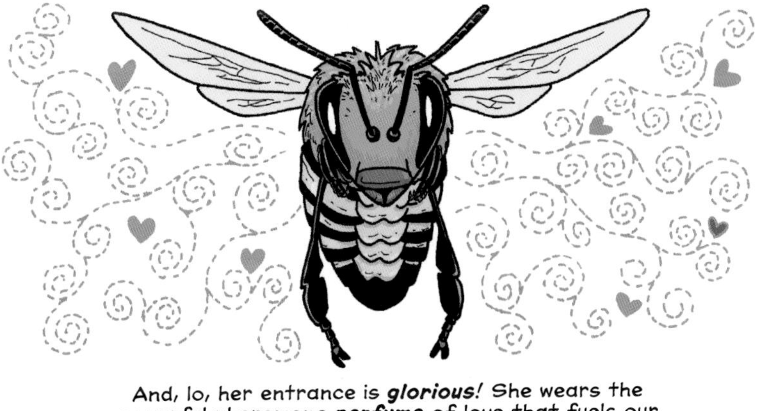

And, lo, her entrance is ***glorious!*** She wears the powerful pheromone ***perfume*** of love that fuels our desire to mate and sends us all into a passionate ***frenzy!***

We all valiantly vie for her attention, for she will only visit the great gathering once in her life, and of the hundreds of drones who gather, she will accept only ten to fifteen as mates.

Each drone she chooses will couple with her and give her a genetic gift, which she shall store and use to fertilize her eggs in the years to come. The diversity of her mates will give variety to her young and keep her hive strong.

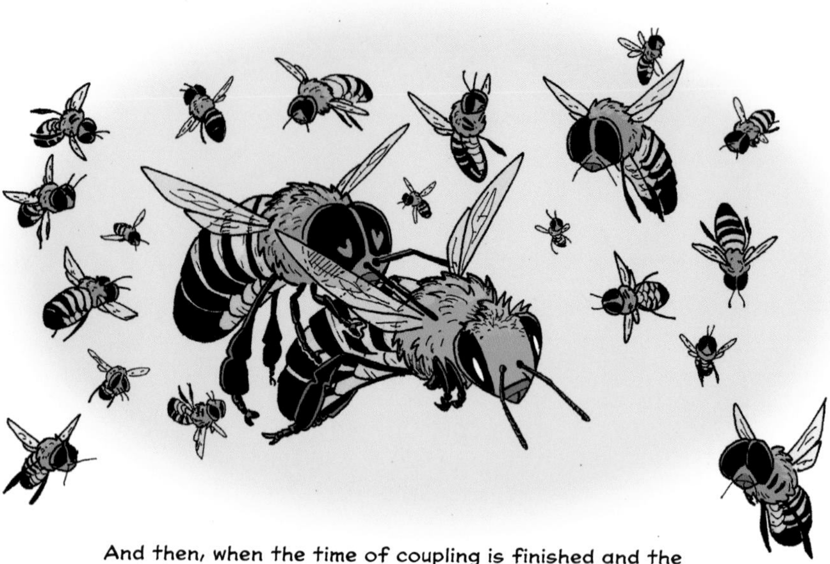

And then, when the time of coupling is finished and the male has imparted his mating gift, he breaks off from the queen and falls dead to the forest floor below.

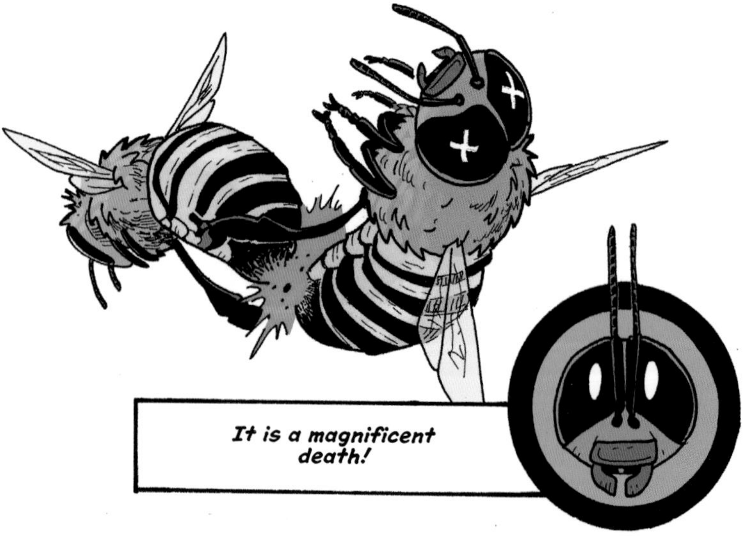
It is a magnificent death!

I just gave you honey so you can mate with a queen?

Yes!

And you'll die if you're successful?

Most definitely!

Give it back.

What?

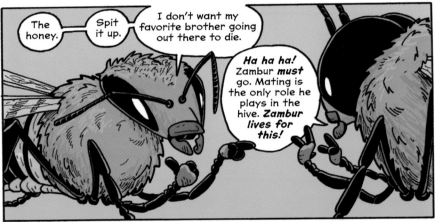

The honey. Spit it up.

I don't want my favorite brother going out there to die.

Ha ha ha! Zambur *must* go. Mating is the only role he plays in the hive. *Zambur lives for this!*

You live to die?

I live to die so that the clan may live.

That's *absurd*.

That is the way of the hive.

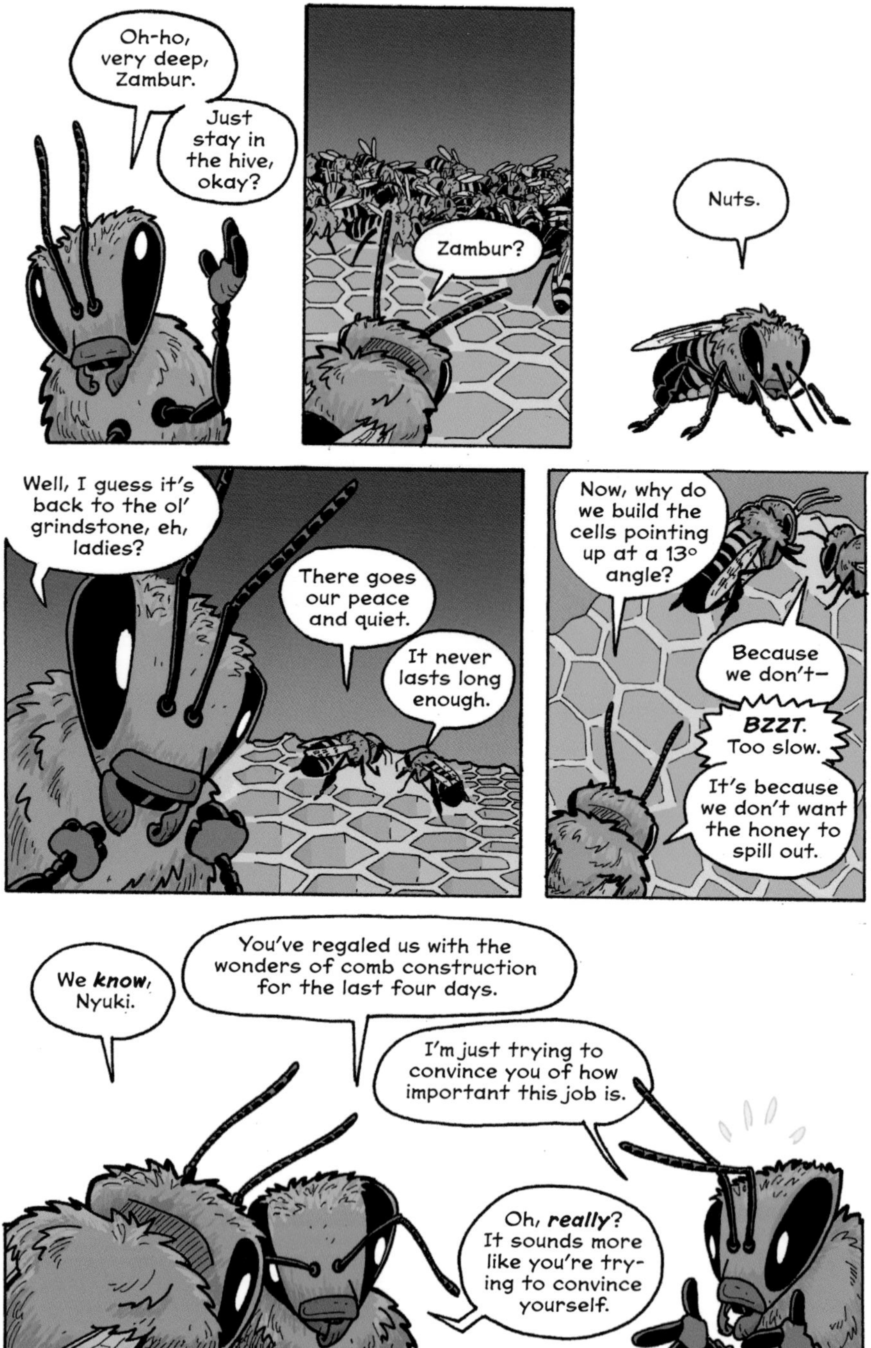

Oh-ho, very deep, Zambur.
Just stay in the hive, okay?
Zambur?
Nuts.
Well, I guess it's back to the ol' grindstone, eh, ladies?
There goes our peace and quiet.
It never lasts long enough.
Now, why do we build the cells pointing up at a 13° angle?
Because we don't–
BZZT. Too slow.
It's because we don't want the honey to spill out.
We know, Nyuki.
You've regaled us with the wonders of comb construction for the last four days.
I'm just trying to convince you of how important this job is.
Oh, really? It sounds more like you're trying to convince yourself.

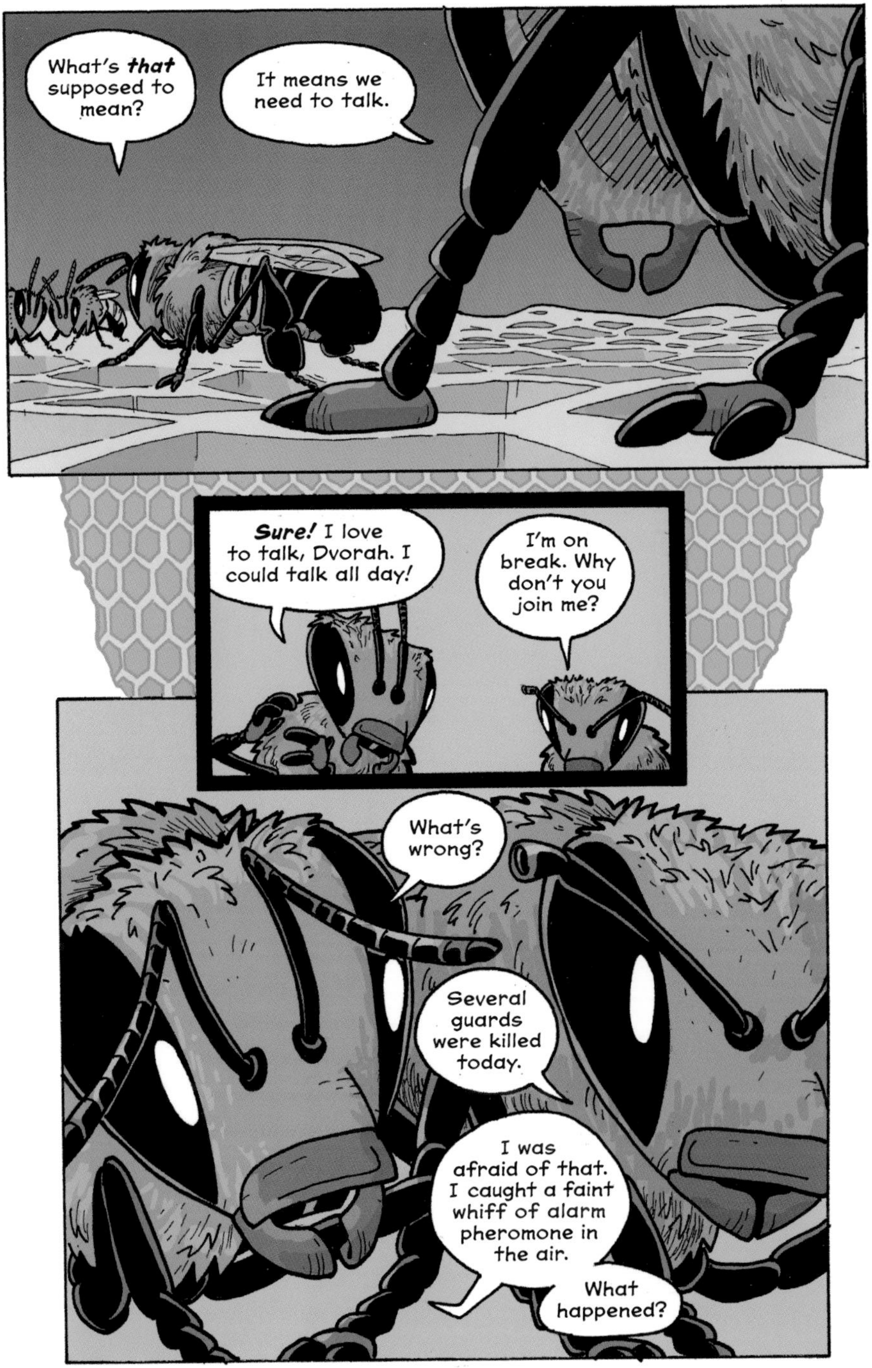
What's ***that*** supposed to mean?
It means we need to talk.
Sure! I love to talk, Dvorah. I could talk all day!
I'm on break. Why don't you join me?
What's wrong?
Several guards were killed today.
I was afraid of that. I caught a faint whiff of alarm pheromone in the air.
What happened?

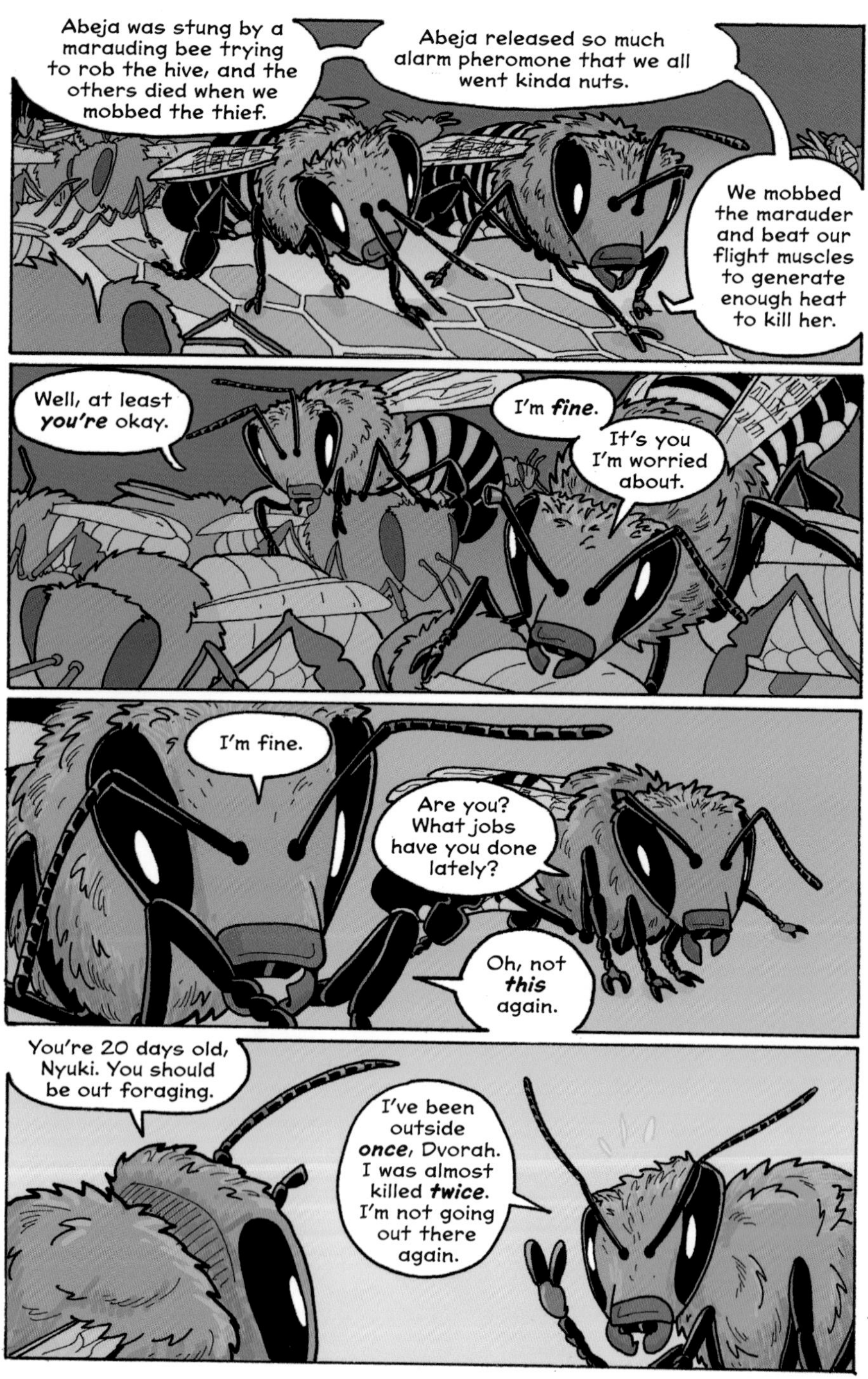

Abeja was stung by a marauding bee trying to rob the hive, and the others died when we mobbed the thief.
Abeja released so much alarm pheromone that we all went kinda nuts.
We mobbed the marauder and beat our flight muscles to generate enough heat to kill her.
Well, at least *you're* okay.
I'm *fine*.
It's you I'm worried about.
I'm fine.
Are you? What jobs have you done lately?
Oh, not *this* again.
You're 20 days old, Nyuki. You should be out foraging.
I've been outside *once*, Dvorah. I was almost killed *twice*. I'm not going out there again.

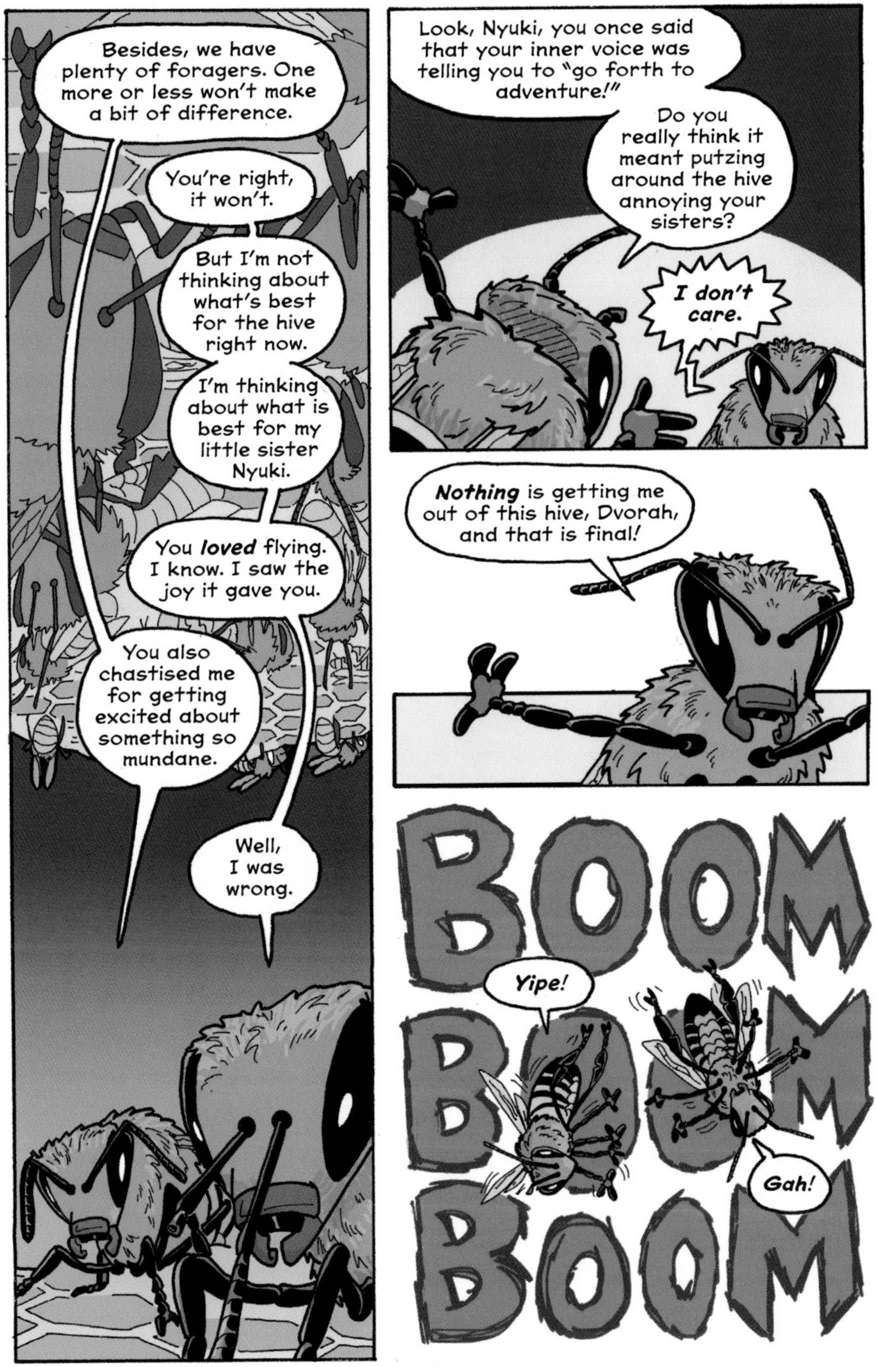
Besides, we have plenty of foragers. One more or less won't make a bit of difference.
You're right, it won't.
But I'm not thinking about what's best for the hive right now.
I'm thinking about what is best for my little sister Nyuki.
You ***loved*** flying. I know. I saw the joy it gave you.
You also chastised me for getting excited about something so mundane.
Well, I was wrong.
Look, Nyuki, you once said that your inner voice was telling you to "go forth to adventure!"
Do you really think it meant putzing around the hive annoying your sisters?
I don't care.
Nothing is getting me out of this hive, Dvorah, and that is final!
BOOM
BOOM
BOOM
Yipe!
Gah!

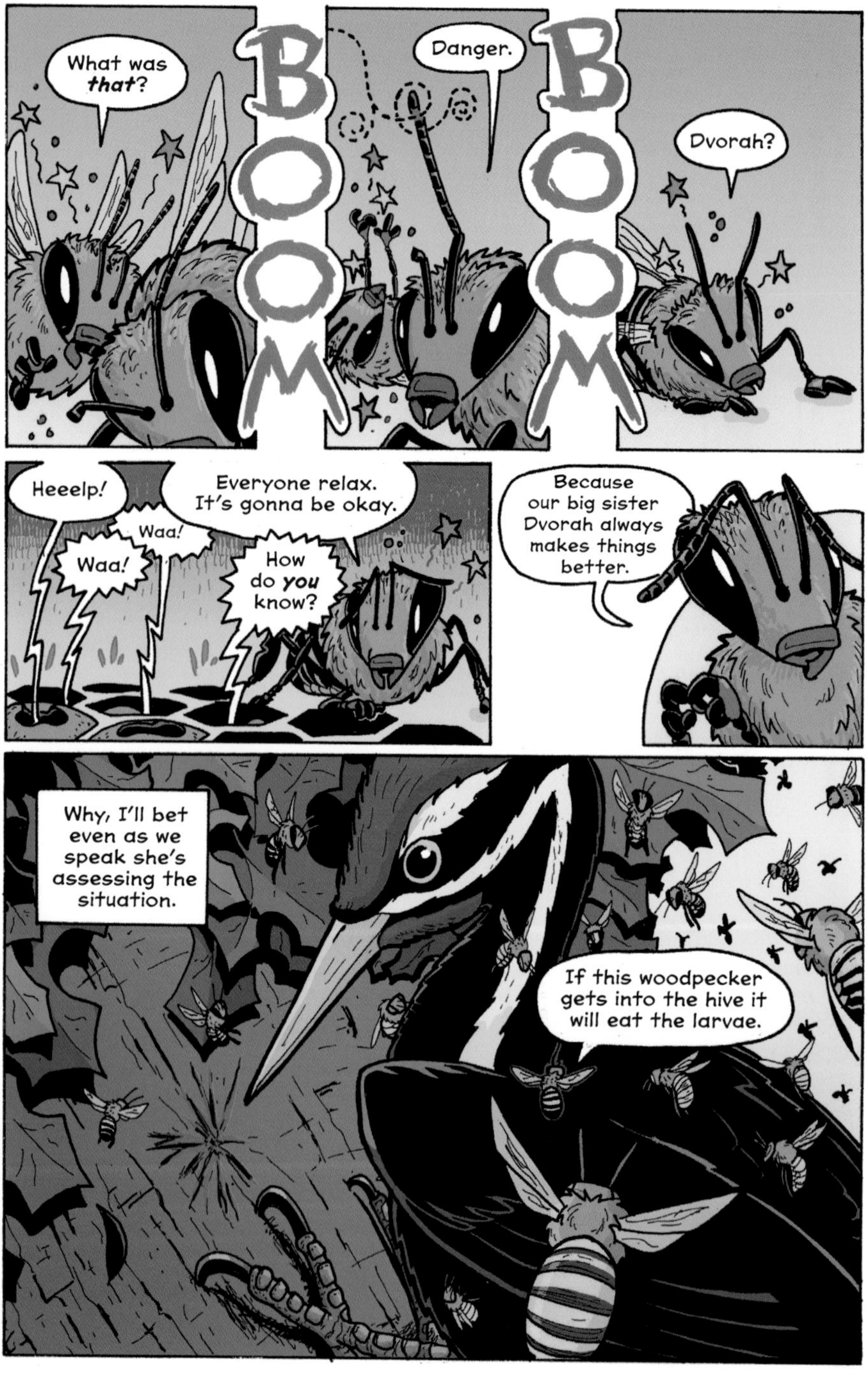
What was *that*?
BOOM
Danger.
BOOM
Dvorah?
Heeelp!
Everyone relax. It's gonna be okay.
Waa!
Waa!
How do *you* know?
Because our big sister Dvorah always makes things better.
Why, I'll bet even as we speak she's assessing the situation.
If this woodpecker gets into the hive it will eat the larvae.

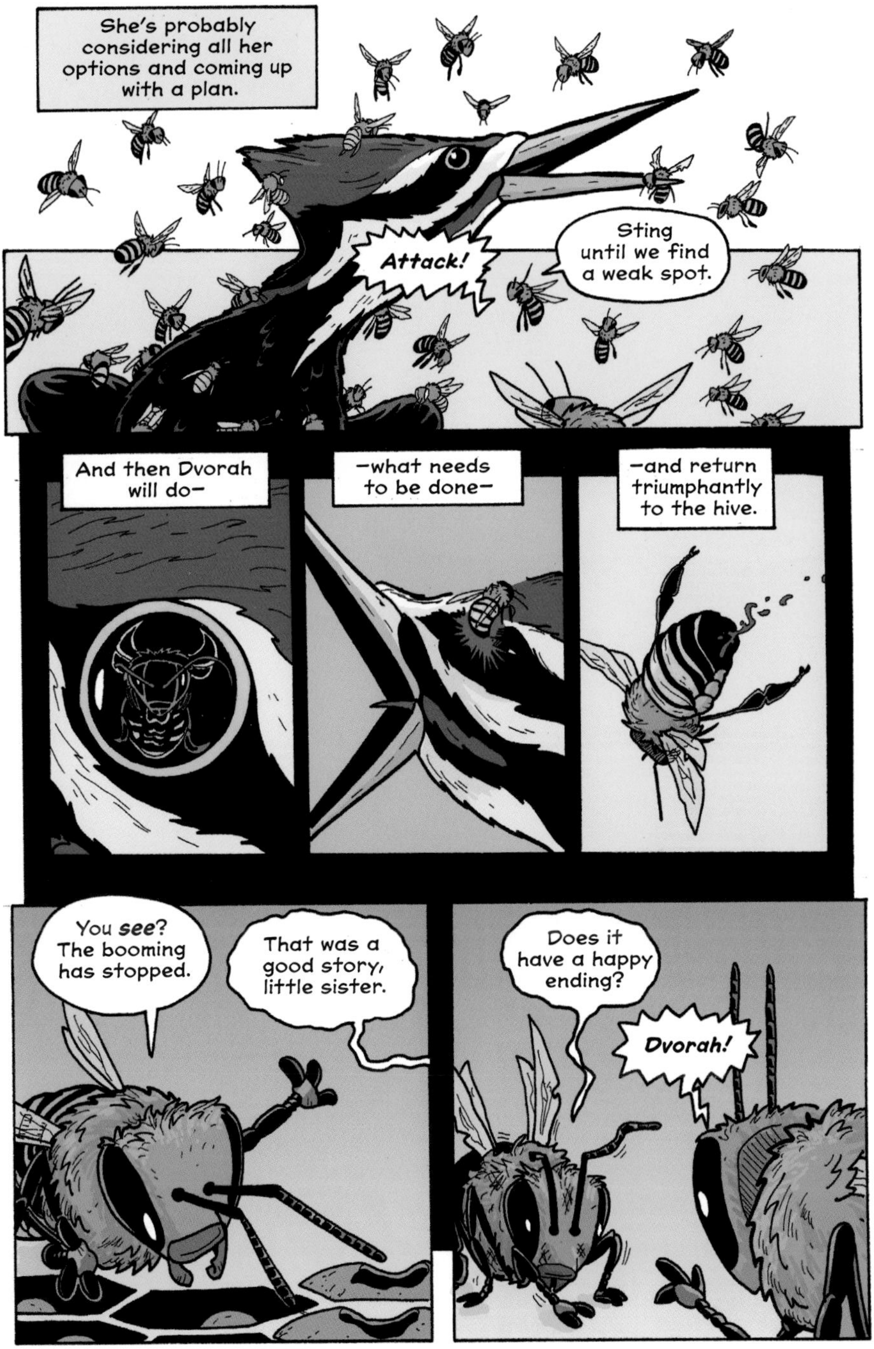

She's probably considering all her options and coming up with a plan.
Attack!
Sting until we find a weak spot.
And then Dvorah will do—
—what needs to be done—
—and return triumphantly to the hive.
You **see**? The booming has stopped.
That was a good story, little sister.
Does it have a happy ending?
Dvorah!

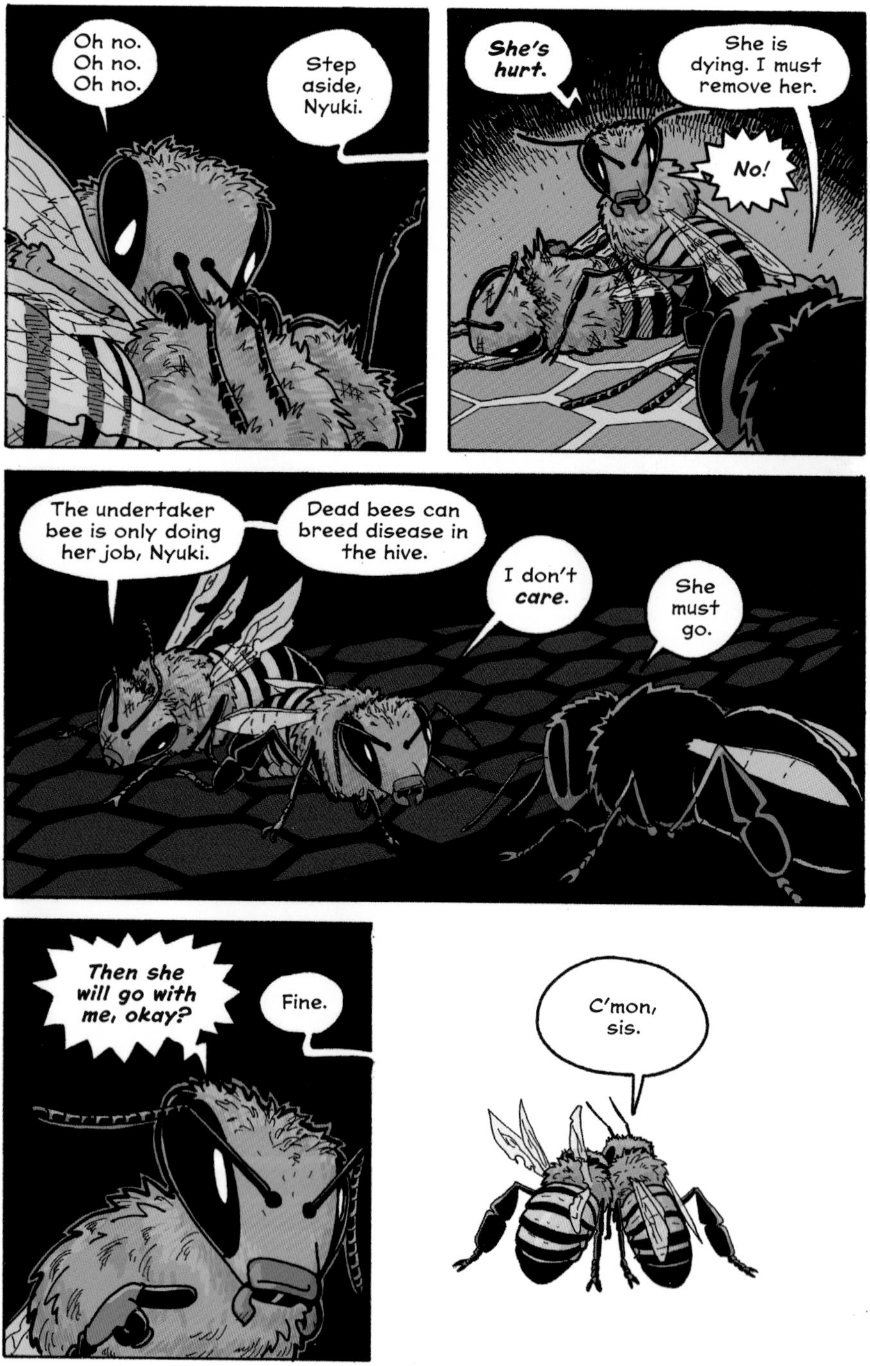

Oh no.
Oh no.
Oh no.
Step aside, Nyuki.
She's hurt.
She is dying. I must remove her.
No!
The undertaker bee is only doing her job, Nyuki.
Dead bees can breed disease in the hive.
I don't *care.*
She must go.
Then she will go with me, okay?
Fine.
C'mon, sis.

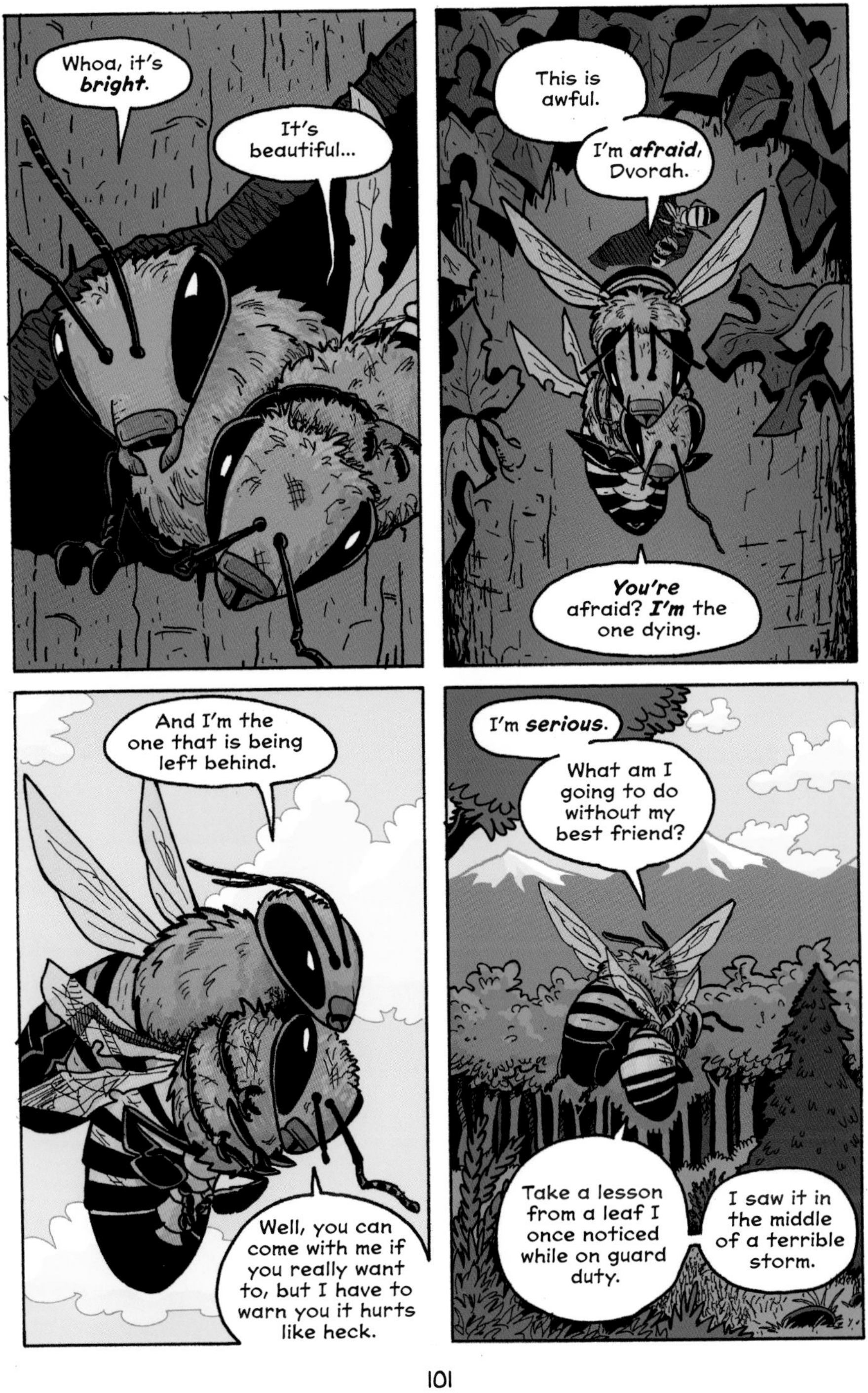
Whoa, it's ***bright***.
It's beautiful...
This is awful.
I'm ***afraid***, Dvorah.
You're afraid? ***I'm*** the one dying.
And I'm the one that is being left behind.
Well, you can come with me if you really want to, but I have to warn you it hurts like heck.
I'm ***serious***.
What am I going to do without my best friend?
Take a lesson from a leaf I once noticed while on guard duty.
I saw it in the middle of a terrible storm.

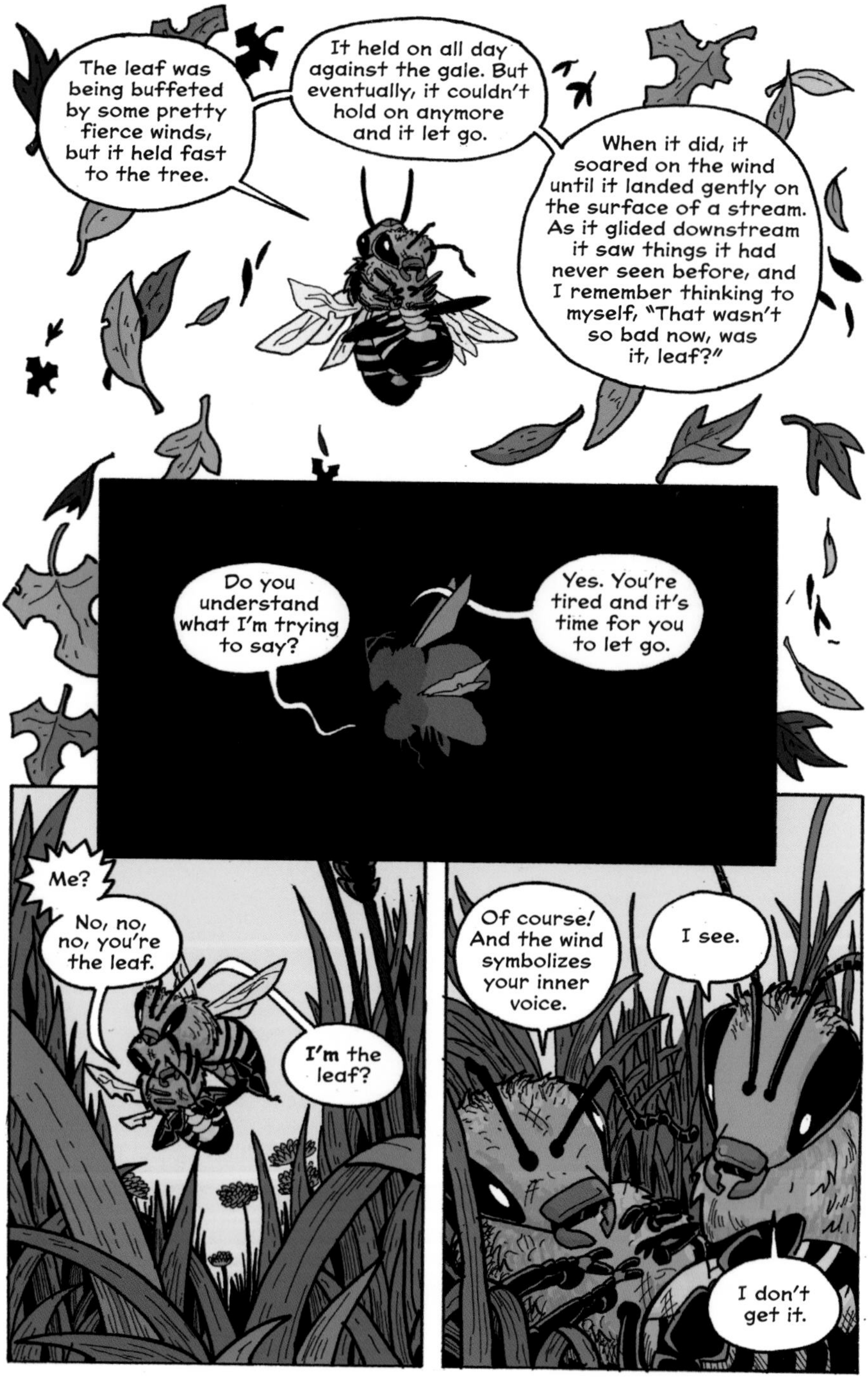
The leaf was being buffeted by some pretty fierce winds, but it held fast to the tree.
It held on all day against the gale. But eventually, it couldn't hold on anymore and it let go.
When it did, it soared on the wind until it landed gently on the surface of a stream. As it glided downstream it saw things it had never seen before, and I remember thinking to myself, "That wasn't so bad now, was it, leaf?"
Do you understand what I'm trying to say?
Yes. You're tired and it's time for you to let go.
Me?
No, no, no, you're the leaf.
I'm the leaf?
Of course! And the wind symbolizes your inner voice.
I see.
I don't get it.

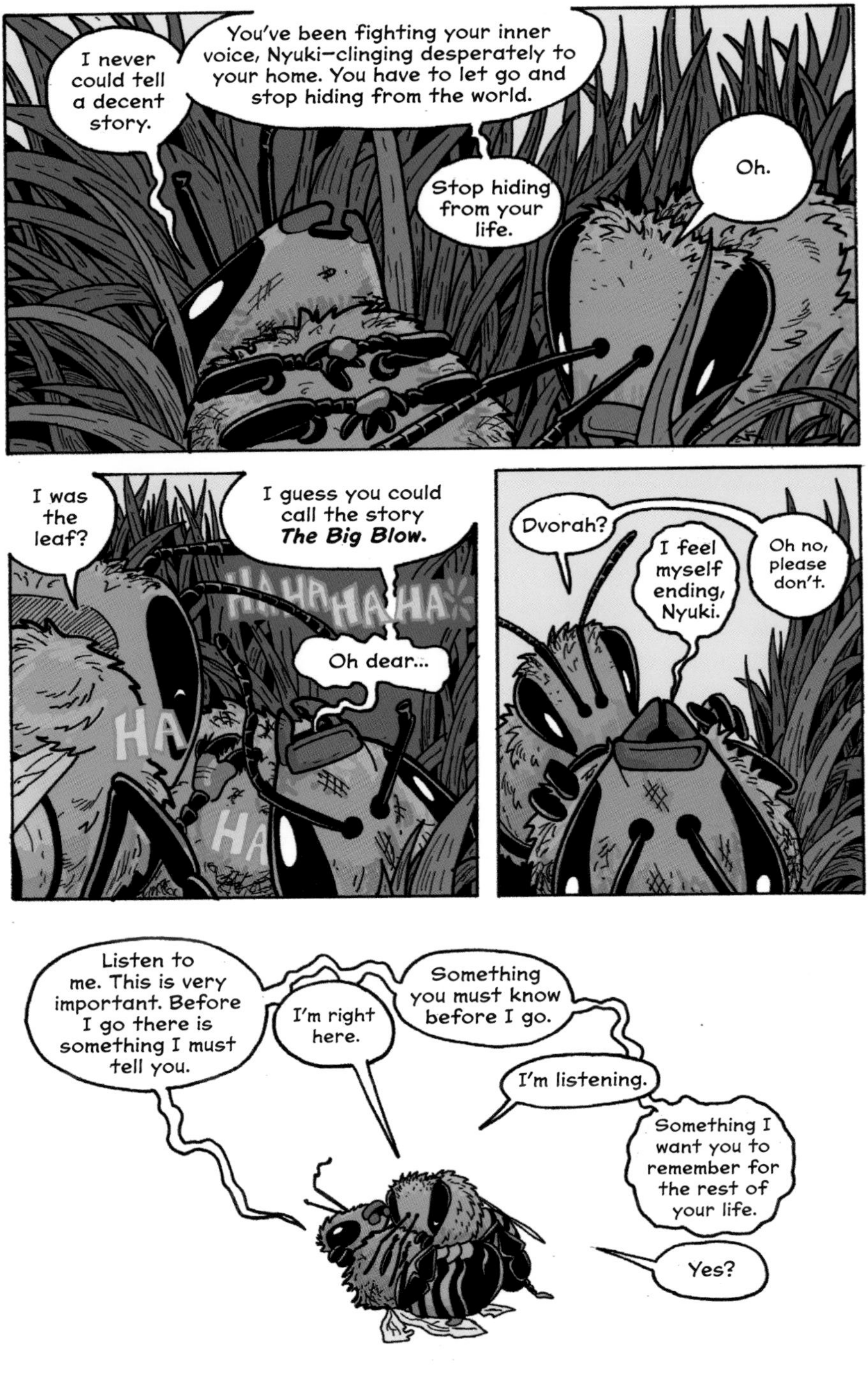

I never could tell a decent story.
You've been fighting your inner voice, Nyuki—clinging desperately to your home. You have to let go and stop hiding from the world.
Stop hiding from your life.
Oh.
I was the leaf?
I guess you could call the story *The Big Blow.*
HAHAHAHAHA
HA
HA
Oh dear...
Dvorah?
I feel myself ending, Nyuki.
Oh no, please don't.
Listen to me. This is very important. Before I go there is something I must tell you.
I'm right here.
Something you must know before I go.
I'm listening.
Something I want you to remember for the rest of your life.
Yes?

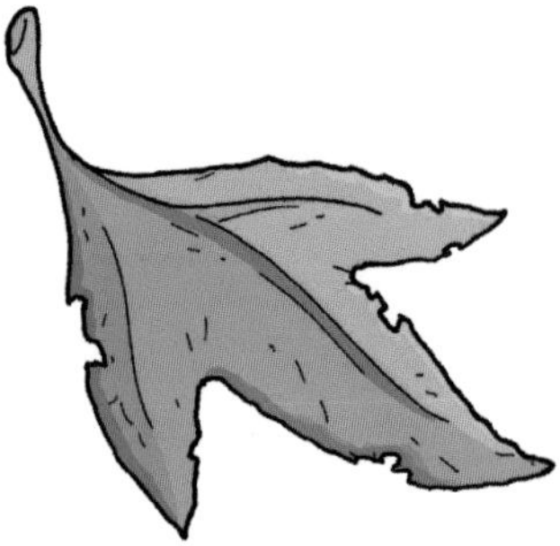

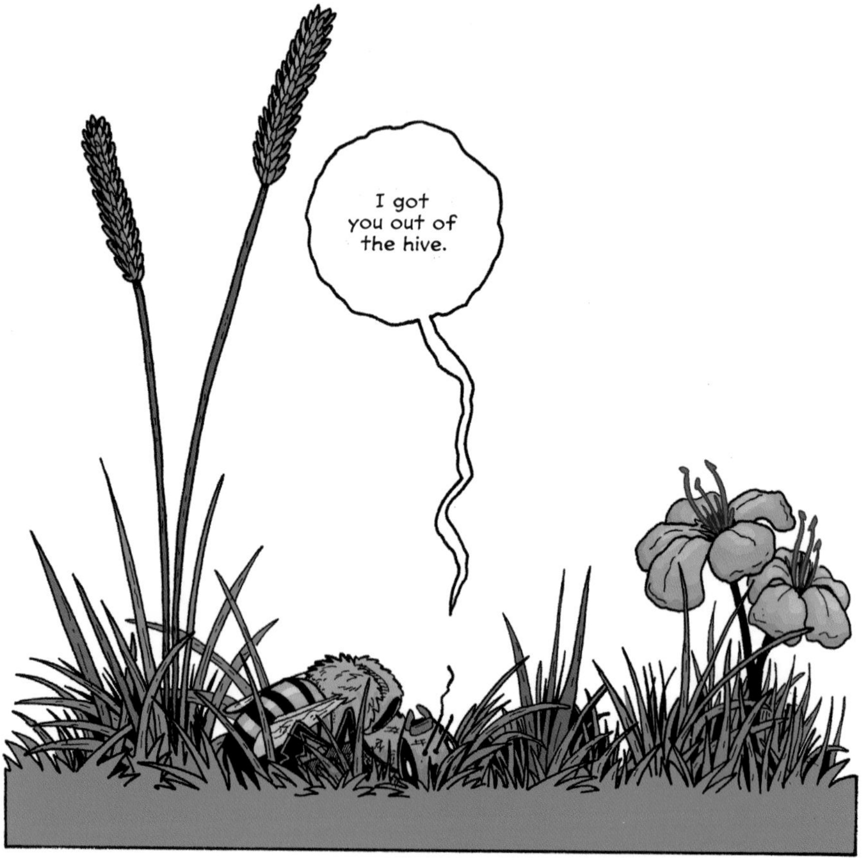
I got you out of the hive.

5

THE PLAN

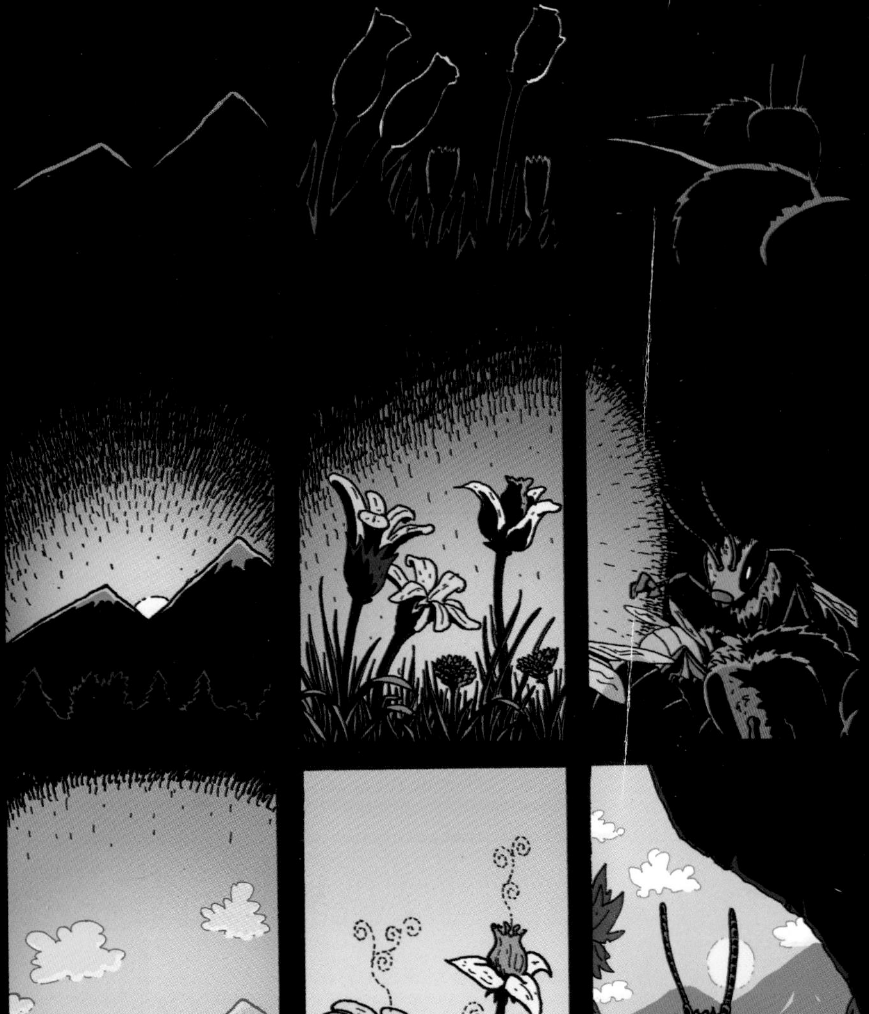

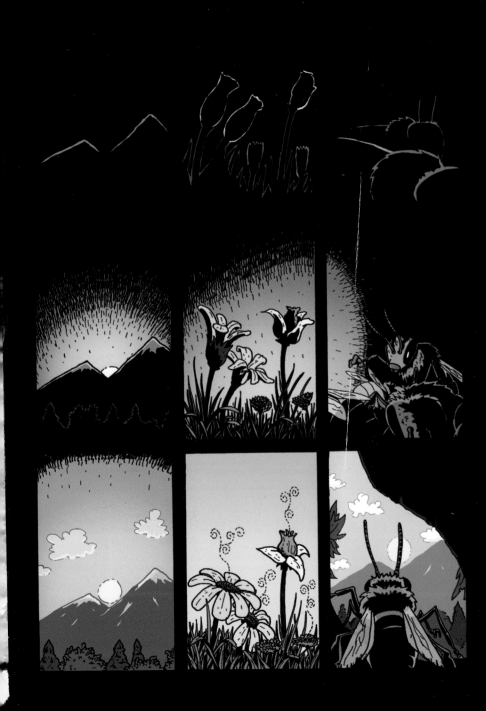

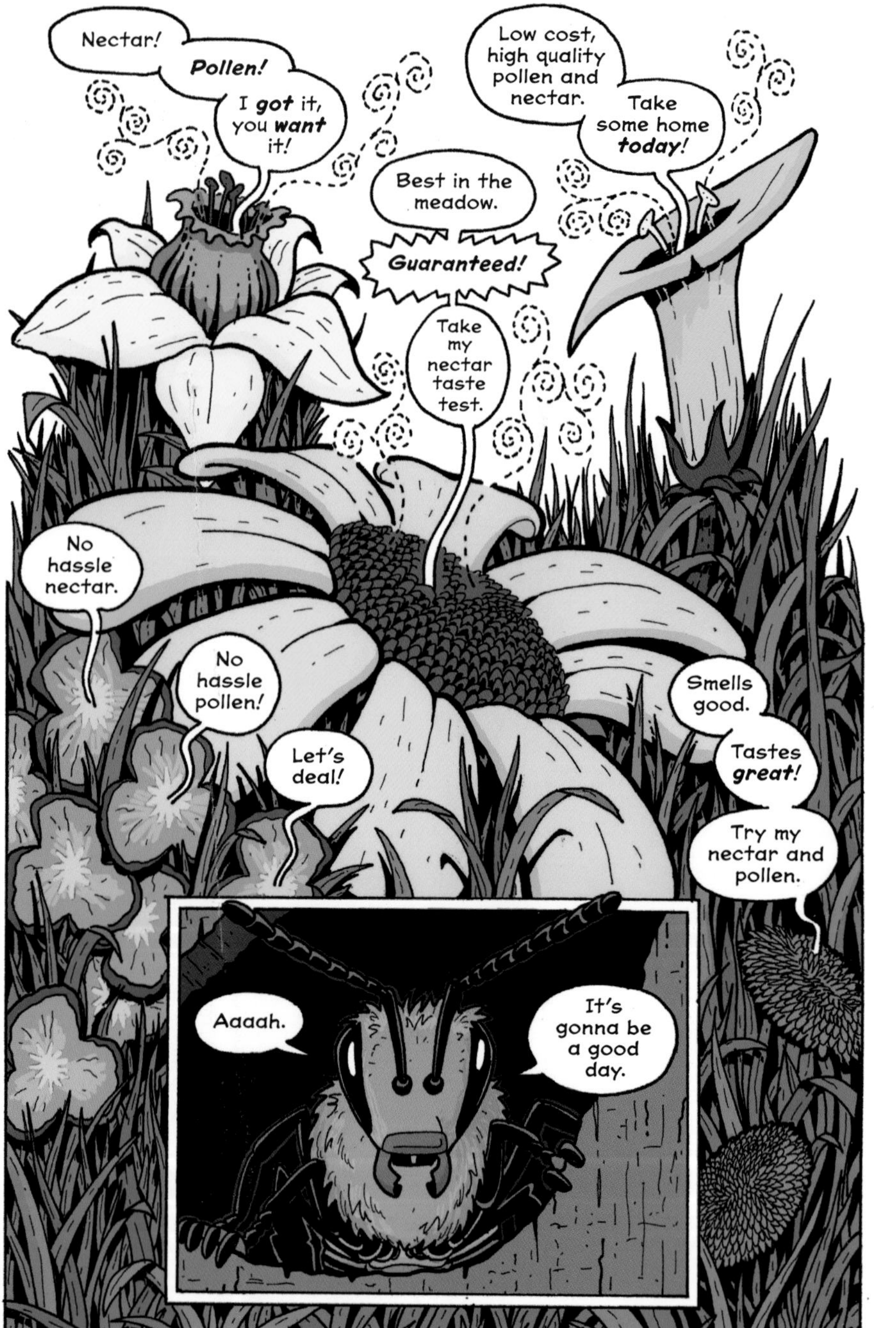
Nectar!
Pollen!
I got it, you want it!
Low cost, high quality pollen and nectar.
Take some home today!
Best in the meadow.
Guaranteed!
Take my nectar taste test.
No hassle nectar.
No hassle pollen!
Let's deal!
Smells good.
Tastes great!
Try my nectar and pollen.
Aaaah.
It's gonna be a good day.

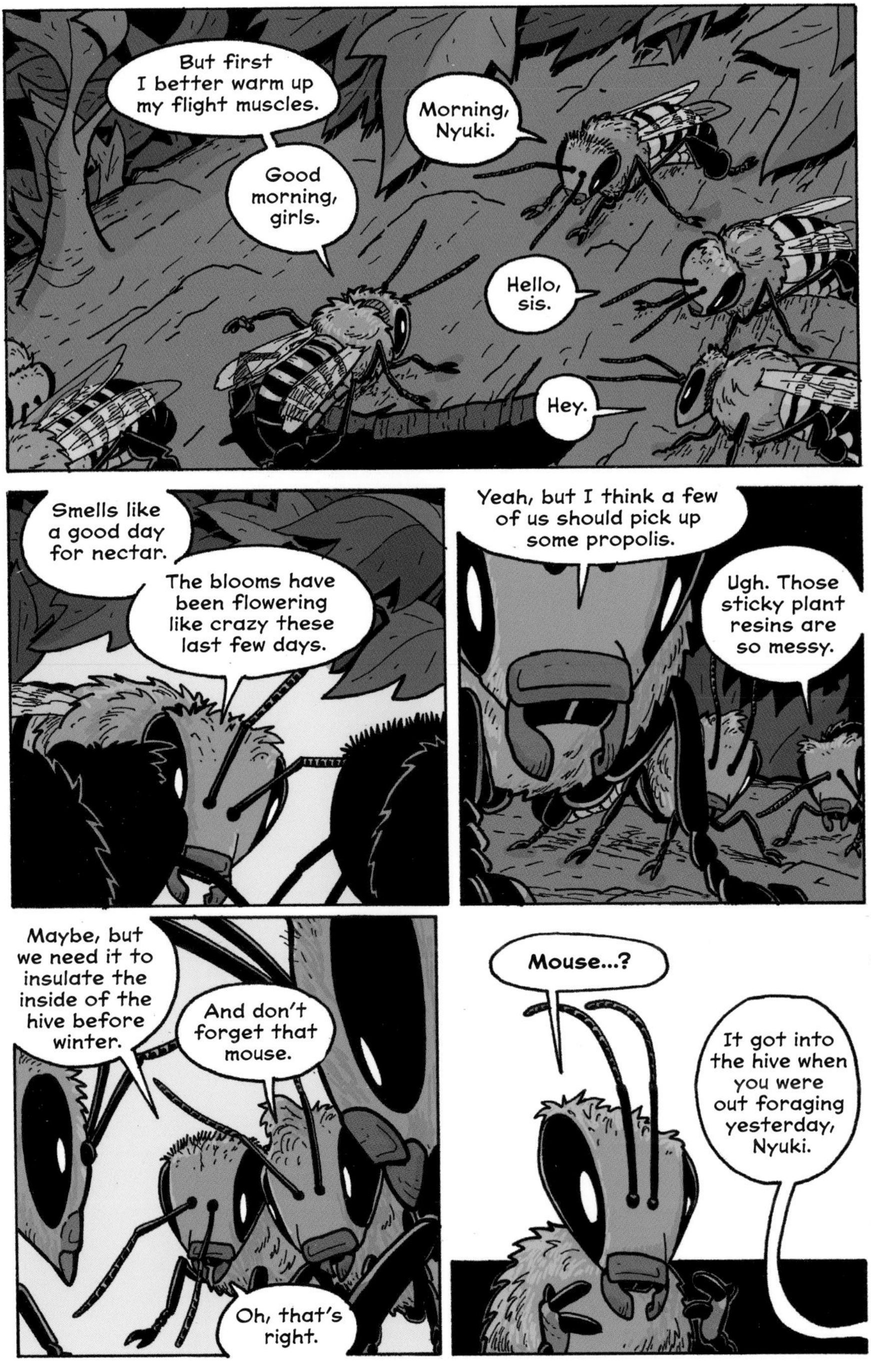
But first I better warm up my flight muscles.
Good morning, girls.
Morning, Nyuki.
Hello, sis.
Hey.
Smells like a good day for nectar.
The blooms have been flowering like crazy these last few days.
Yeah, but I think a few of us should pick up some propolis.
Ugh. Those sticky plant resins are so messy.
Maybe, but we need it to insulate the inside of the hive before winter.
And don't forget that mouse.
Oh, that's right.
Mouse...?
It got into the hive when you were out foraging yesterday, Nyuki.

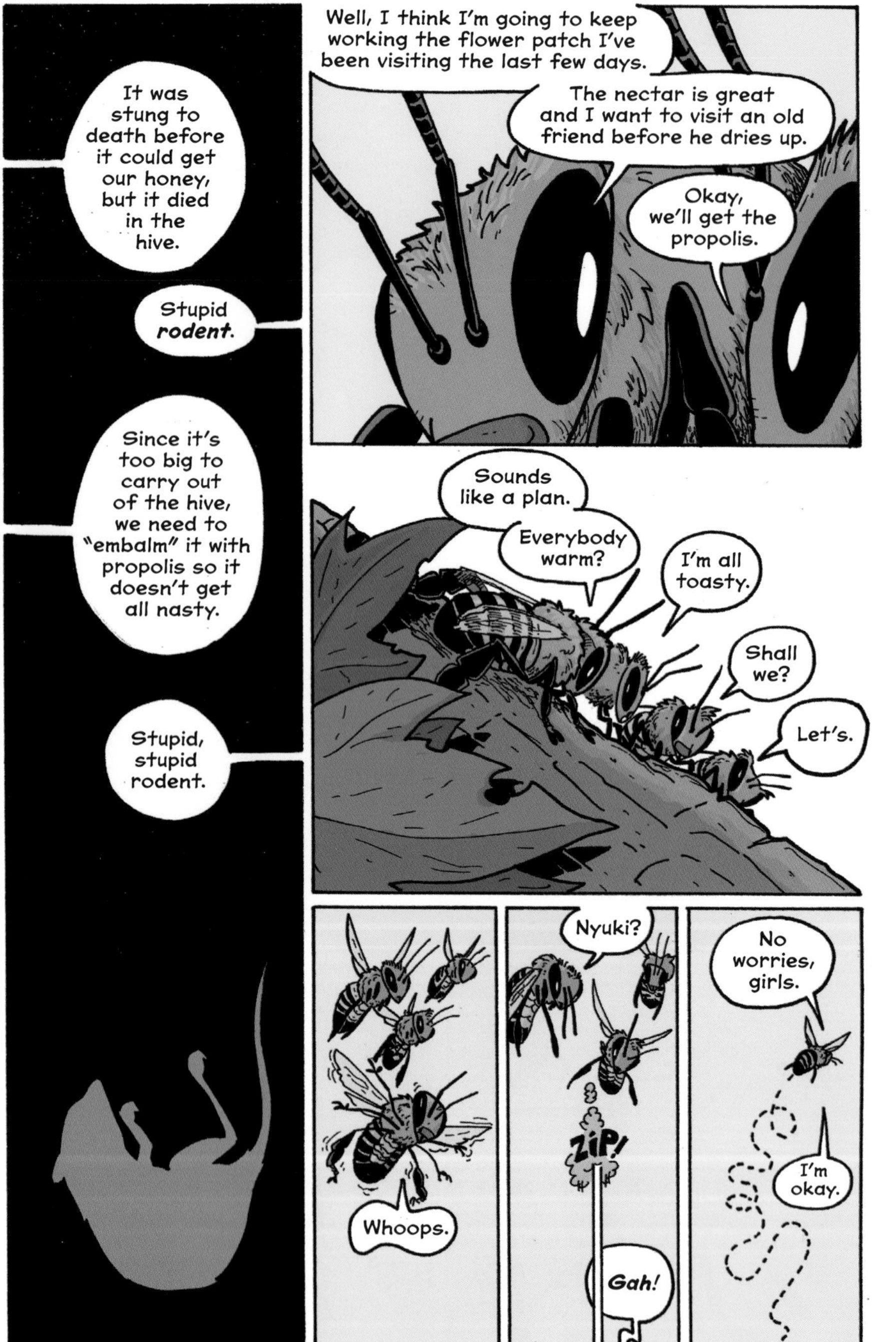
It was stung to death before it could get our honey, but it died in the hive.
Stupid *rodent*.
Since it's too big to carry out of the hive, we need to "embalm" it with propolis so it doesn't get all nasty.
Stupid, stupid rodent.
Well, I think I'm going to keep working the flower patch I've been visiting the last few days.
The nectar is great and I want to visit an old friend before he dries up.
Okay, we'll get the propolis.
Sounds like a plan.
Everybody warm?
I'm all toasty.
Shall we?
Let's.
Whoops.
Nyuki?
ZIP!
Gah!
No worries, girls.
I'm okay.

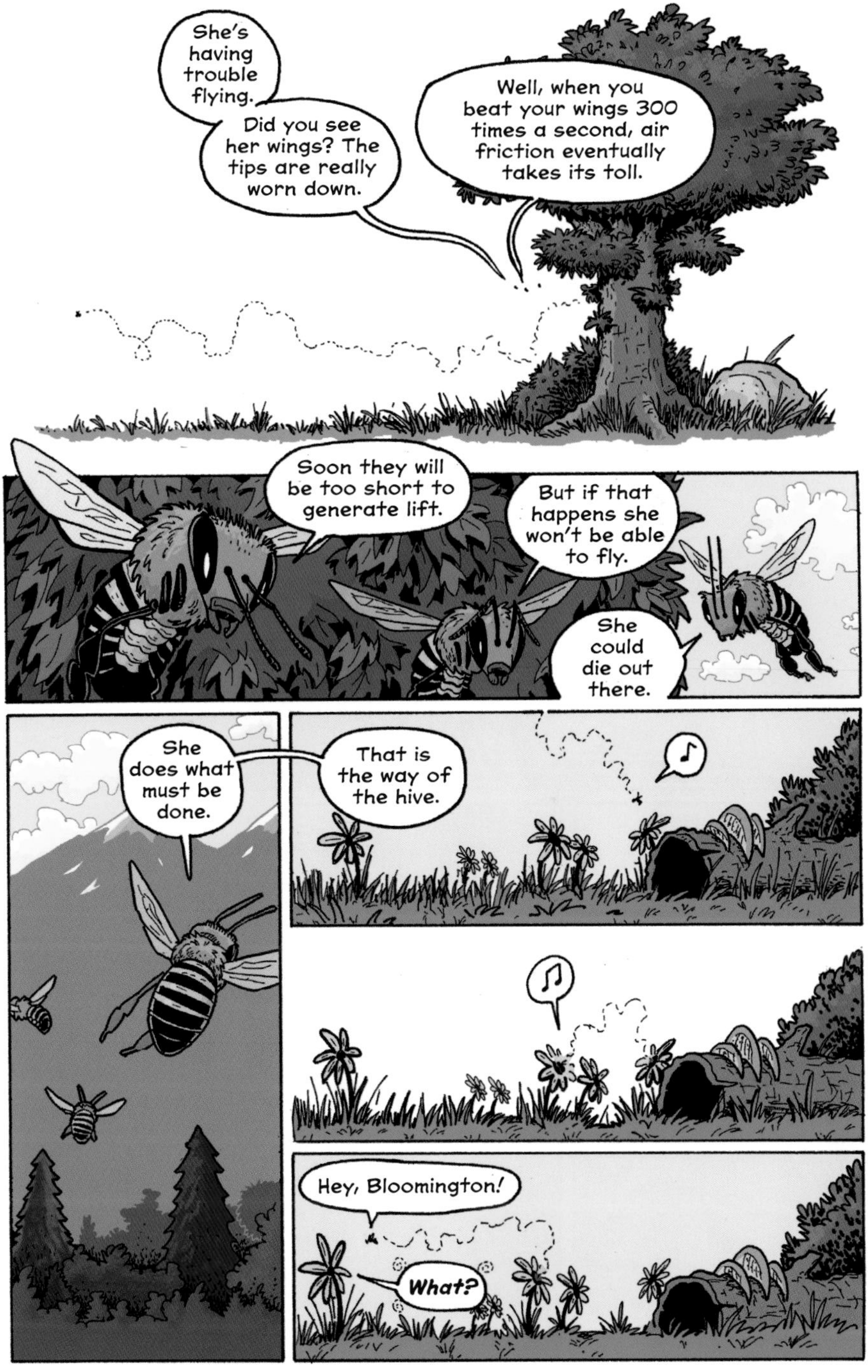

She's having trouble flying.
Did you see her wings? The tips are really worn down.
Well, when you beat your wings 300 times a second, air friction eventually takes its toll.
Soon they will be too short to generate lift.
But if that happens she won't be able to fly.
She could die out there.
She does what must be done.
That is the way of the hive.
Hey, Bloomington!
What?

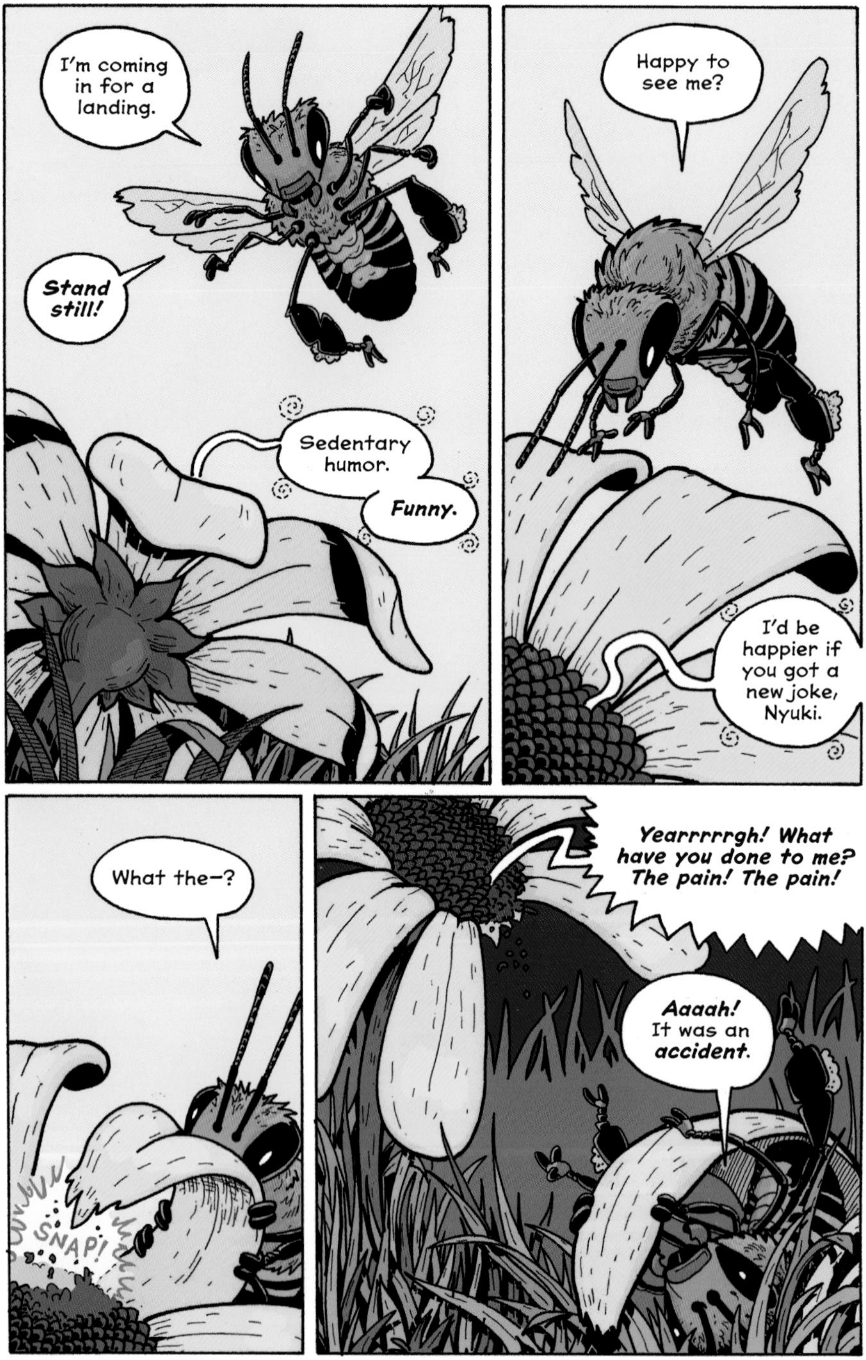
I'm coming in for a landing.
Stand still!
Sedentary humor.
Funny.
Happy to see me?
I'd be happier if you got a new joke, Nyuki.
What the–?
SNAP!
Yearrrrrgh! What have you done to me? The pain! The pain!
Aaaah! It was an accident.

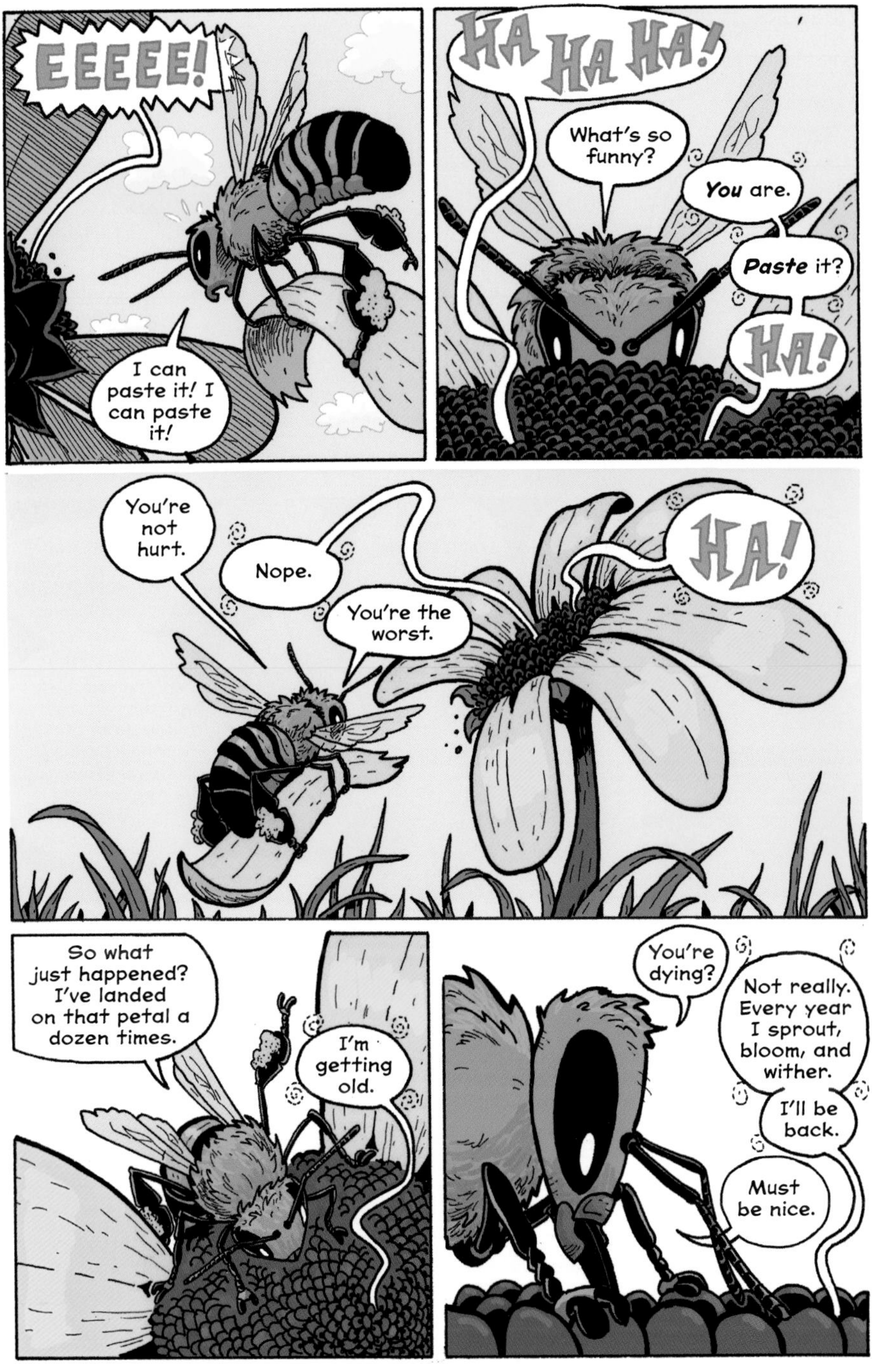
EEEEE!
I can paste it! I can paste it!
HA HA HA!
What's so funny?
You are.
Paste it?
HA!
You're not hurt.
Nope.
You're the worst.
HA!
So what just happened? I've landed on that petal a dozen times.
I'm getting old.
You're dying?
Not really. Every year I sprout, bloom, and wither.
I'll be back.
Must be nice.

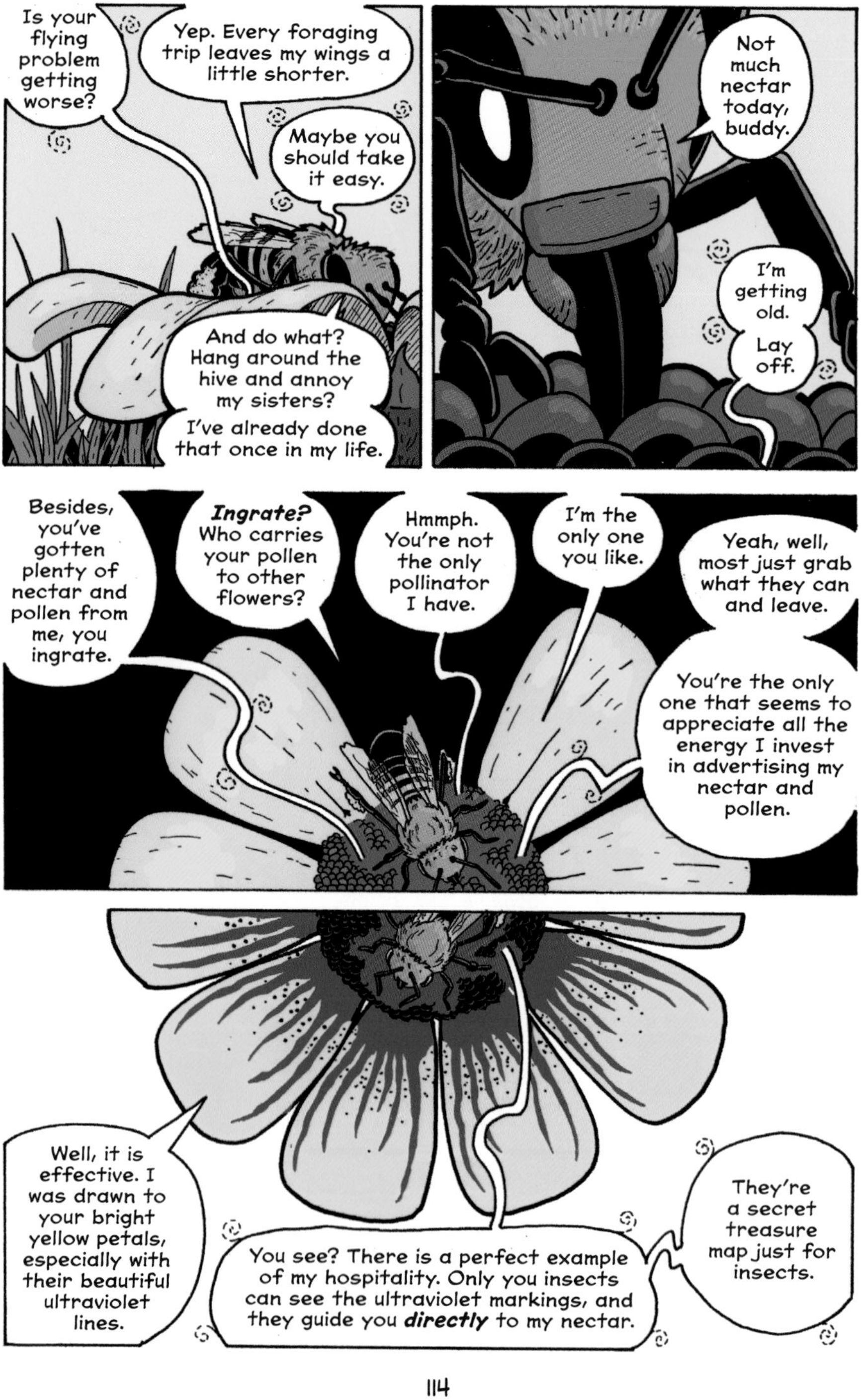

Is your flying problem getting worse?
Yep. Every foraging trip leaves my wings a little shorter.
Maybe you should take it easy.
And do what? Hang around the hive and annoy my sisters?
I've already done that once in my life.
Not much nectar today, buddy.
I'm getting old.
Lay off.
Besides, you've gotten plenty of nectar and pollen from me, you ingrate.
Ingrate? Who carries your pollen to other flowers?
Hmmph. You're not the only pollinator I have.
I'm the only one you like.
Yeah, well, most just grab what they can and leave.
You're the only one that seems to appreciate all the energy I invest in advertising my nectar and pollen.
Well, it is effective. I was drawn to your bright yellow petals, especially with their beautiful ultraviolet lines.
You see? There is a perfect example of my hospitality. Only you insects can see the ultraviolet markings, and they guide you *directly* to my nectar.
They're a secret treasure map just for insects.

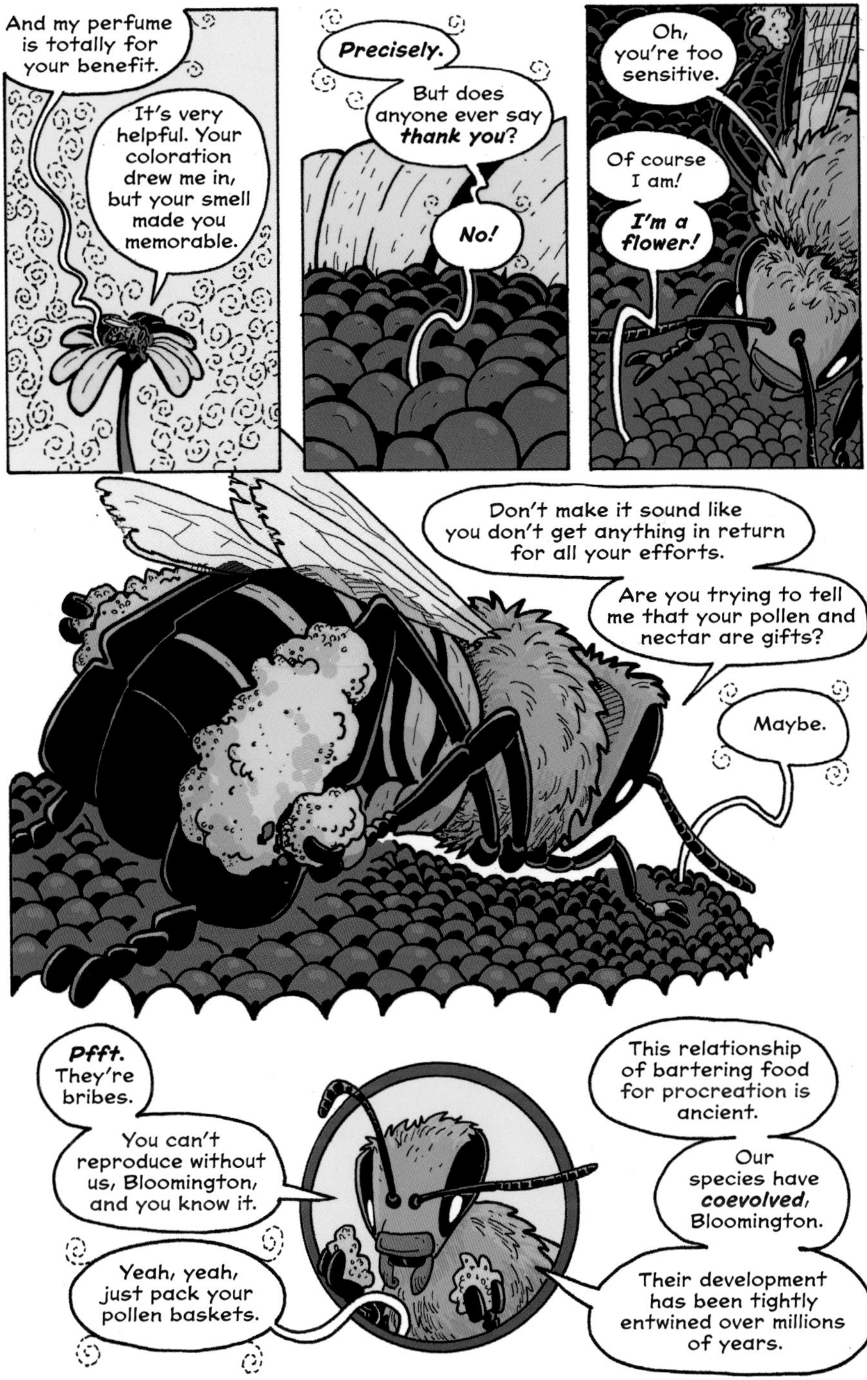
And my perfume is totally for your benefit.
It's very helpful. Your coloration drew me in, but your smell made you memorable.
Precisely.
But does anyone ever say thank you?
No!
Oh, you're too sensitive.
Of course I am!
I'm a flower!
Don't make it sound like you don't get anything in return for all your efforts.
Are you trying to tell me that your pollen and nectar are gifts?
Maybe.
Pfft. They're bribes.
You can't reproduce without us, Bloomington, and you know it.
Yeah, yeah, just pack your pollen baskets.
This relationship of bartering food for procreation is ancient.
Our species have coevolved, Bloomington.
Their development has been tightly entwined over millions of years.

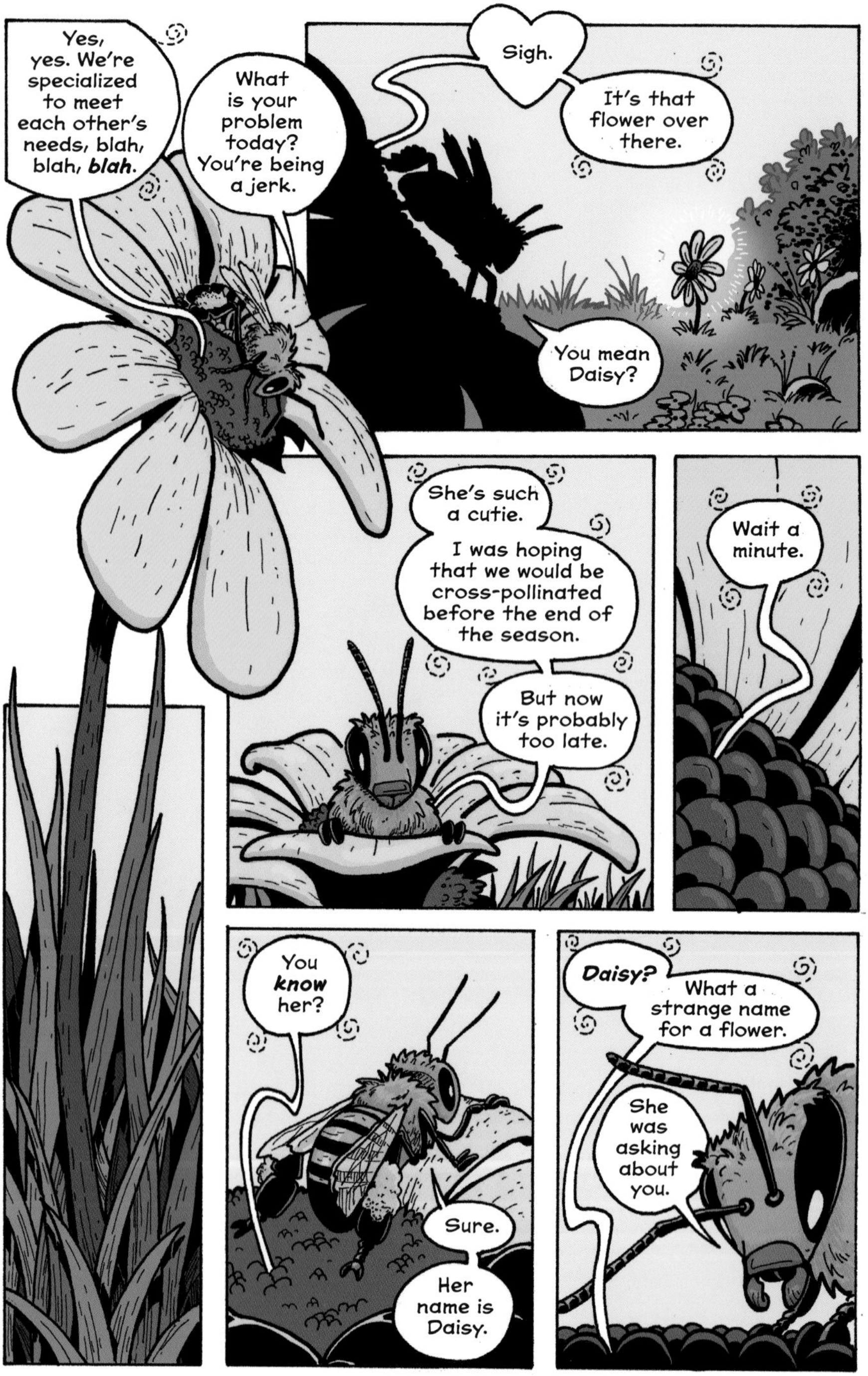
Yes, yes. We're specialized to meet each other's needs, blah, blah, *blah*.
What is your problem today? You're being a jerk.
Sigh.
It's that flower over there.
You mean Daisy?
She's such a cutie.
I was hoping that we would be cross-pollinated before the end of the season.
But now it's probably too late.
Wait a minute.
You *know* her?
Sure.
Her name is Daisy.
Daisy?
What a strange name for a flower.
She was asking about you.

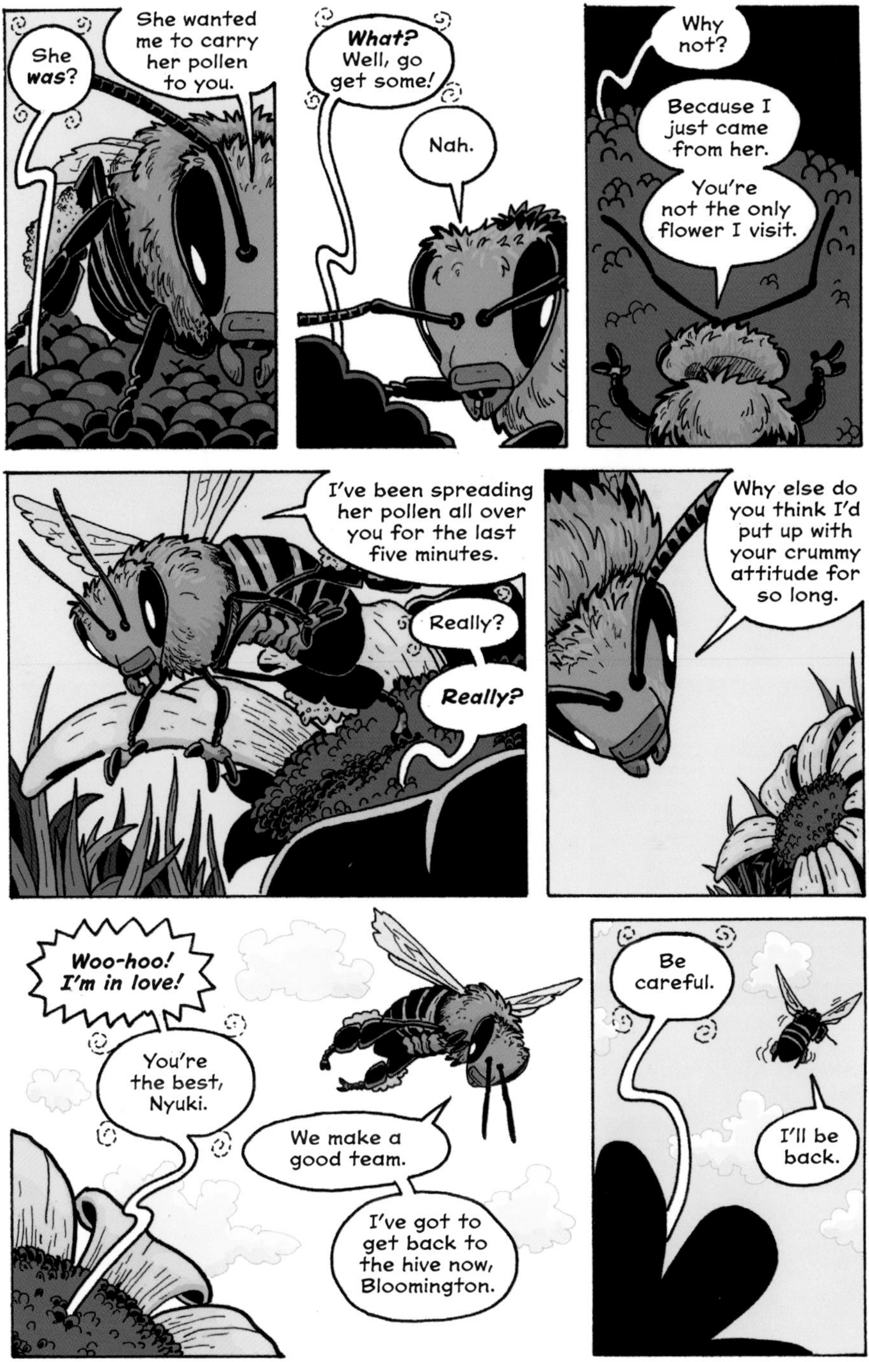
She was?
She wanted me to carry her pollen to you.
What? Well, go get some!
Nah.
Why not?
Because I just came from her.
You're not the only flower I visit.
I've been spreading her pollen all over you for the last five minutes.
Really?
Really?
Why else do you think I'd put up with your crummy attitude for so long.
Woo-hoo! I'm in love!
You're the best, Nyuki.
We make a good team.
I've got to get back to the hive now, Bloomington.
Be careful.
I'll be back.

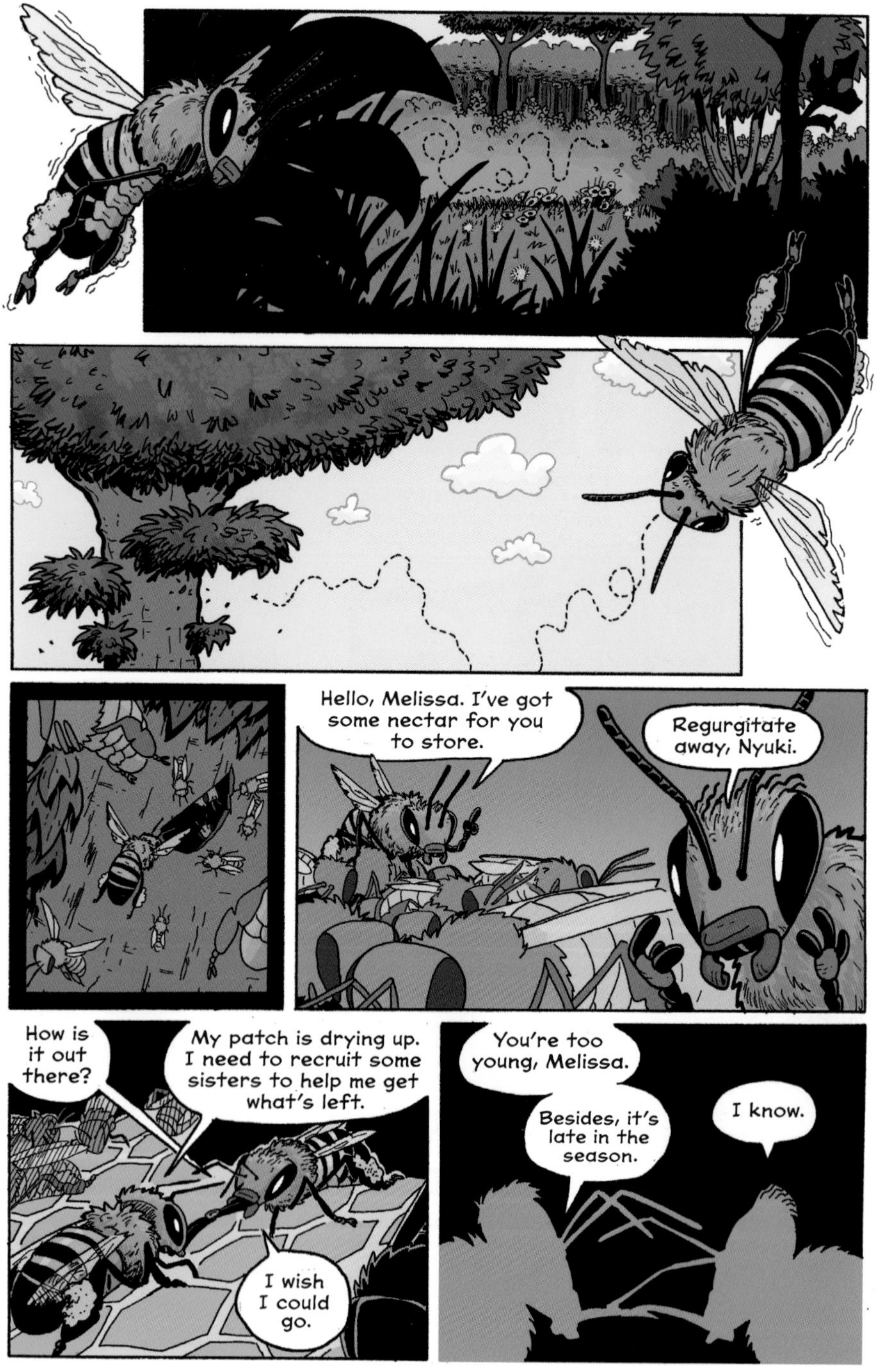
Hello, Melissa. I've got some nectar for you to store.
Regurgitate away, Nyuki.
How is it out there?
My patch is drying up. I need to recruit some sisters to help me get what's left.
I wish I could go.
You're too young, Melissa.
Besides, it's late in the season.
I know.

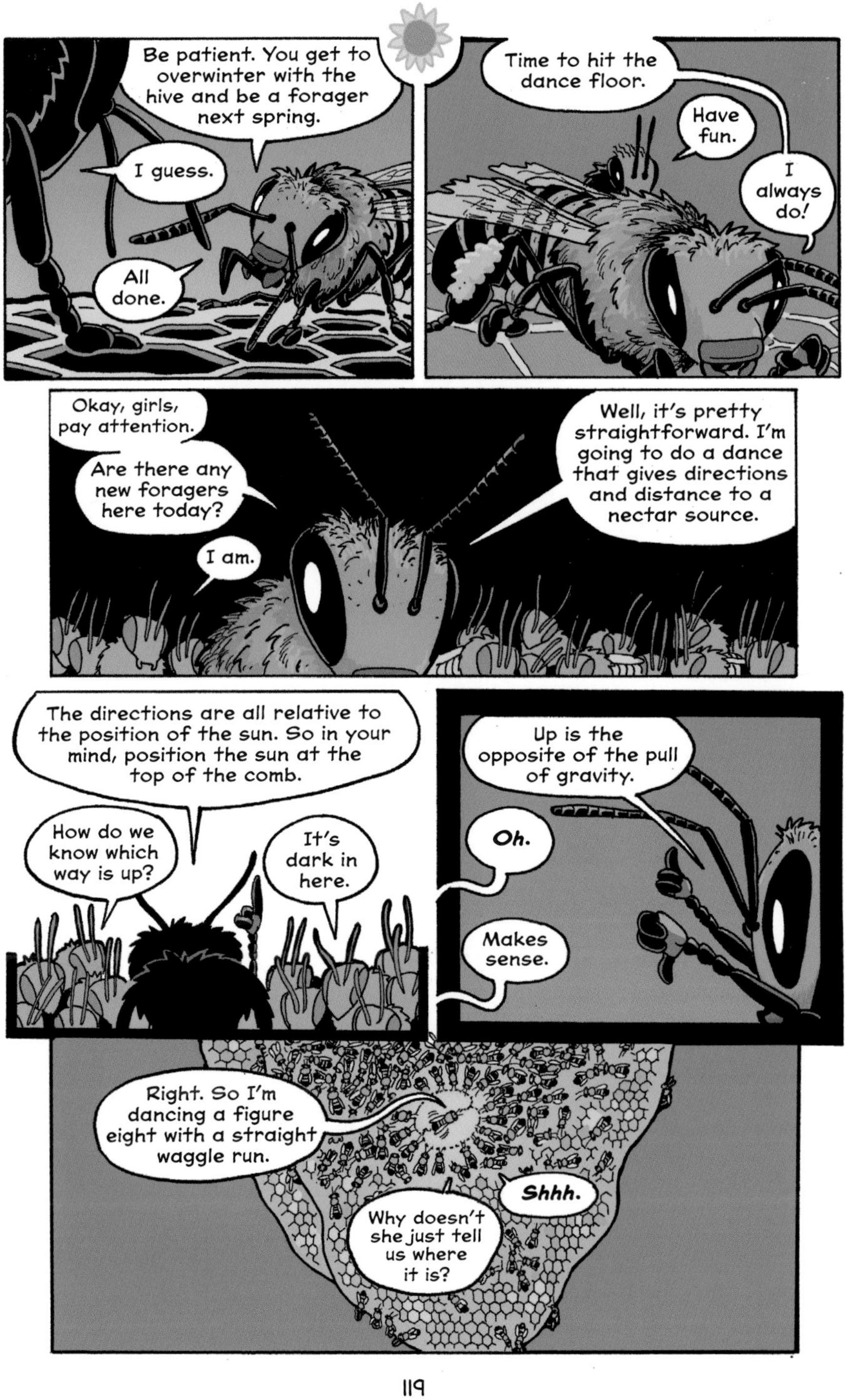
Be patient. You get to overwinter with the hive and be a forager next spring.
I guess.
All done.
Time to hit the dance floor.
Have fun.
I always do!
Okay, girls, pay attention.
Are there any new foragers here today?
I am.
Well, it's pretty straightforward. I'm going to do a dance that gives directions and distance to a nectar source.
The directions are all relative to the position of the sun. So in your mind, position the sun at the top of the comb.
How do we know which way is up?
It's dark in here.
Up is the opposite of the pull of gravity.
Oh.
Makes sense.
Right. So I'm dancing a figure eight with a straight waggle run.
Shhh.
Why doesn't she just tell us where it is?

She can really dance, can't she, Melissa?

Yes, Queen Hachi. Her enthusiasm is mesmerizing.

Heh. It used to be annoying.

There is desperation in this dance. I fear it may be her last.

Her *last*?

I doubt she survives her next foraging trip.

What??! But she's my friend!

I'll take her place. *I'm ready.*

No, you're not.

Nyuki would *want* me to go.

I know Nyuki has told you to be patient, Melissa.

So how am I supposed to know when I am ready?

It's different for all of us.

You will know.

She was impatient like you once.

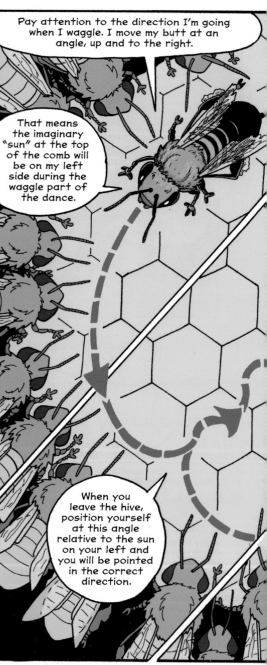

Pay attention to the direction I'm going when I waggle. I move my butt at an angle, up and to the right.

That means the imaginary "sun" at the top of the comb will be on my left side during the waggle part of the dance.

When you leave the hive, position yourself at this angle relative to the sun on your left and you will be pointed in the correct direction.

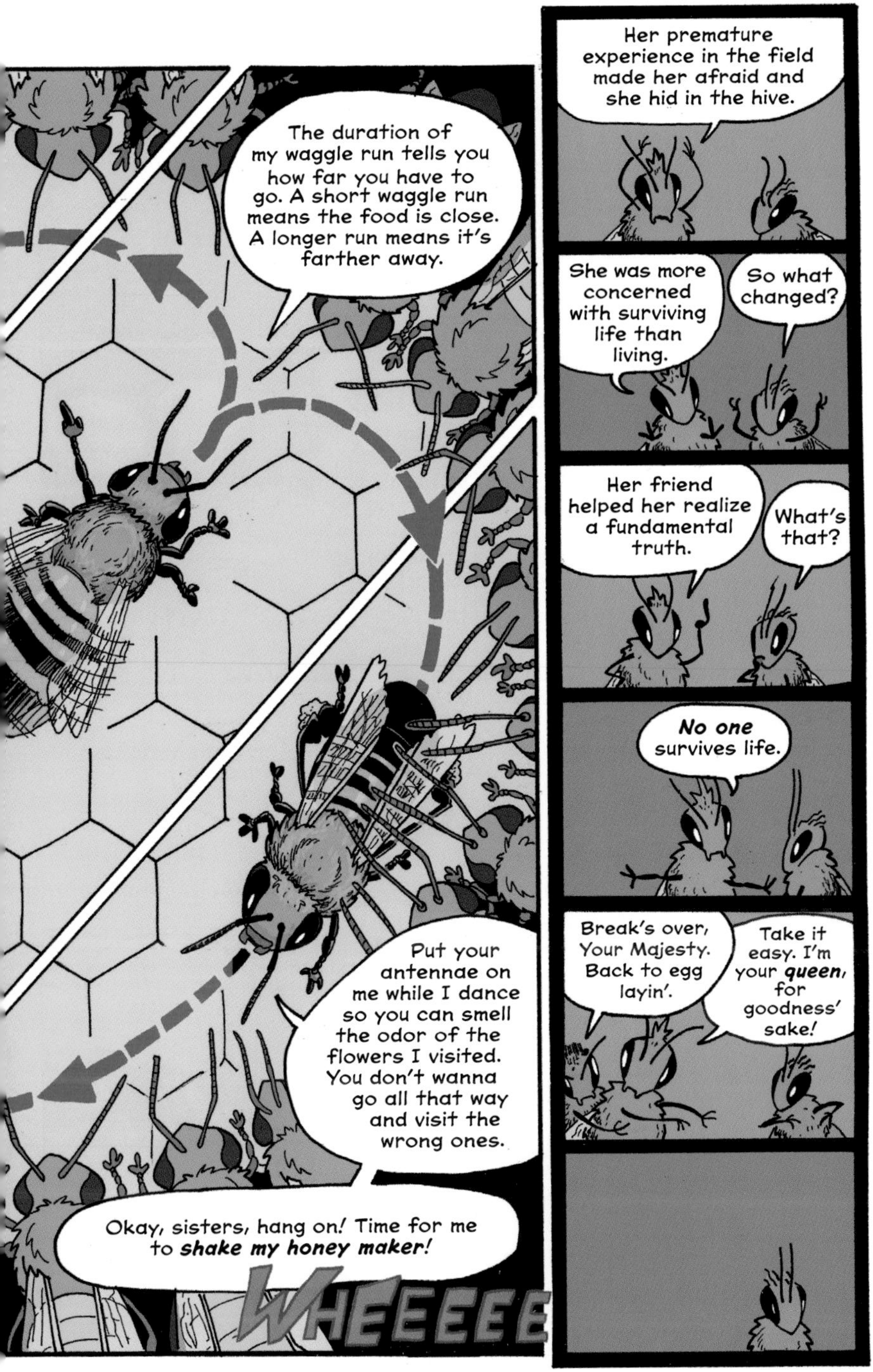
The duration of my waggle run tells you how far you have to go. A short waggle run means the food is close. A longer run means it's farther away.
Put your antennae on me while I dance so you can smell the odor of the flowers I visited. You don't wanna go all that way and visit the wrong ones.
Okay, sisters, hang on! Time for me to **shake my honey maker!**
WHEEEEE
Her premature experience in the field made her afraid and she hid in the hive.
She was more concerned with surviving life than living.
So what changed?
Her friend helped her realize a fundamental truth.
What's that?
No one survives life.
Break's over, Your Majesty. Back to egg layin'.
Take it easy. I'm your ***queen***, for goodness' sake!

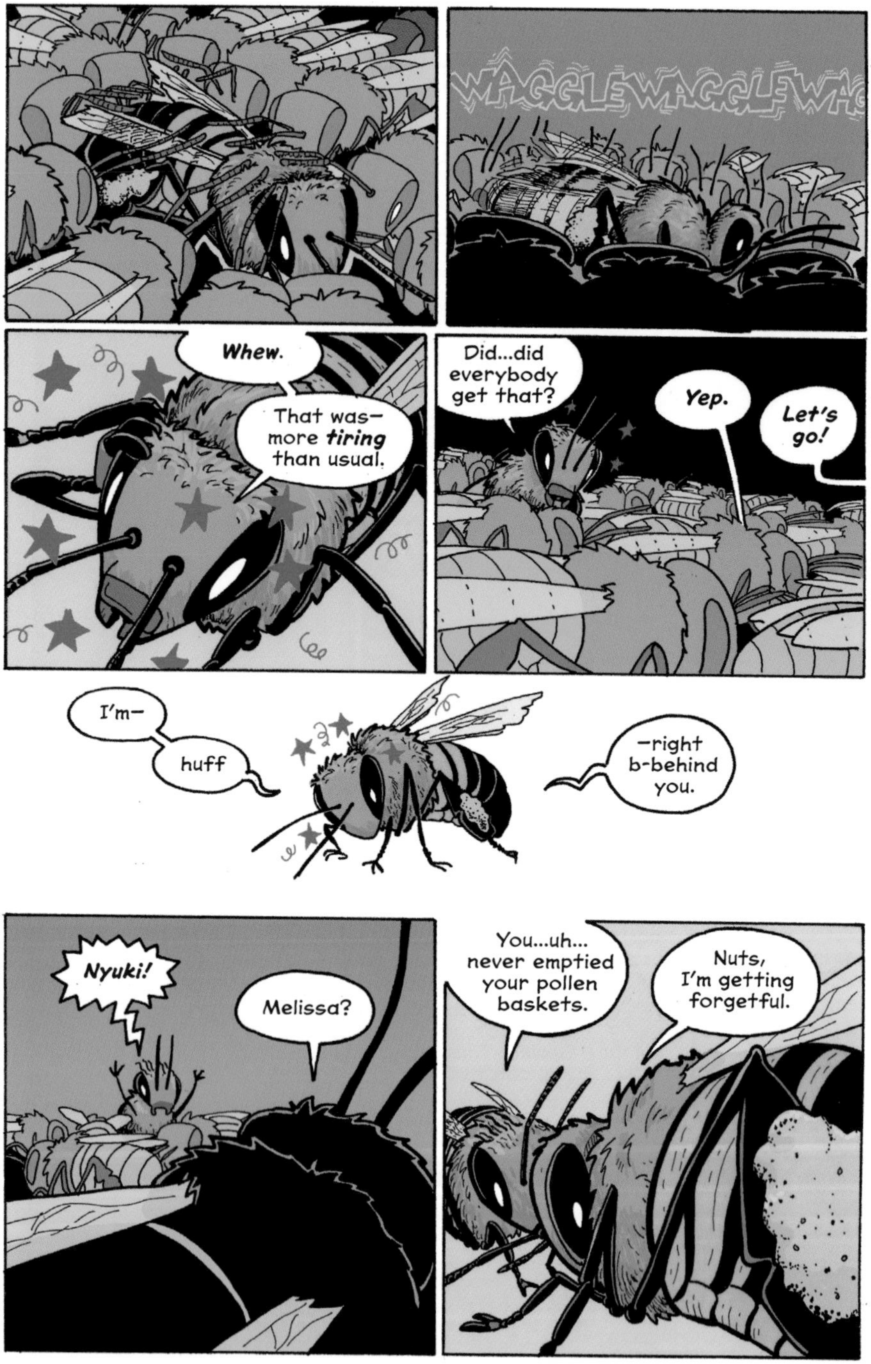
WAGGLEWAGGLEWAG
Whew.
That was—
more tiring than usual.
Did...did everybody get that?
Yep.
Let's go!
I'm—
huff
—right b-behind you.
Nyuki!
Melissa?
You...uh... never emptied your pollen baskets.
Nuts, I'm getting forgetful.

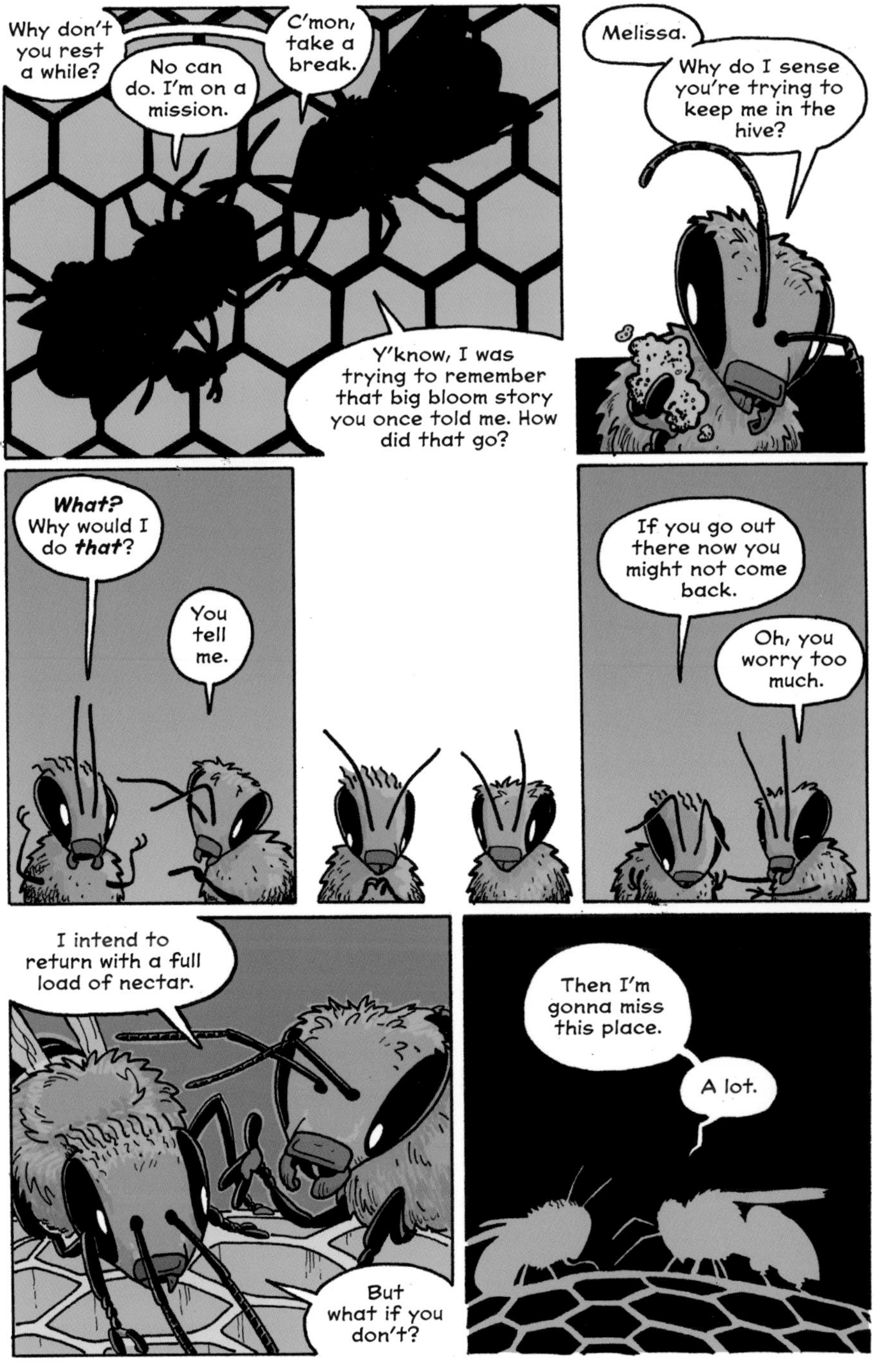
Why don't you rest a while?
No can do. I'm on a mission.
C'mon, take a break.
Y'know, I was trying to remember that big bloom story you once told me. How did that go?
Melissa.
Why do I sense you're trying to keep me in the hive?
What? Why would I do *that*?
You tell me.
If you go out there now you might not come back.
Oh, you worry too much.
I intend to return with a full load of nectar.
But what if you don't?
Then I'm gonna miss this place.
A lot.

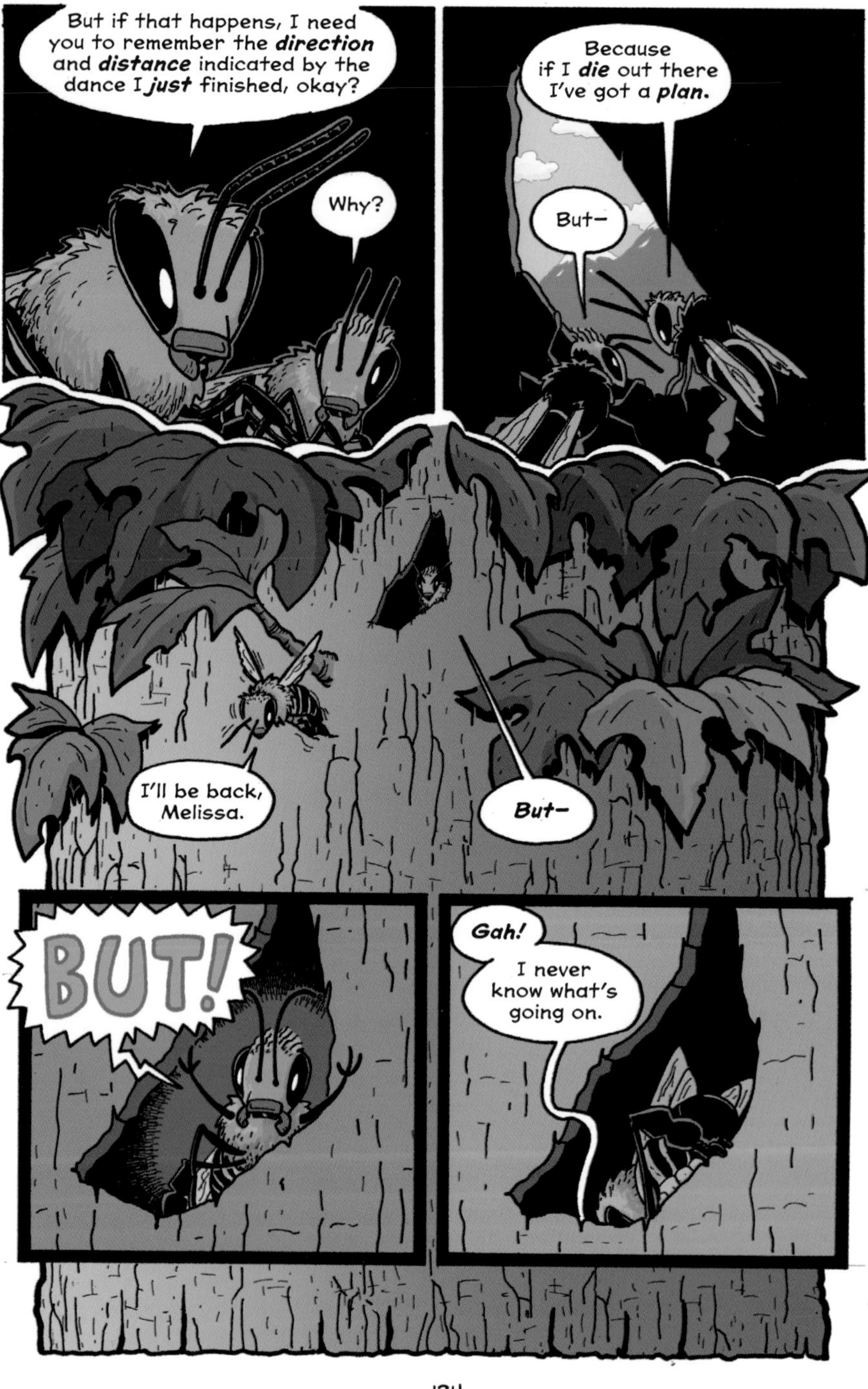
But if that happens, I need you to remember the *direction* and *distance* indicated by the dance I *just* finished, okay?
Why?
Because if I *die* out there I've got a *plan.*
But–
I'll be back, Melissa.
But–
BUT!
Gah!
I never know what's going on.

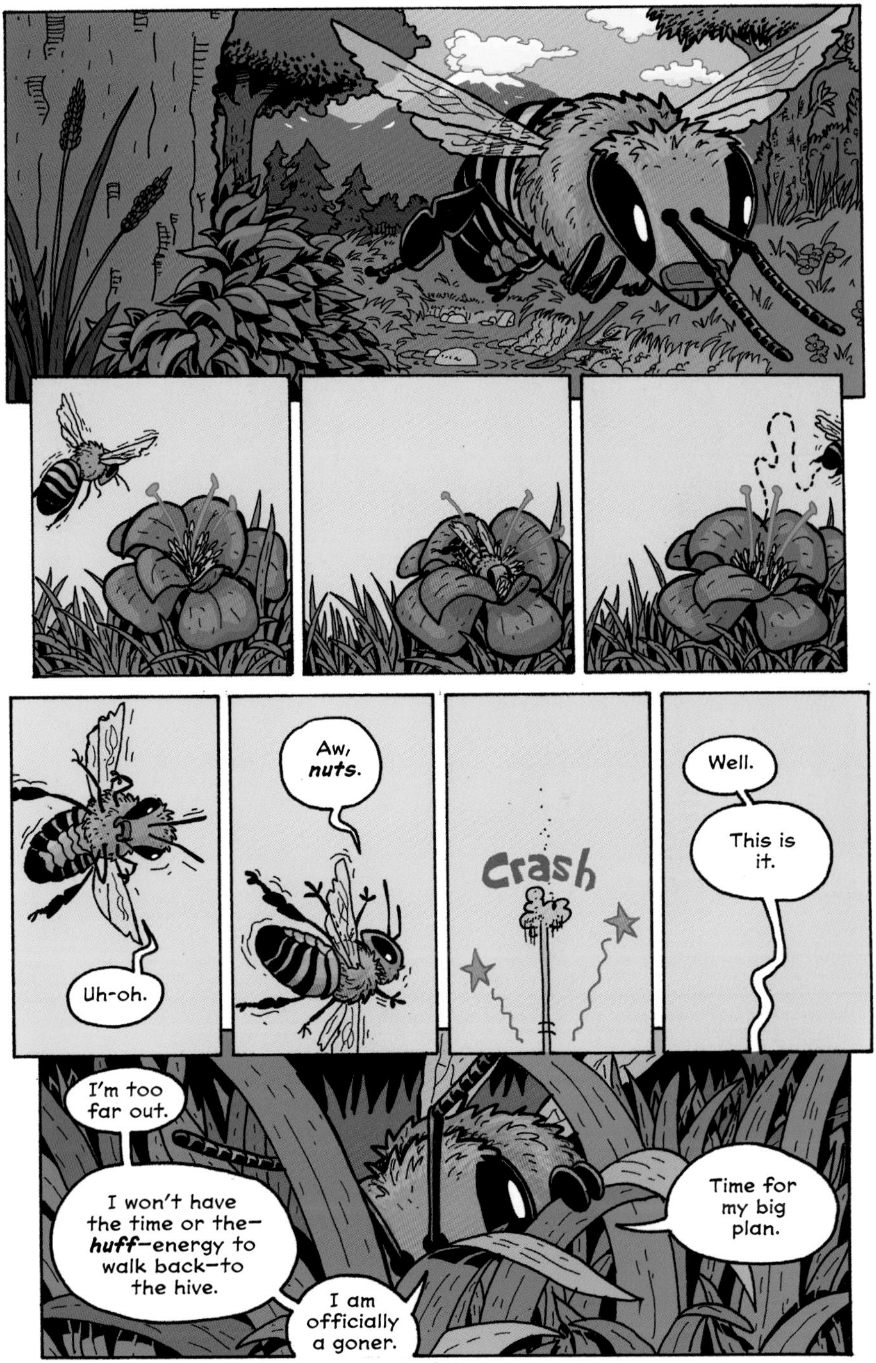
Uh-oh.
Aw, **nuts**.
Crash
Well.
This is it.
I'm too far out.
I won't have the time or the—**huff**—energy to walk back—to the hive.
I am officially a goner.
Time for my big plan.

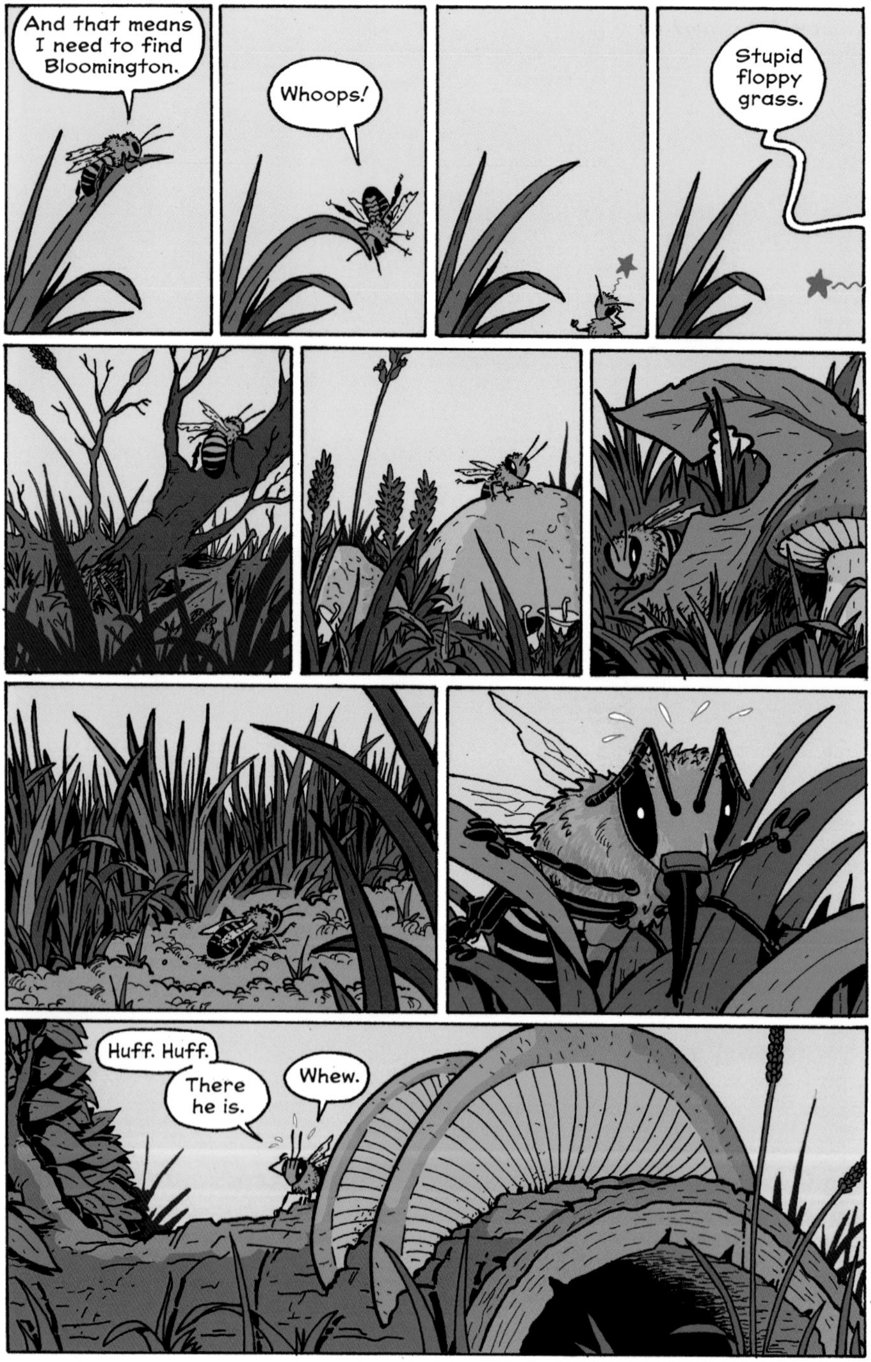
And that means I need to find Bloomington.
Whoops!
Stupid floppy grass.
Huff. Huff.
There he is.
Whew.

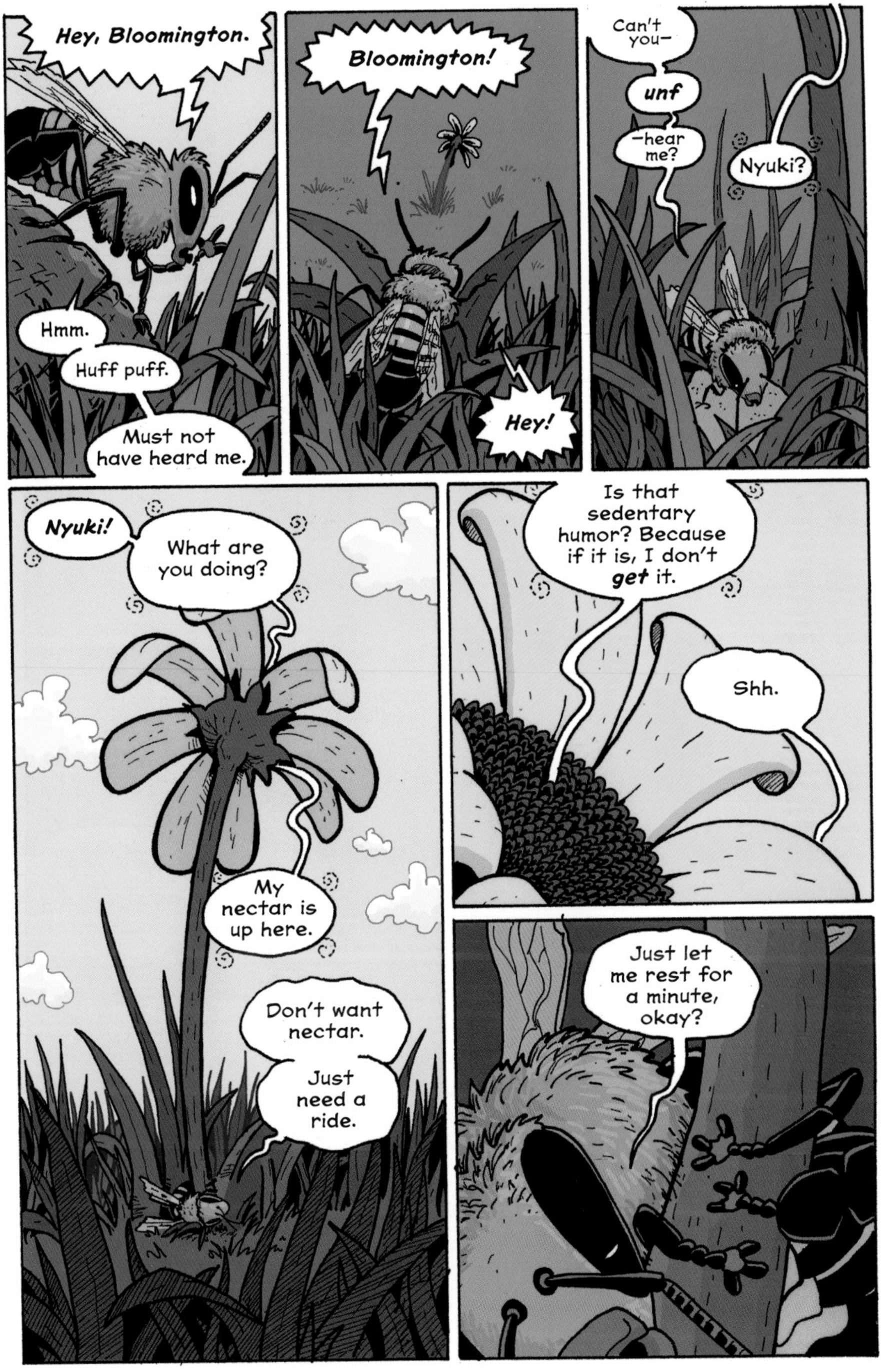
Hey, Bloomington.
Hmm.
Huff puff.
Must not have heard me.
Bloomington!
Hey!
Can't you—
unf
—hear me?
Nyuki?
Nyuki!
What are you doing?
My nectar is up here.
Don't want nectar.
Just need a ride.
Is that sedentary humor? Because if it is, I don't *get* it.
Shh.
Just let me rest for a minute, okay?

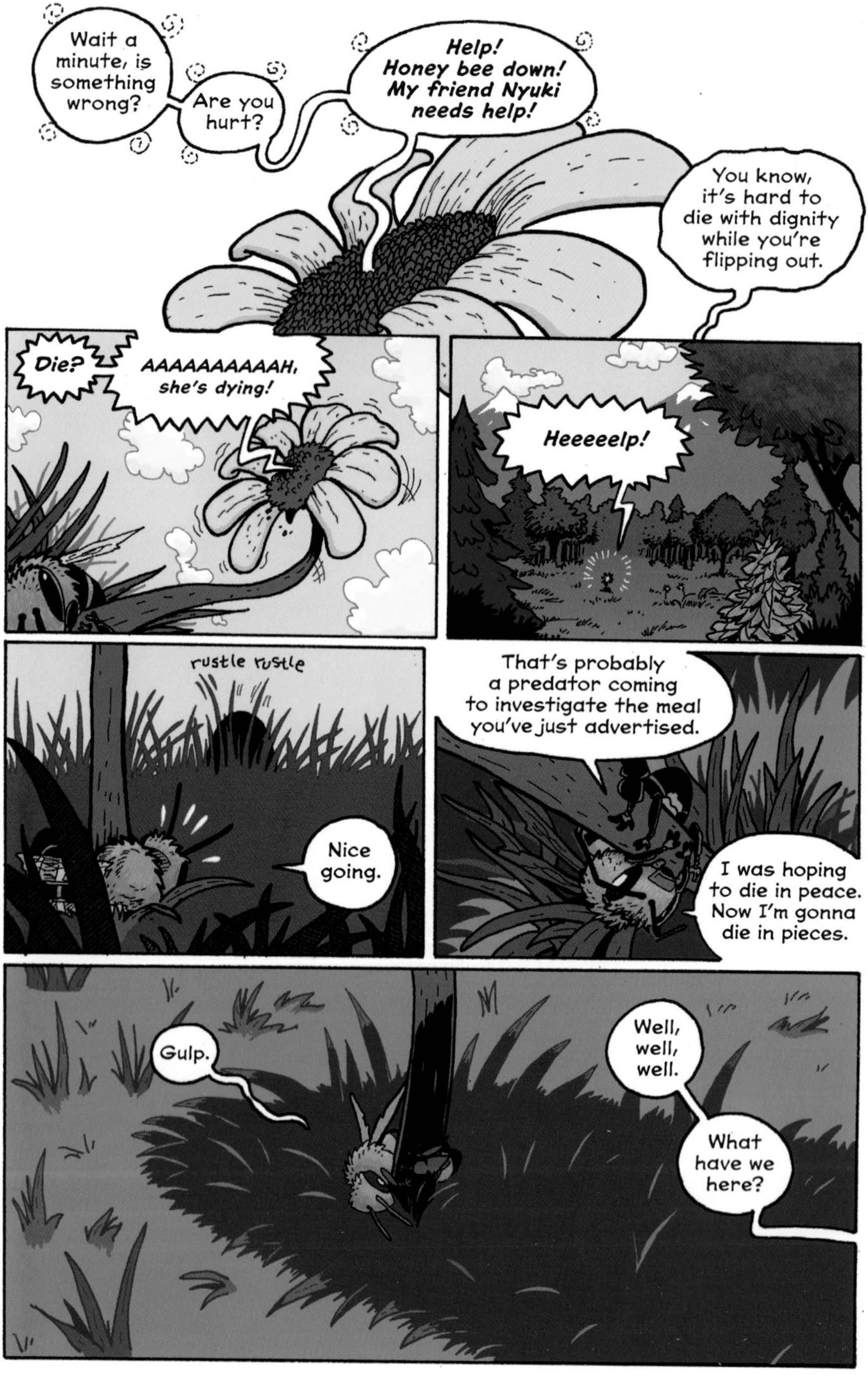
Wait a minute, is something wrong?
Are you hurt?
Help! Honey bee down! My friend Nyuki needs help!
You know, it's hard to die with dignity while you're flipping out.
Die?
AAAAAAAAAAH, she's dying!
Heeeeelp!
rustle rustle
Nice going.
That's probably a predator coming to investigate the meal you've just advertised.
I was hoping to die in peace. Now I'm gonna die in pieces.
Gulp.
Well, well, well.
What have we here?

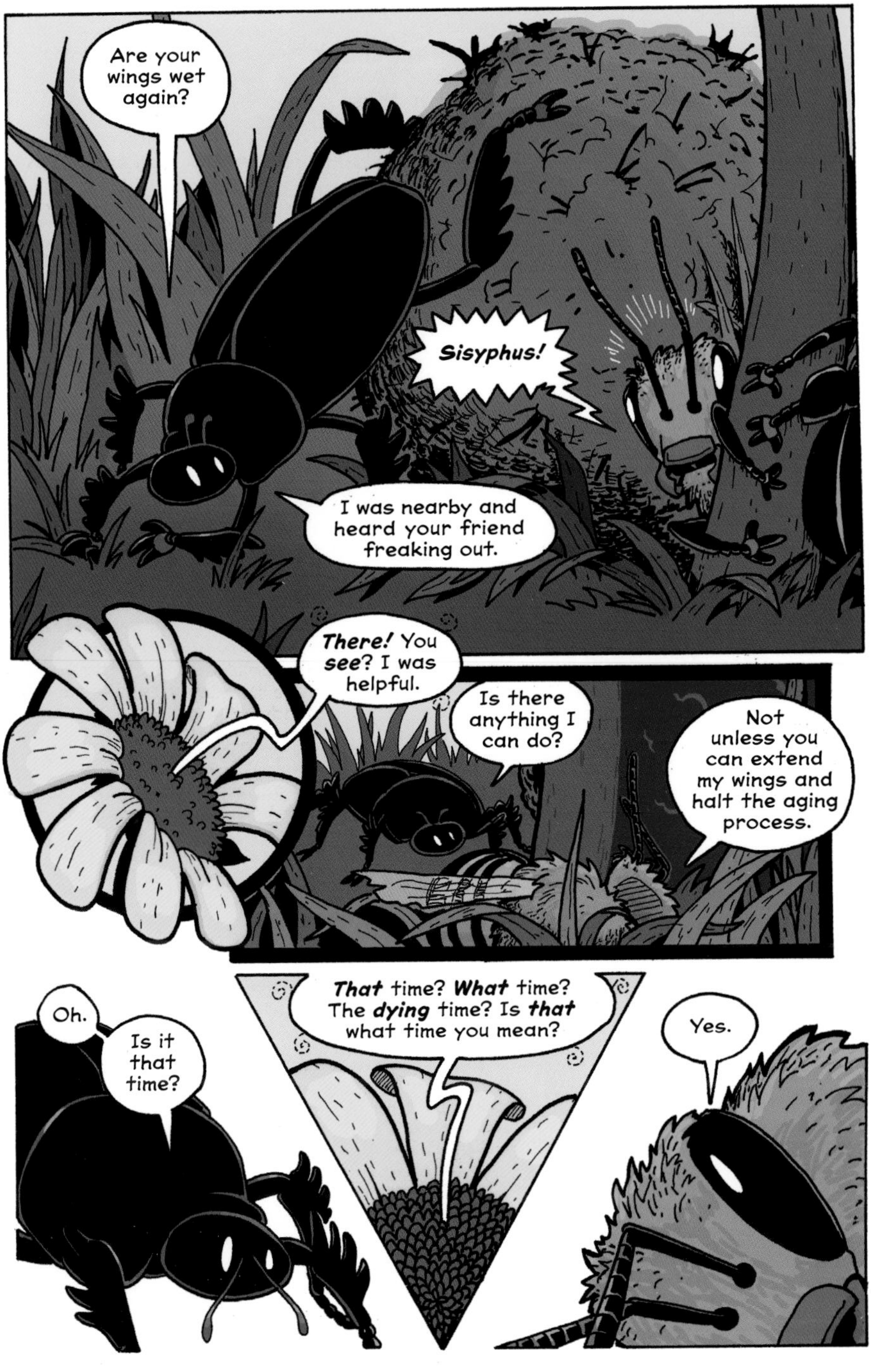
Are your wings wet again?
Sisyphus!
I was nearby and heard your friend freaking out.
There! You see? I was helpful.
Is there anything I can do?
Not unless you can extend my wings and halt the aging process.
Oh.
Is it that time?
That time? What time? The dying time? Is that what time you mean?
Yes.

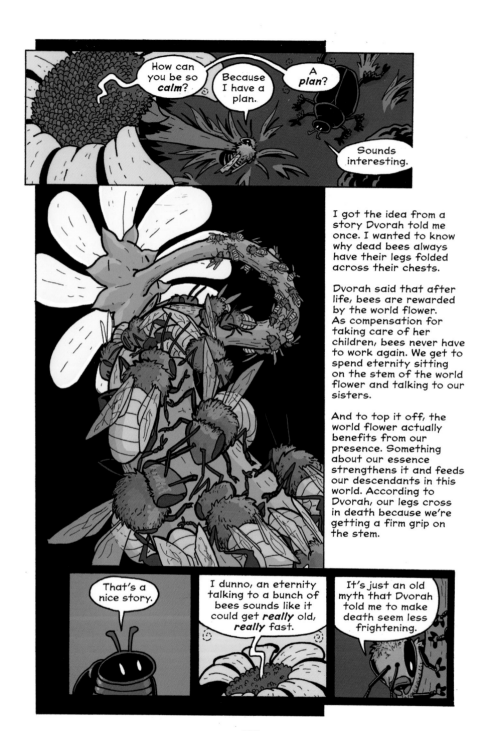

How can you be so *calm*?

Because I have a plan.

A *plan*?

Sounds interesting.

I got the idea from a story Dvorah told me once. I wanted to know why dead bees always have their legs folded across their chests.

Dvorah said that after life, bees are rewarded by the world flower. As compensation for taking care of her children, bees never have to work again. We get to spend eternity sitting on the stem of the world flower and talking to our sisters.

And to top it off, the world flower actually benefits from our presence. Something about our essence strengthens it and feeds our descendants in this world. According to Dvorah, our legs cross in death because we're getting a firm grip on the stem.

That's a nice story.

I dunno, an eternity talking to a bunch of bees sounds like it could get *really* old, *really* fast.

It's just an old myth that Dvorah told me to make death seem less frightening.

130

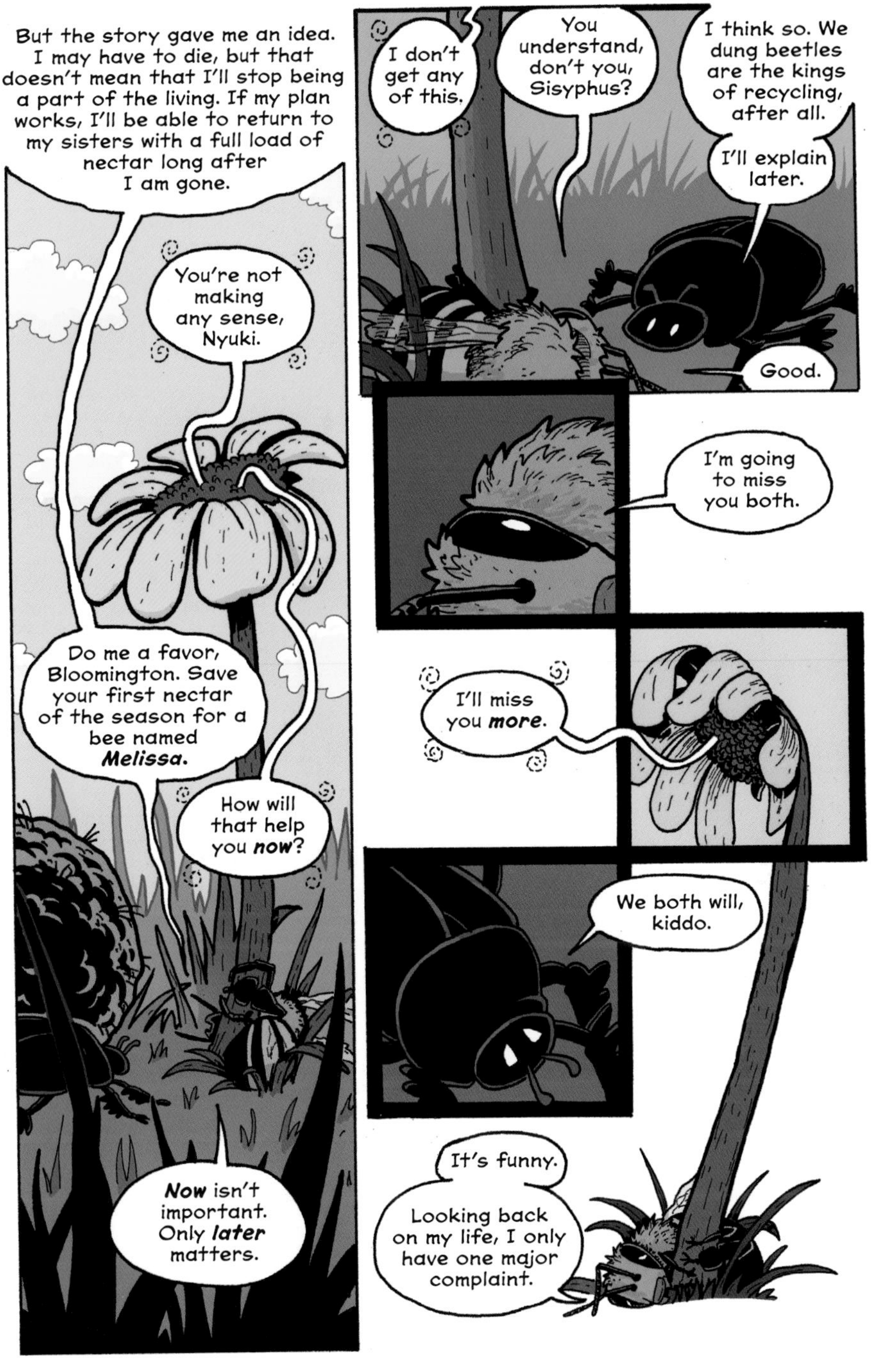

But the story gave me an idea. I may have to die, but that doesn't mean that I'll stop being a part of the living. If my plan works, I'll be able to return to my sisters with a full load of nectar long after I am gone.
You're not making any sense, Nyuki.
Do me a favor, Bloomington. Save your first nectar of the season for a bee named ***Melissa.***
How will that help you ***now***?
Now isn't important. Only ***later*** matters.
I don't get any of this.
You understand, don't you, Sisyphus?
I think so. We dung beetles are the kings of recycling, after all.
I'll explain later.
Good.
I'm going to miss you both.
I'll miss you ***more***.
We both will, kiddo.
It's funny.
Looking back on my life, I only have one major complaint.

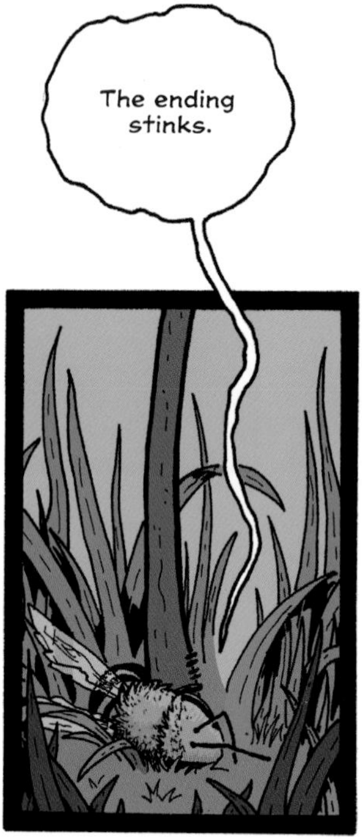
The ending stinks.

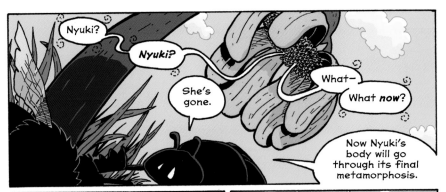

Nyuki?

Nyuki?

She's gone.

What—

What *now*?

Now Nyuki's body will go through its final metamorphosis.

The seasons will change, your flower will wilt, and her body will be broken down bit by bit by an invisible kingdom of bacteria.

Her parts will return to the soil, where they will feed your roots in the spring.

What was once Nyuki will become part of your new flower.

By the time you bloom next year, I think you will understand her plan.

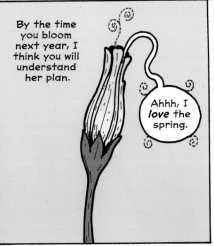

Ahhh, I *love* the spring.

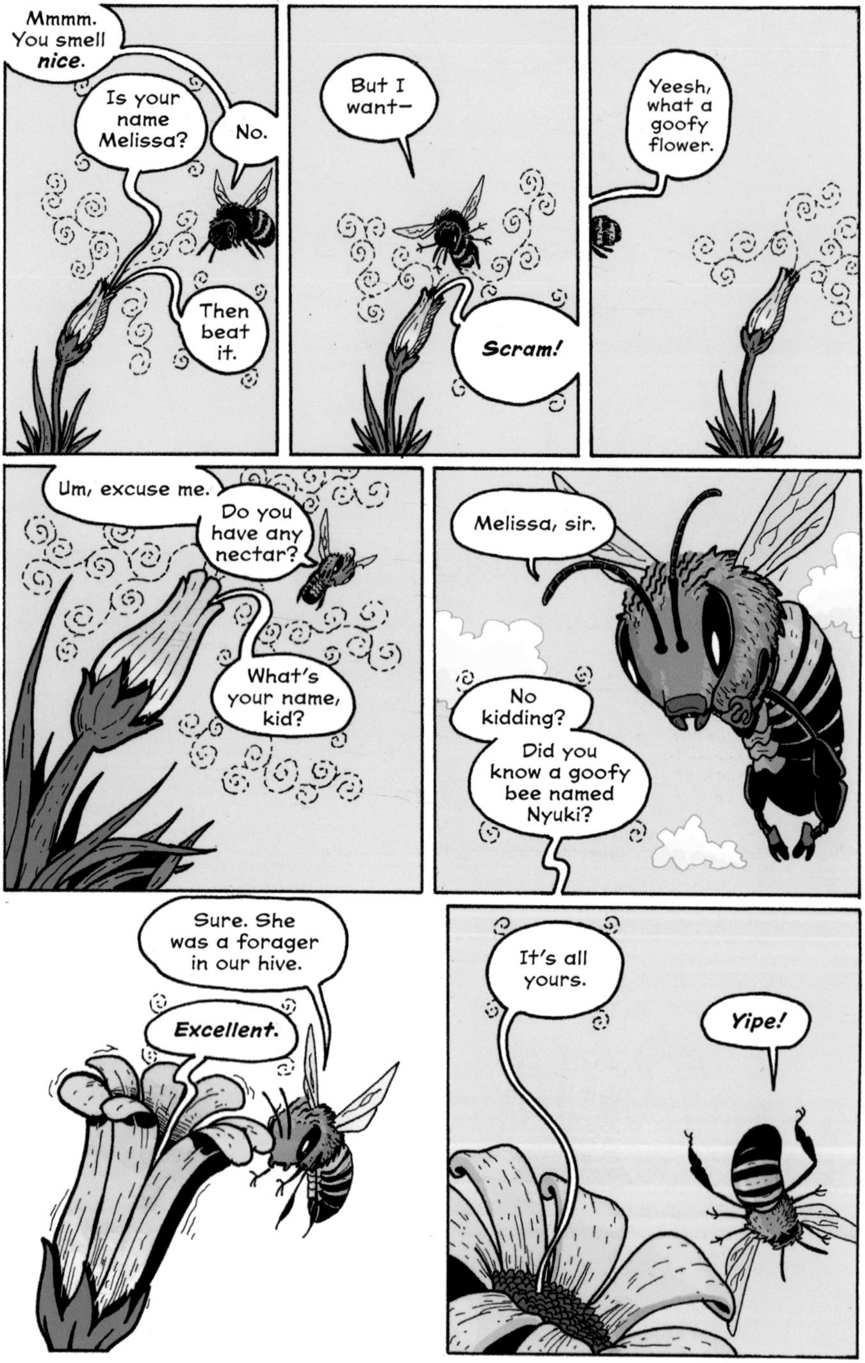
Mmmm. You smell *nice*.
Is your name Melissa?
No.
Then beat it.
But I want—
Scram!
Yeesh, what a goofy flower.
Um, excuse me.
Do you have any nectar?
What's your name, kid?
Melissa, sir.
No kidding?
Did you know a goofy bee named Nyuki?
Sure. She was a forager in our hive.
Excellent.
It's all yours.
Yipe!

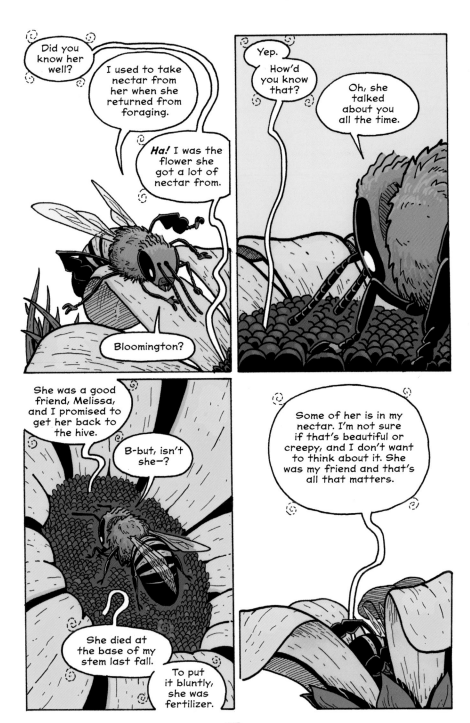

Did you know her well?

I used to take nectar from her when she returned from foraging.

Ha! I was the flower she got a lot of nectar from.

Bloomington?

Yep.

How'd you know that?

Oh, she talked about you all the time.

She was a good friend, Melissa, and I promised to get her back to the hive.

B-but, isn't she—?

She died at the base of my stem last fall.

To put it bluntly, she was fertilizer.

Some of her is in my nectar. I'm not sure if that's beautiful or creepy, and I don't want to think about it. She was my friend and that's all that matters.

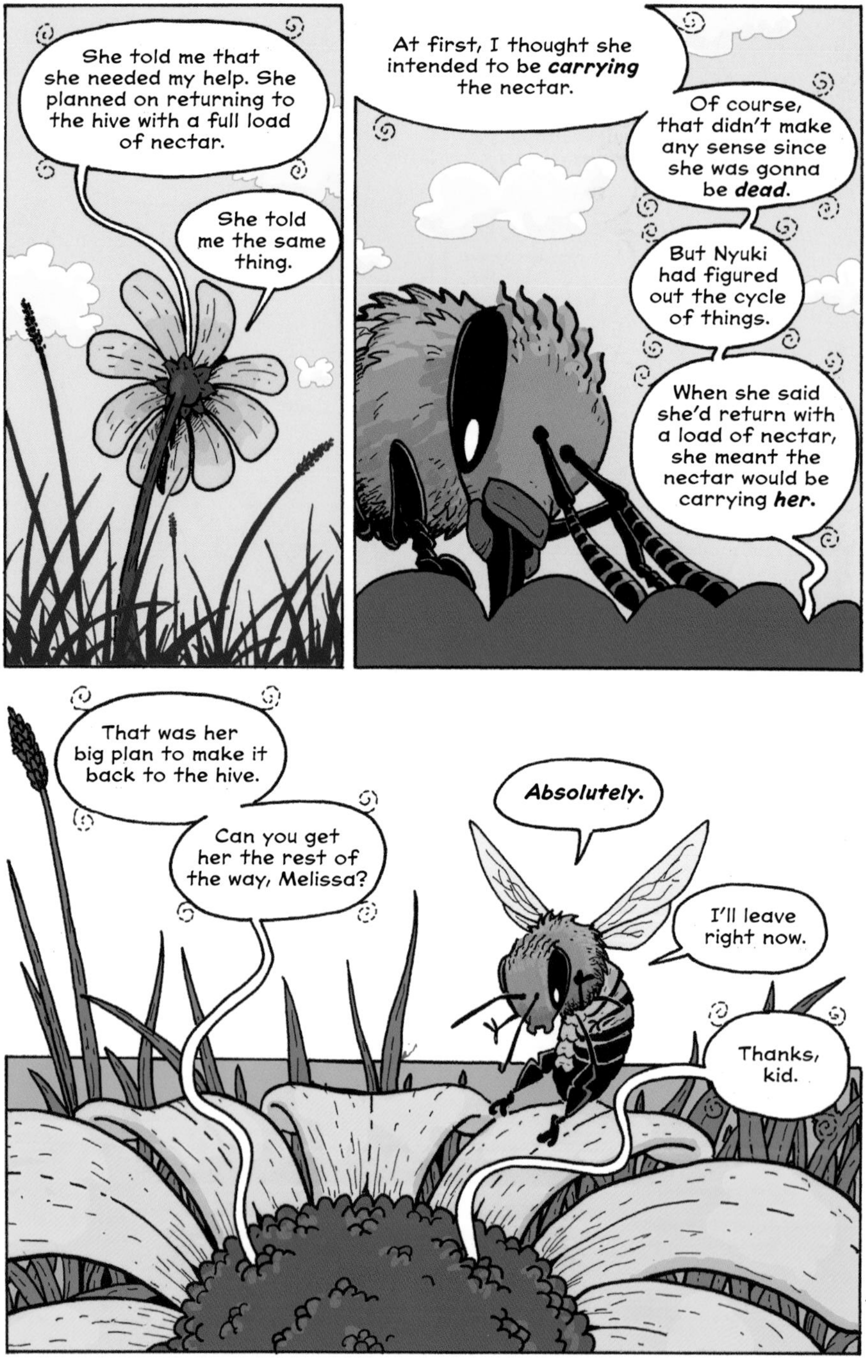

She told me that she needed my help. She planned on returning to the hive with a full load of nectar.
She told me the same thing.
At first, I thought she intended to be *carrying* the nectar.
Of course, that didn't make any sense since she was gonna be *dead*.
But Nyuki had figured out the cycle of things.
When she said she'd return with a load of nectar, she meant the nectar would be carrying *her*.
That was her big plan to make it back to the hive.
Can you get her the rest of the way, Melissa?
Absolutely.
I'll leave right now.
Thanks, kid.

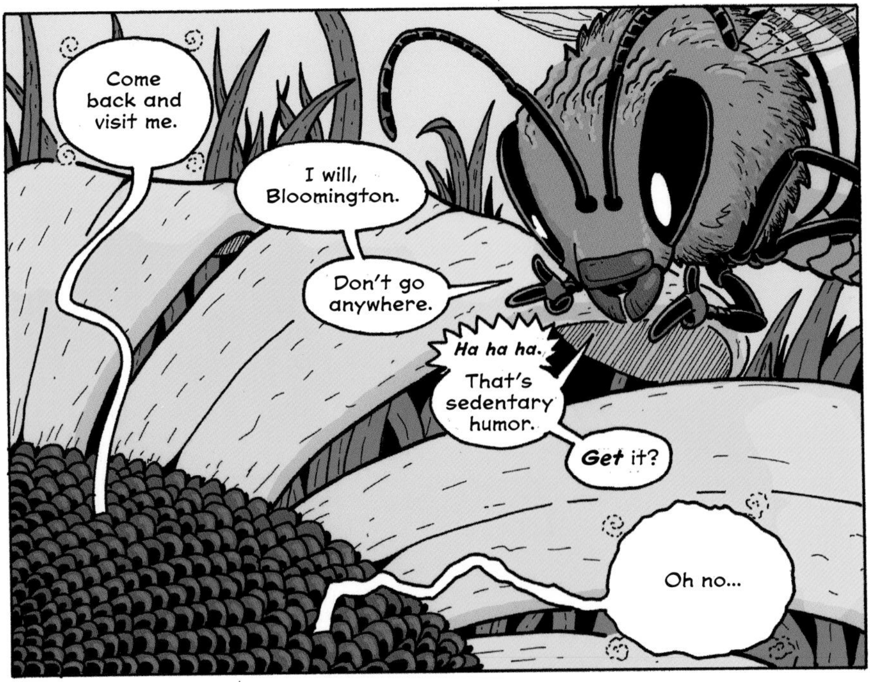
Come back and visit me.
I will, Bloomington.
Don't go anywhere.
Ha ha ha.
That's sedentary humor.
Get it?
Oh no...

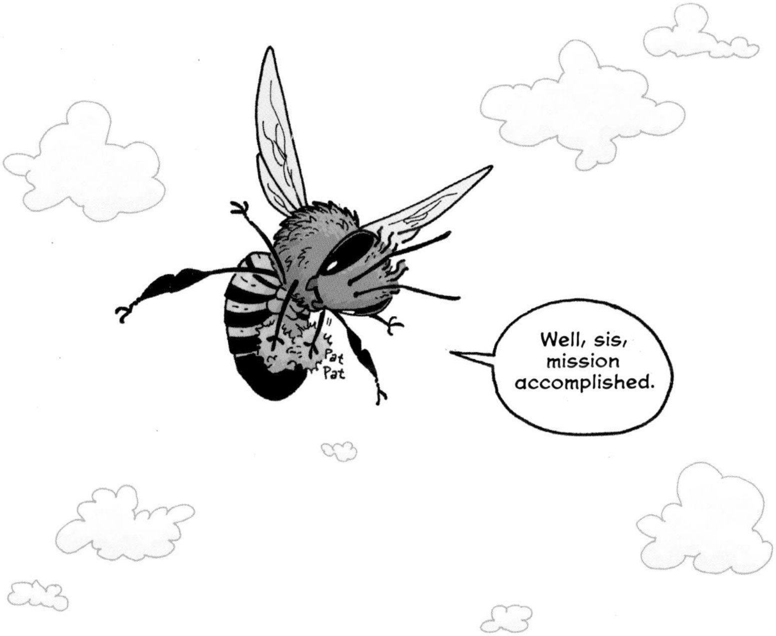
Pat Pat
Well, sis, mission accomplished.

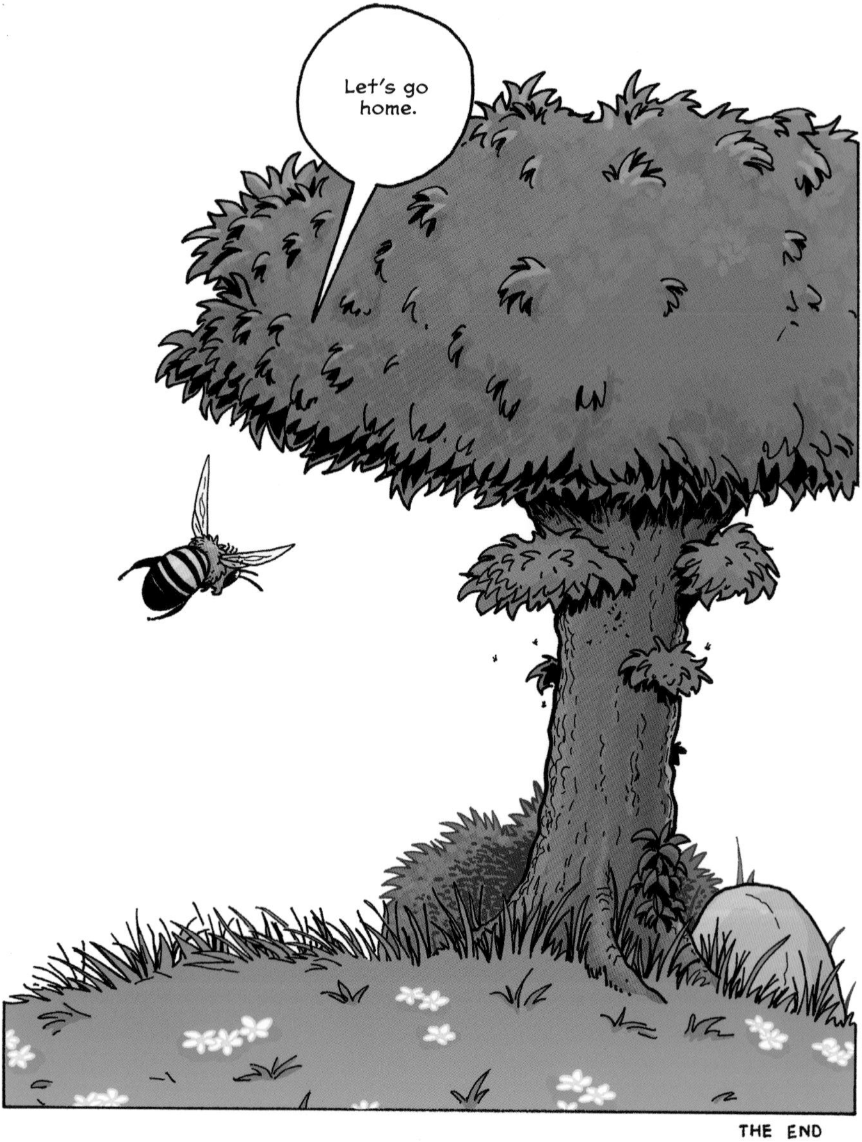
Let's go home.

THE END

ODDS & ENDS

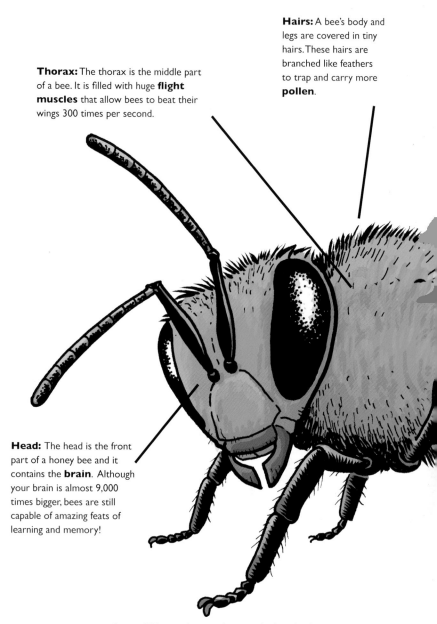

Thorax: The thorax is the middle part of a bee. It is filled with huge **flight muscles** that allow bees to beat their wings 300 times per second.

Hairs: A bee's body and legs are covered in tiny hairs. These hairs are branched like feathers to trap and carry more **pollen**.

Head: The head is the front part of a honey bee and it contains the **brain**. Although your brain is almost 9,000 times bigger, bees are still capable of amazing feats of learning and memory!

Legs: All insects have six legs attached to the thorax.

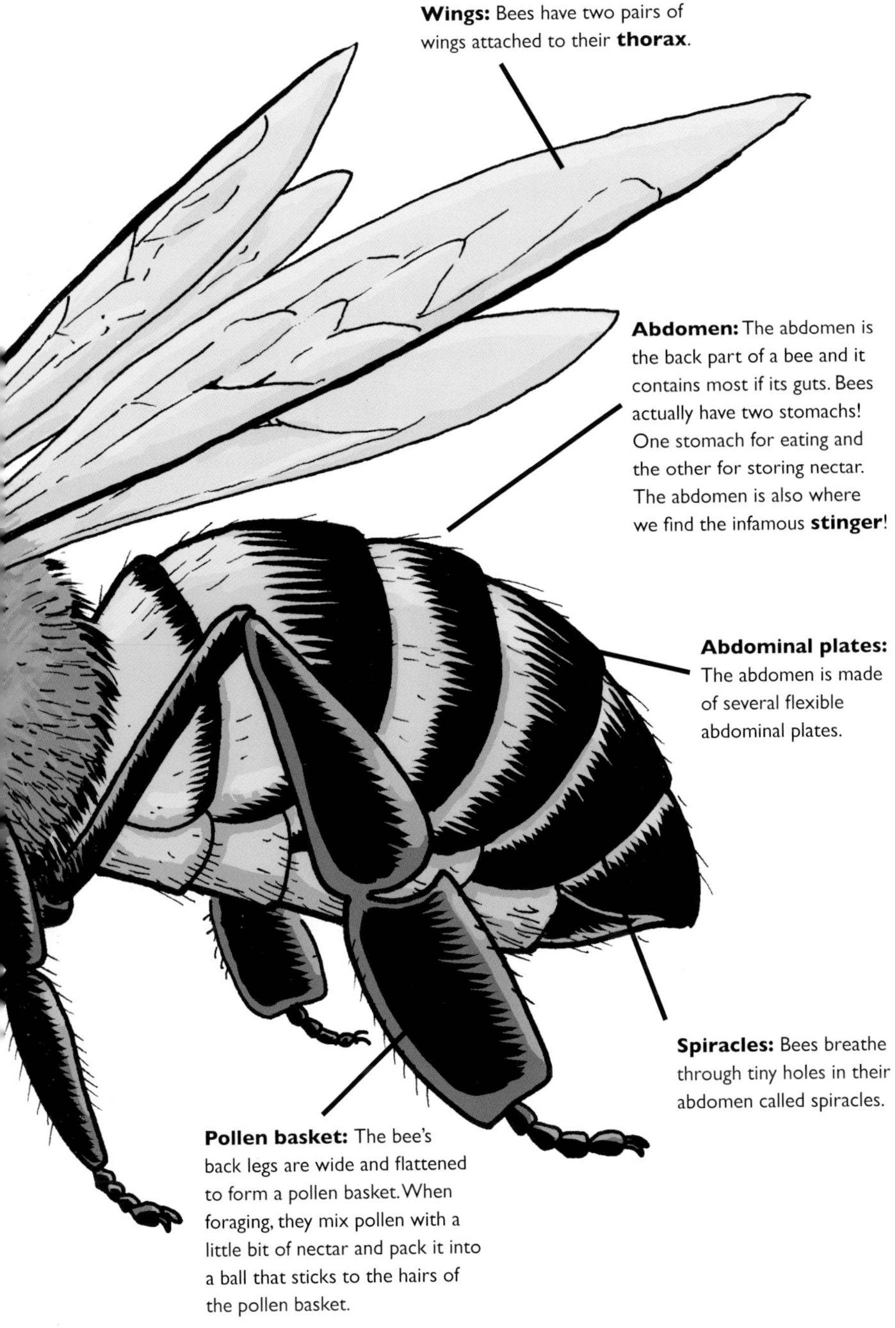
Wings: Bees have two pairs of wings attached to their **thorax**.
Abdomen: The abdomen is the back part of a bee and it contains most if its guts. Bees actually have two stomachs! One stomach for eating and the other for storing nectar. The abdomen is also where we find the infamous **stinger**!
Abdominal plates: The abdomen is made of several flexible abdominal plates.
Spiracles: Bees breathe through tiny holes in their abdomen called spiracles.
Pollen basket: The bee's back legs are wide and flattened to form a pollen basket. When foraging, they mix pollen with a little bit of nectar and pack it into a ball that sticks to the hairs of the pollen basket.

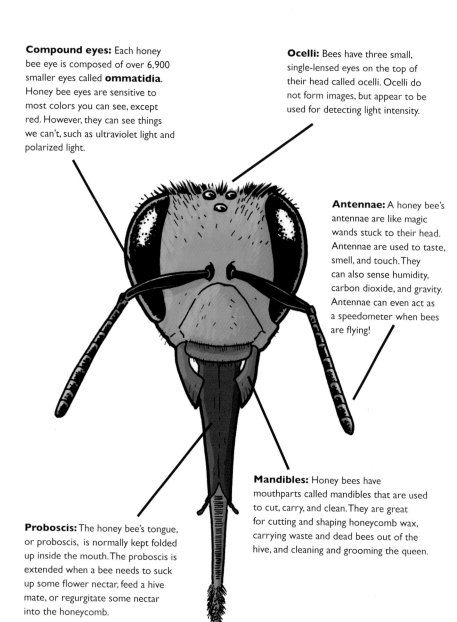

Compound eyes: Each honey bee eye is composed of over 6,900 smaller eyes called **ommatidia**. Honey bee eyes are sensitive to most colors you can see, except red. However, they can see things we can't, such as ultraviolet light and polarized light.

Ocelli: Bees have three small, single-lensed eyes on the top of their head called ocelli. Ocelli do not form images, but appear to be used for detecting light intensity.

Antennae: A honey bee's antennae are like magic wands stuck to their head. Antennae are used to taste, smell, and touch. They can also sense humidity, carbon dioxide, and gravity. Antennae can even act as a speedometer when bees are flying!

Mandibles: Honey bees have mouthparts called mandibles that are used to cut, carry, and clean. They are great for cutting and shaping honeycomb wax, carrying waste and dead bees out of the hive, and cleaning and grooming the queen.

Proboscis: The honey bee's tongue, or proboscis, is normally kept folded up inside the mouth. The proboscis is extended when a bee needs to suck up some flower nectar, feed a hive mate, or regurgitate some nectar into the honeycomb.

ANNOTATIONS

These annotations are designed to expand upon some of the science described in the story and answer questions that might have popped up as you read.

A few notes about cartoon bees:

Insects aren't the most . . . expressive critters in the world. Their rigid exoskeleton makes it impossible for them to smile, and their lidless eyes mean they cannot close them into slits when they're really, really mad. So one of the big challenges in writing this book was illustrating emotions in my characters without giving them human mouths and eyes.

Antennae are useful stand-ins for our expressive eyebrows. They can also look like hair standing on end in surprise. Opening and closing the mandibles works for talking, and by accentuating the inner curve of the bees' mandibles, they even look like they're smiling sometimes.

Anger and frustration were a little tougher, but ultimately the bees offered inspiration. When I was a postdoctoral student, I studied how bees learn odors. They can be taught to dislike a smell, and when they are exposed to the offensive odor, they will sometimes dramatically cross their mandibles. This mandible crossing with lowered "eyebrow" antennae worked pretty swell to make Dvorah, Bij, and Ari look annoyed.

We humans depend on our eyes to convey a lot of emotional information. Much of that is expressed with our eyelids and eyebrows, so the bees' antennae did a lot of that work. But the other component of our eye that is important is the pupil. It tells us where the character is looking. Bees don't have a pupil, but when light reflects off a honey bee's 6,900 eye facets, it creates a white spot in the middle of the eye. I used this white reflection as a stand-in for a pupil.

There was one instance, however, when I tossed science aside and went straight for cartoony. Honey bee larvae are really just an elaborate bag with a mouth designed for eating. Their mouths aren't very big or expressive. Larvae don't have teeth and they do not have uvulas (that little punching bag at the back of your mouth). But I wanted baby Nyuki to be adorable, so I gave her a big toothy grin. And when she yells, she has a great big uvula rattling in the back of her cartoon throat.

Finally, bees don't speak. I just want to be clear about that for anyone in doubt. But they do communicate with each other. Odors and dances are capable of conveying tremendous information in a hive.

CHAPTER 1: TRANSITIONS

Big Bloom Theory

Our story starts with a creation myth. All cultures have them and I wanted to imagine how a bee imagined the beginning of everything. The stories we tell say a lot about how we envision the world and our place in it. Not surprisingly, a life-sustaining flower sits at the center of Nyuki's universe.

Big Bloom Theory is a reference to the **Big Bang Theory**, which is our current model for how our universe came into existence. In this model, the universe started as an incredibly dense and hot singularity that exploded 13.772 billion years ago. In the aftermath of the explosion, all the particles, elements, and radiation of our universe were formed as the universe rapidly expanded out from the epicenter of the explosion. It must have been a whopper of an explosion, because the universe is still expanding.

The Primordial Soup

The earth didn't form until about 4.55 billion years ago. At first it was a roiling, boiling ball of nasty gases, but after about 550 million years of that, the first molecules of RNA and DNA started to form in the ancient oceans. RNA and DNA are the information molecules that are the foundation of living things. About 500 million years after the appearance of RNA and DNA, the first single-celled organisms made their appearance on Earth.

The Cambrian Explosion

Single-celled organisms would be the only type of life on Earth for approximately 3 billion years. Then, about 500 million years ago, there was a rapid evolution of big organisms made of many cells. This occurred at the start of the Cambrian period and so this rapid explosion of life is called the "Cambrian Explosion." On page 7 of this book, you can see some delightfully weird Cambrian critters like Trilobites, Wiwaxia, Anomalocaris, and, my favorite, Opabinia.

Crawling onto Land

One of the most exciting discoveries about the transition of our ancestors onto land has been a fossil named Tiktaalik. Tiktaalik lived about 375 million years ago and it looked like a cross between a fish and an amphibian. Like a fish, it had scales and gills, but its fins were very unique. Unlike other fish, its fins had bones in them that allowed Tiktaalik to support its body like a salamander. The bones in Tiktaalik's fins are remarkably similar to the bones in your arm (just a lot smaller)!

Planet of the Insects

Insects were masters of the air long before people got airborne. But, to be fair, insects had a head start on us. The first fossil evidence of insects' ancestors suggests they crawled onto land over 400 million years ago. That means insects and their relatives were on land adapting to new and different environments 30-40 million years before our ancestors crawled out of the sea, and hundreds of millions of years before humans showed up.

The Hexapod Welcoming Committee

Millipedes, centipedes, spiders, and insects invaded the land long before our amphibious ancestors crawled ashore. The insects that were on land then probably wouldn't be super recognizable, so I cheated a little to use familiar insect types. Of the ones you see on page 8 of this book (beetle, mantis, grasshopper, cockroach, butterfly, and dragonfly), only the dragonfly and roach would have been around to greet their new neighbors. I did make sure to exclude honey bees. Honey bees evolved alongside flowering plants 100 million years ago in the Cretaceous period.

Counting Critters

Insects and their relatives comprise more than 80% of all the organisms in the world. Their small size, quick reproduction, and ability to adapt to numerous different environments have made them incredibly successful. Scientists have used a wide array of different techniques to look for insects and refine our calculations of how many species are on Earth. One of the last regions of the world that hasn't been thoroughly described is the tree canopy in rain forests because it's tough for big heavy humans to access the high spindly branches. Our current best guess is that there are anywhere between 9 million and 30 million different insect species on the planet. If we count each individual ant, bee, beetle, etc., we come up with the monstrous number of 10 quintillion insects skittering and flying around us.

Odd Jobs

Honey bees go through a series of jobs in the hive, but there are no set rules about who does what. While on average most bees follow a general series of jobs, starting with cleaning cells and culminating in foraging, bees aren't programmed robots. They can skip around doing different jobs based on the needs of the hive or continue to do one job for their entire life. On average, a honey bee lives a little over 52 days and the general sequence and time range for doing these jobs are below:

- Cell cleaning (1–7 days old)
- Capping brood (2–10 days old)
- Queen tending (4–14 days old)
- Tending brood (7–15 days old)
- Receiving nectar (10–16 days old)
- Handling pollen (9–19 days old)
- Hive cleaning (9–23 days old)
- Comb building (12–23 days old)
- Ventilating (13–23 days old)
- Guard duty (15–27 days old)
- Foraging (18–52 days old)

One of the biggest behavior transitions for honey bees is moving from a **worker** in the hive to working outside as a **forager**. These two jobs require very different behaviors. Scientists have shown that workers and foragers have unique sets of genes turned on in their brains. These genes are controlled by a process known as epigenetic methylation. That's a mouthful, but it is a relatively simple idea. When a bee is a worker, there are molecules called methyl groups stuck to their forager genes, which block the bees from turning on the foraging genes, so they

behave as workers. When bees become foragers, the methyl groups are removed from the foraging genes and they are stuck on the worker genes.

But how do the bees know to make that switch? This is because of an environmental cue that we will talk about later . . .

Butt, Butt, Butt . . .

As we saw in the story, when Nyuki was a larva she spent most of her time eating and eating and eating some more. When the time came to build her cocoon, she used her own feces in the construction. But what kept her from excreting her poop earlier in development? Well, she couldn't. A honey bee larva doesn't grow an anus until very late in its development. So she just had to hold it.

Discs

I agree with Nyuki: metamorphosis sounds terrifying. All your larval cells disintegrate and you are rebuilt? Brrr. The secret group of cells that do the rebuilding are called imaginal discs. Imaginal discs are made of cells that are responsible for building the adult structures in a bee. Entomologists call adult insects "imagos," so these cells are imago-making discs or, more succinctly, imaginal discs.

Chitin

A honey bee's exoskeleton is made of a substance called chitin. When a bee first emerges, the chitin molecules are disconnected like a pile of loose bricks. However, those chitin molecules start to make chemical connections in the 24 hours after emerging. These chemical connections are like the cement between bricks, making the bee's exoskeleton tough armor.

The Big House

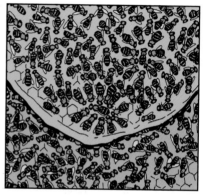

A honey bee hive can contain between 10,000 to 60,000 honey bees.

CHAPTER 2: SWARM

Pollen

The comb of a hive is full of cells that are used for three basic purposes. Brood cells are where baby bees are incubated, honeycomb is where nectar is stored, and pollen is stored in its own set of cells. Since pollen can be many different colors, the pollen comb can be quite beautiful depending on which flowers are in bloom.

Calm Before the Swarm

Nyuki wasn't just making another dumb joke when she made a silly play on the phrase "calm before the storm." The hive really does get strangely quiet a few hours before swarming. Spooky, huh? And then when the hive is ready to swarm, the waves of activity rippling across the hive rapidly crescendo. The bees get more and more worked up as they prepare to swarm, until they literally fall out of the hive, carrying the helpless queen with them.

A Caste of Three

In the honey bee hive, there are three types (or castes) of bees. The vast majority of bees in a hive are **workers** like Nyuki and Dvorah, and they do almost all the important work. A fertilized egg that is fed lightly on brood food (a mixture of honey, pollen, and glandular secretion from the nurse bees) plus a teensy bit of royal jelly will grow into a worker bee. All workers are sterile females, so they can't lay eggs. They are also all sisters since they all have the same mother: the queen.

There is only one **queen** in every hive. She's bigger than her daughter workers and is responsible for laying all the eggs. The queen leaves the hive only once early in her life to mate. When she does, she will mate with as many as seventeen drones and store their sperm for the rest of her life. When she lays an egg, she can control whether or not she fertilizes it with sperm. If she fertilizes an egg, it grows into a worker or a new queen. When she lays an unfertilized egg, it grows into a male called a drone. Since a drone develops from an unfertilized egg, it doesn't have a father, but it does have a grandpa (the queen's dad). The prodigious queen bee can lay up to 1,500 eggs in a single day!

There are only a few **drones** in the hive relative to workers and, as we saw from Zambur, they look very different from their sisters. Drones have bigger bodies, no stinger, and enormous eyes that spread all over their head. This different appearance is mainly because they develop from unfertilized eggs. Behaviorally, they don't do much around the hive. In fact, the workers have to take care of the drones since they don't take very good care of themselves.

To make a queen, nurse bees feed larvae from a fertilized egg large amounts of royal jelly. Royal jelly contains a much higher concentration of glandular secretions than regular brood food. Queen larvae also get fed more often.

House Hunters

Bee scouts are picky house hunters. They are looking for a potential home that meets certain specific criteria. They need an empty cavity that is at least 15–40 liters in size, a relatively small hive entrance near the bottom of the cavity, and nice exposure to the sun so the colony stays warm. The scout has to do all those calculations with a brain that only has 950,000 neurons and then return to the swarm cluster to tell her sisters.

Dung Beetles

Dung beetles play an important ecological role. Sisyphus will eventually bury his dung ball and his mate will lay an egg in it. When the egg hatches it will munch on the dung and start growing. This lifestyle does a couple very important things. First, by burying the dung, dung beetles fertilize the soil, providing food for a whole host of plants and decomposers. Second, dung that is buried can't be used by pests such as flies to lay their eggs. So dung beetles fertilize the land and help keep insect pest numbers low.

Stingers

Only female bees have stingers because stingers evolved from a structure called an ovipositor. The ovipositor is a tube-like structure that extends off the backside of a female insect. Female insects use their ovi-

positors to drill into the ground or the bark of a tree and then squirt an egg into the hole. But worker bees don't lay eggs, so over time their ovipositors have evolved for a different function. Instead of drilling into wood or dirt, they drill into an animal. And instead of squirting an egg into

the hole, they squirt a nasty venom that rips open the animal's cells and causes pain and swelling. As we see in the story, bees die when they use their stinger on an animal with rubbery skin like us, but that isn't true for all stinging insects. Wasps can sting you over and over and over again. They really are the worst. The reason wasps can do this is that they have a smooth sheath they can slide over their stinger before they pull it out, so their barbs don't get caught on our rubbery skin.

As we learned in Chapter 4, bees can sting other insects without dying. When a bee stings another bee, they insert their stinger into the weak points in the chitin. Since the chitin isn't rubbery, the barbs on the stinger don't get caught.

CHAPTER 4: HOMEFRONT

The Big Stinky World of Bees

The first half of a bee's life is spent in the pitch-dark hive. Without any light, they can't see a thing, but they get along just fine using their antennae. Bees use odors to identify their hive mates and strangers, dancers transmit the odor of the flowers they visit to dance attendants, and queens use pheromone odors to control and direct the activities of the workers. At the mouth of the hive, bees release volatile pheromones to signal alarm. And out in the field, foraging honey bees remember good flowers based on their perfume and mark good flower patches and water sources with a scent they emit. Bees live in a world of odors and their ability to smell (olfaction) may be their most important sense.

Bee Wars

You may be wondering why Dvorah and her fellow guards took such extreme action against a bee who was trying to rob their hive. Well, it turns out that one of the fiercest predators honey bees face is other honey bees. In fact, the behavior that guards display at the hive entrance has evolved primarily to protect their hive from members of their own species. Robbing usually only occurs when there is a dearth of nectar in the field. In fact, when resources are plentiful, bees from other colonies are often admitted and adopted into a hive. But when things are bad, foraging bees may seek out honey stores in other hives. They are attracted to the smell of honey coming from a hive entrance. If a robber manages to get past the guards and get a load of honey, she will return to her hive and recruit her sisters to help her plunder the other hive. The resulting conflict can lead to a bee war that may leave thousands of bees dead. The robber bee at the beginning of Chapter 4 was darker than Dvorah and the other guards because robber honey bees tend to become smooth, polished and black after multiple fights with other bees.

Trophallaxis

Bees often exchange honey or nectar using a process called trophallaxis. Trophallaxis can take place three ways: between workers (as when Nyuki gave Melissa the nectar she had collected), between workers and the queen (workers feed the queen), and between workers and drones (just like when Nyuki gave Zambur some honey to go on his mating flight). During trophallaxis, a worker regurgitates the nectar or honey in its crop out through its proboscis and onto the waiting proboscis of another bee. Queens rarely feed themselves and receive most of their food from workers. Trophallaxis is also important during the waggle dance. Dancing foragers will often stop dancing and give their sisters a taste of the nectar they have found.

Why the Eye?

When the hive was under attack, Dvorah stung the bird in the eye and helped drive it off. But why the eye? Well, when bees get into attack mode one of the things they zero in on to sting is dark colors, just like that bird's big black pupil.

Bees are also induced to sting by animal scents and sudden movements.

CHAPTER 5: THE PLAN

An Ancient Partnership

Flowering plants and bees both appeared in the Cretaceous period, and since then have been coevolving alongside each other. As the dinosaurs were stomping around in their final glory days on earth, insects and plants were just beginning to forge an intimate relationship that would entwine them for millions of years. Bees need protein and sugar to survive. Flowers need to have their pollen reach another member of their species so they can reproduce. Some plants use wind to carry their pollen, but if the wind is blowing the wrong way, a plant's pollen may never find its target. It's much better to have a go-between like an insect carry it to other flowers. By providing pollen (protein) and nectar (sugar), the flower encourages bees to stop by for multiple visits. Over time, some flowers and pollinators have coevolved exclusive partnerships, so the extinction of one partner could lead to the loss of the other.

Warming Up

Every morning in the summer, bees crawl out onto the face of the hive and sit in the sun to warm up. Unlike humans, who maintain a relatively constant body temperature, insects

are typically the same temperature as their environment unless they warm themselves up. One way to do this is to bask in the sun and let the big ball of thermonuclear fire in sky heat them up. But sometimes when it's a bit chilly, bees have another trick. They can contract all the flight muscles in their thorax at the same time. Contracting the muscles this way allows them to shiver and generate heat without beating their wings. Sometimes it is just so cold that shivering doesn't work. Under these conditions bees can get so cold that they slip into what is called "chill coma." During chill coma, bees (and all insects for that matter) get so cold that they stop moving and topple over. They look dead, but if you warm them up they will spring back to life. The research for my PhD focused on what happens to muscles during chill coma. It was pretty fun work.

The Pollen Basket

The back legs of a honey bee are broad, flat, hairy, and slightly cupped. This area is known as their pollen basket. Honey bees mix the pollen they collect with a little nectar (just to hold it together) and pack it into their cupped back legs. The hairs in the pollen basket help hold the pollen on the leg.

Depending on the time of year, bees return to the hive with a rainbow of different colored pollen packed on their legs.

How to Make a Forager

When Melissa receives nectar from Nyuki, she is getting more than just sweet plant juice. She's also getting a chemical message designed to delay her development into a forager. Foragers carry their nectar load in their honey stomach. The honey stomach secretes a chemical called ethyl oleate that gets mixed into the nectar. Ethyl oleate inhibits worker bees from becoming foragers. As long as the hive has a lot of foragers, most of the workers receiving nectar are being inhibited. But foragers eventually die, and as they die, there are fewer bees to inhibit the workers. That means that some of the workers are no longer inhibited and can start becoming foragers. In this way, the colony can maintain a fairly constant number of foragers working to get pollen and nectar for the hive. Nyuki clearly doesn't think Melissa is ready to be a forager and she is sharing ethyl oleate with her to make sure she doesn't become one.

I'd Rather Fly

It requires more energy for a bee to walk than it does for a bee to fly, so Nyuki's final stroll to the base of Bloomington was probably exhausting.

Overwintering

To survive winter, a colony of bees will cluster together in a mass surrounding the queen and the larvae in the honey comb. The workers contract their flight muscles to shiver and generate heat to keep everyone warm, and feed on the honey in the comb to keep their energy up. With a little luck, enough bees will survive the long, cold winter to get the hive up and running again in the spring.

Extra Cool Bee Stuff

Where are all the Monster Bees? How come bees don't get as big as you and me? Well, it all comes down to skeletons and breathing. We have our skeleton on the inside and it can support a lot of weight. Bees (and insects in general) have their skeletons on the outside. This exoskeleton (exo = outer) is a hard shell made of a substance called chitin, and even though it is pretty tough, it couldn't support too much body weight.

The other thing that limits an insect's size is how it breathes. In our lungs, our blood picks up oxygen and carries it to all the cells in the body. Bees and other insects don't have lungs. Oxygen comes into their bodies through little holes called spiracles and then flows through tiny tubes called tracheae. These tubes must branch to almost every cell in the bee's body. If the bee got too big, there would have to be tons of tracheae and oxygen still probably wouldn't get to all the cells.

How to Build a Bee

Like all insects, honey bees have three basic parts: the head, the thorax, and the abdomen. The head contains the brain and much of the bee's sensory apparatus. The bee's antennae are two feelers that extend out from its face. They are used for taste, smell, and touch. The eyes are on either side of the bee's head and each is composed of about 6,900 facets. Each facet receives a little bit of light independently and contributes one "pixel" to the image that is formed in the bee's brain. The mouthparts are also on the head. This includes the bee's proboscis, which it uses to suck up nectar and water. The thorax is the transportation center for the bee. This is where the four wings and six legs attach. The inside of the thorax is full of the very large muscles that beat the wings.

A Microprocessor in the Head

Bees have 950,000 nerve cells in a brain that is only 1 cubic millimeter in size. Despite the small size, they are capable of some astounding behaviors. They also have a remarkable capacity to learn and are a model organism for many researchers studying learning and memory. My work as a postdoctoral researcher focused on the mechanisms underlying how bees learn floral odors.

WHAT'S IN A NAME?

All the bee names in Clan Apis are the word for "bee" in different languages.

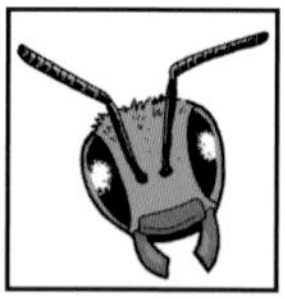

Nyuki *is Swahili for bee.*

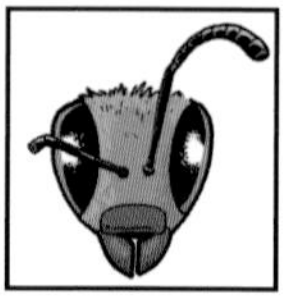

Dvorah *is Hebrew for bee.*

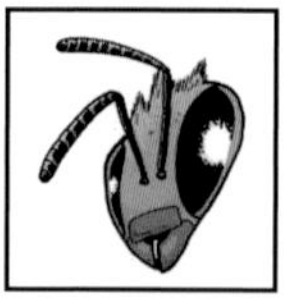

Hachi *is Japanese for bee.*

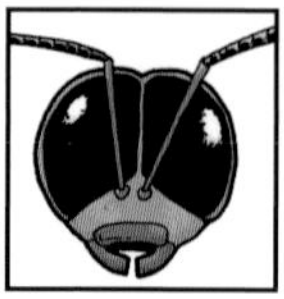

Zambur *is Farsi for bee.*

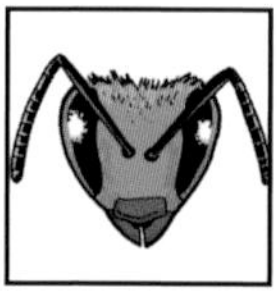

Abeja *is Spanish for bee.*

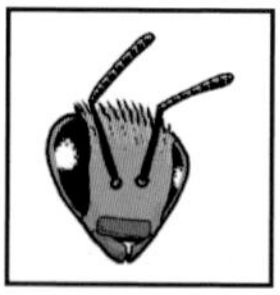

Melissa *is Greek for bee.*

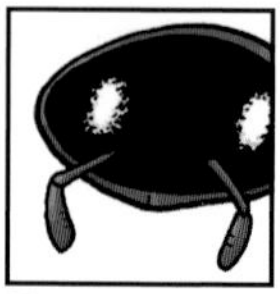

Sisyphus *the dung beetle was named after that mythological fellow who was condemned to the futile task of rolling a rock up a hill. This name springs from my past as a graduate student. I was in an insect quiz game and my team was asked what the Sisyphus beetle does. I was the first to give the correct answer. Since that happens so rarely, the experience really stuck with me.*

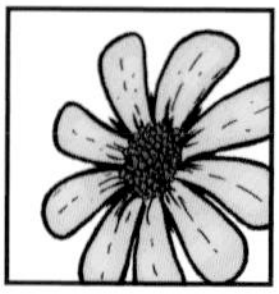

Bloomington *is named after the hometown of the world's greatest college basketball team.*

REFERENCES

The following books were core reference materials for this book. Each is a well-written, rich source of bee knowledge with several photographs and diagrams that served as valuable visual reference.

Herb, Brian R., Florian Wolschin, Kasper D. Hansen, Martin J. Aryee, Ben Langmead, Rafael Irizarry, Gro V. Amdam, and Andrew P. Feinberg. "Reversible Switching between Epigenetic States in Honeybee Behavioral Subcastes." *Nature Neuroscience* 15, no. 10 (2012): 1371–73. https://doi.org/10.1038/nn.3218.

Hosler, Jay S., John E. Burns, and Harald E. Esch. "Flight Muscle Resting Potential and Species-Specific Differences in Chill-Coma." *Journal of Insect Physiology* 46, no. 5 (2000): 621–27. https://doi.org/10.1016/s0022-1910(99)00148-1.

Hosler, Jay S., Kristi L. Buxton, and Brian H. Smith. "Impairment of Olfactory Discrimination by Blockade of GABA and Nitric Oxide Activity in the Honey Bee Antennal Lobes." *Behavioral Neuroscience* 114, no. 3 (2000): 514–25. https://doi.org/10.1037/0735-7044.114.3.514.

Leoncini, I., Y. Le Conte, G. Costagliola, E. Plettner, A. L. Toth, M. Wang, Z. Huang, et al. "Regulation of Behavioral Maturation by a Primer Pheromone Produced by Adult Worker Honey Bees." *Proceedings of the National Academy of Sciences* 101, no. 50 (2004): 17559–64. https://doi.org/10.1073/pnas.0407652101.

Misof, B., S. Liu, K. Meusemann, R. S. Peters, A. Donath, C. Mayer, P. B. Frandsen, et al. "Phylogenomics Resolves the Timing and Pattern of Insect Evolution." *Science* 346, no. 6210 (2014): 763–67. https://doi.org/10.1126/science.1257570.

Roh, Chris, and Morteza Gharib. "Honeybees Use Their Wings for Water Surface Locomotion." *Proceedings of the National Academy of Sciences* 116, no. 49 (2019): 24446–51. https://doi.org/10.1073/pnas.1908857116.

Rothenbuhler, Walter C. "Behaviour Genetics of Nest Cleaning in Honey Bees. I. Responses of Four Inbred Lines to Disease-Killed Brood." *Animal Behaviour* 12, no. 4 (1964): 578–83. https://doi.org/10.1016/0003-3472(64)90082-x.

Shubin, Neil. *Your Inner Fish: A Journey into the 3.5-Billion-Year History of the Human Body.* New York: Vintage Books, 2009.

Whitfield, Charles W., Anne-Marie Cziko, and Gene E. Robinson. "Gene Expression Profiles in the Brain Predict Behavior in Individual Honey Bees." *Science* 302, no. 5643 (2003): 296–99. https://doi.org/10.1126/science.1086807.

Winston, Mark L. *The Biology of the Honey Bee.* Cambridge: Harvard University Press, 1991.

ACKNOWLEDGMENTS

My wife, Lisa, had to endure countless readings of initial scripts as I hashed out the events of Nyuki's life. She was always the first (and sometimes the only) person to see the story and art as they evolved. She assumed her role as unofficial editor without protest and was always honest with me (sometimes brutally so). But when I made her laugh (or once, cry), I knew that I was moving in the right direction. We didn't always agree on things, but her proximity to me and the work was vital for its creation. This book would not be the story it is if not for her.

I started working on this book before Lisa and I had children. Now we have two sons in college. I've learned so much about storytelling talking to Max and Jack. Like their mom, they are unflinching critics, and I am so thankful for their honesty, wit, and creativity.

This work originally appeared in the late 1990s as a five-issue comic book series called Clan Apis. I am deeply appreciative of the financial support Peter Laird, cocreator of the Teenage Mutant Ninja Turtles, and the Xeric Foundation gave the first issue of Clan Apis. Without their help, I couldn't have afforded to get the ball rolling.

My deepest thanks and admiration go to Hilary Sycamore for her beautiful colors. Nyuki's adventures were originally published in black and white and it was a thrill to see Hilary bring a new vibrancy to these pages. Her colors have infused the bees with life in a way I didn't think possible.

Special thanks to Daryn Guarino and Active Synapse Comics for publishing the first collected volume and valiantly keeping it in print for almost two decades.

Thanks also go out to Gib Bickel, K. C. Engelman, Rod Phillips, Harold Buchholz, Jim Ottaviani, Sue Cobey, Brian Smith, John Wenzel, Sharoni Shafir, Levi Lawson, Jeff Mara, Satish Chandra, Harry Itagaki, Stan Sakai, Leah Itagaki, Paul Chadwick, Sarai Itagaki, Elizabeth Bickel, Tara Tallan, Wendy Guerra, Adam Guerra, Mathew Guerra, Austen Julka, Mark Crilley, Simon Smith, Nathan Stegelmann, Andrew Stegelmann, Samuel Stegelmann, Marc Hempel, Kurt Stegelmann, Grant Stegelmann, Seth Stegelmann, Kim Field, Ken Lemons, Toni Thordarson, Kim Preney, Kevin Johnson, May Berenbaum, and Geraldine Wright.

HarperAlley is an imprint of HarperCollins Publishers

The Way of the Hive
Copyright © 2000, 2021 by Jay Hosler
This book was previously published as Clan Apis.
All rights reserved. Printed in Bosnia and Herzegovina.
No part of this book may be used or reproduced in any manner whatsoever
without written permission except in the case of brief quotations embodied in
critical articles and reviews. For information address HarperCollins Children's
Books, a division of HarperCollins Publishers, 195 Broadway, New York, NY 10007.
www.harperalley.com

Library of Congress Control Number: 2020942249
ISBN 978-0-06-300736-9 — ISBN 978-0-06-300735-2 (paperback)
Colors by Hilary Sycamore
The artist used a 0.7mm color Eno mechanical pen and soft blue graphite to draw
the art on smooth Bristol paper. The illustrations were inked using Koh-i-Noor
Rapidograph technical pens (#1, 2, 3, and 4) and a Kuretake Brush Pen. All the goof-
ups, errors, and embarrassingly bad drawings were eliminated using a Staedtler
Mars Plastic eraser and copious amounts of Bic Wite-out EZ correct tape.
Typography by Chrisila Maida
21 22 23 24 25   GPS   10 9 8 7 6 5 4 3 2 1
❖
Originally published in 2000 by Active Synapse